The Girl from Liverpool

Elizabeth Morton

The Girl from Liverpool

MACMILLAN

First published 2022 by Macmillan
an imprint of Pan Macmillan
The Smithson, 6 Briset Street, London EC1M 5NR
EU representative: Macmillan Publishers Ireland Ltd, 1st Floor,
The Liffey Trust Centre, 117–126 Sheriff Street Upper,
Dublin 1, D01 YC43
Associated companies throughout the world
www.panmacmillan.com

ISBN 978-1-5290-6027-0

1 3 5 7 9 8 6 4 2

A CIP catalogue record for this book is available from the British Library.

Typeset in Sabon by Palimpsest Book Production Limited, Falkirk, Stirlingshire
Printed and bound by CPI Group (UK) Ltd, Croydon, CR0 4YY

Visit **www.panmacmillan.com** to read more about all our books
and to buy them. You will also find features, author interviews and
news of any author events, and you can sign up for e-newsletters
so that you're always first to hear about our new releases.

For my sister, Ruth

One

1930

'Stand still, Peg!' said Moira O'Shea, brandishing a hairbrush. 'Stop making a face. The wind will change and you'll stick like that. Now turn around, and give over fidgeting.'

Peggy, still in her nightdress, perched on an old milking stool in the cramped parlour of their shabby terraced house in Feather Street, and raised her piercing blue eyes. She squirmed away from her mother, who had just taken the last of the cloth strips from Peg's mousey brown hair and was now doing her best to drag the brush through a clump of it. Peggy doubted the tangled, limp ringlets would last the morning, despite all the yanking and twisting she had suffered with her ma's effort at rag-rolling the night before.

'But I hate church. Why are you making me do this? Can't I make up me own mind about Jesus when I'm big?'

'Don't be daft. It'll be grand to see you in a pretty frock for once.'

'You'd not do me out of a few bevvies with your uncles to celebrate your first Holy Communion, queen?' said her father, who had just wandered in.

1

A few bevvies. Peg was only eight, but she knew that with the O'Sheas there was no such thing as a few bevvies. They would all go to the room upstairs at the Throstle's Nest after church and there would be a right royal knees-up. There would be dancing and they'd all get sloshed. Gram would fall down the stairs. Uncle Davey and Uncle Seamus would start a fight about something over nothing and they would never remember why in the morning. Her mother would sing that stupid song about a woman called Mary and sad mountains and being back in Ireland. Her brother Brendan would be sick after furtively drinking the dregs of the unfinished beer bottles. Everyone would end up crying and the next day they would all be walking around with sore heads and saying *never again, I swear on our Peggy's life, never again*.

Her grandmother bustled in and shoved a pair of white rosary beads and a battered white Bible with an embossed gold crucifix into her hands.

'You look like that Clara Bow, love.'

'Who's Clara Bow?'

'Clara Bow?' echoed ten-year-old Brendan. 'She's got proper curls. And movie stars have rosy cheeks. Freckly Peg doesn't.'

'Well, we can soon sort that out,' said Gram, lunging forward and pinching Peggy hard on each cheek.

'Ow!' cried Peg. 'Gerroff!'

'Don't speak to your Grammy Nora like that. Bit of respect for your elders,' said Dennis O'Shea, winking as he stuffed a heel of bread smothered in margarine into his mouth. He belched unapologetically.

Peggy gave a theatrical sigh. There was no way out of this. She would just have to bear it.

Half an hour later, after Peggy had changed from her nightie into her communion dress, she came into the kitchen scowling.

'Don't you look a picture, our Peg!' said her dad.

'No I don't, Da. This stupid thing is too short,' she replied, tugging at the hem of the white dress. It barely covered her knees. It had seen better days as her mother's wedding dress, and her grandmother's wedding dress before that. Taken up, let out, taken in, re-hemmed, re-seamed, and now wreathed in a bit of an old white net curtain to hide the frayed and stained satin underskirt.

'I mean it. I don't like this get-up, Mam,' moaned Peg.

'Yes, you do. You love it,' replied Moira.

'Surely to God, today will be that dress's final outing,' Grammy Nora said, sharing her unwanted thoughts on the matter.

There were more arguments over where they would all sit at church, and what should be done with baby Jimmy, and where they should put the jam and sugar butties to keep them cool and stop them from curling. But all these vexations were forgotten when Da, noticing four-year-old Sheila was having her own heated conversation with one of the chickens that had come in from the yard, scooped his youngest daughter up and plonked her on the table out of harm's way. When he was done with chasing out the clucking hen, all flapping and feathers, making

Philomena, who was nine, sneeze loudly, and Sheila yelp, and little three-year-old Peter giggle, he kissed Peggy and told her how pretty she looked in a dress.

'C'mon, kids, we best be off then.'

'Can I be an angel?' asked Sheila, beaming, as she scrambled off the table, crashing into the dresser as she jetéd across the room, wrapped up in white netting. She pulled at the ruffles of her ma's skirt. 'Can I be the Virgin Mary? Can I wear this veil?'

'You can, love . . .' replied her mother.

'It's not a fancy dress party, it's church,' said Gram, squashing her hat onto her head and pursing her lips. She looked at herself in the mirror and rubbed away the pink lipstick marks from her teeth, making little squeaking noises with her finger.

'She can if she wants. Peg's refusing to. Right then. Let's go. It's half an hour's walk to Holy Cross and we're already late.'

They set off down the hill in the sunshine, but not before someone realized they had forgotten the baby. 'I thought our Brendan had him!' cried Moira, running back to get chubby Jimmy out of the pram in the yard where he was still snoozing.

They headed off again towards Scottie Road, all gleaming white gloves, summer dresses, white socks, all bobbing and skittering and swinging and twirling of rosary beads, picking up random stones and chucking them.

'I'll bloody crown you if you get those dresses mucky! Brendan! Phil!! Get down off that wall now!'

People washing their steps sat back on their heels, wiped their foreheads and smiled, others leaned out of windows to see what the commotion was and waved. They were a sight all right, the O'Sheas. Philomena and Sheila, with their wild, untamed curls, who dressed identically and finished each other's sentences; and Brendan, with his father's short, muscular legs and long body. Peter being dragged along by Dennis, and distinctive, feral Peggy with her curtains of flyaway hair, poker-straight now and hanging limply about her shoulders. Those O'Sheas from Feather Street, people would say, oh they're trouble, and the skinny one with the upturned nose and face full of freckles is the worst, that Peggy girl. *You want to watch her*, they would whisper, raising their eyes as if to suggest some secret.

Irish as a peat bog and mouths on 'em like the Mersey Tunnel, that lot.

The church was full by the time they got there and Mass had already started. There was much 'make way, make way, budge up, budge up' and shuffling and squeezing through the four-strong throng of men who lined the walls at the back, and 'it's the O'Sheas, late again, always late' and tutting and loud sighs and ripostes of 'we're here, aren't we, move, move, Peg coming through!'

A wide-hipped nun swept forward and grabbed Peggy by the arm, pinching her flesh. 'Peggy O'Shea, I said you needed to be here half an hour early,' she snapped, shoving her in the back. 'Get up there with the others.'

Peggy laughed over her shoulder at her sisters and brothers, and grinned and winked as she was dragged off down the aisle. In the front pew, decorated with white lilies and curling white ribbons, the whole row twitched and shuffled up to make a space for her. This caused more whispering, and complaints of her treading on someone's toe, and the priest paused mid-gospel and raised an eyebrow to see what the fuss was about. Finally, Peggy settled into her seat.

The nun sitting behind her leaned forward and jabbed her between the shoulder blades. 'Peggy O'Shea, if I hear a peep out of you!' she hissed.

Peggy turned away, bowed her head, smirked, and whispered 'Peep, peep,' just loud enough to be heard, which made everyone packed together in the pew giggle into their white-gloved hands and squeeze their noses to stop them from exploding into laughter, praying the nun wouldn't crack them one. One thing Peggy could always be relied on to do was lighten the mood.

The priest droned on, and Peggy soon began to get bored. She started fidgeting and writhing, gazing up at the ceiling, examining the end of her hair, sucking it into a point, examining it again, sighing, fanning herself with the Mass sheet. How long was this going to go on? It felt like forever.

The only reason she had been persuaded to do it was because she'd been told she could make a few bob from the aunties and uncles out of this communion lark. The nuns at school had said it was going to be miraculous, eating Jesus's body. But Peggy's friend Frances said her cousin had told her it wasn't miraculous, it was just like eating a stale Jacob's cream cracker, the ones that always got stuck on the roof of your mouth. Frances had stood Peggy in front of a mirror and taught her to poke her tongue out while she pretended she was the priest so that Peggy could practise. They had collapsed into giggles on the bed when Peggy backed off and yelled 'You get your dirty big hairy hands off me, Father O'Mahoney!'

Jolting Peg back into the present, the priest started to read from the Bible. 'Take your son, your only son Isaac, whom you love, and go to the land of Moriah, and offer him there as a burnt offering on one of the mountains of which I shall tell you. And so it came to pass . . .' When he boomed out the word *pass* he pronounced it with a long-drawn-out *ahh* sound, not the flat 'a' Peggy was used to.

'He says *parse* like arse,' she whispered to Frances. 'Is that how posh people talk?'

Frances sniggered.

The girl on the other side nudged her. 'Shove up. Why d'you keep squashing me, Peg?'

But Peg didn't answer. An altar boy in white robes, with the white lacy hem grazing his ankles, olive skin and glossy thick brown hair, had appeared from the side altar. Mesmerized, Peggy watched him walk solemnly and reverently forward in his shiny shoes and place a candle on the altar.

'Who's he?' she hissed to Frances. He looked so different to the freckly, pale-faced, unruly lads she was used to. He was poised, tanned, with a smooth, warm skin tone, brown velvet eyes and full lips.

'He's from Holy Cross School. There's a bunch of them. From Little Italy end of Scottie Road. Look, they're all sitting over there in the side chapel.'

7

Peg craned her neck. The splash of colour, the bright oranges, lemony yellows and sky blues of the beautifully coordinated outfits, smart boleros over sleek A-line dresses with white piping and matching high-heeled shoes, strings of pearls and colourful beads, all made for an arresting sight. The women all seemed to have luscious brown or black hair tumbling over their shoulders, and red or fuchsia-pink lips. The sunlight sloping in through the high stained-glass windows above the altar warmed their lustrous skin and made their glass earrings glint. Even the grandmothers looked wonderful, wearing black lace mantillas, their dresses neat and perfectly ironed. And oh, the hats! Some of them were like rare wild birds perched on the top of the women's heads, some had polka-dot lace veils, others wore pretty raffia pill-boxes.

She pictured her own mother, whose battered straw boater had got wet in the rain so many times that its ribbon was crinkled and falling loose on one side, her untamed curls escaping from underneath it.

The Italians looked so beautifully put together, an orchestrated vision of loveliness. The men wore suits with the sheen of money to them – not just the grownups, the boys as well. In their tailored three-piece suits, clean shirts and tightly knotted neckties, they looked more like miniature men, with an air of seriousness and high-mindedness. Not like the O'Shea boys: the cow-keepers. The dairy lads. Although a dairy was a perfectly respectable business, it was mucky, there was no getting away from it. The smells followed you. Worse, you stopped noticing that they did. *Pungent* was the polite way of putting it when it came to the O'Sheas. Peggy wondered what this Italian lot smelled of. Of scented flowers and sweet perfume and cologne and Parma violets, no doubt.

She turned her head again to the back of the church where her own family stood. Brendan was there, chewing his shirt cuffs, Peter playing with a marble, Sheila and Philomena teasing baby Jimmy; Ma, bored, yawning, and Da with his hands thrust deep in his pockets, jangling coins. Uncle Seamus took out a handkerchief, wiped his sweating forehead and then blew his nose on it loudly. Disgusting.

Suddenly little Peter darted out down the centre aisle. It looked like he had dropped something from his pocket, one of his marbles perhaps. Peggy twisted around to see her da run after him, hook a finger under his jumper and swipe him over the head. Baby Jimmy let out a yell to make his presence felt and shoved a stubby fist into his mouth as Ma thrust him at Brendan, who in turn thrust him into Philomena's arms. She began walking back and forth at the back of the church, jiggling him up and down, with Sheila following behind demanding she should also be allowed to carry the baby. Such fidgeting and twitching and wriggling and squirming. Peggy looked back to the Italians.

'Peg, what are you staring at?' said Frances.

'Those people.'

'Don't you know them? The Giardanos. There's a whole bunch of them,' Frances whispered. 'They live around Gerard Street.'

That was a pretty run-down part of town, thought Peg. She had been there a few times with her father,

9

on the milk round. And yet the kids all looked like princes and princesses.

'Roberto Giardano is making his communion with us.' Frances gestured towards the end of the pew at a small boy in white shorts, white shirt and red bow tie, with white knee-length socks. 'And that altar boy, that's his brother. Anthony Giardano. The handsome one.'

Anthony Giardano, with his smooth skin and soulful brown eyes, was now standing in front of a bank of flickering votive candles stuck on rows of metal spikes. His silhouette shimmered, oscillating against the light of the flames. As he walked forward, his vestments swished. He was carrying a huge, heavy Bible. He looked so serious.

If that was me, thought Peggy, I would pretend to trip over and everyone would laugh. But Anthony, with a solemn expression, bowed his head and kissed the Bible and then offered it to the priest. She watched, rapt, as the boy then turned around and knelt on one knee, a lock of his shiny black hair falling over his face. The priest placed the Bible over the back of his shoulders.

'What's he doing?' whispered Peggy as the priest opened the Bible, turning over the pages.

'He's making himself into a table.'

Anthony wobbled, but still he was steady and serious. He's going to start laughing, thought Peggy, he's going to start laughing any minute. But his expression remained earnest and grave. And he stayed like that; Frances was right, the boy was to be a human lectern until the end of the reading. When it was all over and the priest closed the Bible with a flourish, Anthony calmly stood up, brushed down his cassock and made the sign of the cross.

Peggy couldn't quite put a finger on what she was feeling, but whatever it was, it made her quiet for a few moments.

'The O'Shea girl has finally shut up,' Sister Veronica murmured to the nun sitting beside her. 'I suppose we should be thankful for small mercies.'

'Bring your candles onto the altar, children,' thundered the priest. One by one, the nun lit everyone's candle with a taper as they came out of the pew. Peggy took her place with the others as they all began to sing gustily, *'The King of love my shepherd is . . .'*

'Look at dozy Peggy O'Shea, fiddling with the blessed candle,' hissed Sister Veronica. The candles were elaborate affairs, adorned with netting and bows and curling ribbons. Discs of paper shielded the children's hands from the dripping wax. As they all shuffled into a semi-circle, Peggy paused, distracted by the lit candle. Fascinated, she tipped it to one side and watched the wax dribble and pool onto the paper. She pushed her finger into the melted wax, feeling the heat from it, enjoying the sensation of it hardening and crackling on her skin.

'Move, Peg,' said Frances.

Peggy felt a sharp shove in her back and twisted round to object, but when a globule of hot wax rolled off the paper and dripped onto the back of her wrist, she withdrew her hand quickly, fumbled . . . and dropped the candle.

There was a scream from Frances. But it was the

altar boy who brought everyone's attention to the drama unfolding. 'Fire! That girl's on fire!' he said.

The candle had become entangled in the net over-skirt of Peggy's dress, and within seconds it had set the gauze alight. The flames leapt up suddenly and frighteningly. The shock of it made Peggy's whole body rigid with panic.

'Stand back!' someone shouted.

'Do something!' someone else yelled as Peggy yelped and screamed, trying to bat the flames away as they whooshed up dramatically.

Everyone was frozen in shock. A few on the altar bolted off in fright, a few backed away in horror with hands over their mouths, before a great rushing forward of bodies, more shouting, the communion hosts tumbling off the altar and onto the floor as someone raced towards Peggy. There was a huge gasp – and then an equally huge sigh of relief, as the good-looking altar boy grabbed the jugs of water and wine and chucked one, then the other, over Peggy's dress. Their eyes met for an instant. Then, with his hands wrapped in communion napkins, he tore at the lacy overskirt, ripped it from the flimsy bodice and stamped and smothered out the flames. And it was all over in seconds, as quickly as it had started.

The organ had honked to an abrupt end, but a few bewildered voices dribbled on: '*I nothing lack if I am his, and he is mine forever . . .*'

Peggy stood there, dazed, all scabby knees and limp curls.

'Trust Peggy O'Shea,' spat Sister Veronica.

It had been an accident waiting to happen, people

would say later. The circular discs of paper were too flimsy. And who would be so stupid as to trust a girl like Peggy O'Shea with a lit candle?

'Show a bit of decency, girl! Cover yourself up!' Sister Veronica said as she dragged Peggy off by a clump of her dishevelled hair. 'You've turned this into a circus! You'll go to hell for this, Peggy O'Shea.'

In a matter of minutes, everything returned to calm and order. The altar boy was standing back beside the priest, his hands held gracefully together in prayer. The Italians once again looked as if they were posing for a painting, like the one on the domed ceiling of chubby angels blowing trumpets above the heads of saintly shepherds and kings.

Still slightly in shock, Peggy took her place back on the altar for communion. By contrast to the Italians, the O'Sheas nudged and tittered, trying to see her. They hissed to those beside them.

Peggy, who seemed not at all worried, only a little bemused at the amount of fuss, didn't help matters as she kept looking over her shoulder and smiling back at her family. They grinned back at her as though she had done something to be proud of. Sheila, who was leaping around at the back of the pews wrapped in the floaty veil like a demented Isadora Duncan, gave her the thumbs up.

At least she had made it a day to remember, her mother said later. And as there was no harm done, no one cared. It had all happened so quickly that a good many had missed it, which was why the story had to be related in loud whispers, passed along the pews: *Did you see what happened? Peggy O'Shea nearly set herself on fire and burned the church down. Never seen anything as funny in my life.*

'What a hoot,' said Uncle Seamus. 'That's the best craic I've had in weeks. In fact, months. *Years.*'

And it was true. It was the kind of incident that would be talked of for years to come. *D'you remember when Peggy O'Shea nearly set herself on fire? We still laugh about it now. Do you remember the look on Father O'Mahoney's face? How the nun cracked our Peggy over the head and pulled her by her hair while she stood there practically in just her knickers on the altar? It's true what they say about clean drawers. You never know. You just never know.*

'Hey, Peg, you're famous now,' laughed Uncle Seamus as they came out blinking into the sunshine after Mass. There was more laughter and slapping of thighs.

'Peggy, you dozy mare. You made a right show of yourself,' said her mother, but even she couldn't help her face crinkling up into a smile.

'What happened, Peg? What did I miss?' said her pal Martin Gallagher. News had somehow reached Feather Street, where he also lived, and he had run all the way to the church to ask her.

'I dropped the candle and it set fire to me dress.' Martin grinned.

'The altar boy saved the day. Wait'll I go and get him,' Peggy said, and turned, ready to dart off. 'His name's Anthony Giardano.'

'Get back here, our Peg,' said her dad suddenly and darkly. He reached out and grabbed her arm so tightly, she felt him pinching her. She didn't under-

14

stand why he had gone so quickly from laughing to looking so very serious and angry. 'The altar boy? He's one of the Giardano boys?' he asked.

'I don't know.'

She followed her father's gaze towards a handsome, dark-haired man in a suit who stood on the church steps. Over the bobbing heads of the crowd, the man was looking in their direction and returning an equally unfriendly stare. Sucking on the end of a cigarette, he flicked it contemptuously into the gutter.

Dennis O'Shea pulled Peggy roughly to one side, knelt down and spoke directly into her face, gripping her forearms.

'Peg, love, you've given us all a laugh as usual. But that's all it was, a laugh. I don't want you to go anywhere near those Giardanos. If I find out you've disobeyed me, you'll feel the back of my hand,' he said.

'Why?' she asked, bewildered.

'I don't need to tell you why,' he answered brusquely.

And so that moment in the church, one that might have entertained them for years if only things had been different, would instead turn out to be a moment that haunted them. It stuck like a thorn in their flesh, worrying and niggling; and as some said much later, if old wounds hadn't healed by now, they would never heal at all. No wonder it all ended badly.

'That Giardano boy saved me life. I could have been like the son of Abraham, Da. Could have been a crispy burnt offering right there on the altar.'

'Eh?' he asked. 'What the heck are you going on about?'

'Weren't yer listening to the priest, Da?'

'Less of the cheek, love. You keep away from him, and the Giardano lot.'

'Why? You can't make me.'

'Never mind why,' he replied.

Narrowing her steel-blue eyes, she turned around to see if she could spot the boy amongst the small group of glamorous Italians gathered under the magnolia tree, with its beautiful pink buds ready to burst into flower.

But he had gone.

Or rather, he had quietly slipped into the shade beneath the tree, discreetly placing himself behind its knotty trunk, where he had watched and listened to every word of the exchange. And just like Peggy, he too wondered why her father was saying she wasn't allowed to speak to him. What hidden secret lurked? He had seen the fury in the girl's father's eyes and the answering glare from his own father, and his curiosity grew.

'Come on! Lead the way!' someone shouted. 'Time for the shindig to start!'

They all drifted off to rooms above pubs, back parlours and parish halls for their communion parties.

The boy remained for a moment or two, staring at Peg's scowling face. She had a wild temper; but there was something about her silver-flecked blue eyes, and her generous mouth with its curving, tulip-shaped lips, that he would not forget in a hurry.

Two

The Giardanos' communion breakfast was laid out in the back room of Albertini's ice-cream bar in a side street behind Fontenoy Gardens. Each booth, with its red banquette seats and fringed lampshades hanging over the table, was squashed full of bodies.

Anthony Giardano, fresh from his heroics with the girl who had set herself on fire, watched his smiling aunt drift around the room pressing little net bags of sugared almonds tied with blue bows into the palms of the children who had just made their communion. They each squealed when they opened them and saw that there was also a five-shilling note tucked inside. When she reached Anthony, she kissed the top of his head and gave him one of the little bags. 'Antonio. For you a *bomboniera* gift also. Bravo boy with the stupido girl.'

Anthony's uncle took out his beloved violin from its case. The grownups raised their heads and paused their conversation as he played 'Maria Mari', and for a brief moment they were transported back to Bardi, or Napoli, or Roma. Anthony, meanwhile, sat in one of the booths, popped a sugared almond into his mouth and rested his chin in his palm. Mr Albertini joined his uncle and began to sing. The words of the song meant little to Anthony; he couldn't understand much Italian, just snatches, the consequence of his parents being so keen for him to be accepted as British. But he enjoyed listening to the sound of the violin and now to the others singing along. After a few songs, his uncle took his bow and a burly, thickset man stood up on the raised dais and began singing 'O Sole Mio' in a high contralto.

The Giardanos would always feel the tug of the old country, the old way of life, and even though many in this room had left Italy behind decades ago, these songs still had the power to fill their eyes with tears and remind them of the warm sun on their faces and the scent of bougainvillea.

Little cakes and ricotta pastries were handed around on a plate by a young woman wearing a pretty yellow dress and matching shoes. Ice-cream wafers dripping with raspberry juice appeared from nowhere. There was a group of girls perched on a high table in one corner, waiting for a teetering pyramid of sticky profiteroles that everyone said was on its way: white beaded purses looped over wrists, bare tanned legs swinging, feet in frilled socks crossed at the ankles. Anthony was crossing the room to join them when he felt a shove in his back.

'Come on, Tony. Let's get out of here. You coming with us to the pub?' It was one of the older boys, his cousin Matteo. 'No one will notice, what d'you say?'

It felt more like an order than a question.

Following Matteo outside because he couldn't think of an excuse not to, Anthony joined the other older cousins in a game of pitch and toss. The fresh air filling his lungs was a welcome relief after the smoke-filled room. After finishing the game they set off along the pavement, passing stubby rows of terraces and sooty factories, heading towards the Dock Road.

This part of Liverpool was ravaged from the beginning of the slum clearances, but there was enough of it standing undefeated, especially the pubs and the grocers and the pawn shops. With hands thrust deep in their pockets, chins stuck out proudly, they swaggered in concert, swigging from bottles of pale ale. They knew they were an eye-catching sight to passers-by, especially in their best clothes, starched white shirts, waistcoats and smart shoes, and they weren't surprised when people looked back over their shoulders at them and stared.

'Can I come to the pub?' asked a small voice, and Anthony felt someone tugging on his shirt. They all whirled around and laughed at little Roberto, who had run to catch up with them.

'Eh, no, bambino. Go back to the shindig.'

Roberto humphed and turned on his heel.

'Fancy the Boot?' Matteo said to everyone, with a smirk.

'Why would we go to that dive? I'd rather go to the Throstle's Nest,' said a tall, heavy-set boy. 'The O'Sheas are having their communion bash there. The cow-keepers.' A grin spread across the tall boy's face, and they all grinned back. They carried on walking and fifteen minutes later, prickling with excitement, emboldened by booze and lightheaded from the fags, they arrived at the pub.

19

Matteo indicated towards the hinged, blackened board with his beer bottle. At an upstairs window they could see a crowd of children dangling a ribbon from the sill, leaning out dangerously.

'They're O'Sheas, I swear. They know how to cause trouble. They've either got red hair or a face full of freckles, or both. That girl who set herself on fire in church? She was one of them. You know her, Tone?' asked Matteo.

Anthony frowned. 'No,' he said warily.

'You don't know the O'Sheas? Well, it's time you met them,' Gino Riozzi said, cracking his knuckles and smiling. 'Ciggie before we go in?'

He handed the packet round. They stood in a small semi-circle, lighting one cigarette from another, occasionally glancing up at the window in between flicking ash into the gutter and letting the smoke curl up languidly, blowing out perfectly formed, shivering smoke rings.

'Cig, Antonio?'

All eyes were on Anthony as Gino thrust the packet under his nose. It would have been impossible to refuse so he took one, lit it and sucked as hard as he could. Spluttering smoke and gasping, his purpling face and coughing made them all burst into laughter.

'Hey, who's the bambino now? You need to man up! You ready for the O'Shea challenge?' said Gino, slapping him on the back.

Anthony nodded nervously. But he had seen those O'Shea men. He had watched them from under the tree. They had fists like hams and thighs carved out of rock.

Matteo took a long drag of his cigarette and blew a plume of smoke out of the side of his mouth. He pushed open the double doors of the pub. Anthony was hit by the sweet smell of beer and hops and cigarette smoke. The air was tinged with a bluish fog.

'They're all upstairs,' Matteo said over his shoulder, then nodded towards the stairs in the far corner of the bar. 'This is where the fun starts.' He clapped his arm around Anthony's shoulders. 'We have a beautiful game, Tony. Think you can nick a bottle of beer from the O'Sheas' beano?'

Anthony frowned. The two older boys smirked.

'That's it. That's the game. Easy as pie. Or it would be, if it wasn't the O'Sheas. You have to be quick and crafty. If they realize a Giardano crashed their party, they'll kick ten lumps out of you. You up for it?'

What could he say? No? Gino leaned into his ear and shouted above the din of the pub, 'The one who nicks the most bottles is the winner. The one who gets his head kicked in by the O'Shea lads is the loser.'

They all laughed. 'Go on. You first, Tone. You're smaller than us. You're like a little ship rat. They won't notice you. Get up them stairs.'

'We'll have a pint waiting for you when you get back!' cried Gino. 'If you don't get your own to drink!'

Anthony took a deep breath. He separated from the group. For a moment he was going to run, but turning back and seeing them grinning, he realized he had no choice but to go up the rickety winding staircase.

21

'Gerra move on, soft lad,' said a voice behind him. He turned. It was the man who had been laughing at Peggy in the church, with the shock of ginger hair and burly frame that blocked out light, slightly slurring his words, speaking with a thick Liverpool accent.

Anthony darted up the stairs. When he reached the landing, the door swung open and the man overtook him and walked into the room. The smell of beer filled Anthony's nostrils. The blast of noise, an accordion, clapping, singing and shouting, the blur of bodies, caused him to shiver. The few people who casually looked round at him when he quickly stepped through the open door thankfully didn't comment; most of them seemed too drunk to notice. There was louder clapping and more music, the accordion roaring now and someone blowing a penny whistle, and people shouting. A woman had climbed onto the table and was lifting her skirts and each time she lifted them a little bit higher, people cheered. Someone cried, 'Give us a decko! Just another inch, Doreen, pet!'

Anthony pressed himself back against the wall, trying to make himself invisible.

'Are you Peg's brother?' a man asked, clutching a bottle of beer in each hand, steadying himself by leaning onto the wall. He squinted at Anthony as he tried to focus. 'Can't find our Martin. You seen him? Big lad? Carroty hair?' Anthony turned away, looked at the floor and didn't answer. He was thankful when the brute sank into a chair and appeared to be too drunk to keep asking.

A long trestle table ran along the centre of the room, covered in a white tablecloth stained with spilt beer, orange squash and yellow piccalilli. There were plates of half-eaten sandwiches, pork pies alongside pickled eggs. Someone pushed back a few chairs and started to sing 'The Galway Shawl'; there was a man playing a battered old accordion and beside him another man on the drum, another blowing into something that looked like a trumpet but wasn't. They all laughed, and someone started to clap and stamp their feet.

'Ah, this is the craic,' Dennis O'Shea said to a woman handing out a fresh plate of sausage rolls. He winked as he took three and stuffed two in his mouth at once. 'Wetting the baby's head, birthdays, funerals are grand, but sure, Holy Communion is what the family love most.'

Anthony watched all this, amazed. He had assumed the O'Sheas were dirt poor – they certainly looked it, from their mismatched clothes and wild hair – but there was no expense spared here. They seemed to have found the money for piles and piles of sandwiches squashed into triangles, biscuits and jelly; and cakes! Sponge cakes oozing with jam and sugar, and rich fruit cakes with dollops of icing on top of them. Not like the pretty, delicate, dainty fancies and biscotti his own family was eating down the road in the ice-cream bar.

'Make way! Make way! More scouse coming through!' someone cried.

A savoury smell filled the air, making Anthony's mouth water. There was a surge of activity as people

23

got up from chairs and moved forward to the table, pushing and jostling as they gathered around the tureen. 'You'd think these lads and lassies hadn't eaten a hot meal for months,' someone remarked.

Three screeching and giggling girls raced around a table chased by two boys, and a second woman with a huge steaming bowl of mutton stew shrieked, 'Mind out the way, eejits!' An ancient, papery-skinned lady sitting on a chair, legs splayed and leaning on a walking stick, slyly slid the stick out with a grin and a wink, causing a freckly red-haired boy to fall head over heels as he raced past her, banging down on the floor head first with a loud thwack. Cruel as it was, they all laughed and slapped their thighs when they saw the boy rolling around on the floor clutching himself in agony. When they saw the bruise purpling on his forehead, they laughed more and cried to the old woman, 'You're a devil, Maud! What did you do that for?'

'Arse over tit, our Martin went!' said a woman who rushed forward, and everyone grinned as she hugged him to her skirts. 'We'll rub a bit of marge on it and find a cabbage leaf to stop the swelling when we get home. That'll do the trick, son. You'll be right as rain.'

Head down, big round brown eyes staring up from under his thick fringe, Anthony watched all this drama, enthralled. At the far end of the room, he could see a table with crates of beer piled up on it. A few people moved away and he had a clear view of it. Steeling himself, he scurried towards it, reached out and took a bottle and quickly moved away. No one had questioned him, no one had noticed him, and with his heart beating so hard it might have burst out of his chest, he made his way back across the room. He was about to go out of the door, but not before he grabbed another half-finished bottle from the long table, took a sip and shivered, his lips curling in distaste.

And then he felt someone poke him.

'You again?' Peggy O'Shea said. 'What you doing here? Nicking our beer?'

She had a currant bun in her hand and she was idly picking the currants out, putting them in her mouth, slowly and deliberately, one at a time.

'Sorry,' he stuttered, putting both of the beers back on the table quickly. 'It's a game.' There was no mistaking her. This was the girl who had set her dress on fire.

'What game?' She narrowed her eyes, tipped her head. 'Tell me.'

'Who's this?' It was the boy who had tripped over the stick.

'No one,' replied Peggy. 'Go away, Martin.'

The boy stood staring, chewing his lip. Anthony felt his blood run cold. But then the boy turned, distracted by someone calling his name, and walked off.

'Here,' Peggy said, shoving two beers from the table into Anthony's hands. 'You can have all you want. For saving me life in church. But scram.'

'Thanks,' he said.

But then there was noise, shouting, and his heart leapt to his mouth as he just stood there, frozen.

'The Giardanos! There's a load of them down-stairs,' a man was yelling.

'The nerve!' said the warbling woman, climbing down off the table.

'The bloody cheek of them!' cried another. There was a rush of bodies over to the window and others trying to barge through the door to go downstairs and find out what was happening.

'In here,' Peggy hissed to Anthony, pulling him by the sleeve, pushing aside a bead curtain near where they had been standing. Behind it was another door, which she opened. 'Quick, hide in this cupboard with me.'

They pressed themselves against the wall, squashed together in the dusty alcove alongside mops and buckets and a smell of damp and Vim.

'What's your name?' she whispered.

'Antonio. You can call me Tony.'

'Margaret-Mary. You can call me Peg.'

He nodded, seriously. He ran his tongue over his dry lips. Peggy could hear him breathing raggedly. The light bleeding in from the keyhole meant she could see his shoes. Those shoes. Shiny, with laces like liquorice. And then, from outside, there was more shouting and thundering down stairs – or was it up? It was hard to tell.

'In the bar! The Giardanos!' cried a voice.

'You, wind your flaming neck in!' someone cried.

Peggy opened the door an inch and peered out. 'They're all scrapping,' she said, grinning. People were crowding around the open windows, trying to get a look at the punching and kicking that had spilled out onto the pavement. 'You frightened?' she asked him.

'No,' he replied.

'Yes, you are. I can see you're sweating. There's another way down if you don't want to get involved or anyone to see you. There's a door behind the table with the cakes on it. It leads to the back stairs.'

'Ta,' he said. He took a deep breath. Right now, everything in his body was screaming at him with one single word: *run*. Flinging open the door, he shot out and, head down, dipped, curved and swooped round the trestle tables and between the chairs.

Watching him go out the door, Peggy smiled and smoothed down her skirt. Then, out of the corner of her eye, she noticed something on the floor by her foot. It didn't look like it belonged there. She bent down and picked up the little net bag, turning it over in her hand, undoing the small blue ribbon with the holy medal tied on one end. Her eyes widened when she saw the five-shilling note stuffed inside. It must have fallen out of the boy's pocket when they had crouched down, trying to hide themselves. Anthony Giardano.

'Anthony Giardano,' she murmured, rolling the *r* on her tongue and enjoying the strange sound of it in her mouth. Anthony Giardano had forgotten his sweets and a five-bob note.

As the sound of more shouting rose up in the street, a cry went up. 'The coppers! Scarper, everyone!'

'Leg it!' said another voice, as the clanging of a bell rose in pitch from somewhere far off.

27

Three

Moira O'Shea lay in bed on her back in the hollow of the old horsehair mattress, staring at the creeping patch of damp on the ceiling. She could hear her husband bumping around downstairs. Baby Jimmy was in a drawer beside her. She was exhausted. Turning her head, she looked at him lying there. He was a small peachy bundle, his velvety head poking out of the top of the swaddling. She reached out a hand and touched him. Sometimes she did that, just to feel him breathing. Lying on her side, she luxuriated in the silence and felt relieved there was nothing to fill it for a moment. There was so much noise in this house. So many children. And they just kept coming. She curled herself into a ball.

She felt her eyelids going heavy, prayed she would be asleep by the time Dennis came upstairs. It wasn't that she didn't love her husband. But she was so tired. So very tired. And the Holy Communion bash had been so eventful, what with Peggy setting herself on fire and the bust-up with the Giardanos. It had just about finished her off.

'Christ on a crutch,' said a voice at the foot of the stairs. It was Dennis. It sounded like he had tripped over something. One too many at the Throstle's Nest lock-in again.

28

She winced. Should she pretend to be asleep? Please God, he would leave her alone tonight.

'Are you asleep?' he said. The bed creaked as he sat on the end of it and pulled off his boots. She heard the thwack of the laces. 'Are you asleep or awake, Moy?'

'I was asleep. I think.'

He took off his trousers.

'What a day . . .' he said. When he got in the bed and under the eiderdown with a puff of feathers escaping from gaps in the stitching, he curved his body around hers. She felt his hands pull up her nightdress and touch her bottom. He smelled beery and when he kissed her neck, she squirmed away.

'Too tired,' she murmured. 'The kids . . . You'll wake them.'

'Ah, come on now, Moy. I need to sleep too, but you wouldn't leave a fella all twitching next to you because he couldn't find a bit of peace with his wife.' His hands were moving down her body now, between her legs. 'Don't be such a tease, Moira.'

A tease! She thought of herself, pale and wan and worn out after all these babies. When she was young she hadn't been able to keep her hands off him either, but she was lithe and pretty then. Now she felt old and tired, but it seemed to make no difference to her husband. 'Ah, come on now,' he said. 'I love you, Moira.'

He had never stopped telling her how much he loved her. If she was half dressed, he would pause and reach out to touch her breast, or place his hand on the cheek of her bottom and cup it gently, saying he couldn't help himself, it was because he loved her. There was always another baby to feed, another toddler to wash, but it didn't stop him. He would take what he could. A handful of flesh here, a kiss on the lips there, a nuzzle, a suck, a lick, a sniff.

She felt his arms circle her waist and his hands cup her bottom. She felt him part her legs with his knee, and she twisted her head, looked across at her sleeping children. There was an art to doing it with a one-year-old in a drawer and a three-year-old in a cot bed lying next to them without waking them, and Dennis had perfected it. He knew how to do it quickly and quietly. Sometimes he gently put his hand over her mouth, sometimes he did it with barely a movement, just breathing and sighing, and it was over in minutes.

'Wait,' she said, fumbling in the side drawer. 'I'm not having another baby.'

There were six of them now. And that was enough. Father O'Mahoney said to her that each child was a blessing. But it was less of a blessing when you couldn't feed them, when they got sent home from school or ticked off by the bobbies, or day in, day out when they kicked and screamed and never seemed to do what you asked. Sure, she loved her children, but a blessing? A curse, more like. But Father had said it was wrong to use a rubber. Not that he'd used that term, but he'd said it in so many words from the pulpit.

Doreen, her sister-in-law, had told her about something called the rhythm method. She'd given Moira a chart, and Moira had tried to remember counting the days, even ticked them off with a red pencil. But she could barely remember what day the bread man was coming or how much she owed the coal man, or what night was Brendan's Boys' Brigade, or if this was the week the girls needed a bath and fresh drawers. She had even forgotten the baby that morning, for goodness' sake. More often than not, the red squiggles and crosses were never remembered until Dennis came upstairs and started putting his hands all over her. Then she tried to count backwards through the days in her head, but that was hopeless as well.

'We can't have another baby. I mean it, Denny.' She was groping in the dark in the back of the drawer, searching for the rubbers Doreen had given her.

But he wasn't listening. He pulled her back to him and kissed her, mumbling about how they'd manage – 'Put them johnnies away, let's take a chance just this once, I like it the natural way, the way God intended' – and now he was moving inside her, moaning and pulling open her nightdress to expose her breasts and kissing her, and she was weakening because the truth was she took such comfort from the fact that he loved her, and it allowed her to forget that they were poor because she revelled in the fact that this was a pleasure that was hers to enjoy just as much as those who had all the money in the world. No one loved her like Dennis. But he obviously hadn't listened to a word she'd said; why would he?

'Well, Father O'Mahoney will be praising God that we didn't use a johnny,' she said, after they both flopped in exhaustion. 'But if I'm flaming pregnant,

I'll kill you, Dennis O'Shea. So I bloody will.' There was a pause as shadows moved across the room. You could hear the baby breathing.

'That was a party and a half, wasn't it? Those Giardanos, I ask you. Our lads gave 'em what for, though.'

'They did indeed,' she murmured, drifting off into sleep.

Four

When Peggy arrived at school on Monday morning, late as usual, there was a gaggle of children waiting for her at the gates. As they followed her in, they began singing to the tune of 'London's Burning': *'Peggy's burning, Peggy's burning, fetch the engine, fetch the engine, fire fire! Fire fire! Pour on water, pour on water . . .'*

'Shurrup,' she yelled, but there was just more laughter. 'Leave me alone,' she snapped.

'What's the matter, moo-cow?' someone said.

She pursed her lips, gave one of her signature scowls. She was used to the constant jokes about cows and mooing, because of the dairy. And she had long since learned how to pretend that she didn't care. But she had also learned that if you stood up to this kind of boy, they usually backed down.

'Next time, Rickets Roberts, when your skint ma comes begging me da to give her another week to pay for her milk, me da'll say she should sling her hook,' she said.

'Ha! Says a flamin' O'Shea. Your brother doesn't even come to school wearing shoes some days. You're so poor, the only toy the O'Sheas have got to play with is a mouldy cowpat,' he retorted.

Despite her cocksure thrust of the chin and firm hands on hips, the words stung Peggy like actual fire. It was true; she had lost count of the weeks her da would drink away any money they made on a Friday night, and their two mangy, tired cows hardly made a dairy. But she wasn't going to hear it from Rickets Roberts.

'Say that to me face!' she yelled and ran forward, nostrils flaring, head down like a bull. With a shriek, she crashed into the boy's stomach. Winded, he turned puce, clutched himself and doubled up as he staggered groggily around the playground.

'*Pe-ggy, Pe-ggy, Pe-ggy,*' chanted everyone as Peggy, bringing her hand around, started striking whoever got near her with a ringing blow, swinging punches wildly.

And then suddenly there was a great flapping across the tarmac. It was Sister Dorothea rushing forward, a huge great black crow shouting, 'No fighting, Peggy O'Shea! Is that you? I heard about the communion party, and now you're at it again!' As she stepped into the scuffle and prised the children apart, the rosary beads hanging from her waist became tangled in Peggy's wild, straggly hair.

'Ow! Sister, you're hurting me!' yelled Peggy as she was dragged off, head bent, still attached to the nun.

'Peggy O'Shea. What are you good at?' said Sister Veronica half an hour later, squinting at Peggy through wire spectacles.

They were in her office. Peggy, sitting on a hard

chair in front of the sister's desk, stared into her lap and picked at her nails.

'Lift your head up and have the decency to look at me. What exactly is the point of you, Peggy O'Shea? Playing the fool and fighting like the rest of your boneheaded family?'

'I don't know, Sister.'

'Don't know what?'

'I don't know what's the point of me, Sister Veronica.'

For a moment Peggy let the silence stick between her and the nun. Sister Veronica sighed. 'Surely you're better than that? You've a brain in that head, not stuffing. Use it, girl.'

'Sorry, Sister,' she mumbled.

'Don't let it happen again. You're only eight. You've got your whole life ahead of you. It's not been a good start, but you've still plenty of time to turn things around.'

'Aye, Sister.'

'Yes, Sister. Not aye, Sister. For pity's sake. Sit up straight. Don't mumble. Now I'll say this only once. Find something you're good at. And stick to it. Find a path in your life, and good things will come. It doesn't have to be like this. Always doing stupid things. Pegging yourself to the washing line, getting your head stuck in the railings . . .'

'Aye . . . yes, Sister.'

'Now get out of here. And make sure you confess all this nonsense to Father O'Mahoney next time you're in church. If we're having a fresh start, you'll feel better when you've cleaned your slate with God, not just me and Sister Dorothea. Pull up your socks and go.'

Peggy nodded. But as she was about to leave, the nun stopped her.

'By the way, your ma, how is she? I heard it was the Giardanos who turned up at the communion party. Was that hard for her?'

Peggy shrugged. 'She's grand. Me da said we knocked seven bells out of them Giardanos.'

The nun winced. 'Can't have been easy to see, though, can it?'

They were strange words to hear from the nun, and it was a question Peggy didn't know how to answer.

Later, in the classroom, things had become calmer. As Sister Dorothea walked between the desks with a long ruler in her hand, pointing and poking and prodding at everyone's open arithmetic exercise books, Peggy leaned over and whispered questions behind her hand to Frances.

'Fran. Franny . . . Anthony Giardano, you said he goes to Holy Cross School? Next to the church? At the bottom of Fontenoy Street?'

'Yes. Why do you want to know?'

'He's an altar boy?'

'Mmm. All the Italians are altar boys. They're dead holy. He's there every Sunday with his family. Unlike your lot. You'd know that if you went to Mass. Be quiet, Peg, I'm trying to do this sum. If you have six apples in one hand and seven in the other, then times that by thirteen, what d'you have?'

'Big hands? Who knows, who cares,' Peg replied, sucking the end of the ruler pensively.

It was Saturday afternoon and Anthony Giardano was with his father in the Fascio Club in a side street off the bottom of Bold Street, perched on a high stool, drinking a milkshake through a red and white straw. Behind the bar stood a pretty, olive-skinned waitress, drying glasses with a tea towel in front of a gold-framed picture of a smiling King Vittorio.

'I don't like it,' said Enzo Giardano, sipping a glass of grappa.

He was resting his foot on the brass rail, a cigarette drooping from his lip. The glasses lined up on the glass shelf and the rows of bottles filled with exotic-coloured liquids, aniseeds and garish turquoises and the vibrant yellows of limoncello, threw back reflections which made prisms of coloured light shimmy across the ceiling and bounce off the mirrored walls of the room.

'Mussolini cosying up to the generals like that,' Enzo went on. 'Gives me the willies.'

'Me too. Tickling each other's bellies,' said a man stirring heaped spoonfuls of sugar into a tub of cream.

'Nonna is upset.'

'That's not surprising.'

'Mussolini? I'll not have a word said against him,' said the barmaid.

'*Sì.* He's doing so much good for Italy,' said a third fellow in a neat suit sitting at the far end of the bar, staring with love into his grappa.

Anthony, listening to all this, wiped his finger

around the inside and sucked it. He wasn't quite sure what they were talking about but he was happy to just listen; he enjoyed it when they switched between Italian and English, peppering their sentences with expansive hand gestures and expletives and exclamations he didn't quite understand.

'We loved him at first, but I'm not so sure now. And while we're on the subject, I think you should change the name of your cafe, Luigi. Fascio Club – it doesn't sound good. It's bringing a lot of attention lately. People don't like it round here.'

Sofia Giardano, Anthony's mother, bustled about behind the bar carrying a tray of washed gold-rimmed glasses.

'Why should we?' the barmaid said. 'All we do is play bingo and dominoes and meet with friends for supper. It's our social club.'

'It's not good, though, now they've started asking us to send more of our wages home. I don't like it.'

'Enjoying the milkshake, son?' asked Enzo, changing the subject. Anthony slurped at the remains of the drink with the straw and squirmed away as his father ruffled his hair.

The girl behind the bar laughed also, showing her large white teeth. 'You heard about those O'Sheas? You hear about our boys going to their party?'

Anthony paused, felt his heart beat a little faster.

Enzo frowned and shook his head. 'I told them to stay away. I heard there was a big bust-up.'

'There was. Pretty bad. They were brawling outside on the pavement. Joseph came home with a shiner.

38

The police had to break it up. Our boys held up, but it was an idiotic thing to do. Don't know why they decided to go to the Throstle's Nest.'

The girl behind the bar puckered her lips. 'What I don't understand is why you Giardanos hate the O'Sheas? Funny, you get on so well with the Flanagans. You designed the mosaics at their shop, didn't you, Enzo?'

She was talking about the entranceway of Flanagan's Grocers – a beautiful design with the words 'James Flanagan' picked out in swirling Italian mosaic tiles above the door. 'And the Liverpool Irish and us Italians have so much in common. We're all Catholics and we're in church together all the time. Parading up and down Scottie Road with our statues and dressing up our little girls as May Queens in lace curtains. Kiddies at the same schools. Mr Albertini doesn't have a problem with them. What is it with you and the O'Sheas?'

No one answered. Enzo and Sofia glanced at each other. Anthony waited to hear their reply.

'They've had it in for us for years,' said Enzo carefully. 'It started when they refused to deliver milk to us. Then they tried to get everyone else round here to stop doing business with us. Someone lost an eye in a fight in a pub over it.'

The girl chewed her lip. She wasn't convinced that he was right.

Gloria Giardano, with a coolness beyond her thirteen years, in white socks and a red and white polka dot dress with a nipped-in waist, appeared from behind a beaded glass curtain with a jug of lemonade on a silver tray. 'The O'Shea boys call us dirty tallys,' she said. 'That's why.'

'I know about all that. I know a fight breaks out whenever the O'Sheas and the Giardanos catch sight of each other. And I know our boys call them filthy Fenians. But why?'

Gloria shrugged and tossed back her shimmering, glossy hair. They couldn't quite remember the details. Exactly what had caused this hatred between the two families, no one could say, and the silence in the room spoke for itself. But from the looks on their faces, it didn't really matter, either. They just knew that it was so.

Sunday morning, and usually Peggy would be up and out of the house, milking or helping her father with a delivery. Either that or someone would be asking her to clean the grate or take baby Jimmy out in the pram, feed him or change him, or walk Peter and Sheila to the boating lake, or stop the chickens escaping. But today, calculating her mother would be in a good mood, she got up before everyone else and hoped no one would ask her to do any chores.

She dug out an old but pretty floral dress from the bottom drawer that she had worn once, for her brother's christening. Looking at her reflection in the mirror, she was amazed to see that it still fitted. It was a little tight and the seams of the ruched bodice strained a little, and perhaps it was too short, but she still managed to do it up, fiddling with the small round pearlized buttons, using her thumb to push them through the buttonholes. She slipped her feet into her scuffed boots.

'Ooh. Look at you, Peggy love,' quipped her mother when she came into the kitchen.

'Where are you going dressed up like that?' her father said. 'What's all this about?'

She narrowed her eyes at him. *Shut up*, her expression said. She sat down and began tightening her boot laces.

'You're all dressed up. You're usually never out of your dungies,' said her mother.

Peggy scowled, irritated. As she angrily pulled the laces too tight, one of them snapped. 'Blast. Now look what you've made me do,' she said, which just made them laugh.

'That wasn't my fault,' said her mother.

'Yes, it was.'

'So come on then, why are you all glammed up? You've even brushed your hair. Have you really put that dress on to do the cows? Sit down and eat up your breakfast.'

Peggy grimaced at the plate of cold leftover scouse from the communion party that her mother plonked in front of her. She picked up the food and pushed her fork into a lump of gristle, held it up and twirled it, inspecting it as if Moira had just prepared it with the intention of poisoning her.

'I'm not eating scouse for brekkie. And I'm *not* doing the flaming cows,' she said, putting the fork down and pushing her plate away. 'I'm going to church.'

'Church?' said her father.

41

'Church?' echoed her mother with a splutter of laughter. 'Christ alive! What's brought this on?'

'I'm full of Jesus's love,' Peggy replied flatly. 'My heart is brimming with the Holy Spirit.'

'I've heard it all now,' said her father.

'You're mad,' said Brendan, wandering in chewing a bit of bacon rind. He wound it around his finger, examining it, and stuck it back into his mouth.

'Never mind all this Jesus talk. I want you to clean the grate.'

'Sorry, Ma, God is calling me,' Peggy said, jumping up, pushing the chair out from under her and grabbing her cardigan. 'And if God is calling me it's only right that I should answer.'

Her mother and father looked at each other in open-mouthed shock.

Peggy whirled around in a flurry of humphs and stomps and raised eyebrows, and then she was gone.

'What's going on with her?' Dennis said to Moira.

'I haven't a clue.'

'Me neither. She's certainly behaving very strangely.'

'Aye. Very bloody strangely indeed.'

Holy Cross was already filling up. Peggy slipped in and took her seat in the back pew. A sense of anticipation settled upon her. She turned over the bag of sugared almonds nestling in her palm, felt it going hot in her hand. A nun entered and lit a candle, bowed in front of the altar. Peggy craned her neck and waited.

The choir began singing the entrance hymn, 'Praise, My Soul, the King of Heaven'. The Monsignor and another priest and three altar boys that Peggy didn't recognize, carrying candles, began slowly and reverently walking down the centre aisle towards the altar. Disappointment took hold of her. Damn it. Frances had got it wrong. There was no Anthony Giardano here today. Annoyed with herself that she had gone to the trouble of putting a dress on, one that itched and scratched and she couldn't properly breathe in, she slumped back in the pew, feeling foolish.

After ten minutes she left the sound of murmured prayers behind, unabashed by the stares she received as she pushed past people in the pew to make her way outside.

But as she set off down the road in the direction of the tram, there he was: Anthony Giardano, with a stick in his hand, trailing it across the railings and enjoying the sound of it. He stopped and stood blinking in the sunlight, navy blue tones picked out in his glossy black hair. He was wearing shorts and a newly ironed white shirt. His long legs looked tanned and smooth in contrast to Peg's scabby knees and the pink marks where she'd enjoyed picking at grazes before they had properly healed. Usually she was proud of her scars and would talk them through with relish to anyone who cared to listen: this is where I fell off the wall, this is where our Brendan walloped me with a bike chain, this is where I stepped on the rake.

'Anthony Giardano?' She lingered by the railings, pushed a foot between the bars, tipped her head to one side. 'Why aren't you serving?'

'I was.' He absent-mindedly peeled a piece of bark

off the stick before throwing it down and wiping his hands on his shorts. 'Half eight Mass. Father asked me to stay and help with the mission boxes.'

She felt the bag of sugared almonds in her pocket. She had come here to give him it; there had been the crisp five-shilling note inside, and she wondered if he even knew. That's why she was here and that's what she was going to do.

'You left your bag of sweets. There was money in it. Five bob. Here.'

He looked surprised. 'Ta,' he said, taking the bag. 'My auntie gave it me for altar serving. Must have dropped it.'

She nodded seriously.

'What you going to do with it? The money, I mean?'

'Save it, I suppose,' he answered, frowning.

There was a pause. Peggy rubbed at an invisible mark on the stone flags with her scuffed toe, then shoved a piece of hair behind her ear. 'Why?'

Lines creased across his smooth brow. He pondered the question for a moment. 'Don't know,' he replied.

'You know Hegarty's sweet shop down Scottie Road? D'you like sweets? You like them sugared almonds, don't yer?'

'Course. But I'm not allowed to go there,' he replied, and squinted away into the distance.

'How would anyone know? Just lie. Say you're doing the mission boxes for the poor. Say there was a whole load of them. You ever had a flying saucer? They taste like Holy Communion but nicer.'

He chewed his bottom lip, shook his head.

'Come on then. Shall we go?' The way she said it, so purposefully and direct, it would have been impossible to refuse. 'We can go to the reccy after. Our Brendan knows how to get a rope and throw it over a lamp post to make a swing and I play steeries with one of me ma's old prams. But in Fontenoy Gardens reccy they've a witch's hat.'

'I'm not supposed to.'

'Don't be a baby. Are you daft or summat? Don't you want to?'

'Yes,' he said, earnestly.

'Well, come on then.'

They walked along the dock road and through the maze of sooty back-to-back terraces with their puny outhouses. Peg leapt back and forth over the handrail that ran all the way up Havelock Hill, before hopscotching along the pavement. Anthony jogged along behind. 'Bet you can't catch me, slowcoach!' she yelled at him.

The bell jangled loudly in the sweet shop when they went in. Fat Mr Hegarty came out, wearing a white apron. They rested their chins and fingertips on his polished wooden counter. With his bulbous nose and his white hair and beard, he had a look of Father Christmas. Lined up on varnished wooden shelves were glass jars of sugared almonds and cinder toffee. The sweet smell and the sight of the metal scoops dusty with sugar, tied onto chains and hanging from the shelves above the gleaming linseed-oiled wooden floor, were intoxicating.

'I'll have sixpence of orange bonbons. And he'll

have ten flying saucers. And ten penn'orth of pear drops,' said Peggy. 'And a bag of sugared mice.'

'Now Peg, how can you afford that? I'm not giving it you for nothing.'

'He's paying,' she said, and nodded at Anthony.

Anthony put his hand in his pocket and tentatively held out the five-shilling note. Mr Hegarty raised his eyebrows; as they moved upwards, it was like white spiders coming to life. 'A five-bob note? Who's this? Rockefeller?' he said.

'His auntie gave it him for being an altar boy.'

'Oh really?' Mr Hegarty sounded suspicious, but he turned towards the shelves.

They waited, rapt, as he took down the jars. There was the sound of the twist of the lid, the rattle of the scoop as it plunged into the glass jars, the clatter of the pear drops and bonbons as he spilled them into the metal weighing scales and the rustle of the paper bag as he tipped in the sugared mice and flying saucers. Deftly twisting the corners of the bag, he handed it over to an enthralled Peggy and Anthony.

When they got outside they both squatted down on the pavement. Peggy opened the bag, her mouth watering at the sweet smell as she went solemnly through it. 'You choose first. But I don't like the yellow pear drops. Too sour. You can have 'em.'

'I don't like bonbons much. Too tangy.'

They each decided on a sweet, put it in their mouth, and fell quiet as they savoured the taste, cheeks bulging, their tongues and the insides of their mouths prickling as they sucked.

'D'you want to be my friend?' said Peggy.

He nodded in reply.

'Here.' From her pocket she produced a large purple gobstopper.

'Where'd you get that from?' he asked, wide-eyed.

'Nicked it,' she said, her eyes full of mischief.

'From the sweet shop?'

'Aye. I'm good at it. Me brother Brendan taught me. Tastes even nicer when you don't pay for it. You'll see.'

'You really nicked it?'

'Nicked it for you.'

When they got to the witch's hat at Fontenoy Gardens, Anthony and Peggy sat on the wooden seat, legs dangling over the side of it, resting their forearms on the metal bar at chest level as they used their feet to push themselves off. The metal frame, shaped like a cone, swung round wildly from left to right then right to left.

'Me da would kill me if he knew I was talking to you.' She took out the lollipop she was sucking, regarded it, put it back in her mouth again.

'Mine too.'

'Why?'

'Dunno. Because I'm Italian, maybe?'

'Because I'm Irish? Except not all Italians hate the Irish. We know the Riozzis. We deliver our milk to them and me da likes the craic with them. And the Macari girl whose dad owns the music shop is in my class, and she comes to the dairy to stroke the cows.'

'I don't know why, then. My Papa just says you O'Sheas are a bad lot.'

She pursed her lips. 'Lots of people say that about us. Mainly because of Brendan nicking stuff, but lots of people love us an' all. Say they couldn't do without us.'

'Mm,' he said.

'Maybe it's just because I'm an O'Shea and you're a lying, cheating Giardano,' she said, and laughed and thumped him playfully on his upper arm.

'Or maybe because I'm a Giardano and you're a thieving, feckless O'Shea,' he said, giggling, and then a pear drop somehow lodged in the back of his throat and caused him to choke a little and gesture to Peggy to wallop him on his back, and they both laughed harder as she did it.

'What's feckless?' she asked.

'You lot,' he replied, and they giggled again.

'See you tomorrow after school to finish the sweets?'

'Kay. See you, Peggy O'Shea,' he replied.

Five

The letter that Enzo Giardano found on the table when he arrived home came in a buff envelope with a pink Italian stamp on it. He peered at the round, fat letters scrawled across it.

'Read it to me, my eyes aren't good in this light,' said Sofia, when she got back from the ice-cream parlour. The weather had changed unexpectedly, and she peeled off her coat.

They went inside. Enzo opened the crisp envelope and unfolded the contents. As soon as he set eyes on it, he wished he hadn't.

'Are you sure you don't want to read it yourself?' he asked.

Sofia faltered. She went and sat at the table, close to the fire on the range. 'No,' she said, and closed her eyes and winced, her head thrumming with anxious thoughts about what was coming. 'Tell me later.'

There was a note from his cousin Giuseppe, and a sketch on a piece of paper folded into quarters. Enzo looked at the sketch first. It was a design for a mosaic his father had been commissioned to do for a butcher's shop in Bardi. Then his attention was drawn to the note.

Dear Enzo,

I'm not quite sure where to start. I don't trust what Mussolini is doing. We went down to the square the other day and it was all everyone was talking about. There was a group of men, and they had banners and flags and they were standing on boxes shouting. And Father Paolo came running out of church because they were creating such a racket. Waving flags and slapping each other's backs like they were the kings of the world. Thankfully Father Paolo chased these clowns off with a broom. But it gave me a bad feeling. You certainly are in the right place. How lucky you are that Liverpool welcomed you with open arms like it did. But I'm still worried about Lucia on her own. She's refusing to move. And I'm sure she's dying. Your cousin in New York is insisting I go and stay there.

Mussolini looks such a fool with his arms waving about like he's directing traffic in the square. I'm sorry to bring it up again but I can't get the newsreels out of my mind. We all went to see it at the cinema. Pathé filmed it. A whole load of red-faced, over-excited fools. I can see this escalating, can't you? He would love a war. Any war. Would love to go stomping his boots all over Albania. And Europe, for that matter.

Make sure you have all your papers in order. They've set up committees here to go

*looking into the affairs of those Italians that
live abroad, now insisting they send money
back to Italy. It's happening in New York, so
it will be happening there in Liverpool soon,
no doubt. Keep away from Luigi's Fascio
Club. He says it's harmless, but it's not like it
used to be.*

*Please write. I still can't quite decide what
to do next. You could come home I suppose.*
Giuseppe

Enzo folded the piece of paper slowly, slipped it
back into the envelope. Go home? To Italy? Why
would he do that? They had been here ten years now.
He raked his fingers back through his hair and rubbed
his scalp, trying to make sense of what he had just
read. Why was his cousin suggesting that he return
to Italy? He had made a life here. His children already
had Liverpool accents and they had been brought up
barely speaking Italian, so desperate had Enzo and
Sofia been for them to fit in.

No, for now, he would put the letter in the drawer
and not say anything to Sofia apart from showing
her the sketch. That way nothing would change. He
liked his life here. And most of all, he liked spending
time at the club with Luigi. What a fuss Giuseppe
was making. He didn't wear the fascist party lapel
pin like some in Liverpool still did. He had stopped
that years ago. He wasn't that stupid.

Six

The following day, at half past three, Anthony arrived at the reccy. He was in his school uniform and looked neat and clean. He wore a grey sweater with yellow lines around the V-shaped neck. A blue and white striped tie. Shorts. Socks with elastic around the top of them and a little coloured label sticking out.

Peggy, with her hair in plaits, was sitting on a low wall, her jumper pulled over her knees. Her clothes were baggy, holes at the elbows, one of the pockets torn off, cuffs so frayed they looked like lace edgings.

She watched him jog across the playground, amazed at how smart and clean he looked. Neat as a new pin, and after a whole day at school. The O'Shea family were too poor and had never managed to look like that, even at weddings and funerals. Too many mouths to feed. That's what her mother always seemed to be shouting all over the place. 'You lot eat me out of house and home. How are we supposed to pay the rent? I'm worn out. You're the worst, Peg. State of you, and look at the mess in here!' The Italians had things in their lives that her ma and da would never have dreamt of: ice-cream carts, fish and chip shops, music shops, hairdressers. O'Sheas just have too many bairns and too many flaming cows, she thought.

'I thought you were going to be late. You're out of breath. You've been running.'

'I had to go with Papa to the town hall after school to help with the mosaics.'

'What's mosaics?'

'Little pieces of shiny glass and stone. You make pictures out of them, on floors in halls and in shop doorways and gravestones and things like that . . .'

'What for?'

'Not for anything.' He smiled. 'Just cos people like them. Kirkland's bakery have just done their name above the entrance. Some rich people decorate their front doorsteps with mosaics.'

'Me ma decorates our front step with her scrubbing brush,' she said, grinning. 'She decorates me and our Brendan with it, 'an all.'

He laughed. 'The Giardano family is famous in Liverpool for our mosaics . . .'

She tipped her head to one side, chewed her lip.

He took her hand. 'Come with me . . .' Leading her down the entry passage and into the courtyard, they stood under the arch of Fontenoy Gardens. 'Look down,' he said, his voice bouncing off the curving brickwork.

He held her under her elbow and repositioned her so she moved back an inch. He indicated the paving slab under their feet, studded with beautifully arranged stones with the words 'Fontenoy Gardens' picked out in green and glass square tiles. 'This is one of ours. All those tiny bits of glass. The Giardanos did that.'

She squatted on her haunches, traced a finger over

the intricate patterns made by the tiny pieces of glass in swirling patterns. 'Right nice.'

'Right nice,' he echoed. 'Papa says it another way. *Bellissimo*.'

'*Bellissimo*,' she repeated, turning the word round in her mouth. She liked the way it sounded when he said it.

'You want to see where we make 'em?' he said.

'Aye,' she said seriously.

They caught the tram from outside. It was a short journey, but one Peggy had made many times before. She rested her forehead flat against the window, enjoying the feel of the vibrations rattling through her body.

'Me brother Brendan comes down here on a Saturday to mind people's bikes.'

'That's nice,' he said.

'Eh?' she said, and then laughed. 'Penny to mind your bike. It's daylight robbery, more like. He punctures their tyres if they don't cough up, and everyone knows it.'

They got off the board. On the short walk through a maze of back streets, from her pocket Peggy took the bag of sherbet they had bought. She licked a finger, stuck it into the sugar and sucked it.

'Your turn,' she said, offering the bag to him.

'Ta.'

The sign on the outside of the building read 'Giardano Mosaics'. A straggly wisteria wound its branches around the lintel, dripping purple flowers. Anthony glanced over each shoulder as he approached the building. She watched as he reached inside the letterbox and pulled out a key that was on a string. He put it in the keyhole and opened the door, and she followed him in.

In the half-light she could see barrels stacked up, a long table, and vague shapes. But when he switched on the light the shapes began to take on recognizable forms. The room was large and airy with high windows. A long, wide table with low benches either side stood in the centre. Along each wall there were cupboards with shelves above, holding jars and bowls in various shapes and sizes. There were sinks at each end of the room, and containers full of an assortment of brushes.

She followed him as he walked over to a barrel. He slid off the circular lid to reveal stacks of square glass tiles. He picked the top one off, blew the dust away, and rubbed the surface with his fingers.

'We cut these tiles into tiny pieces.' He nodded towards a shelf from which hung hooked and pointed metal instruments and sharp knives. He took one of the knives, laid the tile on the marble-topped table and sliced the stone in half. Peggy was amazed that it seemed to cut as easily as butter. 'Sometimes you just break them into tiny pieces by smashing them with a hammer. We put them in the putty.' He pulled out a drawer under the table. In it were sheets of what looked like baking paper.

Lifting the top sheet to the light, Peggy saw that on the paper there were beautiful intricate designs drawn in pencil.

'The little pieces are called tesserae, by the way,' he said.

'Tesserae,' she repeated. She had never heard such a word. It felt soft around the edges when she spoke it.

'Papa gets the tiles sent over from Italy. His brother has a business there. All these little stones and pieces of glass are shipped over from Napoli. Simple really. He just makes pictures, but with bits of stone and glass.'

'Instead of tubes of paint? That's nifty.'

He pulled off a sheet covering something on the table. Laid out on a beautiful slab was a frame with a half-finished collage of blue and green mosaics in the shape of a fish.

'Do you like it?'

'Mosaics,' she said, tracing her hand over the swirls. 'Aye. I do. They're . . . more than pretty . . .'

She walked around the room, stopping occasionally and touching things: a knife, a jar, a tile, a crescent moon made from stone. Her big blue eyes widened. 'I didn't know about any of this lark. Mosaics,' she repeated. 'They're like diamonds,' she said, half to herself and half to Anthony. 'Can I look at them ones up there?' she asked, pointing at a high shelf.

He nodded, went up the wooden stepladder and took down a glass jar. Inside it were pieces that had already been cut into fragments, each as small and fragile as a fingernail. He poured the contents of the jar into a bowl.

Digging her hands deep into the bowl, Peggy scooped the pieces of glass up, spread her fingers wide and let them fall through, enjoying their exquisite beauty. She felt embarrassed by the dirt pushing up under her fingernails. Such delicate, beautiful pieces of glass deserved better than her grubby hands.

'Look at this,' Anthony said. With a flourish, he pulled off an old dustsheet covering a tall shape on a wooden plinth and revealed a large stone statue of an angel, bigger than he was. It was only half finished, but one of its wings had already been studded with pieces of yellow and white glass.

Peggy felt her throat tickle, and she coughed. Anthony pushed the angel an inch towards the centre of the room.

'It's all glittery. Like it's alive.'

He laughed. 'Which is funny, cos it's going in a cemetery.'

'Will you be a mosaic man like your da when you grow up?'

'No,' he said. 'I want to be a soldier. Join the air force. Or the army. *Pow pow*,' he said, squinting with one eye and miming firing a gun at her.

'Why not mosaics?'

He shrugged. 'All the Giardanos do mosaics. I want to do something different. What d'you want to be?'

'Dunno.' She paused for a moment, as though thinking about her future for the first time. 'I don't want to work in the dairy. I'm not going to be a cow-keeper. Don't want to do the milking. Don't even like helping my cousins in the shop with the jug-filling. They hardly give me a penny,' she said, rearranging the handful of glass fragments on the saucer. 'Me ma and da would just have me doing cows forever. But not flipping likely. Maybe I'll be an explorer. Or I'll join the circus and walk the tightrope.'

57

'Eh? That's silly.'

'Why? I'm good at balancing. You saw me on the top of that wall. Watch me walk in a straight line. I could be one of those ladies who wobble on balls. I fancy that.'

Jumping up onto the low bench, she stretched out her arms and walked along it, carefully placing one foot in front of the other. 'Have you ever been to the scaldies?'

'I've seen kids swimming in there.'

'You mean you've never done it yerself?'

He shook his head. 'My mamma told me the chemicals from the factories swoosh around in there. That's why it's so warm. I heard you can get sick from it and turn yellow.'

'Codswallop. Me and my brother and my sisters always go in there. I've never had a dicky tum from it. Not once, it's right lovely. Roll up your keks and dip your feet in and wiggle your toes in it, you'll see how warm it is.'

'Does it smell?' he said.

'Pongs a bit,' she answered. 'A bit like rotten eggs, but it's grand. I'd choose that instead of having a bath any day. Don't like being in the nuddy in our kitchen. It's like Lime Street Station, our house. Our Brendan's got curly hairs growing round his todger, and when he strips off to gerrin' tub everyone laughs.'

He bit his lip. 'Isn't it just lads swim in scaldies?'

She turned down the corners of her mouth. 'There's no rules to say lasses can't go in. You want to meet me at Chisenhale Street tomorrow after school.'

He shrugged a reply.

'Well, do yer or not?'

He nodded.

She paused. 'I made a recorder out of a carrot the other day,' she said as she jumped down from the bench.

'Did you?'

'Yes. You make holes in it. It's easy. Don't suppose . . . Can I have a couple of them stones to keep?' she added, gesturing at the jar.

'Yes.'

She looked at him wide-eyed. 'Honest?'

He nodded, scooped out a handful.

Wrapping them up in her small handkerchief, she quickly put them deep into her pocket, as if she was afraid he might change his mind.

When Anthony got home to Hunter Street, the oil lamp was burning on the parlour table.

'Where've you been?' asked his mother, a bundle of sewing on her lap.

'The Macaris',' he said. 'Helping unload some mandolins from their van.' But there was a catch in his voice. 'I'm going upstairs to practise my violin.'

'Wait a minute. You've got purple all around your mouth. Antonio?'

He shrugged. The gobstopper, he thought. The remains of it was still wrapped in his handkerchief, a white ball now that all the colour had been sucked off.

'Nothing gets past your mother,' said his father, grinning as he paused from polishing his shoes. 'Remember that. She has the eyes of a rat.' He put down the shoe and the rag he was using, came and stood behind Anthony and put his big hands on his shoulders. 'What have you been up to, son? Have you really been with Mr Macari?'

'Yes. I swear on my life. Catholic's honour. Cross my heart and hope to die,' he replied, shrugging his father's hands away. He felt a prickle of excitement. He had just lied, and the words hadn't lodged in his throat like a plum stone the way they usually did.

Peggy was *right*, easy as pie, he thought.

When Peggy got home, she found her sister Philomena thumping a ball against a wall of the end of their terrace, bouncing it under her leg and twirling to catch it.

'Where'd you get that?' asked Phil, noticing the pear drop bulging in Peggy's mouth.

'Me and Anthony Giardano went to Hegarty's the other day. Used his altar boy money,' she replied.

'Who's he? Is he your fella? I'll tell Martin Gallagher.'

'Yer what?' Peggy said. She did a handstand against the wall, continued the conversation upside down with her skirt making an umbrella over the top half of her body. She didn't care about her bare thighs on view, dirty knees, or her knickers, the sagging elastic and the washed-out colour of them. 'He's not me fella, stupid. And neither's Martin Gallagher. He's me pal. Anthony Giardano bought me sweets and gave me mosaics.'

Philomena stopped whacking the ball against the wall, shoved it in her pocket, tipped her head to one side.

'Mosaics? What's that?'

'Never mind.'

'Can I have a sweet?'

'No,' Peg replied.

Philomena suddenly, without warning, dropped the rubber ball and barged into her. Peg tumbled onto the ground and Phil pinned her down, sat astride her, grabbing for her pocket and yelling, 'Our Peg's got sweets!'

Bodies appeared from nowhere.

'Peg's got sweets!' cried Brendan and his two friends, hurtling out of the passage.

'Leave off,' shouted Peg.

A head poked out of an upstairs window.

'Peg's got sweets? Give us one, Peg?' cried Sheila.

'Flamin' 'ell. Are you lot scrapping again?' cried her mother at the next window. 'Haven't you had your fill of fighting lately? Phil, leave her alone. Peg. Need you to do the cows. I'm off to the washhouse in a minute. I don't know. You lot'll be the death of me,' she muttered, wandering back indoors. 'Come inside and have a bath now, Phil. It's Friday! Sheila! Bath time!'

Peggy followed her sister into the house. Their mother was moving around the kitchen, picking things up, throwing potato peelings into the range. She took the blackened kettle and poured boiling water from it into the tin bath that sat on the stone floor in front of the dresser. The water hissed as it splashed against the cool metal and steam rose into the room.

'I'll take the milk to the Riozzis tomorrow,' piped Peg.

Brendan spun a coin on the table, squinting at it

as the heads and tails merged into one. Baby Jimmy was now sleeping in a wicker basket that they usually used for laundry, but lined with blankets, at least it was comfortable and clean. Her father was sitting in the rocking chair, reading the *Liverpool Echo*. He looked up at her in surprise.

'Well, that's a first. You volunteering for work.'

She shrugged.

Sheila wandered in and pulled her arms out of her sleeves, trying to keep some modesty intact.

'Get a move on before this water goes cold,' her mother said, and yanked Philomena's shift dress up over her head. Phil stood there, naked and shivering, her arms wrapped around her small skinny body.

'Heavens to Betsy! I don't know how you kids get so filthy. Get in, you two,' she said.

'It's the flaming cows,' said Peggy. 'They stink. And they make us stink.'

Sheila carefully lowered herself into the bath and yelled. 'Too cold!'

'Stop whingeing,' said her mother, pouring in the hot water from the kettle. Using an old rag, she lifted Sheila by the hand and started scrubbing her armpit. Sheila squirmed and yelped more. Finally she settled, slipping beneath the water right up to her neck, feet sticking out one end of the tin bath, luxuriating in the warmth.

'Our Peg's got a boyfriend,' she said, as she rubbed her shin with the cloth. 'Phil just told me. They bought sweets. Peg loves him. Peg lets him kiss her and—'

Peggy, like a hissing and spitting cat, sprang across the room and with both hands pushed her sister under the water. The splashing soaked them all as Sheila's arms flailed and her feet kicked in a frenzy.

'Take it back!' cried Peg, pulling back her fist.

Sheila spluttered and choked and emerged rubbing her eyes. She said sorrowfully, 'I take it back, Peg.'

Peggy threw her down with another splash.

'Stop it, Margaret-Mary! Give over, wasting all the precious water!' cried her mother.

'What's all the commotion?' said her father, glancing up and brushing splashes off his trouser leg.

'Peg's been seeing that Giardano boy. That's what Phil says.'

'Peg, is that true?' He threw down his newspaper angrily. 'Peg!'

'She's lying. She made it up. Liar, liar, pants on fire.'

'Why would she do that?'

Peggy twisted round, widened her furious eyes at her sisters. 'I don't know. Ask Phil.'

'Peg, if I find out you've been hanging about wi' him . . .' He scowled at her.

'The hole I have!' she cried.

'If I find out you've disobeyed me!'

You'll what? Peggy wanted to say. *Wallop me? Tan my hide until I'm black and blue?* But instead she pursed her sulky lips. A secret, that's what she and Anthony Giardano would have to remain. And wouldn't that be the craic, she thought.

Seven

The whole week, Peggy had been thinking about the scaldies. It wasn't that she didn't have friends at school to go with her; there was Frances, and stupid Martin Gallagher always following her around trying to get her to show him her drawers. He had even given her a penny once to do it. But Anthony Giardano was different. She skipped all the way from school to the reccy, to find him sitting on the wooden seat of the witch's hat. Striding towards him and breaking out into a run, she waved at him. Leaping onto the witch's hat, sitting with her legs astride the seat, she made it swing wildly in the other direction.

'Tell me mother I saved your life!' she said, laughing, as he wobbled and she caught him. Then, climbing up to the highest level on the witch's hat, pulling herself up by her hands, first one bar and then another, she pushed it back and forth again, shifting her weight from one foot to another and giggling as he curled his fingers tightly around the edges of the seat.

Eventually the contraption lost momentum and she joined him as it lulled to a stop, plonking herself down, out of breath and smiling.

'You bring your trunnies for the scaldies?' she said,

wiping her forehead with her sleeve. 'You can go in in your grundies. Some lads go in actual starkers. No one cares.'

'Got them on under me keks. Fancy a ciggie before we go?' he asked, casually. He took a bent cigarette out of the packet he produced from his pocket, straightened it and stuck it in his mouth and, as if he had been doing it all his life, struck a match and lit it. He looked every inch the movie star, thought Peggy, as he squinted and sucked hard on it and blew the smoke away and looked into the distance. After a few more drags, he offered it to her.

Casually, she took the lit cigarette, and like she had seen her mother and her father and her uncles doing a million times before, sucked deep and hard on it. She felt her eyes watering and wanted to cough badly, but she managed to swallow it down. Waving the smoke away and handing it back to him nonchalantly, she shrugged.

'Ta.'

After a few more drags, he dropped the butt end and crushed it beneath his foot.

'Shall we go?' he said.

She smiled and nodded, dizzy with excitement. She saw the summer stretching out in front of them like this: making paper boats and floating them across the lake at Stanley Park and raucously chucking stones to sink them; climbing over the wall at Croxteth Park to steal apples; playing cowboys and Indians; clinging on to the back of delivery vans with the wind in their hair as they rattled down the road; rolling in the Derby Hall copse and picking sticky buds off each other's socks; sharing a cream slice at Sayer's, or a pennyworth of chips from Vince's chip shop at Paddy's market.

They took the tram to Chisenhale Street Bridge, where the hot water flowed into the river, pumped straight from the Tate and Lyle factory. On the way, she leaned her forehead on the window and let it rattle as she always did.

'Quick, it's our stop,' she said, and they jumped down off the board, setting off down Coniston Street, which took them in the direction of the canal. When they got there she scrambled up a high wall that ran along the street, pulling herself up by her hands.

'Look at me,' she said, as she stood on top and grinned down at him. 'Told you I was the best at this.' Stretching out her arms, she placed one foot in front of the other slowly.

'Careful!' he cried, laughing, as she slipped and wobbled.

'Sister Veronica says, what am I good at? What d'you think she'd say if she could see this?'

'Top of the class.'

'Aye. I'm top of the class at cursing, an' all.'

'Are yer?' he asked, trotting along beside her, enthralled.

'Balls and bloody brick dust!'

'You can't say that!' he said, his eyes widening.

She grinned. She liked the sound of the words in her mouth. 'Why not? Balls and bloody brick dust!!' she yelled. He giggled. 'Me da said the eff word the other day. He said it about me Uncle Seamus.'

'What's the eff word?'

She giggled, leaned into him, covered his ear with her hand and whispered so close it tickled.

'Sometimes if you really want to say it and you can't help it, and you feel like it has to just come out, you say *fudge* instead. *Fudge off.* Or, what the fudge are you doing now, our Peg?' They reached the canal. 'I'm going in. Come on,' she said, grabbing his hand and pulling him along with her as she cantered down the slope, whooping loudly.

Steam was rising from the surface of the water. There was a group of kids already splashing around.

'Take your keks off.' He was embarrassed. 'Don't be shy,' she said, determined to coax out the mischief in him. She kicked off one shoe and the other and then pulled her dress over her head, dropping them in a little pile. He looked nervous as she hopped on one leg in the act of taking off her socks and said, 'What's the matter? Are you scared?'

'No,' he replied.

But he just stood watching as Peggy ran to the edge in her baggy knitted swimming costume, held her nose, cried 'Fudging heck!' and jumped straight into the water. She disappeared underneath the surface. Then her head bobbed up and, gasping for breath, she smiled and stuck one arm out of the water and waved. Lying on her back and paddling her feet, she cried, 'It's toasty warm. Gerrin! Don't be a sissy.'

Overtaken by a sudden energy, he tore off his jumper and shorts and then slipped off one shoe and then the other and dumped them on top of the pile of Peggy's clothes. He ran to the edge and, with an encouraging nod from Peggy as she cried 'Don't be scared. *Geronimo*!', he shut his eyes, held his nose and jumped with his knees drawn up to his chest.

There was a huge splash and for a moment she thought he had sunk without trace, as the water stilled and rings appeared on the surface; but then there he was, shaking his head from side to side, his hair throwing off an arc of silver droplets, gasping and laughing. Peg splashed water into his face and laughed as he squirmed away, returning the splash. She yelped and shouted 'Surrender!' Paddling their arms and bobbing about in the water, feeling the warmth wrap around their bodies, they floated on their backs, squinting up at the sun as they idly splashed their arms and legs.

'This is the life, eh, Anthony? Fudging marvellous.'

It was Anthony's father's hands on his collar that he felt first, his feet lifting off the floor. 'Didn't I tell you?'

His face was knotted with anger, contorted into such rage that each vein stood out on his neck. Anthony was shocked and frightened.

'What were you doing with that dairy girl? Didn't I tell you to stay away from her?'

He frowned. 'But Papa . . .'

'Do I look like a fool? Eh? I don't want you going anywhere near those O'Sheas. D'you think I liked hearing from Gloria you've been wasting your time with her at the back of Fontenoy Gardens?'

Gloria! What a snitch, he thought. Had she been spying on them?

'Why can't I see her?'

'It is not for you to ask me why,' Enzo said, steely and angry. 'It is for you to do as I say.'

'You can't make me!'

'Who's been putting those thoughts into your head? The O'Shea girl? I can smell the stink of her on you, boy.'

'Papa, no—'

Enzo reached out with his other hand to swipe him, but Anthony ducked away.

When Sofia Giardano came in, her hand flew to her mouth. 'Leave him alone, Enzo!' she said, seeing him puff out his chest and tower over her son, who he had backed into a corner. 'He's ten years old. He's not to know. And I don't even know myself. You're just in a state because of the news,' she said, darkly.

His father shrugged, let him go and walked out the door, letting it shut behind him with a bang.

Sofia knelt down and spoke into her son's tearful face. 'He's worried about other things, Anthony. But stay away from the O'Shea girl. Promise?'

'Promise,' he said with a shrug.

That night, Anthony lay in his bed in the attic and stared out of the skylight up at the sliver of moon. He had heard the low voices of grownups talking indistinctly behind closed doors so often lately. Sometimes they spoke in Italian, but Anthony didn't know what they were talking about. They used words he didn't understand, apart from 'Mussolini'. That name was mentioned over and over.

It was all so confusing. During the World Cup Anthony had pretended to cheer for Italy to please his father, but really he'd wanted England to win, like all his school friends.

'What's the matter with Papa?' he said to his mother the next day. 'Why's he so angry?'

'Never you mind,' she retorted.

'Is it Peggy O'Shea?'

'No. It doesn't help, but it's not about Peggy O'Shea. It's your uncle. More trouble again. It's complicated grown-up stuff. Blessed Mussolini behind all the bother.'

Eight

That evening, just like every Friday evening, all the O'Sheas – including Uncle Seamus and Auntie Doreen and all their kids – gathered round the kitchen table at Feather Street for a fish and chip supper. There were so many grasping for greasy chips and flakes of cod and dollops of mushy peas that no one noticed Peggy slip outside to meet Anthony.

She found him waiting, just like she'd told him to, under the sign on the side of the brick building that could have just been another house in the street. The sign read 'O'Shea's Dairy'. It was owned by her Uncle Seamus, who lived in the flat upstairs with his sons, but all the O'Sheas, including her da, worked there. On the ground floor there was a shop where people came to fill their jugs with milk. When you went through the back kitchen it led into a yard with a jumble of outhouses. The end of terrace suited the small shippen that had been built on to house cows.

Going through the door, first through the shop, then into a back room, down a narrow dark corridor and into a rudimentary kitchen, she then opened a second door. There was a smell of hay and damp straw. It was what Peggy sometimes smelled of, thought Anthony. It was strong, but it had a sweetness to it.

'Shush,' she said, putting her fingers to her lips. 'If you follow me into the shippen, I'll show you the cows. Just be quiet. Nettie and Glenda don't like it if you give them a fright.'

Anthony grinned when he saw the silhouette of two large cows chained in a small stall. As his eyes grew accustomed to the light, he watched as they swished their tails back and forth quietly. There was the sound of their hooves on the floor and the cows' steaming breath swirled from nostrils as big and round as the Mersey Tunnel.

'Go on, touch Nettie,' she said, and she walked forward to the stall and climbed onto the second rung of the gate and reached her hands through the bars. The cow was different to the dray horses Anthony was used to, the ones that took Mr Albertini's ice cream around the city and were kept in the stable at his uncle's. When he touched Nettie's hindquarters, her hide was coarse and as prickly as a porcupine.

'Touch here,' she said, 'this is the soft bit. She likes that. Don't you, Nettie?' She stopped for a moment, then took his hand and placed it on the cow's ear. 'See? Look at her face.'

Anthony smiled. The cow shivered and swished its tail back and forth.

'Look, I can get her to move her ears.' Peggy flicked the tips of the cow's ears. 'See?'

'Don't they need a field?' he asked.

'There's hay and straw. But as long as they have grass. We collect the rake-offs from Stanley Park. Me da knows the park keeper. Once a month there's a bit of a bunfight at Anfield when all the cow-keepers can go and have their pick of the cuttings after they mow the football pitch. We have to feed them twice a day. Look.'

She opened a bag that she dragged over from the corner, dug her fingers in and let the grass clippings fall through her splayed fingers. They gave off a fresh, sharp scent.

Anthony stroked the cow as she continued, 'There's always an argument. There's deliveries and someone has to be in the shop for filling jugs. Me da says there are more than four hundred dairies from Scottie Road to Saint Ann's and Toxteth, so no wonder we're always worrying about getting enough business. There's all sorts of other animals round here. People have pigs and chickens, and one fella in Pansy Street had a tiger in his yard.'

'A tiger!'

'Well, that's the story. Think it was just for a little while when the circus came to Stanley Park and they had nowhere to keep the animals.'

'That's a lot of cows, though.'

'Everyone needs milk.' Peggy nodded to where the milk pail was set back against the wall, which was lined with long shelves.

'My Uncle Luigi has a fridge at the ice-cream bar. You know, like the Americans?'

'Me da says fridges are the enemy. Does your da have an enemy?'

'My papa says time is the enemy. Mosaics is slow and everyone wants things to be done in a rush these days.'

She nodded seriously.

'And those that don't like the Fascio Club is the enemy,' he added.

'What's that?'

'Our club. Mr Albertini's ice-cream bar. Men in suits who come round asking questions. Never trust a man who walks into your bar wearing a suit and tie casually asking for a Knickerbocker Glory, Papa says.'

'Once, when Nettie was out in the yard, she got bit by the dog. She was so mad she kicked the door down and charged out into the street and nearly got run over by the tram. Shall I show you something? Promise you won't tell?'

He nodded, his dark eyes widening.

'I've made a den in the back, behind the coal hole. Sometimes I come here instead of going to school. They never think of looking here for me. If ever you want to hide, crawl in here. This is my special place.' She lifted a small trap door in the wall. The small space behind it could have been a dog's kennel. 'Come in,' she said. Crawling through on their hands and knees, they both wriggled inside. Sitting in the inky blackness, they lapsed into silence. After a few moments, the darkness and the sound of the cows sneezing and mooing made them giggle. They just sat there: Anthony chewing the cuff of his sleeve, Peggy twisting a strand of hair around her finger.

'No one knows this place. If you're ever in trouble, you can come here and be safe. It's right nice,' she said.

'Right nice,' he echoed.

'*Bellissimo*,' she said. 'You got a best friend, Anthony?'

'Just my cousins and brother, Roberto. Giardanos are a tight lot. My sister, Gloria, got wind of us palling about and she told Papa and he wasn't pleased.'

'She jealous or summat?'

He shrugged. 'Just kind of fiery.'

'You want to be my best friend? You can if you want.'

'Ta,' he said.

'Best friends for life?'

'Best friends for life, Peg.'

When they went outside and walked back along the dock road towards Feather Street, the sun was sinking into the Mersey and the sky looked like it was on fire.

'See you tomorrow,' she said. 'I'll bring you me cherry stones that I've been collectin'. We can go down to the houses by the Dockers' Umbrella and play cherry wobs up the spout.'

'Cherry wobs? What's that?'

'You don't know?' Peg was amazed. 'I'll teach yer. You get your cherry stones and stick 'em up the spout, and the one whose stones come furthest in the gutter when the water gushes out, wins.'

He grinned.

'Meet me at the reccy after school? Bring me some more of those little pieces of shiny glass, will yer?' she called after him.

He turned and waved, raised a thumb and smiled.

Peggy's mother called this time of the day the golden hour, and with his face bathed in the aureate hue of the summer evening, to Peggy he looked like the most beautiful thing she had ever seen.

Nine

It was the end of August, and yet some of the brambles that had sprung up at the edge of the paving stones were still in flower. The blackberries in the shadier part of the bushes had hard green knobs, but in sunnier spots they had turned to delicious berries plump with juice.

Peggy reached forward, avoiding the prickles, plucked off some of the berries and curled her palms around them. Flushed with happiness at the thought of Anthony waiting for her, she broke out into an excited run towards the reccy. Breathless, she stood scanning the playground when she got there. He hadn't arrived.

She must be early, she thought. She looked down at her hand. The berries had stained her fingers and the creases of her palms. Maybe he was still at school? Detention, perhaps? she wondered, as more time passed. She opened her fingers. The blackberries had turned into a sticky mess. Another half-hour and she looked like she had plunged her hands into blood. She threw the berries into the gutter, wiped her hands on her skirts, humphed when she saw the red marks, and sat hugging her knees on the edge of the pavement. Still he didn't appear. Her mood soon turned to frustration.

'Knew you'd be here,' said a voice. It was Phil, a mass of shivering russet-coloured curls, hurrying towards her across the playground.

'What d'you want?'

'You have to come home and do the chores. Ma needs you to help her blacken the stove.'

Peggy screwed up her face. 'Can you do it? I'm waiting for someone.'

'I helped her scrub the step. Me fingers are raw. Who?'

'Someone.'

'It's getting dark. Mam says she needs you.'

Peggy sighed and rose to her feet. She would come back tomorrow, she decided, as she stomped home behind Phil, tired, hungry and bracing herself for a telling-off.

Ten

The following day, in school, she pestered Frances.

'Fran, where d'you think Anthony Giardano lives?'

'Why?'

'I was supposed to meet him yesterday and he didn't come.'

'Little Italy. Top end of Scottie Road. Where all the hairdressers and ice-cream bars are and there's a pub on every corner.'

'Which house?'

'How would I know?' Frances shrugged. 'If you can't find him, go to the church like you did before.'

'Good idea, Fran,' said Peg.

On Sunday morning, after sliding into the pew at Holy Cross, she watched people coming in and out. After Mass, as everyone slowly filed out down the aisle, she went over to the bank of votive candles. She was planning to go to the presbytery and see if Anthony was milling about with the mission boxes or folding the vestments.

Suddenly there was a nun beside her, speaking in a soft, lisping voice. She pressed a little card into Peggy's hand.

'Isn't she beautiful?' she said, pointing at the card. 'Saint Theresa of Aquinas.'

'No, ta,' said Peggy, giving it back. 'I'm here to try and find Anthony Giardano.'

The nun looked surprised. She had never known anyone to refuse her delicate little cards with the pretty coloured pictures of saints on them. She bristled and moved away.

'You never know when you might need it,' she snapped. 'I have no idea who Anthony Giardano is.'

On her way to Little Italy, Peg made a detour past the witch's hat. There were a few kids hanging around, kicking an old battered football, but no Anthony. Undeterred, she set off to try and find his house in the jumble of back-to-backs and terraces that was Little Italy, sloping down towards the river.

She stopped outside a small, squat house with a little statue in the window. Jesus was wearing a strange pointed hat and his arms were outstretched to show off his beautiful gold-encrusted cloak. It wasn't like the two bits of wood nailed together that was the crude crucifix in the hall of her own home. She knocked on the door.

'*Sì*,' said the woman who poked her head around it.

'I'm looking for Anthony Giardano.'

'Who are you?' she said.

'Peg. I'm one of his friends.'

'Not here,' the woman said gruffly, and slammed the door shut. Peg stared at it for a moment. She rapped on the letterbox, knelt down and shouted through it.

'I'm looking for him, missus. You know where he lives?'

The door opened. A man stood staring at her, wearing a string vest and with his braces looped about his thighs.

'Who's asking?' he said.

'Peggy O'Shea,' she said, standing up quickly.

'No one here by that name,' he said, rudely slamming the door once more in her face.

Shouting through the letterbox again, she called, 'Where is he?'

An upstairs window slammed open. A head stuck out, one Peggy didn't recognize. 'Git,' the voice cried. 'Or I'll poor a bucket of water on yer.'

'What's wrong with you, Peg? You've been moping around for days . . .'

For a moment she thought about telling her mother. *Best friends forever*, he had said. So why had he just disappeared? But no – he *was* her best friend. She even had the tiny glass fragments still wrapped up in her handkerchief to prove it.

But her mother wouldn't want to hear that about a Giardano.

Another day passed, and another, and doubts began to creep into Peggy's head. Had she been smelling? Was it the cows? she wondered, burying her head into the crook of her arm and sniffing. You could wash and wash yourself, but the smell would never go.

And then one day, on her way to do the messages, she made another detour and passed the reccy – and there he was, sitting on the witch's hat. Just like that. As if the days since she had last seen him hadn't happened at all. Her heart leapt as she raced over to him. Pure joy? Is that what she was feeling? Sometimes you just needed a little bit of sad before happy comes along again, her mother always said. She was right! She ran over to him excitedly, calling his name. 'Anthony!'

As she drew near and saw his face, she knew something was wrong.

'Stop looking for me,' he said.

She felt her legs wobble underneath her. 'What?'

'I can't see you any more,' he said, head bowed, fiddling with the cuff of his jumper, pulling the sleeve out of shape.

'Why not?'

'Never mind. I just can't,' he stuttered, raking his hands back through his hair. 'I can't.'

She frowned. 'I won't let you,' she said angrily.

'Well, I'm not gonna be here any more. We're going away.' The words hung in the air, then dropped like a bomb and shattered.

'Why?'

'My father has a job. And we're all going with him. I can't say where. Can't say any more.'

Peggy sensed he wasn't telling her the whole truth. She had done enough lying herself in her short life to recognize that.

For a moment, he wavered. 'I'm sorry,' he added quietly.

'Well, you're a flipping coward for going,' she said. 'I wish I never met you. I thought you and me were like peas and carrots, but turns out we're not.'

'Peas and carrots?'

'Go together like peas and carrots. I don't know why I wasted my time with you,' she spat.

'It's not my fault,' he said. 'What d'you think I can do? I'm only ten.'

'Shurrup,' she said. And she folded her arms crossly and turned away, kicked the kerb of the pavement. 'Think you're too good for us cow-keepers, don't you? You're just like the others.'

'No,' he said. 'No, it's not that.'

'Is it your flaming snitching sister?'

'No.'

'But you won't tell me where you're going?'

'I'm sorry. They say it's complicated,' he added mysteriously. There was a far-off look of sadness and worry in his eyes, but it was one that an eight-year-old girl full of pique was too young to recognize.

'Tell me. You sure it's not your sister?'

He sighed. 'It's nothing to do with Gloria. But I have to do what my family tells me to do now, Peg.'

'But I wanted us to have the craic. I had planned so many things. The Pier Head, and worm fishing and crab catching in Otterspool, and . . . and . . . the fairy dell at Sefton Park and sink paper boats on Stanley Park boating lake . . . bunk a ferry to Birkenhead. New Brighton fair!' she said, petulantly. She slumped against the wall, drew her knees up, pressed her hands flat over her ears. 'You said we were going to spend the rest of the summer together. Me da's right. You can trust a thief, but you can't trust a liar!'

He hesitated. But then the cloud of worry descended again. 'I can't, Peg.'

'Like I bloody care,' she muttered. She picked up a stone and chucked it against the wall before stomping off, furious, let down and miserable.

Eleven

1940

It was cold, and the air was heavy with that far-away feeling that comes when snow is about to fall. The windowsills and gutters were hung with fifteen-inch icicles. The milking room at O'Shea's Dairy was dark and dank.

Peggy sat on a stool. An oil lamp gave off noxious fumes and made the air wobble. The blackout didn't help. She could hardly see her hand in front of her face. She shivered. There was only the sound of the cows' breath, the feel of the warm moisture coming from their nostrils. She leaned her head flat against Nettie's flanks as she squeezed the milk from her teats.

Outside, in the street, she could hear someone laughing. She paused, stood up and looked out of the small window at a group of girls and boys in uniform walking down the road. They looked like they were having a good time, linking arms and singing gustily. And here she was, milking a cow, knee-deep in manure.

She unbolted the door. OPEN UNTIL AIR RAID WARNING, said the sign propped up in the window. Her father, who had taken over the running of the dairy after Seamus hastily left to help at the family farm in

Lancashire when Davey's sons had both joined the army, had scribbled a clumsy rhyme and stuck it next to the sign:

Though Hitler's bombs might come our way,
We'll milk our cows both night and day.
STAND FIRM LIVERPOOL, WITH O'SHEA'S DAIRY!

Time had a habit of moving on and taking you with it. So much had taken place in the last ten years. Her mother had had two more children, which made eight of them. Eight! That meant ten people living in their tiny, cramped house at times. Baby Kitty and Liam, who was six, were the latest additions.

Hitler had actually started the war that he'd threatened. And although no bombs had dropped in Liverpool yet, one thing was for sure: it had upended their lives in ways no one had ever imagined. Her mother still insisted it was true what they were saying, this was a phoney war that would be over soon. But with Sheila, Jimmy and Liam evacuated in Wales, Brendan in the merchant navy, daily blackouts and the air raid practices, blimps and soldiers everywhere, it felt very real to Peggy.

She stretched and yawned, absent-mindedly rubbed the callouses on her fingers that had built up into hard knobs of skin. The handles from the milk buckets she lifted every day for their customers had rubbed and chafed the skin on her palms, as well as blistering her fingers.

She swore her arms were inches longer since she'd been working here with her uncle and cousins after leaving school. To think that she had been so desperate to leave, and how much she'd hated the nuns! At least there she would have been given a hot meal, and she would have had children her own age to play with. She was even beginning to think fondly of Sister Veronica. 'I only want the best for you,' the nun had said so often. She should have listened to her. And now, just as the nun had predicted, her life was knee-deep in cow muck. It was often left to her to fill people's jugs and do the twice-daily milking, at seven in the morning and seven at night. It was no life for an eighteen-year-old girl, no life at all. Her brothers and sister helped – Brendan when he was on leave and Peter when he wasn't at school; Philomena when she wasn't at the parachute factory – but not as much as she felt they ought to.

Peggy blamed her mother. Moira hadn't tried hard enough to make her finish her homework or get her to school on time, or even get there at all. Peggy had been a useful spare pair of hands, and the eleven plus would have been a waste of time because she would be leaving when she was fourteen anyway; that was what all the O'Sheas did. Better to give someone else a chance who could make something of books and learning, like her friend Frances, her mother had said. 'You're lucky with the dairy. You've got a job to go to and one that you'll enjoy.'

It seemed strange to Peggy, weary and old beyond her years, that all this time Frances had still been at her desk, doing her certificate, dodging the nuns, singing Allelujah hymns and saying the Angelus every day at noon. There was even talk of Frances becoming a teacher. A teacher! You would hardly believe it, the trouble they'd both got into at school.

Sloshing milk over the side of the pail onto her boot, Peggy went through to the front room where there was a counter, carrying the pail to transfer into jugs for their customers the next day. The smuts from the gasworks stippled the window pane in the back door. She stood up and rubbed a circle in it with her cuff, trying to brush away the dirt from the smear.

'Eh, Peg, look who's here,' said a muffled voice in the gloom on the other side of the door. 'You on your own?'

The light was strange and unnatural, liquid soft, Mersey estuary light. The body that the voice belonged to was just a silhouette.

'Who?' she asked.

'Me, you dozy mare,' said Martin Gallagher.

She opened the door to him. He looked handsome tonight, she thought as she opened it, broad-shouldered and strong, with his shock of red hair tumbling over his face full of joined-up freckles.

'Where did you get to last night? You left without me,' he said.

The dancehall had been packed. They had almost been overwhelmed by the crowd queuing to get in. There had been a sign at the box office: IN THE EVENT OF AN AIR RAID WARNING, THOSE WHO WISH TO LEAVE THE HALL SHOULD DO SO IMMEDIATELY. MEANWHILE THE DANCING WILL CONTINUE. But as soon as Martin and Peggy had taken three steps into a foxtrot, the sirens had gone off.

'No one's going anywhere! Down with Hitler,

you'll not spoil our fun!' Martin had said as he climbed onto a chair and punched the air. The whole place erupted with a *boo!* when the band stopped playing, and then a loud cheer as the orchestra leader put on her tin hat and the music started up again. There had been no real air raids yet, but this war was certainly giving Martin some purpose. Peggy wasn't sure, however, that this was a good thing. Martin was always bristling for a fight, on edge at all times, hands bunching up into tight fists at the merest provocation.

He came in now, took the pail from her and put his arms around her waist.

'Gerroff,' she said.

He laughed. 'Come on,' he said. 'Be a sport. Give us a kiss, Peg.' He put his mouth on hers. 'That's nice,' he said, sliding his tongue between her teeth.

She returned the kiss then squirmed away, but he took her by the back of the neck and parted her knees by placing one of his legs between them. She felt her nerves jangle as he kissed her harder.

'Where did you end up last night? Looking for more trouble? You and Paddy get into a fight?' she said, wiping her mouth and wriggling out from his embrace.

'Our Paddy! Couldn't punch his way through a wet *Echo*. I went home. I was listening to the wireless wi' me ma, wishing you were with me. *ITMA*. Tommy Handley. Bloody funny.' He followed her across the room and nuzzled into her again. 'Please, come on, love . . . Bit of sinning for you to confess to Father O'Mahoney.'

The smell of the manure filled her nostrils.

'Why do we have to always do our courting here? Amongst the flaming cows. I'm sick of going home with straw in me hair.'

'Where else d'you suggest we go? Don't be a tease. You know how much I love you, Peg.' He started to kiss her again. 'Go on, Peg,' he pleaded. He undid his belt, grasped her hand suddenly, pushed it down inside his trousers. She withdrew it sharply. 'Touch it. Just for a minute. You know how much I like it.'

Did this even deserve to be called courting? she thought.

'Not here,' she said. 'It stinks.'

The cows snuffled. Their breath swirled in the air, a white stream from their wide nostrils.

'You feel good, Peg. I don't mind the pongs. That's because I love you.'

'I mind.'

'C'mon, Peg. This war could reach our shores any minute. Hitler is about to start invading Finland and Denmark. Could be us next. I might die soon. You don't want me to die a virgin, do you?'

She faltered. Her mother's words came searing into her head again. *Don't let Martin Gallagher have his way with you. He's no different to any other man. They only want one thing. You'll end up up the duff like I did – you'll have a kiddie hanging round your neck like a millstone before you know it. Eight times over.*

The nuns had taught her at Saint Joseph's that purity was a gift from God, only to be offered up on her wedding night in His presence in a sacred union with her husband. But Peggy didn't much like the sound of that – God right there, looking down on her, like he might even be jumping into bed and joining in the fun. At least her mother was a realist, she thought.

'I'm just as likely to die as you. You're not even going away to war. There's them risking their lives in France right now, but you're skiving off out of it.'

'Skiving! I thought you were happy that I was staying put. We even had a party when we found out us dockers were essentials.'

She chewed her lip. 'I just thought you might want to do your bit?'

'We've always done our bit. And we'll carry on doing our bit. People couldn't survive without us dockers. It's dangerous now. We're first in the line of fire for Hitler and his bombs.'

He leaned into her, pursing his lips up for a kiss, but she pushed him off.

'Anyway, you can talk. What are you doing? Nowt. Pulling at the tit of a cow,' he said crossly.

Her brows knitted together fiercely.

'I might join the WAAF. Or the Wrens.'

'Don't talk stupid. Your ma and da need you to do the cows.'

'I might. There's not so much to do now that Sheila and Jim and Liam have been evacuated to Wales. I could at least help with them lasses who do the mobile teas. Or knitting socks. Maybe fire-watching. Why not?'

'Have you forgotten you still have to help your mam with the baby on top of the milking?'

'I'm joining the WAAF. I like the uniform. I like the little hat. I like the red lipstick they wear. Bright red to keep the fellas' spirits up, d'you know that? It's Lord Chamberlain's orders.'

'To look like a hussy? Don't talk daft.'

'It's true. Ma can't stop me.'

He shrugged.

'Whatever you say. But come on, Peg. You can't leave me like this.' He grasped her hand again and kissed it.

'Gerroff!' she cried, snatching it back as though she had stuck it into a fire. 'Stop pestering me!'

'You certainly know how to ruin the mood,' he said. 'Why you going all frigid on me?'

She didn't exactly know what *frigid* meant but thought it must have something to do with Frigidaires. Cold and icy.

'Please yourself, love. I'll sort myself out,' he grunted. He moved away, fastening his belt.

She watched him turn, resentment bubbling up inside him, no doubt. Touching him lightly on his arm, she said, 'Marty . . .' but he jerked away from her. She did it again and he shrugged her off for a second time. She was about to say sorry for giving him the brush-off, but then she thought to herself, was she sorry? No. Not one bit.

He turned to face her. 'What d'you want from me, Peg?' he asked.

What was it that she wanted? She thought of her mother and all those children, and how tired she seemed to be all the time. She certainly didn't want that. Right now, she wanted him to stop sulking.

She touched his arm again in another conciliatory gesture. 'I don't like it when we fight.'

It worked. He embraced her and rested his chin on the top of her head, spoke gently into her hair. 'I love you, even when you're gnarly with me, you little wild pretty thing. I just want you so much. Every minute of the day. Let's not bicker. We should be celebrating.'

'I suppose,' she replied.

'Ah, look at the state of me, Peg,' he added, gesturing towards his crotch. 'You could hang your flaming hat on that.'

She blushed. She was only just eighteen. She had her whole life ahead of her. But sometimes it felt as if Martin, who was two years older, was closing it down before it had even started.

'Martin. This war – I mean it, I'm going to join the WAAF. I want to do something. I do love you, but this is a chance to make something of meself. Get away from the dairy. You do understand that?'

'Whatever you say, Peg.'

A week later, Peggy picked up the clothes that were scattered around the parlour, folded them and placed them neatly on a chair. Please God, the practice air raid warnings weren't going to start up again. The previous evening they had gone off late, and the wardens had knocked on the door, and they'd all had to traipse off to the shelter at the bottom of Feather Street. By the time they got back it had been past midnight, and she hadn't had a wink of sleep. She had gone to bed tired and woken up exhausted.

She moved around the room, collecting pots and

glasses to put in the sink and soak. Warming her baby sister's bottle on the stove in a pan of hot water, she began stirring the oats into the milk. Baby Kitty waddled in on stubby legs, her thumb stuck into her mouth, tugging at Peggy's skirt with her free hand.

'Miwk,' she said.

Peggy recognized the threadbare darned and patched cardigan she was wearing as Brendan's. Good grief, had it lasted this long? Just like the pram outside in the hall: it was the same pram that had held all eight of them now. The children had kept coming; it had had three new wheels and a few springs replaced, but amazingly, it was still in working order. It was bearing up better than her ma, Peggy thought ruefully.

A picture flashed into her head of her mother in better times, taking down her hair, standing on a chair and laughing and singing at a party. Had it been a christening party? Communion, maybe? She couldn't quite remember.

Peggy held out her hands to the range to warm herself. She looked around, then sat down and hauled Kitty onto her knee.

'Let me clean your face,' she said, and spat on the corner of her skirt and rubbed the baby's cheeks as she wriggled away. Thankfully Kitty was now old enough to grasp her bottle in her hands, so Peggy could get on with washing the pots. She lifted the child off her knee and onto the rug, trying to ignore her mother's old coat draped over the chair, with the sagging hem and the gaping stitches and the badly sewn patches at the elbows she was supposed to be mending.

Moira bustled in from the washhouse and put a bundle of clothes down on the table.

'Letters from Wales,' she said. 'Just met the postie. Read them to me, Peg. My eyes.'

Peg took the envelope. She hoped these letters would be better than the last ones. She sat down, opened the envelope and began to read the first letter.

'Dear Mam . . .' She paused. 'It's from Jimmy.' She took a deep breath, rested her bottom on the edge of the range, crossed her feet at the ankles.

I ate something called a Welsh teacake. There is a rabbit here. It has a name. Treacle. No one finks ['thinks', corrected Peggy] to skin it and eat it. And when I asked when we was going to boil it they was shocked. I don't like semolina. It's like frog spawn. I tried feeding it to the dog under the table when they weren't looking, but they caught me . . .

Peggy's words trailed off.

'Carry on,' said her mother.

Peggy continued.

I don't like digging for victry either. I don't think tis for victry. I think it's for the farmer who wants me to plant his potatoes cos he's dead lazy. He sits on a bale of hay smokin a pipe and saying "many hands make light work". I had a baff the other week. But I had to wait for the water after his two kids, and then his dog, and then it were me. I've

95

*got nits again and bites from the bed bugs, so
mebbe that's why he doesn't like me. I still
haven't seen our Sheila.*

When she reached that part of the letter, Peggy's
mother snatched it from her, scanned it, and threw
it down with a sigh of exasperation. 'Didn't I tell
Jimmy to stick with his sister?' she said. 'Stupid silly
article, never listens to a word I tell him.'

'You want to hear Sheila's?' said Peg.

'Go on,' sighed her mother.

*Dear Mam, Mrs Wilmington took me in her
car and when you wind down the handle, the
roof opens, and we went really fast and the
wind blew in my face. Mrs Wilmington made
me a lemon meringue last night. Mrs
Wilmington has got lovely hair, she told me
she wants to be a blonde bombshell. She
paints stuff on it to dye it which stinks more
than our cows. Mrs Wilmington took me to a
hairdressers called Touch of Class. When she
came back all her hair was piled on top of
her head in sausages. My hair was cut and
done into something called a Pompa door
pin-up Pixie cut. There was a girl having hers
done with ring curls. Mrs Wilmington lets me
sleep in the big bed with her.*

'Good grief! What on earth is she thinking of! Mrs
bloody Wilmington,' spat Moira. 'Lemon meringue!'
she cried. 'And Sheila is fourteen years old! What's

the world coming to! Sheila has breasts and probably she's got her Auntie Mary by now! Why I got swept up with the panic and agreed to let the children be evacuated just because everyone in the street was doing the same . . .'

'You sure you want me to read the last one, Ma?' said Peg. 'It's from Mrs Jones.' Moira nodded. Peg continued.

Dear Mrs O'Shea, I'm afraid Liam is still not settling. We can't keep washing his clothes every morning and every night. Even when he comes home from school his underclothes are wet. We've tried everything. We have tried separating him from the other children, we have tried punishing him with a paddle.

Peggy went over and placed a hand on her mother's shoulder. They were all used to a swipe around the head or a quick slap on the back of the legs or a rap across the knuckles; her brothers had all received the cane at school, and the strap. 'Six of the best' and 'the bitter pill' were not phrases that were unfamiliar to any of the O'Sheas. But they had never had the belt from their father, like some of her friends had. Punishing Liam? A paddle? What was that? It sounded horrible.

'They're coming home,' said Moira, 'and that's final.' She exhaled and slapped her thighs decisively then stood up from the chair, as if she was bringing an end to the conversation. 'Plenty of other people in Liverpool are doing the same. I should have brought them home at Christmas like everyone else did.' She picked Kitty up from the rug and started pacing the room with her wedged on her hip.

'Who's coming home?' Dennis asked, having arrived back from work just in time to hear the tail end of the conversation.

'The kiddies.'

'Are you sure? What do you think those big black balloons are? Them blimps that are tied up on the railings at Stanley Park? And the fellas in uniform on every street corner? What about the blessed blackout? Why d'you think we're fumbling around in the dark every night? Nearly got myself killed on this morning's milk round.' He shook his head. 'There might be no bombs at the minute, but I'm not sure they wouldn't be better off staying in Wales in the long run.'

'I don't care,' Moira snapped. 'And anyway, I need them. Admit it. You miss them doing chores and running errands for you. Getting your *Echo*, filling the milk jugs. Emery boarding the stove. No Sheila to sweep up the hearth. No Jimmy to go to the washhouse for me or little Liam to help me do the grate.'

'Have you seen what's happening to them poor devils in Europe?'

'Tough nubs to them that's having bombs dropped on 'em, but still nothing's happened here yet. I'm bringing the kiddies back.'

'Tough nubs!' he echoed, shocked. 'And can we afford three more mouths to feed, now people aren't paying their bills?'

98

'Peg can do more hours at the dairy. Take over more of the milking. And you can collect the bills.'

Peggy's heart lurched. 'But I wanted to join the WAAF.'

'Well, you can't. I need you here, Peg. Put those ideas out of your head right now,' her mother snapped.

Peggy humphed. With Philomena out working in a factory, she was always the one wiping someone's nose, kissing their forehead, telling them everything was going to be all right. Why should it always be her who had to make sacrifices? No one did it for her, she thought glumly. 'If our Sheila comes back she'll be an extra pair of hands to help with the baby, so you won't need me here as much. Why can't Pete do more dairy hours? Or Phil?'

'Phil's harder to pin down each day now she's working at the parachute factory, and Pete'll be threatening to join the merchant navy like Brendan. Baby Kitty has started to walk now. Another bloody nightmare. I need all of you here. One of you runs off, the others will want to do the same.'

Peggy looked at her baby sister, who had wandered in and stuck her head under a chair for no reason, and tried not to resent her: the constant threat of a little hand tugging a tablecloth, or being burnt by the fire or the range, or grabbing the handle of a mug of steaming tea.

'I want to do something for this war.'

'You can help this family. Now, I've an idea we should paint the skirting boards brown, the same colour as the brown rug. Makes the room look bigger, apparently. Why don't you do that for me?'

'How does that help with the war effort?'

'You'd be helping me and dad. And cow-keepers, we're essentials, love.'

'That's not fair,' Peggy moaned.

'You're telling *me* it's not fair,' her mother replied. 'Life's not fair, and you better get used to it, love. Anyway, I know you don't really want to join up. You just fancy yourself in that uniform and that red lippy.'

Peggy scowled.

Her father stood up and announced he was off to the Throstle's Nest for a pint. He had barely been in the house five minutes.

She felt the weight of disappointment crashing about her head. Just when she was about to go off and do something exciting. Something that would take her away from this overbearing family bursting at the seams; something she would be doing for herself, that she would have enjoyed so much. And now here she was, back to more grind, and more chores, and more flaming mothering while she was barely an adult herself.

Twelve

'We can't be late. We're always late but I don't want the kids to be left on the quayside on their own,' said Moira, jamming her hat on her head and checking herself in the mirror as she smeared her lips with the bright red lipstick Peggy so wanted to wear.

'You're the one who's making us late, Ma,' said Peggy.

Moira smiled. She looked happy for the first time in months, thought Peggy.

They went outside. The flimsy coat Peggy was wearing didn't do much to shield her from a biting March wind blowing off the Mersey as they got off the tram and set off to the Pier Head. It was a sunny, blustery day, and there were bubbles of brown foam where the crosswinds whipped up the surface of the river into a soapy froth. The sinister black barrage balloons, which had been tied to the railings ever since war was declared six months earlier, jerked about in a frenzy, looking like they might break loose from their moorings. The small boats anchored in the river bobbed up and down, bucking and tossing in the fierce wind. The Liver Buildings, with the magnificent bronze Liver Birds perched on top of two plinths, dazzled in the sunshine.

They hurried along, her mother gripping Peggy's hand.

By the time they reached the chalkboards at the Pier Head, crowds had gathered. Peggy fixed her eyes on the blue smudge of the horizon. Other people waiting on the quayside were exchanging stories of how their children had been treated, some well, some not so well. Stories of them going hungry, and stories of them being used as hired hands for gratis, cruel teachers and miserly farmers; but then, some were talking of great kindness and generosity, trips to the beach, blackberry picking, trips to Llandudno, being fed nourishing homemade food, chicken pie, sausage stovies and plum crumble.

'My kids have been mucking out pig pens and haymaking – would you believe that were possible, when they don't lift a finger at home? Still, I'm glad they're coming back,' said one woman.

'So am I,' chipped in Moira. 'Flipping prime minister thinks he knows better than us mothers. And our priest. What do these priests know about how much a wrench it is to be without our kiddies?'

There was another story as well, one spoken in low voices: that the people in Wales had got sick of looking after the hordes of unruly, wild children from Liverpool, especially the scruffy nit-infested scurvy kids like the O'Sheas, and they were glad to see the back of them.

The harbourmaster stepped onto the quayside with a flag in his hand, signalling the boat was about to arrive. Moments later, it slipped into view. The sunlight refracting off the Mersey created sparkling splashes of silver on the water. The first sight of the

Mersey Princess was blurred, fuzzy and shimmering, but gradually it began to take shape and sharpen into focus as it glided slowly into the estuary. As it grew closer, across the water came the sound of children's excited shouts and cheers, along with a joyful blast on the foghorn that sent a frisson of excitement rippling through the crowds.

The boat finally slid into the dock. There was a rush of people towards the railings. Some of the children who had come out onto the decks began to recognize their parents' faces. They pointed and shrieked, 'Mam! Dad!' and put the fear of God into everyone as they raced to the rails and waved.

Peggy strained forward and stood on her toes to see. 'Mam! I think that's our Jimmy! He's just chucked his hat into the Mersey like they're all doing!' she said, pointing at the top deck.

'Daft apeth. I might have known he'd be one of the ones playing silly beggars. What did he do that for? Thinks the war's over, probably.'

'Not over yet,' said a sailor, pulling on the ropes as he prepared to wind them around the cleats. 'Hasn't even started. But Hitler is most probably delighted you lot think so. You've made a mistake bringing your kiddies home. The bombing will begin any day. Mark my words. We could all be dead soon.'

Moira threw him a look and tightened the belt on her mackintosh.

'Come on,' said Peggy, gently steering her away to the other end of the landing stage. She gestured to the other end of the boat. 'There's Sheila! And Liam too! Here they come! Good grief, they've grown!'

'Jimmy! Sheila! Liam!' shrieked Moira as the gang-plank banged down on the landing stage, all clanking chains and buffeting up against the huge rubber tyres, and water slopping and slapping against the ship; and then her children were running into her open arms. Scooping them up, she kissed their warm heads, and tears sprang to her eyes. 'You're back!'

'Mammy, it was horrible,' said Liam. 'I had to sleep on the floor, and they wouldn't feed us until we finished our jobs, and Jimmy got poorly, and they wouldn't even let him change his clothes, and his shirt has still got sick on it . . .'.

They looked thinner, their cheeks were hollow and they had dark rings under their eyes. They were wearing threadbare clothes; Sheila's skirt had a hem with gaping stitches, and Liam's shoes were split down the back seams. Maybe her mother was right after all, thought Peggy. Maybe it had been as bad as some had said.

Moira pulled them to her. 'Never mind. You're home now. That's all that matters. I've got a treat for you, and I'll get you a nice warm bath – Liam, you look like you haven't washed since you left.'

'He whiffs,' said Sheila.

'I can see that. Look at the dirt under your nails! You could grow potatoes in them ears!'

Peggy ruffled the tops of her siblings' heads. Her mother knelt down, buttoned up Liam's top buttons, kissed him on his cheeks, kissed Sheila and Jimmy on their hair, kissed all their fingers.

'Been horrible without you all,' said Peggy, kneeling to pull up a sock that had sagged around Liam's

104

ankle. She pecked him on the lips. She was shocked to see how thin his little legs were.

All around her, people were doing the same, Peggy noticed. Some had hiked up their children onto the curve of their hips, a few fathers and older brothers carried their boys on their shoulders, some were sobbing snottily into their mothers' skirts; but there was an overwhelming feeling of happiness at having these kids back home in Liverpool. How long this would last, no one dared think of. The news of ships being armed and the terrible stories of what was happening in Poland were forgotten about for the moment.

Liam and Sheila's and Jimmy's words tripped over each other all the way home, vying for Moira's attention.

'We got new curtains? What's them kisses on the windows?' asked Liam, charging into the front room when they went in the house.

'Kisses for Hitler, to stop the window panes shattering. Blackout curtains. Stop the Germans seeing what's what, if we have the lights on. Didn't Farmer Jones have it in Rhyl?'

'No,' said Liam. 'I hate him. Made me dig for him, dig, dig, dig, for victory, that's all I did. Bloody digging.'

'Liam O'Shea!' cried Gram, who was bustling about with glasses of Vimto. 'Language! I'll wash your mouth out with soap if you curse again! Who taught you to speak like that?'

'Farmer Jones,' said Jimmy. 'Move your bloody lazy arses, lads!'

And Grammy Nora shrieked again, although Peggy knew she could outdo Farmer Jones with her potty mouth any day of the week.

After racing around the house, marvelling at how much their baby sister had grown in six months ('Kitty can say *pig*! And *miwk*!'), they squashed round the table in a corner of the tiny room and ate Spam fritters and scouse, ladled out from a huge porcelain tureen in the centre of the table.

'So nice to have you kiddies home!' Philomena cried when she came back from work.

Peggy came in with another tray of drinks and a plate of biscuits. Sherry for Moira. More juice for the children. A glass of milk for Sheila, who was so excited to be back with her baby sister that she just looked at her, round-eyed and with silent wonder, as if she had lost the power of speech.

When Brendan came downstairs wearing his merchant seaman uniform there were more kisses and hugs, and everyone remarked how tall he had grown; or was it just that the uniform made him look a proper young man? He laughed and slapped the arm of the chair when Jimmy spoke a few words in Welsh, 'Coc y gath,' which they all mimicked, laughing some more when he gleefully told them it meant 'the cat's willy'.

'When is Da home?' asked Peggy, in a lull.

'Soon,' replied Moira. 'Soon.'

Dennis O'Shea was on his way home from the dairy. Rubbing his hands together vigorously and blowing on his fingers to warm them up, he popped his head around the door of the Throstle's Nest pub. 'The kiddies are back!' he announced. 'Anyone fancy a bevvy at Feather Street?'

Half an hour later, after a pint of Guinness, then another, he came barrelling in through the front door. Leaves swirled around his feet as he shook out his coat, and they could all hear raucous laughter coming from the hallway. He picked up the children, smothered them in kisses, ruffled their hair, pinched and squeezed their cheeks.

'Guess who I found!' he said. 'Go and see who's outside, Peg!'

Peggy came out, shivering, into the street. Martin was standing there, lingering under the street lamp as he finished a cigarette.

'Can I come in? Hear there's a knees-up?' he said. She could smell the tobacco on him, and the beer, from the front doorstep. She smiled and nodded, and he came towards her and kissed her full on the lips. He followed her in, undid his scarf and clapped his big hands together.

'Hey, it's the O'Sheas all together again!'

The children flung themselves at him and he gathered them up in his strong muscular arms. They had grown up with Martin: he had worked at Gallagher's Dairy in Everton, but now he had a job hauling crates at Huskisson Dock, and he was like a brother to them. It was no surprise he and Peggy were now 'going steady', which was how everyone described it in low whispers and winks and taps to the side of the nose.

Peggy smiled at him, and he winked back at her as he sat down on the battered sofa and roughly pulled Liam onto his lap. Sheila came around the back of the sofa, draped her arms around his neck. 'Mind me drink!' he cried, as Dennis handed him a glass of beer.

Moira smiled. 'Can't tell you how happy I am to have you kids back,' she said, raising her glass.

And Philomena whooped, Liam and Jim cheered, Sheila clapped her hands.

Martin stood up and moved closer to Peg now, one arm around her waist. He turned his head to her. 'This is grand,' he whispered, speaking into her hair. 'This is what I want for you and me, Peg.'

'You don't mean it? Eight kids. It's killing me mother. She can barely get by from one day to the next. Look at her.'

He shrugged. Dennis brought in a big pie on a huge plate. 'Turnip and potatoes, it's not half bad.'

When the excitement died down and they were all settled in chairs and on the stairs, lounging on the sofa or sitting with their backs against the wall, the conversation turned towards the war.

'I went down to Saint George's Hall today and it's been confirmed in an actual certificate. We cow-keepers *are* essential,' said Dennis.

They all laughed. 'How does it feel to be essential?' someone said.

Peter chimed in. 'I want to join the merchant navy like Brendan. I'm joining up as soon as I can.'

'You'll do nothing of the sort,' Moira retorted. 'You're only thirteen. Might as well measure up your coffin now, lad. Martin, do you want to join up?' she asked.

'Not bloody likely,' Martin responded.

Peggy wondered why not. She had a feeling it was because he knew how the last war had torn his family apart. His father dead when he was a baby, and both of his uncles too. The older brother he had never known because he was too young to remember, but who had left a gaping hole in their lives when he had been killed in the trenches. Martin wouldn't say any of that to anyone – he couldn't say it out loud – but Peggy had guessed as much.

'We're alive and healthy. We're all alive and kicking. Let's fudging drink to that,' said Dennis, drunk now.

'We had our first proper air raid practice the other day at work, now they've finished the shelter at the end of our street. We all had to go traipsing down to the basement. There were a rat sitting on one of the bunk beds waiting for us. Not going to be fun,' said Philomena.

Martin leaned into Peg amidst all the chatter. 'Fancy nipping out for a walk along the canal while they're gassing?' he asked.

'So you can put your wandering hands all over me? You know what nearly happened last time we went for a walk along the canal,' she said, squirming away from him. 'And in broad flipping daylight.'

'It were nearly dark. Behind a load of coal sacks. No one could see us. Don't tell me you didn't like it.'

She rolled her eyes. 'I have to be up again at half-past six to do the milking,' she said.

'Can't Jimmy do it?' he asked. He shouted across the room through the fog of cigarette smoke. 'Hey, Jim? Will you do the milking tomorrow?'

'I didn't come back from Wales to do the milk,' Jimmy said. 'I did fire-watching. I want to do it here.'

'You're ten. Too young,' said Moira.

'No, I'm not,' he replied.

Martin and Peggy exchanged smiles. He picked up a broom, put it under his arm and started marching across the room, singing and clapping. '*Now imagine me in the Maginot Line, sitting on a mine in the Maginot Line, now it's turned out nice again, the army life is fine . . .*'

Suddenly Jimmy charged across the room, ran straight at him and rugby-tackled him to the floor. 'I'm Hitler!' he shouted. And everyone laughed, and Martin cried, 'Go on, smash Hitler's face in! Beat him to a pulp. Kick his head in!'

They all laughed even more as Martin picked up Liam, held him right up in the air, spun around and dropped him to the floor and then mimed punching and kicking, yelling, 'I'm Hitler too!'

Everyone except Peggy. She didn't like that side of Martin. It was pretty ugly. But he had been brought up scrapping and boxing and looking for trouble; his hands curled naturally into fists, the muscles tautened in his neck and you could see his veins pulsating, and this war had already brought out the worst in him.

'Hey, guess who I saw on my way back from the Boot. The Giardanos. The flaming Giardanos are back in Liverpool.'

Peggy started. It was the first time she had heard that name in years. Though she had often thought about the boy, the memory of him sitting on the witch's hat sucking a gobstopper had faded. But now

110

here he was again, a picture of him in her head, sharpening into focus.

Martin reared up, grabbed a chair and stood on it. Raising his fist, he cried, 'Oi oi! Tell them to steer clear of here or they'll get a knuckle sandwich from me!' Everyone hooted again. Everyone except Peg.

'Come on,' she said. 'I'll walk with you across the street. Think you've had about enough to drink.'

When they got to his front door, she could hear the wireless playing from inside the Gallaghers' neat terraced house.

A smiling Martin slurred his words slightly. 'You look pretty. Come on in, Peg.'

She touched her hair, which was done in a plait hanging over one shoulder, and shrugged.

Every evening, Mavis Gallagher would sit hunched in the armchair with a piece of embroidery on her lap, listening to the wireless. She usually sat with the linen stretched flat by a metal hoop, pushing the needle in and out, cross-stitching the hours away, and Peggy expected tonight would be no different. No wonder Martin wanted lots of babies, she often thought. Here, unlike across the street at the O'Sheas', it was always deathly quiet; when you stopped talking you could hear the clock on the mantelpiece ticking in between sentences, and it felt unsettling. Who could live with so much silence?

'Where's your ma?' asked Peggy, when they went inside and she saw there was no Mrs Gallagher, just a flickering brass lamp.

Martin walked across the creaking varnished floorboards and snapped off the wireless. 'Ma's at Legion of Mary. Stay a minute and sit on the sofa with me,' he said, plonking himself down and patting an embroidered cushion. He reached out, grasped her hand and pulled her to him.

Peggy positioned herself awkwardly at the end of the sofa. She tried to avoid his eyes and looked around at the open-mouthed fish ornaments made of coloured glass, delicate china birds and shepherdesses, the willow-patterned blue and white plates on the wall and the stuffed squirrel on the mantelpiece. When she glanced back at Martin, he winked at her. What was that stupid wink about? wondered Peggy, as she fiddled with the end of her plait.

'Time I was off,' she said, standing and then walking back across the room decisively. Martin smiled and winked at her again, then grabbed her arm, pulled her to him.

'Oh, I get it. Your ma's off out for a couple of hours, so you think you can do a bit of courting. Canoodling on the sofa and whatnot.'

'No, Peg.'

She raised an eyebrow. 'Well, that'd be a first.'

'I've been thinking for a while, Peg. About what you said. About you thinking all's I want from you is a bit of how's your father, quick roll in the hay. And, well, I'm wrong to get the hump when you push me away. I know that. And I'm sorry. So, I've come to a decision,' he said.

'What about?'

'I'm going to marry you. Sooner rather than later. Maybe next month. What d'you say?'

Her mouth fell open. 'Marry me? Next month!'

'Aye. I love you.'

'You're kidding?' She looked shocked.

'Shurrup, Peg,' he said, embarrassed. 'I'm serious. Wait . . .'

Peg frowned as he moved towards her, took hold of both of her hands in his. Now what was he doing, good God, kneeling down? And taking something out of his pocket? And then the dreadful realization hit her. She looked at him, aghast, as he fumbled with the small box, from which he took out a cheap Woolies ring and held it in front of her.

'I've been waiting for the right time, carrying this around with me for weeks, but tonight, seeing you and the kiddies. Everyone so happy. Peg, will you marry me?'

Her hand flew to her mouth. 'Martin!'

'What's the matter, Peg?' he said, confused.

She stared at the floor, trying to concentrate on the skirting board, as she sucked in her cheeks. Martin frowned. And then his eyes widened.

Snapping the ring box shut, he shoved it back into his pocket. She saw his eyes flash. 'Peg! Why aren't you saying yes?'

'I'm sorry,' she spluttered. 'Maybe, maybe because . . . it's too soon.'

'Do you think it's daft or something? Your mother was married when she was younger than you,' he said petulantly.

'That's because she was in the club,' she said, in a small voice.

'Peggy. I even thought we could have a babby,' he said.

'A baby? What! No. There's this flaming war. And look at me mam. Not on God's earth do I want that.'

He stood up, threw his hat down angrily on the floor and stamped his foot. 'Why not?' he cried.

'I don't know,' she said.

He went back over to the sofa, flumping down, sulkily.

'I'm sorry. I don't mean to be unkind,' she said, biting the inside of her cheeks so hard she was sure she tasted blood. She moved towards him. 'Come here. If I do marry you, Martin, it'll be after this war finishes. Maybe next year, but just not now,' she said apologetically.

'You think this war will be over next year?'

'Ma says it will be.'

'This war could drag on for years.'

'Well, that's another reason to wait. What if we got married and one of us went and died? You wouldn't want me to be a widow, would you? Or you a widower? What if we married and then one of us got bombed, or gassed?'

'What you on about, Peg? I can't wait,' he said.

'For what? Taking me to bed, or getting married?'

He gave her a hostile look from under his tousled fringe.

'Oh, Martin. Don't let's fight.'

He narrowed his eyes and pursed his lips. 'I don't like it that you made a fool of me.'

'I'm sorry,' she said. She reached out and put her hand on his arm.

'It's embarrassing, Peg,' he murmured, sulkily,

looking away from her. 'Turning me down. When I had bought a ring and got down on me knee an' all.'

'No, it's not. I just don't want to marry you right now.'

She felt him thawing.

And then he suddenly hooked his arm around her waist, pulled her down on the sofa and rolled on top of her so that she felt the full weight of him pressing down on her. 'But I love you, Peg,' he said, taking her face in his hands. Barely catching her breath, he started kissing her roughly, biting her lip so hard that it hurt, pushing his tongue between her teeth and deep inside her mouth. Then momentarily drawing breath, tracing his thumb along the line of her jaw, he said, 'Look at you. You're the most beautiful thing I've ever seen. I just want you to be my wife. Promise you'll marry me after the war?' And then he kissed her again, tugging up her skirt with one hand and kneading one of her breasts with the other.

She squirmed. 'Mart . . . what are you doing?' she said, as he undid his belt and wriggled out of his trousers and she felt the blunt shape of him against the inside of her thigh.

'I love you, Peg,' he said urgently. He leaned over the side of the sofa. She thought he was taking something out of his trouser pocket, she heard the sound of snapping, saw his head craning down towards his groin.

'What?' she said, confused, not daring to look. And then before she took another breath he was kissing her harder, telling her over and over how much he loved her as he parted her legs with his knees, saying she was the only girl he had ever loved as he pushed his way inside her, making her gasp with the sudden, sharp burst of pain, telling her that he would love her always, he would love her until the seas parted and the heavens fell in on them, as he thrust his hips back and forth. And finally, moaning like a shot dog, he flopped back on the sofa, and it was done.

'Peg? You all right?'

She didn't answer. She felt she was moving right outside of her body, floating up to the ceiling and looking down at the scene, looking down at herself as though what had just happened had happened to some other girl.

'Peg, love?'

She sat up, began buttoning her blouse. 'Look at the state of your ma's antimacassars, she'll crown you for messing them up.' She couldn't find words serious enough to have a conversation about what had just happened. She had barely known herself, it was over so quickly, and she could think of nothing to say apart from small talk about chair coverings.

'I'm sorry, Peg. I do love you. I used a rubber, you don't need to worry. You're just so pretty.'

She began straightening her skirt. 'You shouldn't have done that to me, Martin. You know you shouldn't have.'

'But it's only natural I want to. Like with your cows. I don't know what came over me. Guess it's because I love you so much. I won't do it again until we're married, though, I promise. You'll forgive me, Peg? You'll still be my girl?'

'I suppose,' she said, blinking away tears.

'When you're ready to do it in a more loving way, you'll tell me?'

Looking at a stain shaped like a strawberry as she fixed her eyes ahead of her on the wall, it occurred to Peggy that whatever it was that had just happened had been a stunning act of selfishness on his part – and her mother was right. Men. That was all they wanted. And Martin, it turned out, was no different.

Thirteen

A week passed. From Martin there were apologies, more apologies, the excuse that it was hardly much more than they had been doing for months . . . and then suddenly, one day, it was never spoken of again.

Peggy's anger had turned to frustration, which turned to irritation. Had he wronged her enough for her to finish with him? Not according to Frances. But then, Peggy hadn't told her the whole truth of it. She had just asked her if it was wrong if a man refused to wait until he married before he did 'it' with his sweetheart. Frances had answered, 'Well, I can bet every pub in Liverpool is full of lads and lasses who don't think it's a reason to go running to the confessional box.'

She tried to put aside the unsettling feelings and resolved to make sure they were never alone for now, even at the dairy. Fortunately, Martin had been busy at the docks – busier than ever, securing the waterfront, keeping the goods moving, all under the imminent threat of Hitler and his bombs. The dairy had also been very busy, the house was always full, and there seemed to be a soldier on every street corner who would be watching if Martin tried to drag her into a passage or kiss her behind a lamp post.

Looking at herself in a small, cracked hand mirror in the parlour of Feather Street, Peggy saw a straggly-haired and unkempt reflection staring back at her. She pulled a slightly bashed-in red pill-box hat tight over her head and blotted bright red lipstick over her full lips. Drawing a line under her eyes with a twig dipped in soot she had scooped from the grate, and pumping perfume at her neck and wrists, she murmured, 'That's better.'

'You scrub up well, Peg,' said her father, and winked at her. 'You meeting Martin later?'

'Aye. I promised Franny and her new fella we would see them at the Throstle's Nest.'

That morning, news had reached Liverpool of land mines being laid in the Channel to defend Norway, and an air raid by the Germans off the coast of Scotland with the first British casualties.

'Not the day to be going out, everyone all het up,' said her mother. 'Probably be trouble, the wardens telling you all to go home.'

Peggy shrugged.

'I mean it. Don't be getting yourself into any fights. Martin's not to be trusted. Hitler has declared war on Britain, not flipping Martin Gallagher personally. We're in enough of a mess as it is without him and his pals roaming the street looking for fisticuffs to liven up their Friday night. Why not stay at home tonight? You can help me bathe Kitty. Or at least come back early.'

'I will not. We're going dancing after the pub.'

'And what if the sirens go off?'

'They just carry on at the Grafton. The conductress wears a tin hat.'

Her mother tutted.

She set off down the hill towards the lights of the pub. At the end of the road a large square metal container had appeared with the letters EWS written on the side in yellow. Emergency water supply, Peggy read as she approached it. There were also bags of cement placed at strategic intervals, with long-handled shovels stuck into buckets of sand. Conversations these days seemed to be full of words that were made of nothing but letters: all this talk of ARP, AFS, WVS was making everyone jittery. It felt as if bombing, like another bucket of sand, was just around the corner.

She could hear an out-of-tune piano plinking and plonking from inside the Throstle's Nest as she approached. There were moving shapes behind the stippled and frosted glass, and a few drinkers were spilling out onto the pavement. The sweet smell of hops and cigarettes laced the air.

She had arranged to meet Frances and Martin at eight. They were going to have a few drinks before dancing. If there was trouble it would probably start in the pub, so they wouldn't stay long.

Someone was singing inside, doing a not-very-good impersonation of Arthur Askey. '*Kiss me goodnight, Sergeant . . . Sergeant Major, be a mother to me,*' they warbled. Through a window she saw someone throw a hat and there was a burst of laughter. A man held out his hand and whirled and twirled a girl. A boy took a bottle, shook it and squirted the beer into his mouth. Two girls fell out of the door arm in arm, laughing. One of them, with fair hair and freckles around the lips, started swinging her handbag around and singing a song. Behind her, a man and a woman were speaking quickly and volubly and there were more gales of laughter. It was lively tonight. Peggy stepped off the pavement.

'Mind where you're going, love,' called a voice from the window of an Austin Ten as it rattled along the cobbled street, swerving just in time to miss her. Its headlights were shaded with metal flaps and the pencil-like beams shone through the two slits, barely enough to warn her it had been coming.

Glancing at the big clock in the window of the pawn shop opposite, she wondered if Martin had already arrived at the pub and gone inside without her. Then, looking up, she saw Frances with her new fella at the kink in the road, hurrying towards her.

'Ah, Peg! You look pretty in that velvet dress. Purple suits you,' Frances said, kissing her on the cheek. 'Like your hat.'

Peggy touched the hat, thinking Frances was getting to look more serious each day in her buttoned-up gabardine. Like a proper person who was going to do proper things in life. She would be a kind and loyal teacher, just as she had been a kind and loyal friend, even if they didn't see much of each other these days.

'Noisy in there,' said her new boyfriend, Trevor, squinting towards the shouting and singing coming from inside the pub. He looked smart. A bookish kind of young man, with round horn-rimmed glasses and polished brogues. It didn't surprise Peg that he wasn't keen to go inside that bear pit.

Martin arrived seconds later. 'What have I missed?' he said, breathless, rubbing his hands together gleefully as he galloped towards them. 'Fella said it would all be kicking off.'

'Nothing,' Peg mumbled, embarrassed in front of Frances and Trevor.

'We were told Mr Vogel, the butcher, was on his way. No business coming into our pub. I want to be here if he tries. Come on, let's get a quick half in,' Martin said, bundling them forward and through the door.

Peggy winced. There it was again. The side of Martin she didn't like, just like the Martin on the sofa. She saw Frances look at her out of the corner of her eye and felt ever so slightly ashamed.

'Let's go straight to the Grafton,' she said quickly.

'Not yet. If the German comes near us he'll get what for from me, all right.' Martin raked his hands through his shock of red hair.

'Give over, Martin. *The German*, as you call him, is our butcher. Mr Vogel is our friend. We've been getting our mutton and scrag ends from him for as long as I can remember.'

'Can't bloody trust them now,' he said. 'I'd start buying me meat from Hoolihan's if I were you. What d'you say, Fran? Hey? Can't bloody trust anyone now.'

Frances shrugged, exchanged a look with Peggy.

'Trevor's working at Burtonwood. He has all the gen on the fifth columnists. It doesn't always mean if you're German, you're the enemy. Plenty of German Jews here who fled the last war to be safe, isn't there, Trev?'

'That's right,' he said. 'What about you, Peg?'

'Oh, I just work in the family dairy, milking.'

'Don't do yourself down,' said Frances. 'She might work in the dairy but she's a laugh, our Peg. She'll keep all our spirits up during this war. Isn't that right, Peg?'

Peg shrugged.

'Remember when you stuffed my shoes with straw?' Frances added.

Martin grinned. 'Daft apeth.'

'She can shoot bottle caps like she's a cowboy, and do the best shadow puppets. Pretty rude, some of them. Peg once made a recorder out of a carrot. She can kick a can further down the street than anyone I know. And you should see her balance on top of walls . . . She's a marvel,' said Frances.

'Oh, Fran. No one cares,' she said, embarrassed.

'And she used to have us all in stitches doing impressions of the nuns. Go on, Peg. Do your Oirish. Do your Sister Veronica. *Peg, if oi've told you once, oi've told you a hundred times . . .* Do that thing where you can twist your tongue into a clover . . .'

'Not now, Fran,' said Peg. She felt even more embarrassed, knew her cheeks were flushing red. 'You like your job at Burtonwood?' she asked Trevor.

'I work for the civil service. Pretty boring.'

'It is not. Classified, the work he does.' Frances winked. 'He has all these little maps and things, little model aeroplanes. He's doing his best for all of us with that brain of his. Takes it ever so serious. Won't tell me a thing. Cracking codes, I bet.'

'Grand,' said Peg, drifting off into thought. *What*

exactly is the point of you, Peggy O'Shea? were the words that had come crashing into her head.

'He's coming!' someone shouted suddenly, flinging the door of the pub open. There was a surge of people.

'German fella. What is he, stupid?' said Martin, beer slopping over the sides of his glass. 'Fool to go into any pub in Liverpool tonight. Lot of bad feeling over what's happening abroad. Hitler has said freight, tankers, passenger ships, they're all fair game for the Nazi submarines. Why Vogel would want to put himself in the line of fire beats me.'

'Mr Vogel's harmless,' said Frances. 'Makes the tastiest schnitzel in Liverpool.'

'Barman wouldn't serve him in the last pub. And now there's trouble. Here he comes!' Martin said, bristling with excitement.

Peggy recognized Mr Vogel, their butcher, straight away, coming around the corner with his strange, shuffling gait and pork pie hat. Chin thrust out defiantly, he caught her eye and nodded at her seriously as he pushed past the people thronging in the open doorway. His face was knotty and red and determined.

As he tried to come through the door, a man whipped his hat off his head. There was a hoot of laughter as Vogel lunged at him and tried to grab it back. Peggy couldn't understand how it happened so quickly; people seemed to be surrounding him, making a wall of bodies so he couldn't get past. In a flash he was being shuffled back out of the door. The mood was becoming more uncomfortable by the minute.

'I'll take me money elsewhere,' he said, storming

back out, followed by jeering and slow hand-clapping. He met Peggy's eyes and looked away quickly, shaking his head. Peggy felt a sharp stab of something in the pit of her stomach. Shame? Is that what it was?

'Bloody idiot, coming here,' Martin said, crushing a cigarette under his foot. 'Tonight of all nights. All our ships in the merchant navy, they're now warships, Hitler says.'

'Everyone home! Air raid!' called an ARP man in his tin hat, appearing at the door.

The sound of the siren went up and there was a collective groan. 'Bloody wardens. Spoiling our fun,' someone muttered. The piano stopped, then started up again a moment later. Everyone cheered.

'Just trying to help you,' the warden said. 'We're here to advise you to go home. Too many lights on here.'

'You can't make us,' said the barmaid. 'Probably just another practice, anyway.'

'No, but we can ask you to leave quietly and safely. And we expect you to co-operate. What if this time it's the real thing?'

'We're not going anywhere. Bloody phoney war.'

'That's right,' said another voice from the back.

There was another cheer. A man, drunk, barged forward.

'Hey, mind where you're going!' said the warden, tipping his tin hat with the letter W painted on the front.

'Move out of the way! You're not wanted here!' someone cried.

'Touch my beer and I'll touch your face!' the drunk man said.

'You're rat-arsed,' the warden replied, and grabbed him by his collar and began jostling him towards the door. 'And you can get out an' all,' he shouted at the drunk man's pal, who was swaying unsteadily on his feet, pointing and laughing at the scene.

Peggy, standing near the piano, watched the drama. How could a tin hat give a nobody like him such jumped-up authority? she thought. No one around here liked that. She felt as affronted as everyone else at being told to go home by this man shouting his mouth off.

She felt someone grasp her arm and, startled, twisted sharply round, jerking her hand back in a fist ready to thump whoever it was. Pent-up energy shot through her body like a bolt of electricity.

'Get your flaming hands off me!'

'I'm not hurting you, just moving you out of harm's way,' a young man in an air force uniform said. 'That lamp nearly fell on you.'

Peggy hesitated and looked at him in a strange way, her head tilted to one side.

'*Caramba!*' yelled Martin, rushing through from the snug, then straight back out again through the same door at the sound of a crash from beyond. 'Whole tray of glasses just smashed!' he yelled as he disappeared.

'Everyone go home!' cried the warden.

Peggy hardly noticed any of this. She was still staring at the airman, with his tousled dark hair and soulful brown eyes. '. . . Anthony?' she said.

He frowned at her, puzzled.

'Anthony – is that you?' she stammered, her mouth falling open as if it were on a hinge. The blood seemed to drain from her in an instant, and her legs wobbled under her.

'Peg! I'd recognize those freckles anywhere! Good God! Peggy . . . well, I'll be blowed,' he said, as he clapped his hand to his head in gradual realization.

There was still jockeying and ripples of laughter and pushing and shoving going on all around. She tried to focus, grappling with what was before her, mesmerized by the sight of Anthony in his air force uniform. Gleaming buttons. A little shiny badge pinned onto his lapel. Shoes you could see your face in. And his face . . . there was something even more handsome in his features than she had remembered from when he was a boy.

He stood back, scratched his brow, looked her up and down and said, 'Look at you, Peg! You look beautiful!'

She smiled and revealed the gap in her teeth, which she then instinctively covered with her hand. Anthony remembered that: the gap that he thought was lovely, but she thought was ugly. His eyes shone. He wanted to reach out and touch her.

'The noise in here. Shall we go outside? Watch out,' said Anthony. She felt him place his hand in the small of her back and glanced back over her shoulder before letting him lead her a few paces through the door.

'Good grief. How are you?' he said, as the rush of cool air hit them both.

'Grand,' she said, smiling, and pushed a piece of hair out of her face.

'Still Peg,' he said with a wide grin. 'Thought you were going to wallop me.'

'You've not changed. Except you're taller.'

'You still at Feather Street?'

'Aye.'

His brown eyes rested on hers with that compelling gaze. 'You look smashing.' She had changed a little, he thought; she was a young woman now with curves and breasts. But her lips were still the shape of a tulip and looked even more lusciously plump, and she still had those huge, wide, mischievous eyes. 'I can hardly believe it's you, Peg. I shouldn't even be here. I should be on my way home. Just thought I'd help out the old WRP fellow when I saw there was trouble.'

'That's an air force uniform. A proper uniform. Give us a twirl, then,' she said.

He smiled, slipped his fingers under the lapels, spun on his heel, and then with his arms outstretched, grinned.

'You look the business,' she said.

'Still training. But hopefully I'll be up in a plane in the next few months.'

She could see how happy he was. No longer the shy boy she had remembered, he looked so grown up and proud. Why didn't Martin want this? she wondered. All he wanted was to smash someone's face in. He wouldn't put his life on the line, not for King and country or anyone. She tried to dismiss the thought, because it wasn't a kind thing to think about the man everyone thought she was going to marry.

'How soon do you start to fly?' she asked.

'Not sure yet. Mostly learning about the engines. Fixing them up. But I can't tell you what it feels like to be in the thick of it,' he said. 'You O'Sheas still got the dairy?'

She nodded.

He smiled again. She liked the way his eyes crinkled up under his slightly tilted cap and he revealed neat white teeth; she had liked it in him as a boy. It was part of why she had found him exciting and different.

Frances put her head around the door. 'We're leaving, Peg,' she said. 'Merry hell in here.'

There was another shout from inside the pub and the sound of a mouth organ and the stamping of feet. Someone thumped a tabletop rhythmically with a fist.

'I have to go,' she said, suddenly panicked, imagining Martin all fired up and throwing his weight around in the pub, then storming outside to find her with Anthony Giardano. 'My friends are waiting for me.'

Anthony nodded seriously. 'I want to hear all about you, though. Every little thing. Oh, Peg, I can't tell you how happy I am to see you again. You've made my day. My week, my year! I'll find you at the dairy!' he called after her as she made her way back into the pub, not sure if she had heard him as she disappeared into the throng. The music was growing louder and the sound of voices swelling. For a moment, he wondered if he should follow her; but then, turning his head at the sound of a roaring ambulance hurtling towards the pub, he decided maybe there was enough drama going on tonight without adding to it.

'Could go to the flicks, Trev, seeing as you don't like it here,' said Martin when Peggy joined him in the snug. 'A lot of stopping and starting with the practice air raids in some picture houses. But we know the ones that just carry on, don't we, Peg? They're the ones we like, where it's warm and dark and cosy and there's always a couple of seats free in the back row. Isn't that true?' He grinned.

'Give over,' said Peggy, blushing. Next thing Martin would be telling Trevor how he'd push his hand right up her skirt and kiss her in the dark and she would come home with a rash around her mouth and her ma would tut and try to act as though she didn't know what was going on.

Trevor squinted away. He looked embarrassed.

'Sorry about Martin. Sometimes I have to pretend I don't know him.'

Martin grinned as Peggy turned her head towards the out-of-tune piano that had just started playing again. '*Love embraces familiar traces, wait for me under the cherry trees, by the brook, amongst the honey bees . . .*' sang a woman standing beside it.

Peggy blinked away the smoke-filled air. Having seen Anthony tonight, after all these years, made it feel oddly as though the woman was singing just for her.

Fourteen

That night Peg tossed and turned in the loudly creaking bed held together with old belts, so much that Philomena and Sheila, who she topped and tailed with, shoved their feet into her face and yanked off the coats in order to make her stop. When she awoke, she found her hair all matted into a clump. She went downstairs, lit a fire in the range, plucked the baby out of the old bassinet and fed her with her bottle, then put her back down gurgling happily.

Leaving the house before anyone stirred, she arrived at the dairy for the morning milking. Her father was there waiting.

'This isn't like you, Peg, you're an hour early.'

She took her place on the milking stool and rubbed her hands to warm them up.

Turning them over, she noticed they looked cracked and sore. Sucking the flesh and rubbing her tongue on the flaking skin soothed it a little. She stood up, wiping her hands on her apron. Down the street she could hear Martin. Passing on his way to the docks, he often stopped by for a pint of fresh milk to take with him.

'Morning, Peg,' he said, slurping from the jug as he stood in the open doorway. 'Hey, look at that.'

He pointed up at the sky, to where an aeroplane swooped and roared. 'Spitfire. It's exciting. It's getting closer.'

Peg frowned. 'I don't know about exciting. I don't like this war. Horrible gas masks and stumbling around in the dark. And I don't much like that we can't get our hands on stuff now. I haven't eaten anything in months that doesn't taste like cardboard,' she grumbled. 'We've got no money at all – no one has got money to spend on anything. Mam is feeling it, now that the kiddies have come back. Kitty's ill with her chest. There's three of us in the bed now. Three in the back room. Not enough old coats to keep us warm. I can't stand it. The only reason Pete wants to join the merchant navy, like Brendan, is so he can get a bit of peace, a roof over his head and a hot meal. Some roof!'

'You can move in with me and my mam if you want.'

'I'm not living in sin with you! Imagine what everyone would say about that. Imagine what your mam would say.'

'I'm not saying we should live in sin. That's why we should get married. It would be one less person in the house in Feather Street. There's room at ours.'

'Oh Martin, I've told you, we're not going to get married yet.'

'I just want to be able to do what we did on me ma's sofa whenever I want, and how many times I like. The thought of just rolling over and doing *it* every morning and every night if we were married. I'd even leave the pub and do it in me lunch hour.

And nip home in me tea break.' He moved towards her, but she backed away until she came up against the shelf of enamel jugs. She wished her father would walk back in the door.

'Your mother doesn't like me,' she said. 'Not since the day I broke her vase when I was swinging that broom.'

'Course she does. Everyone loves you.'

Peggy pushed him away as he came in for a kiss. 'Don't you want to fight in this war? Don't you want to do something noble?'

'Noble?' He frowned, as if he didn't quite understand what she was saying. 'And risk getting myself killed? Not bloody likely.'

There was the sound of boots clumping in the yard and the squeak of the gate. She could see through the stippled glass panel in the door that it was Pete.

'I'm off to work. On the ropes this morning,' said Martin. 'See you at the Throstle's Nest later? Thought I might pop by there for a quick half this dinner time. Buy you a shandy to make up for last night?'

This dinner time and every dinner time, Peggy thought. No doubt shouting your mouth off about Hitler in the pub, and about everyone getting behind our boys. Looking for a fight with anyone who might cross your path.

'I can't. Meeting Frances to go to town,' she lied.

She went out through the back room and into the yard. A distant buzzing sound made her look up. It was an aeroplane again, high above them. It slowly descended, then swooped back up again. She thought of Anthony, and regretted that she'd had to rush off and go back into the pub for fear of Martin coming out and finding them talking together.

Worry overtook her. She felt a tightening in her chest and a terrible sense of foreboding. There was an uneasiness in the streets of Liverpool, and she had an awful feeling that something dreadful was going to happen soon. *You're a witch*, her mother sometimes said to her. Moving back into the house after she had finished up with the cows and to fill up her water trough, she washed out the jugs.

'Ta-ra, Peg,' said Pete. 'There's the fresh rags for tomorrow. I'll just sweep up in the yard and then I'm off.'

'Ta-ra,' she said, refolding the rags and laying them over the rail behind the counter. He left, but just as she was about to twist the lock in the back door, she turned and saw a figure standing outside. Someone come to fill their milk jug? It was early for that.

'We're not open yet,' she said, walking through to the front room.

The figure didn't move away. It knocked at the door: *rat-a-tat-tat*. She sighed as she opened it.

'Anthony!' she blurted.

'Peggy . . .' He was smiling hopefully.

'What are you doing here?'

He faltered, losing confidence, and the hopeful expression slid from his face. 'Just wanted to get some milk,' he said, waving a small porcelain jug that suddenly felt stupid in his hand.

'I see,' she stuttered. She felt uncomfortable, embarrassed by how she looked in her old overalls, the boots with the flapping soles, no ribbon in her straggly hair, no lipstick or rouge to pretty herself up like she had done the previous night.

She blinked away the awkwardness.

He smiled, spoke in a low soothing voice. 'Actually, that's a lie. It's you I'm here for, not milk. Don't be angry with me. I was going to knock at Feather Street, but I guessed you'd be here. I hardly slept last night thinking of you.'

She blushed.

'You got so pretty, Peg. Not that you weren't before.'

When had he become so charming? she wondered. Or were all Italians like this?

'You're lucky you found me. I don't always do the early shift.'

'Good timing on my part, then.' She felt a blush rise to her cheeks. She knew he was trying to be kind. She just didn't want him to feel sorry for her, finding her in this dive, knee-deep in manure.

'You have to go,' she said. 'It's not such a good idea you coming here. My da. If he knew . . . He might not recognize you, but if he did . . .'

'He'd knock seven bells out of me?'

'Something like that. And he'll be back after his round.'

He nodded. 'What time do you finish? How about we meet in Stanley Park? Last time I saw you, we were going to sink paper boats on the boating lake . . .'

'We were kids.'

'You were going to take me on the ferry as well. Show me how we could bunk on without a ticket. I haven't forgotten.'

A knot of worry was building up in her stomach.

'I do remember,' she said. 'But I've changed. I'd pay my way now.' She felt her heart race, thumping like a hammer, afraid her father would come back any minute. She glanced towards the open door and paused. She could hear Pete clomping about in the yard.

'So, will you say yes?'

She dropped her eyes, looked quickly over her shoulder again, and shrugged.

A huge smile broke out on his face. 'That'll do me, Peg. Two thirty, then? I'll meet you at the park under the cherry tree. That all right?'

'I suppose,' she said. She remained serious and solemn.

'Bravo. You got awfully sweet-looking, Peg. Can't tell you how happy I am to have found you again.'

The rest of Peg's morning went past in a blur, but she was a better person for the whole day. She was polite and charming when asking if anyone wanted the jugs filling. She was good-humoured and kind, and as she went up Scottie Road she found herself humming the song Peter had been singing around the house for days now. *'We're going to hang out the washing on the Siegfried Line . . .'*

She got home at twelve and, calculating that her mother would be in a good mood, went about the chores vigorously and energetically. She didn't complain when Moira asked her to emery board the stove, even though she was exhausted – the adrenalin was rushing through her and made everything easier to face.

She began to feel nervous, but tried to squash it

down as best she could for fear that someone might notice. When it was time to leave, she plunged her hands into the sink and used a scrubbing brush to get the dirt out from under her nails. She used baking powder sprinkled into her hair to fluff it up and then put a ribbon in, tying it back into a neat ponytail. She didn't want anyone to see her leaving in her pretty spotted tea dress with the white lace collar – they would only make comments – so she covered herself up in a light coat, which she planned to leave bundled up behind the privy.

'Peg, where are you going?' shouted Moira from an upstairs window.

'Nowhere,' she answered. 'Just to see a friend.' And she jogged off down the hill.

The sun was riding high as she stepped through the gates into the park; the blimps bobbed in a gentle breeze. Anthony was already sitting on a bench under a cherry tree that was beginning to blossom. He looked flushed with happiness. He was wearing neat flared trousers with pleats and well-ironed creases, a linen jacket, smart shoes and a trilby hat. She smiled as she went over to him.

'Peggy, you look lovely,' he said with that easy grin of his. When she sat beside him, he placed his hand lightly on her knee. A bolt of electricity jolted through her. As if on cue, a bright sunbeam broke through a split in the clouds, making the lawns and the trees look greener than green, the cherry blossom pinker than pink and the ruffles on the boating lake sparkle silver.

She felt a flutter of nerves. 'Well, fancy this,' she said.

He smiled. 'Couldn't believe it when I walked into the pub.'

She faltered. 'Aye. I was with my friends. Only stopped by for a quick one.' Friends? She blushed. Martin would hardly consider himself a 'friend'; the thought of what he would say to that crossed her face like a shadow. 'Sorry I rushed off.'

'That's all right. I was in a hurry myself. Papa had invited his friend Luigi around. Any excuse to show me off in my uniform. When I was little he used to make me play the violin, now he shows off about me joining the RAF.'

'I can see why. You looked grand in it.'

And then she hesitated again, fell silent and fiddled with her gloves in her lap. Her brows knitted together and she lifted her face to his and spoke directly, her chin jutting out sharply as it always did when she was about to say something awkward. 'Where did you go, Anthony? After that last day I saw you? You just left.' As soon as the words were out of her mouth, she regretted them. She had hardly been here a minute and she was already scolding him.

'It's a tale and a half,' he replied.

'I'm in no rush. Let's hear it. You just disappeared. Did you run away because you didn't want to see me?'

'Of course not! Don't be stupid.' He placed one of his hands on hers and she felt his fingers curl around hers.

'What happened, then?'

'We had to take cover for a bit. Papa had the wrong kind of folks coming to our house looking for him. Had to lie low. We came back to Liverpool eventually. But they sent me and our Roberto away. I went to boarding school. My aunt paid for it.'

'Boarding school? That why you speak all hoity-toity?'

He smiled. 'Do I?'

'Don't sound Italian much, that's for sure. You used to do that thing with your r's. Sounded kind of foreign.'

'It was a military kind of school. They all spoke hoity-toity.'

'Leaving like that, telling me not to find you. Made me think I'd done something wrong. You sure it wasn't because you were going to a posh school and I'm just a cow-keeper's lass? I'm not ashamed, you know. There's nothing wrong with working in a dairy.'

He hesitated. 'I didn't say there was. Why would you be ashamed? I don't care whether you're a teacher or a cow-girl, or the flipping Queen of Sheba. You're Peggy. Uniquely Peggy. You were my best friend. We made a pact, remember?'

She softened, nodded a yes.

'We Italians say best friends are like the stars: just because you can't see them, doesn't mean to say they're not still there. I wanted to come back and tell you where I was going, but once I was in Scotland, I was stuck there, and then away to school. If you knew how many times I regretted just walking off without explaining! I can still see it. You sitting on the witch's hat glowering, and then jumping up and kicking the wall and clutching your foot.' He grinned.

She peered up at him through steel-blue eyes.

'The truth is, I couldn't have explained, because I didn't really understand myself. Papa was so furious with me when he found out that I had disobeyed him and seen you. It was like red mist. And there was such a lot going on. You've heard of Mussolini?'

'Mebbe,' she said.

'Well, everything changed when Mussolini started palling around with dictators like Hitler.'

He didn't want to tell her the real truth of it all. It was too big, too complicated. To say that his father had also got it into his head that it was the O'Sheas who had driven them out of Liverpool would only open old wounds.

'I tried a few times. To write you a letter. But I didn't know the address of your house or the dairy, and my parents – well, if I had asked them . . .'

She shrugged. 'Doesn't matter. We were kids. I was sore at the time, but it was years ago.'

He knitted his brows together. 'I'm sorry, Peg. Will you forgive me?'

'Fine,' she said. There was a short pause, and then she said, 'Military school? You learn how to use a gun, then?'

He smiled. 'Yes.'

'What were it like? You posh now?'

'Am I heck. It was an awful place. We lived a brutal kind of life. Cold showers. Beds hard as nails. The grub was like pigswill. That's not posh, is it?'

She smiled.

140

'Pretty strict. Flogging, bullying, but I got off lightly on that score. Frozen flannels on winter mornings was about the worst I had to deal with. I hated that.'

'The nuns at Saint Joseph's were pretty strict, an' all. Probably not much different.'

'Hey, Peg. I brought something for you. Look what I got.' From his pocket he took a white paper bag. 'Humbugs and pear drops. Red pear drops. I remembered you don't like yellow ones.'

She let out a small excited squeak. 'From Hegarty's?'

He nodded. 'Bought them for you.'

'I haven't had sweets in months. Just sweet tobacco, and I don't like it when it goes all stringy and soft.'

'I didn't nick them, if that's what you're asking.'

She pulled one out from the sticky clump.

'And your brother and sister?'

'Gloria's got a job at Bertorelli's bar. Still as Italian and as hot-headed as ever. Roberto, he's in the seminary. He's been there since he was thirteen.'

'What's the seminary?' she asked.

'Place where you go to learn how to be a priest.'

'Priest?' she exclaimed. She frowned, genuinely puzzled. 'Why?'

'Everyone just thought it was a good thing. Mamma's idea. She's very proud of him. That's what happens in Italian families.'

'Doesn't your brother like girls, then?'

'Maybe when it was decided that's what was going to happen, he was too young to know. He was only ten. It's not a bad place. It has the pine woods and the beach, and we visit from time to time.'

'Didn't you know if you liked girls when you were ten?'

He smiled. She felt something pass between them as he gazed at her with his beautiful, ardent brown eyes. The conversation lulled into a silence.

'You escaped the mosaics, then?'

'Yes, thankfully. For now. Since I joined up.'

'You fire a gun?'

He pulled something out of his top pocket, showed her the little registration card with his name on. Training corps, it said.

'Not quite yet. Mostly we practise with broom handles. But I'll have a real gun soon. And I can't wait.'

'Why the air force, though? It's dangerous.'

'It's nice that you care, Peggy,' he said, nudging her flirtatiously. 'Can't wait. I feel ready. Ready to fight for this country. I'll take my chances.'

'I know plenty of fellas who've lied about their age. A few only fifteen who've joined the merchant navy. Some join just for the craic. Me brother, Brendan, for one.'

He smoothed down his trousers. 'So, you working at the dairy all the time?'

She hesitated, looked away into the distance across the lake. 'Me?'

'Aye, you, Peg. Let me guess. You joined the circus?' he said playfully. 'Tightrope walker?' She felt her cheeks flame. 'I'm only teasing. Peg, I've never met anyone as clever as you. Street-smart, you were. And bold. Still haven't forgotten you nicking that gobstopper.'

'Working at the dairy full time.' She so wanted

to tell him that she had tried to do something else – how many times she had argued with her parents that she shouldn't have to do this job, why couldn't she work on the glove counter at Blackler's or T.J.'s, like other shop girls she knew? But no matter how many times she had stamped her foot, nothing had changed; and she had finally come to realize that everything in her life had been decided for her by other people.

Anthony wouldn't think much of that, she knew. That here she was, a cow-keeper, who everyone presumed would marry Martin Gallagher one day soon. Martin, who wanted to punch the living daylights out of anyone who crossed him. Her dreams of her future were diminishing, as sure as night followed day and day followed night.

She wished she could tell him she was going to be a teacher like Frances. Perhaps she should just lie and say she was, and hope for the best. But she knew how that would go. 'A teacher! You *did* show 'em then, Peg! I knew you would!' And then he would find out the truth and be disappointed. She felt her cheeks flush crimson with embarrassment at the thought.

'I bet you have all the fellas after you. Like bees to a honey pot. You're gorgeous, Peg. So pretty now. Kind of natural and quirky.'

She blushed, raised her hand to her mouth and rolled her lip between her finger and thumb. 'Don't be daft.'

'You are.'

'Not really. Your folks still doing the mosaics?' she asked quickly.

He nodded. 'Except not so much. They're making these at the moment. For the war. For the soldiers, it's a little crucifix, and it has the name of your town engraved on it. People haven't so much money.' He hooked his finger inside his collar, produced a pretty silver cross studded with tiny pieces of glass on a chain.

She could feel his breath on her face, sweet and intoxicating. 'It's beautiful,' she said. She squinted at it as he turned it over. *Bardi*, it said on the back.

'Lovely,' she said as he tucked it back under his collar.

He smiled. 'Hitler will be coming soon to Liverpool. Knowing what he's doing to the poor folks in places like Poland and France, it's made me look at the world differently. You'd think it would make you feel gloomy, but truth is, it's exciting to me. And it's even made me feel differently about the mosaics. I don't look at every bit of glass and think that's my future any longer. And that makes me feel better about everything else. The RAF will open a world of opportunities for me, Peg. And now, with Norway . . .' She nodded sympathetically. Norway seemed to be on everyone's mind but hers. *Norway, Norway, terrible what's happening in Norway*, everyone seemed to be saying.

'I wanted to join the WAAF. But I have to look after the new baby. Ma's had another two kiddies since you left.'

'There's other things you can do.'

'I don't want to darn soldiers' stinky holey socks. I do enough of that at home.'

'Doesn't have to be socks. There's all sorts of stuff.

Fire-watching. Volunteering with the mobile teas. Helping with the WVS ambulance services.'

She shrugged shyly. She couldn't think of one of the things he had mentioned that would work alongside looking after her baby sister.

'Come with me,' he said. He took her hand and led her to the edge of the boating lake. Pulling an old envelope from his pocket, he folded it in half and then into triangles, then opened it out so that it transformed into the shape of a boat. He knelt down on the shingle bank.

'Here,' he said, picking up a few round, flat pebbles and putting them in her hand. He pushed the boat onto the water and they watched it float towards the middle of the lake. 'On our list. Your turn first. Ready, set, go!'

She drew back her hand and threw her pebble.

'Bingo!' she cried. 'I hit it!' She clapped her hands together gleefully and jumped up and down. The boat sagged and they laughed, laughing even harder when Anthony missed it with his pebble. After more pebble-throwing and more giggling, it seemed natural that he should put his arm around her shoulder. Seemed natural that it should remain there for a moment longer than it might have.

'Oh Peg, I've missed you,' he said, hugging her to him. 'I'm sorry I left you.'

She dropped her head, shyly.

'So, what else is on our list? Palm House? Fairy dell? Ferry across the Mersey? Hey, d'you fancy a trip into town? We could go to the cinema.'

She stared at her feet, at her battered Mary Jane

shoes that forced the flesh to pillow over the T-bar strap. To Peggy, the flicks meant the back row and Martin's hand on her knee. And then creeping up to her thigh, and up her skirt, and her slapping it away and him starting over . . . and it went on like that until the final reel whirred to a halt and the lights came on. Should she tell him about Martin?

'The Luxe has opened up, what d'you say? I've got a few hours off. They're showing *Gone with the Wind* again.'

She didn't want to say to him that she'd seen it already. And at least five or six times. That sometimes after the milking, she and Martin would just sit and watch the same film again and again.

'Yes, if . . .' But her words tailed off.

'If what?'

The figure jogging across the park was unmistakeable. Martin. With his stupid cloth cap and the bag for the rake-offs slung over his shoulder, and whistling. It was something he would do when he was passing on his way back from the pub. He was only being kind, but suddenly she felt intensely irritated by it. He should stick to dock work instead of hanging around the dairy all the time.

He was heading towards the park keeper's shed. The keeper would give him the key to the shed with the grass clippings, and then he would be walking past them at any minute, with that cocky wide-legged gait of his. Her heart thudded.

'Nothing. I need to go,' she said urgently. 'Sorry.'

'Peg! Again! Peg, was it something I said?' he called after her.

146

But she just picked up her skirts and left without explanation or apology.

A goose waddled over to the bench and honked. They made a soulful pair, Anthony Giardano and the goose.

Peggy raced to the dairy. She knew Martin would be walking in any minute. Her heart pounded when she heard the door open. The scent of newly cut grass clippings floated in.

'Peggy!' he called.

She pulled the ribbon out of her hair and stuffed it into her pocket, rubbed the lipstick off her lips with an old handkerchief.

'Cuttings!' he said, tipping the fresh, green, sweet-smelling grass into the stall. 'Don't say I don't love you.'

Fifteen

When she arrived at the dairy the next day, Pete was washing out the pots. 'Someone left this for you. An envelope and this pamphlet. Pushed them under the door,' he said.

She opened the envelope and began to read the note that was inside.

> *Dear Peg,*
> *Here's some of the info I was talking about for volunteering. All sorts of things you could do. Perhaps I could help you decide if anything interests you. By the way, I'm at the Pier Head all morning, manning a stall for fellows who might sign up. Beautiful day. What about a quick ferry trip to the Pleasure Gardens in my lunch hour and we can talk about it then? Fancy it? If so, I hope to see you there.*
> *Anthony*

She quickly picked up the pamphlet from the counter, wandered over to the stool and smoothed out the creases of it on her lap. She looked at the pictures of people cheerfully waving bunches of carrots, wearing tin hats and holding buckets and spades to build air raid shelters, everyone smiling. Squinting as she turned over to the other side, she scanned more headlines in bold and the articles and the reproduced posters. One was of Hitler, moustache-twirling and sinister, crouching over a mother and her child. But it was the bottom corner that caught Peggy's attention. *Pig club*, she read.

'Pig club,' she murmured, and slipped off into thought. She looked up, gazed into the distance, and then looked back down again at the picture of a pig and a smiling woman with a turban around her hair.

'You thinking of volunteering?' Pete asked, glancing over her shoulder as he hauled a sack of grass cuttings and tipped it into the stall. 'Dig for victory. You gonna dig for victory, Peg?'

'No. I'm not digging. What's a pig club, Pete?'

'Pig club?'

'Says here you can start a pig club.'

'I think you all chip in, everyone say from here to Feather Street and down to Huskisson Dock, and you buy a pig, feed it the slops, and when it's fattened up, you share it out. Government's involved though.'

'The Small Pig Keepers' Council,' she said, continuing to read. 'They let you legally buy corn or feed as rations. And when the pig is slaughtered you give half the carcass to the Ministry of Food and keep the rest as bacon and pork. I could run a pig club. We have space at the dairy. That empty stall. D'you think I could?'

'Don't be daft.'

'Why not?'

'Never heard such a thing.'

'Why does everyone have to tell me I'm daft all the time?'

'Because you are, Peg. Remember the recorder you made out of a carrot?'

She stood up angrily.

'Flaming hell! I were eight!'

Picking up her shawl, she shoved away the stool and left the room.

Anthony wouldn't think it was stupid. He had thought the recorder was grand, and he would probably think the pig was grand an' all, she thought.

'You came!' He was at the Pier Head, helping another man wind a rope around a cleat. The other end was attached to one of the large silver blimps.

'Whoa. Steady on,' said the chap, as Anthony dropped the rope and it wriggled free like a snake, twisting this way and that, threatening to come loose completely as the blimp bucked and tossed. Peggy pressed her hat to her head as the gust of wind threatened to blow it away.

There was the sound of the ferry's foghorn. Anthony took the rope again, secured it, nodded to the man and then took Peggy by the hand.

'Come on. I've finished my shift on the stall. I'm taking you to the Pleasure Gardens. Boat's about to leave. Two return tickets to New Brighton, please,' he said brightly, handing a shilling to the ticket collector, who was passing by with a machine around his neck.

Peggy opened her mouth to protest, but before she

knew it he was pulling her up the gangplank. 'Wait! I just wanted to ask about the pig club, that's all! I haven't got time to go to the Pleasure Gardens,' she said, trotting after him.

He grinned. 'We can just go across the water and back, then. Save the Pleasure Gardens for another day.'

He clamped his arm around her shoulder and bustled her on board and down inside the lower deck. Bottles rattled on a glass shelf as the engines started and made her ears throb. She felt her whole body vibrate. The grinding and thrumming sound of the boat made it difficult to even start a conversation.

'Let's sit upstairs,' he said. She felt his hand under her elbow and they went up the metal steps.

Coming out into the moist air, the wind stuck strands of hair to her face and she tasted salt on her lips. She tightened the belt of her light coat another inch. As the ship pulled away, the panoramic view of the waterfront stretched out in front of them: the Three Graces, the Cunard Building, the Liver Birds. Then the front of the boat swung round and they began to head towards New Brighton. She felt her palms prickle with excitement.

'You all right? Why were you in such a hurry, when you shot off out of the park yesterday? You were like a whirling dervish.' He did a strange impression with his arms as though he was running.

'The cows,' she stuttered. 'And my da. Time hasn't softened him. Probably best not to come to the dairy again.'

'I won't. But don't you run off again without telling me where you're going.'

'I won't,' she said shyly.

She felt the fresh breeze on her face: not the sooty smell of coke that had been choking her throat in the bowels of the ship downstairs, but cool, salty air.

'Look,' he said, pointing and leaning over the rail. There was a group of girls in a smaller boat sailing a little way away, wearing uniforms. They waved at the ferry. 'Wrens,' he said, turning to her, crossing one foot over the other and resting his elbows on the rail.

'Anthony, you know about pig clubs?' she asked.

'Oh. Pig clubs are grand.'

'You think I could do that? Run a pig club?'

'I think you could do anything you set your mind to, Peg.'

'You don't think it's stupid? Like making a recorder out of a carrot?'

'Why would I think that? Mr Churchill clearly thinks it's a smashing idea, otherwise it wouldn't be in the pamphlet – he wouldn't want the government to be involved. And by the way, I don't think the recorder was daft, either. Edible musical instruments. Nifty.'

She could see the Tower, and the grass slopes of the Pleasure Gardens. The trees were in flower. People were wandering up and down linking arms, children threading in between their parents. There were faint screams of delight coming from the fairground and the music of an organ grinder floated towards them. You would hardly know there was a war on – apart from the rolls of barbed wire along parts of the shore and the blimps that were becoming so familiar, bobbing in the sun.

'I'll help you with your club if you want,' Anthony said. 'Plenty I know who would sign up. Mr Albertini. Mr Lombardi. The Bertorellis.'

She smiled. Looking at him, seeing the encouragement in his brown eyes, she felt as if she had just awoken from a long sleep and entered a place she hadn't known existed. And even more so after the way Martin was behaving lately. Was this what it felt like to be fully alive? When someone believed in you?

Anthony told her he would be away for a week training at a camp in Morecambe, and they arranged to meet the weekend after that at Albertini's cafe. So she had a week to persuade her mother and father that the pig club was a grand idea. She might as well start as soon as she could.

The following day, her mother announced that they were going to make toffee apples using the precious leftover sugar she had been saving for months. They would take them down to Paddy's market and sell them from a tray outside Elsie's cafe, and if there were any left over the children could share them. It was tantalizing to watch her stirring the pan as delicious smells drifted up from it. This might be the last time sweetness filled their kitchen for a long while.

Earlier Moira had rolled up the tasselled frayed rug, laid out a piece of newspaper on the stone-flagged floor and put down a bundle of wood. With a small axe, she knelt down and began to split the kindling into smaller pieces to use as sticks to poke in the apples.

'More paper, Peg,' she said after a few minutes, sitting back on her heels and wiping her brow.

'Can I stir the sugar?' Phil said, walking over to the stove.

Sheila wandered in carrying Kitty, who was coughing and going purple. 'Give her a teaspoon of sulphur,' said her mother.

Sheila sat down with the baby on her knee whilst Phil fetched a small jar of yellow sulphur from the top of the mantelpiece and unscrewed the lid.

'Open wide,' she said, and blew a spoonful of sulphur into Kitty's open mouth. Kitty coughed even more, and her eyes watered.

'Pig club,' said Peg, speaking over everything else that was going on. 'SPKC. Small Pig Keepers' Council. You all club together and buy a pig. Then you eat it. For the war effort.'

'Yer what?'

'SPK what? What on earth are you on about?' said her mother, standing up and mopping her brow with her sleeve. She took the sulphur powder from Sheila. 'That's enough,' she said and screwed the lid back on the jar, wiping her hands on her apron.

Peg explained it all just as Anthony had. 'You all chip in, everyone say from here to Feather Street and down to Huskisson Dock, and you buy a pig, feed it the slops. Then when it's fattened up, you share it out, give half of the carcass to the government and keep the other half for bacon and pork.'

There was the sound of rain pestering the roof.

'Oh no. Just when we've hung the sheets out to air, Peg,' sighed Moira.

'Did you hear what I said, Ma? I want to do my bit. With the pig club.'

'What the blazes are you on about? Pig club? I've never heard of anything so daft.'

'Mrs Hardstaff's sister has started one,' said Phil.

'I don't know about Lottie Hardstaff, but our Peg?'

'I know about pigs.'

'No, you don't. You know about cows. Cows is very different.'

'We've got the yard. We've got the empty pen that we kept the hens in. How much is a pig, Mam? Do we have any money?'

Her mother snorted. 'Oh, yes, we're rolling in it. We're as rich as Croesus, us O'Sheas. Don't you know your da just won the pools? Go to my room upstairs and get the money box from on top of the wardrobe. Then you'll see how rich we are. You can have what's left.'

Peggy leapt to her feet and galloped upstairs two at a time.

'That was cruel, Mam,' said Phil.

After a moment Peggy came running back down. Rattling the money box against her ear, she felt hopeful. It was a start. She set it on the table. Her mother stood with her back to the range, shook her head, and watched. The girls drew up chairs, rested their chins in their palms.

Peg tipped out the contents. 'Oh,' she said, staring mournfully at a holy medal, a button and a farthing.

'What did you expect?' said Phil. 'We're brassic. We always have been.'

Moira laughed. 'Our Peg wants to start a pig club,' she said as Dennis came into the kitchen, scraping dirt off his muddy boots on the stone step.

'Yer what?' he said. 'What the flaming heck's a pig club?'

She described it. He started to grin. Feeling herself go hot in the cheeks, Peggy glared and turned down the corners of her mouth. 'You always laugh at me.'

'Because you're funny, love. You're a flaming hoot. This even beats you saying you wanted to join an orchestra with a recorder made out of a carrot.'

'Shurrup.'

'Don't you speak to your da like that.'

'I see you've broken the bank. How much money have you got from the money box?' asked her father. 'Couple of farthings?' They all laughed again. 'That's not going to get your pig. That's not even going to get you a rasher of bacon.'

Peggy's cheeks burned. 'Why does everyone have to be so mean in this flaming house?'

She stormed off in a flurry of door slams and stomping and huffs and puffs.

'There she goes again,' said Moira. 'Pouting Peg.'

Two days passed. But despite the constant teasing about the pig club entertaining them all for days – *oink oink, this little Peg went to market* – still the idea remained lodged in Peg's brain. Each morning she woke up pondering on it, and when she went to bed it was the last thing she thought about.

156

Sitting in front of the range, folding and sorting a pile of washing her mother had just brought back from the washhouse, suddenly she leapt up.

'We can bring a pig up from Davey's farm, where we got the cows from. Lancashire's not far away,' she said hopefully.

'Peg, will you drop it! You've been going on about it all week like a broken gramophone record. If you want to do something, go around the houses and see if you can collect some old pots and pans. They're melting them to make bombs and bullets.'

'There's plenty doing that. All the old railings have gone outside the library. The WVS do that.'

'That may be so, love, but if you want to help with the war effort, there's still all sorts of other things you can do. Everyone's pulling together in a time of crisis; people who barely knew each other are making friends. If you must, sign up for your precious WAAFs or WVS or whatever. I suppose I could spare you a few hours a week.'

'What's wrong with pigs?'

Moira grimaced. 'Drop the pig, Peg.'

'They get a bad reputation, but they're clean and clever. Cows smell worse. I'll go around the houses here and see if people would give us five bob to kick things off.'

'No, you won't.'

'Why not? It would bring us all together. If we did that, perhaps those that don't like each other – her across the road always moaning about stringing out the washing line between the houses, Mr Hegarty complaining about kids in his shop – they would all

157

get to like each other, once they were all pulling together over a pork chop.'

'There's plenty round here I wouldn't want to share a pork scratching with, let alone a chop.'

'Like who?'

'The Giardanos,' said Philomena.

'The Giardanos for starters,' echoed Moira.

'I knew one of the Giardanos once,' said Peg, quietly. 'Don't you remember? Anthony. He was my friend. He was nice. They're all right. Nowt wrong with 'em. They're probably better folks than us. I bet they'd give us a few bob for me pig.'

Moira stopped. 'Don't ever say that again. If your father heard you saying things like that, he'd wallop you . . .'

Peggy hesitated.

'Why? And what if I happened to see Anthony Giardano again? You think I wouldn't say hello?'

'What are you on about? One minute we were talking about pigs, and now you're on about the Giardanos.'

'I would cross the road and say hello, and I'd be happy to share a currant bun with him.'

'Stop this stupid talk. Now, Peg.'

Peggy raised her eyes. 'Well, it doesn't have to be the Giardanos. But there's so many others around here. Now, will you write to Uncle Davey or shall I?'

Sixteen

Peggy stepped into the bright sunlight of a late spring morning. She set off down the road, annoyed but still determined. She knew the hidden stories of the streets around here, and she knew people would at least give her a few moments to talk about her pig club idea, unlike her ma and da.

That's what happened when you delivered milk to people's homes. Sometimes their customers would even invite her into their houses, sit her down at the kitchen table and offer biscuits and cups of tea. One morning a woman cried over a custard slice about the son she had lost in the last war when he was gassed; another talked about her brother who had been shot down and survived, but lost the use of his legs. Every Monday Mrs Turpin, a thin lady from across the street, would tell Peg about her husband who would drink his wages away on a Friday. If people needed someone to talk to, Peg always took the time to listen, and so she felt sure they would listen to her now.

'Peg, I like you. I think it's a grand idea,' said Mrs Shufflebottom. 'You've got vim, girl.' She had admired Peg sailing off down the road in the mornings, pushing idlers out of her way, laughing and wiggling

159

her bottom then sticking her fingers up as workmen wolf-whistled at her. 'You'll bring folks over to your side of the argument any day of the week. Everyone loves you. The room goes sunny when you walk into it. Got a knack of making people feel better about themselves.' Now full of energy and excitement, Mrs Shufflebottom banged the table with her fist. 'Do it, Peggy. If you want to feel part of this war, then that's what you should do.'

Peggy beamed and scooped up the coins that Mrs Shufflebottom tipped out of her purse onto the table. She put them into her apron pocket, excitedly.

'Ta, Mrs Shufflebottom,' she said.

She left feeling as if she had awoken from a long sleep and entered a place she hadn't known existed. Did everything seem so much brighter because now she had a purpose?

'Heard about the pig,' Mr Tozer said at the fish-mongers the following week. 'Can I join the club?'

He was holding out a ten-bob note!

She ran home as quickly as her legs could take her. Her mother's mouth gaped when she slammed the money on the table. 'Where did you get that from?'

'Folks around here. Mrs Shufflebottom. Mrs Turpin. Miss Cammidge.'

She waved the bit of paper on which she had scribbled names, ran her thumb down the page, cleared her throat and recited them: 'Murphy, Tozer . . .'

'Stop, Peg. Stop. Get your pig from Davey, all right. But it's *your* pig, you understand? I want nothing to do with it. I've got eight kids and I haven't got the energy for pigs. Or anything else, for that matter.'

Peggy beamed. She leapt up and hugged her mother.

'Thanks, Mammy. I'll show you, Ma. I'll show you. I'll make you proud. This pig'll be good for all of us, I swear.'

She had been on tenterhooks for weeks, by turns excited, wanting to tell Anthony, then worried that Davey's promise to bring the pig from Litherland in his van might not even happen. But the day finally arrived, and a van trundled down Feather Street to the shippen, the horn tooting cheerily. Davey leaned out of the window and waved at her. She jigged up and down excitedly on the pavement and waved back. When he got out, she handed over a bundle of crisp notes. Davey, licking his finger, counted slowly and carefully. 'You'll manage this pig? Will your da help?'

'Da won't have anything to do wi' it.'

'But you're just a slip of a lass.'

'Aye.'

He smiled. 'You need to feed a pig morning and evening, just like the cows. And you know the expression, happy as a pig in muck? That about sums it up. Oh, and they get sunburnt. So you have to keep them cool in summer with plenty of water on their skin.'

He opened the back of the van. A great pink hairy fat sow, with tightropes of mucus hanging from her nostrils, swayed and stomped behind wooden slats and made a strange braying noise. Peggy peered into the darkness. And then, right at the back of the van, squashed next to the sow, she saw another pair of eyes staring at her.

'Is that a piglet?' she asked.

He smiled. 'Weaner. She's three months. From piglet to slaughter is about six to eight months. The hog will be ready for butcher in about three.'

'Can I take the piglet instead?' asked a wide-eyed Peg.

'You can if you want. I don't mind. As long as you pay. What you want to do wi' your money is your choice.'

She clapped her hands together and stood up on the balls of her toes. Davey pulled down a ramp, opened the pen, crawled in and lifted the piglet out over the side.

'Shall I give her a name, Uncle Davey?' Peg said, as he placed it in her arms. It snuffled and snorted and batted its long pink eyelashes. It felt warm, like a baby.

'I wouldn't. Not if you're going to kill it, queen. It doesn't do to strike up a friendship with someone who's about to die, and there's not much different wi' a pig . . .'

'I want to call her Dora.'

'Like I said, you're the boss now.'

'We're all in this together,' she said to Martin an hour later when he arrived at the dairy, having heard the commotion in Feather Street about Peg and her new pig.

'We are, Peg,' he replied, thrusting his hands in his pockets and rocking back and forth on his heels. 'But this pig is already coming between us. I haven't seen you for days. Why haven't you been to the house?'

'Feather Street down to the docks; the Tozers, the Shufflebottoms, Miss Cammidge; they've all joined,' she said, ignoring his question.

Jimmy and Peter turned up then, with armfuls of wood. Phil and Sheila came in as well to have a look and stroke the piglet and giggle and coo over it. The boys had nails and a hammer, but when they asked for help from Martin to shore up the pen, it turned out Martin wasn't in this as much as he had promised; he suddenly remembered he had to help with a new cow at the Gallagher dairy. Leaving them all to go to work on the sty, he departed with a cheery wave.

'Selfish,' said Phil.

When they finished hammering wood against two posts, their foreheads shining with sweat and full of satisfaction in a job well done, they slumped down with their backs against the wall and slurped the syrup water in pop bottles that Moira had made for them.

'Attagirl, we've done it,' said Brendan. 'I hope this works out for you, Peg,' he added.

She pulled the piglet onto her knee, stroked its silky ears.

'So do I, Bren,' she murmured as she tickled its nose. 'Pigs are clever,' she added. 'Davey said.'

'Maybe that's why they're afraid all the time,' he said, raising an eyebrow.

163

Seventeen

Full of optimism about the pig club and relieved that she had managed to avoid Martin for several days in a row, Peg put on her blue velvet hat with the felt roses, fetched her notebook and set off along Scottie Road, smiling up at the cornflower-blue sky and whistling as she walked.

The next thing she had to do was sign people up for the slops, and the first place on her list was the cafe at the bottom of the hill. Poring over the leaflet, she worked out that what she had to do first was find out who would be willing to sign up. If she was doing the milk rounds she would ask the lads to keep one of the buckets on the back of the cart, into which people could chuck their potato peelings, rotting fruit, mouldy vegetables and other leftovers. There were complicated instructions on the leaflet she'd got from the man who had brought her the papers to sign; all about how you needed to inform the government when the pig was ready for slaughter, fill in a form with everyone's name and address. But she wasn't going to bother too much with that. Those details could be worked out later.

Piglets looked like babies, she thought. No one would refuse to sign up when they saw Dora. Perhaps she could wrap her up in a shawl and take her around to meet everyone?

The first stop was the fishmonger's. Of course, being Mr Tozer, he knew all about pig clubs, because he knew all about pretty much everything. Someone in Everton was doing the same, he said to her, promising she could have his leftovers although warning her they might pong some.

She worked her way along the row of shops; the greengrocer's and the butcher's were also pleased to see her.

'Smashing idea – and where will you keep her?' asked Mr Platt. 'Things will get serious now Germany has invaded Norway,' he added. What Hitler was doing in Norway seemed to be all tied up with Dora for Mr Platt, just like all the blonde-haired, big-handed Norwegian sailors drinking in the Throstle's Nest these days. 'Bit of meat will soon be hard to come by,' he said. Peg nodded, happy to take his five bob.

'I keep her in with the cows in our yard.'

'Put me down,' he said. 'And put me down for a packet of sausages.'

Even miserable Mrs Gilby at the baker's brightened when Peggy thrust the leaflet into her hand.

'I've started with a piglet. She's called Dora.'

Mrs Gilby nodded as she read it carefully. 'What do I have to do?'

'Give us five bob to go to the cost of her, if you want. Then you get pork chops and ham when we sell her. Or just give me your slops, and I'll give you free leftover bacon rashers. Pigs will eat anything, potato peelings, old turnips. Even egg cartons.'

165

'When will she go to slaughter?'

Peggy hesitated, flinched. *Slaughter*, she thought. Not a nice word. 'Autumn,' she said.

'Provided we've not all been bombed by then! Keep up the good work,' Mrs Gilby said, signing her name. And on Peggy's way out she thrust a bread roll, warm and fresh, into her hand. Peggy thanked her, hardly believing it. Mrs Gilby had never given her so much as a broken biscuit or a stale rock cake in all her years doing the milk rounds.

When she reached the end of the row, she hesitated. She found herself standing outside Albertini's bar. She wavered. She had been warned never to go in there; God only knew why. Something to do with Albertini and the Giardanos being friends. But this was where Anthony had said he would meet her at two, after his week away. And perhaps if Albertini signed up, the two families, the O'Sheas and the Giardanos, could even become friends themselves? Wouldn't that be something?

Pushing open the door with a tinkling of the bell, she put on her brightest smile and flicked her hair as she approached the man behind the bar. He had a thin moustache and was reading an Italian newspaper and smoking a cigarillo, a thin plume of smoke rising from it.

'Hello there. I'm a friend of Anthony Giardano. I'm collecting for a pig club. You heard of pig clubs? Will I put your name down on the list for slops?'

He paused, took the cigarillo out of his mouth, laid it on the glass ashtray, and wiped his hands on his white apron.

'You like a bit of bacon, do you?' she said hopefully.

'*Sì*,' he replied, breaking out into a smile. 'Especially if a beautiful signorina like you brings it to me.'

He was flirting with her, and even though he must have been a decade older than her own father, he was behaving like a man who thought he was in with a chance.

'Here's the info. Just a piglet now, but she's a pretty little thing and we'll fatten her up well. Will you sign?'

The bell tinkled again, and Anthony walked in through the door.

'Anthony.' She smiled at him.

'You know each other?' the man asked.

Anthony's eyes shone. 'Yes. From a long time ago.'

'She's starting a pig club,' said Mr Albertini.

'I know,' said Anthony. 'That's why I'm here. To tell you to sign on the dotted line.'

'She's going to bring me a nice bit of bacon and some sausages, aren't you, *cara*? Put me down. I like pigs' hooves. With a little bit of gravy, don't I, Antonio? There's nothing like it. Perhaps we can all share a plate with polenta, lovelies?'

'Thank you,' said Peggy, scribbling in her notebook.

After a brief chat and a delicious macaroon, they said goodbye and Anthony offered to walk her to the tram. 'You didn't need me. He was charmed by you the minute he set eyes on your pretty face,' he smiled. She felt him place his hand on the small of her back as he led her to the door. 'I'm proud of you. We'll defeat bloody Hitler. Everyone's pulling together.'

She shrugged, a little embarrassed. 'Pigs are not the same as risking your life.'

'No job too small. Isn't that what Churchill is saying?'

Mr Albertini put his head around the door and spoke into the street. 'Put me down for two pork chops. Let's make this pig club a success.'

Anthony made a gesture of tipping his hat.

'Oh, you should see her,' said Peg excitedly. 'Snuffling about in her sty on her stubby legs. When I put my hand between the wooden slats, she puts her warm moist snout into my palm. Her skin's all bristly and prickly.'

'Bet she's a cracker!' he said.

'She's called Dora. She's gorgeous. Cute. Like a baby. Our Brendan helped me make the sty. She snaffles the slops up like you wouldn't believe.'

He smiled, put his arm around her shoulder. 'Well, I can't wait to meet her,' he replied.

They said goodbye, but she couldn't help thinking about him for the rest of the evening. She thought of how she had allowed his hand to snake around her waist and gently rest on her hip, allowed him to brush a strand of her hair off her cheek, allowed him to thread his fingers through hers.

'Strange kind of friend,' said Frances the following day over a currant bun at Lyons' Corner House, once Peg had told her in halting, back-to-front sentences all about him. 'You told Martin?'

'About the pig club? Not yet.'

'No, you dope. About you taking a ferry across the Mersey with your airman.'

'Oh, Fran, he's just a friend. Nothing could ever come of it.'

'Why not?' she asked, pushing the crumbs around the plate with her finger.

'Well . . . because he's Italian. And my family hates him. And his family hates us.' She laid her forehead on the table and sighed. 'I will tell him, though.'

'Mmm. I can see this is going to end in tears,' Frances said, picking out more of the currants before sliding her plate over to Peggy. 'And as for the blessed pig club, you say this Anthony will help you – but isn't that really just an excuse so that he can be with you?'

'Oh, I don't know. We can never be together.'

'Why, though?'

'I've told you. Because they're the Giardanos and we're the O'Sheas. No one really knows.'

'Doesn't sound a good enough reason to me. Bet it's not enough to stop your legs going to jelly when you see him. I can tell when you say his name. Your eyes change colour. They go from blue to steely grey. You sigh, and your cheeks go all pink and your eyelashes flutter.'

Peg smiled. She grasped her fingertips and reached across the table. 'Oh Frances. He's like a film star, the most beautiful thing on this earth. When he breathes close to me it's like he's breathing Parma violets and fresh roses. And his voice . . . Oh, his voice. And his hands, Fran. He's got these hands. I

169

can't stop looking at them. They're so lovely. Not just his hands. All of him. D'you remember when we first saw him on the altar all those years ago? He was like this person who didn't belong on this earth amongst us rowdy lot. Like he'd been created by a different God to ours. Well, now he's a man, he's even more . . . more . . .'

'More what?'

'I don't know. More everything. Just makes me feel giddy.'

'And you think you can just be friends with this man?'

Peg groaned. 'Oh, I don't know. What about Martin? What exactly d'you suggest I tell Martin? "Oh, Mart, by the way. There's something you need to know: my legs go to jelly when I see Anthony Giardano."'

'Maybe you should think about whether you and Martin ought to be together at all, even if Anthony Giardano hadn't come along to confuse things. No good putting up with second best. The rest of your life is an awful long time to be stuck with second best.'

'I know. I know. Feel my heart.' She took Frances's hand, pressed it onto her chest. 'Does Trevor make you feel like that? Is he your number one?'

Frances smiled. 'Yes. But not because of his film-star looks. God help him, with that funny lopsided mouth and those awful spectacles. You know why? I go giddy when I see him looking at his little maps or his charts, and all those numbers and columns and lists, and he can stare at them without a pen or a paper and just understand what they mean. He's like an encyclopedia. He just knows everything that there is to know. About the sun and the moon and stars, and every battleship, and every aeroplane . . . and I actually love that. I know he talks too quickly, chatters like a woodpecker, and he looks so serious, and he hates the pub and too many people; but when I see him pick up a book that's written in French and then sit there reading it quite calmly, or tell me the Latin names for flowers in our backyard, or play his oboe, I just know – I want to be with this man forever. I suspect we're both of us in trouble, Peg.'

Eighteen

'Good God!' her mother cried when she arrived back from the washhouse. 'I thought you had a baby in your arms! What are you doing, bringing that thing in here!'

'Not a baby. Thought Dora might like to see where we live.' Peggy sat stroking the piglet in her lap. She had just made another list for her club. She had collected more names and had written them down on a piece of paper in pencil, and that evening she had written them in a blue pen in a little notebook.

'It's not a flipping pet! And for goodness' sake, you've given it a name?'

'Yes.' So often, everything Peggy said sounded like she should follow it with 'So what?'

'You're going to eat it, make strings of sausages and bacon, and tripe, and you've given it a *name*?'

'Why shouldn't I?'

'You don't want to be giving it a name. It's a pig. It's a pig and you're going to roast it on a spit and eat it. You should call it Yum Yum,' Moira teased.

Peggy stood and lifted the pig onto the groove of her hip. The piglet really was like a baby. She had small eyes with long eyelashes, and her snout wrinkled when Peggy tickled her so that she looked as though she was smiling. Peggy stroked the part of her head between her ears and was amazed and delighted to see how her curly tail wiggled. When she put her down, Dora trotted about the room on little faltering hooves.

Liam came wandering in. 'I've hurt my hand,' he said. There was always someone in this family needing a thorn or a splinter pulled out of the fleshy part of their palm, or a piece of grit taken out of their eye with a rolled-up bit of rag dipped into water, or a bit of iodine on a grazed knee. But today the piglet made the pain of Liam's splinter magically disappear.

'A baby piggy!' he cried, delighted, and ran over and knelt in front of Dora, hugging her and kissing her between the ears.

'I thought you might want to see her. See how tame she is.'

'I do not. Take it back to the dairy,' Moira ordered. 'It's going to start charging around here and wrecking the place if you leave it. Get it out of here before I start making bacon rashers out of it.'

'Oh, Ma. How can you say that,' Peggy laughed, bending to let Dora nuzzle into her.

At first they didn't notice Dennis with his head bent towards the wireless. But when he stood up, waved his arm and shouted 'Shush your mouths, everyone! Turn that wireless up,' the mood changed in an instant and the kitchen fell silent. A voice crackled out into the room.

'*In a further development, Mussolini has praised Herr Hitler once again, causing grave concern for our allies in Europe.*'

'Would you credit it? As if the Italians didn't make a show of themselves in the last war. Now they're sticking their noses in and getting on the wrong side of the argument again,' said her mother seriously, with Kitty wedged on her hip, rubbing at a smear of soot on her face with her thumb. 'Are you all right, Peg?' she added.

Peggy was frowning. She really didn't have much idea about what the Italians had to do with this war. 'What d'you mean, wrong side of the argument?' she asked.

'If Mussolini goes against the Allies, it's going to cause all sorts of trouble here as well. I've already seen police gathering on the corner of Hunter Street,' her father said, banging his boots together. Pieces of hardened mud fell onto the page of the *Echo* that was laid out on the floor. 'They've been knocking on doors and arresting Italians for weeks. Those in trade unions, or them that seem suspicious. You heard what Churchill's saying now? Collar the lot. There were a group of lads in the pub earlier saying they would do the job for him.'

Peggy worried what this would mean for the Giardanos. Martin, she had no doubt, would already be bristling for a fight. She could picture him, his bones tensing and separating, cracking his knuckles in excitement.

Putting on her coat and telling Phil to take Dora back to the dairy, she headed off to the pub. She needed to find Martin, stop him doing something stupid.

She walked through the doors to find him drinking

a pale ale, squashed up in the pew with James Reilly at his usual place in the snug.

'All right, Peg?' he said.

'There's trouble across the way,' someone cried. 'An Italian fellow, we heard.'

'Mart, you should go home,' Peggy said. 'Don't get tangled up with this.'

The sound of voices thrumming could be heard from outside. A frisson of excitement rippled around the bar. A few scrambled towards the window, standing on chairs to try and get a better view. Beyond the glass there were flashes of light – gunfire? An explosion?

She felt a body of people pushing against her, thronging towards the door to get out and have a look. A foot treading on her toe, a jab in her ribs – she winced with the pain of it, nursed her bashed arm. This was not what she had planned.

Martin drained his pint and stood up. Moving behind her with his hands placed on her hips, he guided her to the door, shouting at people to move out of the way as he did. When they got out into the fresh air she heard a commotion coming from across the street. Someone drew back his fist and punched it into the air, shouting *Oi oi!* It had been a boiling hot day, and the sun had made them all giddy with excitement. Peggy's head jerked round. This city, she thought. Fear everywhere.

'My God! Is he dead? He's bloody dead!' screamed a voice. Whoever it was, they were standing outside the front door of Albertini's across the road.

'What on earth is going on?' someone else said nearby.

'There's a fella lying on the pavement outside! He's not drunk! He's dead!' said a man who, like Martin and Peggy, had joined the small crowd making their way over. 'A dead fella! Did you hear that?'

'Sure did,' replied Martin.

'Open up!' someone cried, barging forward, banging on the glass doors of Albertini's. A second man stepped up and started hammering on the door too. For a moment, Peggy thought his fist was going to go right through.

Inside Albertini's there was the silhouette of someone standing on one of the banquette seats, shading their eyes and looking out into the street.

'Open up!' The hammering grew louder.

'There's a bigger crowd coming up the street,' she said, turning back to Martin. 'Let's keep out of it.'

Mr Albertini flung open the door and gasped at the sight of the mob. But when he saw what they had all gathered to look at, his hand covered his mouth in shock.

A man lay across the front step of the cafe. His head was lolling unnaturally to one side, his clothes dishevelled, tie loose at his neck, eyes swivelled back in their sockets. A dribble of something, white liquid foam, came from his mouth.

A soldier in uniform pushed through, the crowd making way for him. 'Stand back!' someone said. The soldier touched the man with his toe. Was he dead, or just dead drunk? He certainly looked dead.

'Jesus, there's a dead fella there! Jesus, did someone kill him?' someone said to Martin. Peggy clutched the sleeve of Martin's coat and said they should leave.

But she couldn't hold him back, and before she could say another word, Martin had pushed right to the front and joined the excited crowd surrounding the lifeless body, prodding and poking it. Peggy felt her stomach clenching.

'Have I killed him?' asked Mr Albertini, in a daze. 'Was he in the bar?'

'What with? Grappa?' said a woman who had come out of the cafe and was standing with him. 'I don't recognize him. He's not our customer.'

'Jesus, what'll we do?' someone said.

'Call the police,' the soldier said. 'Go back to the pub and call them.'

'Line's down. Been down for weeks,' Mr Albertini said.

And then he caught sight of Peggy, and his expression changed. 'Peggy O'Shea?' he said, looking confused. 'Anthony's girl?'

'Stand back!' said Martin when a policeman arrived, wobbling on a bicycle and blowing his whistle.

Peggy's heart pounded. Had Martin heard what Mr Albertini had just said?

'A dead fella. These Italians. They're a bad lot. D'you reckon Albertini killed him? Or Gloria Giardano? She works here Saturdays, doesn't she?' Martin said. Peggy let out a silent sigh of relief.

'Anthony Giardano's sister? Don't be stupid,' she said. 'What have you got against Italians?'

'Word is they're declaring war soon. Wouldn't be

surprised if this dead fella has been done in by an Italian. Maybe even Gloria,' he muttered under his breath.

Peggy felt her cheeks burn. 'Gloria Giardano is only a lass. Leave her alone.'

'Why are you sticking up for a Giardano?'

'Give over,' snarled Peggy. 'What's that got to do with anything?'

'Dead fellas lying all over the pavement. What's the world coming to? Albertini should be ashamed of himself. Terrible state of affairs.'

A man came nearer, bent to look at the dead man and, with finger and thumb, pulled down his shirt collar, touching it as reluctantly as if it were a dead mouse.

'This fella drinks in the King's Arms,' he announced.

'Aye, he does,' said another. 'And I saw Paddy Doocey drag him over by his feet and lie him at Albertini's front door half an hour ago.'

A mixture of effrontery and relief came over Peggy in waves. 'Is that just to stick the blame on Mr Albertini, Mart?'

What on earth was the world coming to? Dragging dead fellas across the street, she thought.

As the commotion was dying down, an ambulance – one of the many with a matron at the wheel who saw this as a good chance to get in some practice for the real thing – came tearing around the corner.

'Heart attack,' she proclaimed. 'Drink has got him. Died in Paddy Doocey's bar, but Paddy didn't want the trouble of it. Saw an opportunity to shift the blame onto an Italian and took it. This how it's going to be from now on?'

The body was put on a stretcher, a blanket covering his face, and carried into the ambulance. Matron appeared pleased as punch to take possession of a dead fella for her nurses to have a good poke around with, and she cheerfully waved them off.

Blaming Italians for dead fellas! What's wrong with people? thought Peggy.

Nineteen

'Courting?' Anthony said, stern and sad.

Peg fiddled with the gloves on her lap as she sat in the bus shelter, the wind pasting her hair to her cheeks.

'Why didn't you tell me?' he asked.

They had planned to walk along the front at Otterspool. She had been going to tell him about the dead man, about the trouble in street, warn him. It had all come crashing down in an instant.

'I was going to,' she said, squinting towards the horizon.

'And I thought we were hiding from everyone because you were afraid of your father finding out about us. Not this . . . Martin Gallagher. That's his name, yes?'

She stared at her boots and nodded.

'Oh, Peg,' he said, in a flat, disappointed tone. There was another long, awkward pause. 'Guess I'm not so lucky, then, after all. Guess I found you too late,' he added in a small voice.

She pressed her fingers into her eye sockets, trying to push away the tears.

'Bad luck for me. Gloria was right, then.'

'Gloria told you?'

'Yes. Said this Martin fellow was shouting his mouth off in the pub about how he was going to marry you. *I'm going to marry Peg O'Shea.* Gloria has always hated you and your folks, ever since we were kids. She remembered your name.'

'Does she know about us?'

He looked at her blankly. 'There is no *us*, Peg.'

The shock of how she suddenly felt pulled her up short. 'Wait,' she said, desperation in her voice. 'I thought we could be friends. Friends forever, didn't we say?'

'I'm sorry. I don't think I can do that, Peg. Wouldn't be fair on your chap. Having me hanging around, wishing I could take his place.'

His words dropped like a bomb and shattered, crushing her more completely than any of Hitler's missiles could ever do. He placed the palm of his hand flat on her breastbone. The gesture had a finality to it.

'You really are the grandest girl. Feisty. And funny. And so pretty.' He faltered. 'You've no idea how much I thought about you all these years, so I won't pretend I'm not sad. I always wondered what had become of you and whether we would meet again one day. Dreamt what it would be like for you and me to . . . well . . . But I don't think I could bear it to see you with another . . . Not the way I felt when the minute I saw you again . . .'

Peggy bit her lip. For so long she had needed something to give her some purpose, something that would anchor her to the earth. Surely he was that thing?

He stood up from the seat, sighed, turned away from her.

If so, what was she doing, about to let him walk off? Was she mad?

'Wait! Anthony! *I felt it too!*' she blurted out, leaping to her feet and grasping his sleeve.

She could see the rush of relief in his face as he stopped in his tracks, turned back to her.

'Really?'

'Of course. Everyone thinks I should marry Martin Gallagher, but . . . From the first minute I met you again, I couldn't . . . not ever . . . But he has a temper, and I'm scared to tell him . . .'

'Don't speak,' he said. 'You don't need to speak.' He took her in his arms, felt her wet tears against his cheek as he clasped her to him. 'Not right now. Don't speak. Just kiss me.'

He moved her hair away and lowered his face to hers, raised her chin with his finger and then kissed her on the mouth gently, his lips barely grazing hers. His kiss was so delicate but it made her eyelids flutter, made her feel dizzy and desperate. Then he kissed her again on the curve of her neck, kissed her throat, her cheeks, her eyes, her mouth, kissed every part of her that was decently allowed on a June afternoon in broad daylight, with children and mothers and fathers and lovers walking along the seafront and enjoying the warm Liverpool sunshine.

Twenty

'Terrible . . .' murmured Peggy, stirring milk into her tea. She perched herself on top of a high stool. 'Paddy Doocey dragged a dead man across Scottie Road just to blame the Italians.'

'What? Why?' asked her mother, sucking ferociously on a cigarette.

Her father came in from the front room, drinking a glass of stout. When he had drained it and belched he replied, 'Because of Mussolini cosying up to Hitler. They've taken more fellas down to the police station. Classifying them, they said at the pub. Then deciding what they'll do with 'em.'

Peg paled. 'Should we be doing something to stop it?'

'What d'you mean? You gone loose in the head, Peg? These are fifth column traitors. Trade unionists, traitors, Mussolini lovers, the like. Bad as Germans.'

'Leave her alone,' whispered Moira, resting a hand on his arm to stay him.

It alarmed Peggy how quickly people seemed to be making enemies of friends; first Mr Vogel, now Mr Albertini.

'Anyway. No going back now. The Italians'll all have to go.'

'Go where?! That's absurd!'

'Internment camp in Huyton. Then abroad. There's everything you need to know in there,' Dennis said as he waved his rolled-up copy of the *Echo*.

Peggy snatched it from him and scanned the headline. Its ominous, bold black letters confirmed what her father was saying.

'What is it?' Moira asked, sitting down at the table and pushing plates away to make a space for the steaming pot of tea.

'Italy has actually declared war against Britain?' Peggy said, her hands trembling and the newspaper quivering. 'That's ridiculous.'

'It's a rotten thing, that's for sure. This bloody war, turning folks against each other,' muttered Moira.

'We're done for!' Gloria Giardano spun on her heel, directing the full force of her words at her mother. 'Malignancy in our midst – Churchill has called us Italians a *malignancy*! Why did stupid Mussolini have to go and declare war? This is a nightmare!'

Sofia was cooking *brasata* on the stove. There was a smell of rosemary and thyme filling the kitchen. She prodded the beef with a wooden spoon.

'We should get away from here,' Gloria continued.

'Where to? Scotland again? We can't keep running away,' said Sofia.

'If Papa stays here, the only place he'll be going is an internment camp.'

'Should never have joined Luigi's supper club. But how were we to know? Dinner dances and tombolas do no harm,' said Sofia.

'Yes, but the Fascio Club – just the name gets everyone on edge, Mamma.'

'Your father should never have gone round wearing that stupido badge on his lapel. It's come back to haunt us. I said so at the time. All those ridiculous antics. Making us wives swap our gold wedding rings for Mussolini's bits of steel tat with his name engraved on them.' She twisted the cheap metal band on her wedding finger, tore it off and dropped it into a glass vase on the mantelpiece. Turning down the sides of her mouth into hospital corners, she retied her apron strings in a tight knot. 'Is that Anthony?' she asked, glancing anxiously at the door, hearing the sound of the latch being lifted.

But it wasn't Anthony. It was Father Moretti, Holy Cross's curate, who swooped in swirling his black cape. Sofia prepared a strong, bitter Italian coffee in a mocha pot and handed him a cup, then sat down at the table with him. The pot stood between them.

'Get ready as quickly as you can. You could go to the country. We have a convent in Suffolk. I can have a word, if you like . . . ? Father O'Mahoney has agreed.'

'We're not doing anything. And even if they do arrest us, all the people we know in Liverpool are our friends,' said Sofia.

'Apart from the O'Sheas,' said Gloria.

'Apart from the O'Sheas,' she echoed. 'But everyone else. Italians have been here for years.'

Gloria humphed, one hand on her hip, gesturing angrily with the other. 'Is this how it will be from now on? Are we going back to the bad old days?

Liverpool folks enjoyed having their hair cut, eating our ice creams, having us repair their musical instruments, didn't they? Would they really turn against us?'

'Perhaps your father could pass himself off as Irish, if there was trouble,' suggested Sofia.

'Don't be ridiculous,' Gloria scoffed. 'Look at him. Irish don't have our skin. They're pasty as milk bottles.'

'Hitler. What a fool. Who has a moustache like that?' said Sofia.

'Uncle Gianni,' replied her daughter.

'Yes, well, he looks ridiculous too. But we all just laugh at him. I'm finding it harder to see the funny side with this buffoon Hitler.'

There was a sound at the door. Anthony came in and stood in the middle of the cramped room with its picture of King Vittorio hanging on the wall, miniature Italian flags on sticks in a vase, print of the mountains of Bardi propped up on the mantelpiece. He looked in shock, his normally immaculate hair dishevelled, collar undone.

'Mamma,' he said, ashen. 'I just heard. They're arresting everyone. Taking them to the police station and then the camp in Huyton.'

'I told you, Sofia,' said the young priest.

'I'm sorry, Father,' she replied, with a reproachful shrug of the shoulders. 'We're not leaving Liverpool. This is our home. Antonio has just started gunner training with the RAF. He's leaving for Morecambe in three weeks. Surely to God fighting for this country means something.' As if to emphasize her point, she stood, took a bottle of beer, twisted it open and poured it into the pot where the *brasata* was boiling. The liquid hissed as it came into contact with the heat. Sofia jabbed at the pot, taking out her fury on the lump of beef.

'Well, then, your only hope is to get down to the town hall with your papers. Otherwise you really will be arrested.'

'Papers?'

'Immigration papers. To say the exact date when you arrived here. Any male over sixteen who can't prove he was born here will be interned straight away.'

'So many of us Italians don't have them. Didn't bother, just set up shop and got on with what we knew – cutting hair, selling ice cream, mosaics.'

'Papa, you mean?' said Gloria. 'Where in God's name is he?'

Sofia turned to the priest and said, 'This is ridiculous. Scaremongering. The town hall? Are you saying we would have to walk over floors designed by my husband's family, and then be told we aren't welcome here? Nonsense.'

Gloria shuddered. 'All that bonhomie. The Liverpudlians and the Italians . . . communion parties and May processions. It's all over now,' she said, pacing the room in a flurry of hand gestures and head-shaking. 'We're the enemy now.'

There it was. Someone had said it. They had actually said it out loud.

'Of course we're not the enemy . . .' answered Sofia, glancing away. But the tears gathering in her glassy eyes did little to reassure them all.

'They're only rounding up the chaps who have lived here less than twenty years? We've all been here longer,' said Anthony, puffing on a cigarette.

'Not much longer. We need the papers to prove that, that's the trouble,' muttered Sofia. 'I have no idea where they are. Maybe passports . . . do we have our passports? We must have other proof.'

'They will only accept immigration papers,' said Father Moretti.

Gloria threw her hands in the air. Just like her father, she spoke so rapidly and in such a volley of words that it was difficult even for Anthony to understand what she was saying. 'Mamma, go through the drawers. I'll look through the boxes under the bed.'

Sofia began searching through drawers, turning out cotton reels, ribbons, papers, old envelopes. Anthony did a quick calculation on his fingers. His parents had met and married within eight months of meeting. He had come along the following year, so that made it . . . what? Twenty-two years since they had arrived in Liverpool?

'We'll be fine. Anthony is in the RAF. Roberto is still at the seminary. They wouldn't arrest a priest. *Gesù Cristo*, they wouldn't?' said Sofia.

The priest sat there, watching her sift through the mound of papers, peer into envelopes, scrabble in the back of the drawer again.

'Where did Enzo put them?' she said, raking her fingers through her hair. 'Surely they're here. Surely.' She looked up. 'Enzo. Where've you been?' she said, seeing her husband step into the room.

Anthony watched his father taking in the scene:

the turned-out drawers, the priest. Then his gaze shifted back towards his wife.

'Help us find the immigration papers, Enzo. You're just standing there doing nothing,' she said.

Enzo went and sat at the table, watching her moving around him. He leaned back in the rocker and rubbed his temples.

'What's the matter?' she asked, turning out pieces of elastic, a thimble, a ball of string. 'Why are you so quiet?' He seemed unable to meet her eyes. She leaned over him, grabbed his chin and twisted it up towards her. 'What's the matter, Vincenzo?'

'It was such a long time ago,' he said with a shrug. Anthony and Gloria watched with a sinking feeling.

'You never went! Did you?'

'None of us went.'

Sofia gripped the edge of the table for fear her legs would buckle beneath her. 'What?!' she said, her eyes flashing with rage.

'Can't you remember? We went to Luca's bar when he was opening the ice-cream parlour.'

Sofia pressed her hand to her chest as though trying to keep her heart from bursting out of it. 'Please tell me—'

'I never went to the town hall,' he said, cutting her off.

'But you said to me. It was all done. After we moved out, after the business at Luigi's club. You said you had the papers signed. I remember you went to the town hall.'

'I meant to. But one day led to another.'

'But you told me you had done it! Vincenzo Giardano! You do know what this means?'

'Don't go on. All this fuss over a little piece of paper. I'm going out. There are no papers because we didn't get round to doing it. None of us got round to doing it. Don't you remember, it was that day when Luca turned up from Sicily?' he said.

'Oh, and how could I ever forget it? The fools, and everyone drunk as usual!'

'We had a good evening.'

'Is that all you can say?' she asked darkly.

'*Sì.*'

She sprang at him as if on a coil and began hitting him around the head. '*Idiota! Idiota!*'

Grunting, he squirmed away. In a wild, desperate panic, Sofia pulled out more drawers, right out of their runners, letting them smash and tip onto the floor. When there was just the empty casing, exhausted, she sank to her knees.

And then the door slammed open. It was Luigi, breathless and wide-eyed with fear.

Twenty-one

'They've got Roberto. Arrested him at the station.'

'What! Why isn't he at the seminary?'

'He was on his way here. They arrested him at Lime Street Station. He's in Walton police station. I've just been down there. They're already rounding up all the Italians in Scottie Road. Knocking on folk's doors. MI5 have been making lists of all Italian men with connections to the Fascio clubs to be immediately interned if we entered the war against Britain; they've been doing it for years. We all said Enzo should have stopped hanging out at the club. They call us "dangerous characters" – ridiculous.'

'But that's why we went to Scotland! To get away from all that! Where's Papa?' Sofia cried, suddenly noticing that her husband had slunk off somewhere while her back was turned. 'Anyone know where Papa went?' She was hoarse now, dry-mouthed with horror.

'Probably gone to the bar. I'll go and find him. It's gonna be all right,' said Anthony, in what he hoped was a soothing voice.

But no one in that room believed it, least of all him.

*   *   *

It was Mrs Tozer from next door who first rushed into the O'Sheas' house, asking them if they had heard the news, waving the *Echo* above her head.

'They say there'll be another announcement any minute now . . .'

'Oh no,' said Peggy, steadying herself with a hand on the mantelpiece, trying to organize the consequences of what all this might mean in her mind.

Moira, meanwhile, was twisting the knobs on the wireless. Mr Chamberlain's voice floated out into the parlour. '*Italy has declared war. From noon today, the Italians will support Hitler.*'

Peggy grabbed her coat. 'Got to find Martin. Stop him doing something stupid.'

'Peg! Peg!' cried her mother. 'Where are you going? You haven't finished chopping those swedes!'

Rounding the corner into Scottie Road, it was a brick that Peggy saw first, hurtling through the window of the barber's. It smashed the glass and caused the coloured bottles to tumble off their shelves like skittles and shatter. It was quickly followed by another missile.

As she expected, Martin was easy to spot amongst a small group of youths. She felt her whole body tense, felt sick to her stomach. This was sport all right, like a coconut shy – young men chucking whatever they could get their hands on at all the lamps and glass door panels. The night was warm enough for shirtsleeves and she watched in horror as Martin pushed his cuffs up to his elbows, revealing his thick, tensing forearms.

Mr Lombardi stuck his head out of an upstairs window. Seconds later, followed by his terrified wife and daughter and the ancient grandfather and speaking volubly in Italian, he came hurtling out onto the pavement, raised his stick and ran at the small group.

'Crazy! Look what you've done!'

'Traitor!' one of the crowd shouted. The clanging of police bells started up in the distance.

'I've called the police, fools!' he said.

'It's you they'll be arresting, not us!' said Martin. He turned to Peg and seemed pleased to see her. 'All right, Peg? You heard? They're knocking on doors in Little Italy. Giving them half an hour to pack a bag and then slinging them into the backs of vans.'

'Dragging them out of bed, I heard,' said a grinning woman to a shocked Peggy.

There was jostling within the little group gathering on the Lombardis' doorstep, and then one of them broke free. A struggle between Mr Lombardi and another man started, at first a tussle, but soon they were both grappling with each other on the ground. Names were being called and a man ran forward and pulled a clump of hair from the head of one of the fighters, then looked amazed to see it in his hand. A policeman on a horse came charging up the street. The horse reared up.

'Go home, lads!' cried the policeman, waving a truncheon.

Nobody moved.

'Bloody traitors!' someone yelled. 'Collar the lot! That's what Churchill said!'

'I said leave him alone! It's all in hand, lads. Leave it to us. Or I'll arrest you an' all.'

The boys moved away.

'Go back inside, Mr Lombardi.'

There was a gleam in Martin's eye. He was probably drunk. That was it, Peg told herself. People do the most awful things when they're drunk.

By the time the police had put Mr Lombardi and his father in a van – 'For your own safety,' they said lamely – the crowd began to drift off, and things became a little calmer. A few people wandered back and forth in front of the barbers, broken glass underfoot. Others lingered at the corner of the street, but there was nothing much left to see.

'Enough of this, Martin. We're going home now. *Now!*' said Peg, tugging his sleeve.

They set off together. Peggy was numb but Martin was excited and jittery, a tense live wire, adrenalin coursing through his veins.

'Quick,' he said as they walked up Gerard Street, suddenly pulling her by the hand and dashing into a side alley to find another couple and a young man who had also decided it offered a perfect view of the shops opposite. He folded his arm around her waist and clasped her tightly to him.

She frowned. 'What are you doing? I don't like this.'

'Shhh,' he said. He poked his head out, around the corner of the passage.

A woman Peggy didn't recognize called out to him from the shadows of a doorway opposite. 'Mart?' she hissed.

Who on earth is she? thought Peggy. But then, this war had made friends of perfect strangers, people who suddenly found they had more in common than they could ever have imagined.

In the distance there was the sound of whistles, then the clanging of a louder bell. She couldn't see what was happening – just a few more people stepping out into the street, at first only visible as silhouettes. But then, as she squinted into the gloom, there was Kevin Shaughnessy with his girl, who was wearing a long trench coat and long gloves, and another lad she recognized from the Boot.

'Have you heard the news?' a woman said from behind her. Peggy turned to look at her. She was with a few other people, all wide-eyed and agitated; there was something ugly about their manner. It was as if they were moving in a pack, excited by the thrill of the scent.

'Let's go home, Martin.'

And then a girl shot forward from the other side of the street and pressed a stone into Peggy's hand, curling her fingers around it. Peggy looked down at it in horror.

'Go on,' someone shouted. 'Who's going to be the first?'

A pasty-faced man spat noisily, pulled back his arm and threw a lump of brick, which smashed right through the window of Macari's music shop opposite. A cheer rose up from the small crowd. Peggy looked again at the rock in her hand, still appalled.

'Your turn, Peg,' said Martin.

'Are you expecting me to throw this stone? Are you daft in the head? Why would I do that?'

There was the sound of a second rock crashing through the window, and someone inside let out a scream. More people who had been watching from a distance started slinking out of the darkness.

Kevin Shaughnessy's girl laughed in Peggy's face, as though she couldn't quite believe the question she'd overheard. 'Because they're Italians,' she said.

'I know that, but why would them being Italian make you want to throw a stone through their windows?'

'Have you not heard the news?'

'What news?'

'Mussolini has declared war against us.'

'Oh, *that* news!' Peggy said, sarcastically. 'And why would that mean you'd chuck a stone through Mr Salvatore's hairdressers? State of your barnet, you're long overdue for a haircut. Have you thought about that, when you put him out of business?'

Martin's eyes flashed. 'Less of the jabbering, Peg. Get stuck in. We're heading to Granelli's butchers after this,' he said, as he darted out of the dark of the ginnel.

But Peggy remained frozen, livid. 'They live here. This is their home,' she stammered. 'I'd rather eat a rat sandwich than get involved with your dirty work.'

'Your Mart was the one who planned it,' said the girl flatly.

'What?' said Peggy. Her blood ran cold. She felt sick to the stomach. '*My* Mart? Not any more,' she snapped.

She turned on her heel and peeled off down Scarfe Street. Ahead of her was the jumble of terraced houses huddled together and the road where the mosaic work-shop was. She had passed it many times over the years, lingered outside, trying to get a glimpse through the open door of the magical place where she and

Anthony had shared secrets all those years ago. Now she could see, even from the top of the road, that there were pieces of glass where the frosted window had been smashed in, shards littering the pavement.

Hurrying towards it, she picked her way over the debris. 'Oh, good God!' she cried. The door was open on its hinges. The jars had been tipped out all over the floor, the worktop on its side. The whole place was a mess of tiles and glittering glass, as if the floor itself was one huge mosaic.

Her heart thumped at her chest. She had to find Anthony and tell him. Every sinew of her body was screaming that she should go and warn him about what was happening. Arrests and windows being smashed in. Men taken off the street and shoved into vans. Did he know about the workshop? Picking up her skirts, she ran as fast as she could down Scottie Road, along the passages to Mr Albertini's. He would know what to do, he would tell Anthony. It would be him next as well, or Bertorelli's bar.

She arrived breathless at the top of his street. As she scurried across the road, a policeman was tugging a man behind him in handcuffs. It was a shocking sight. She recognized the doleful, hunched figure as Mr Granelli, the butcher. Looking through the window of the cafe next door, she saw someone with a broom sweeping up the glass in between the marble-topped tables.

'Where are you taking him?' she demanded, rushing over to the policeman.

'Police station. Who are you, though?'

'Peggy O'Shea . . .' She tried to appeal to the good

nature of the man. 'My friends, the Giardanos. Giardano mosaics. Would you know anything about them?'

'Go home, love,' said the policeman. 'This has nothing to do with you.'

He pushed the man into the back of the van, shut the doors with a clank and a twist of the lock, and drove off.

When she reached Mr Albertini's bar, she hammered on the door. At first there was no answer, but then his face appeared at the window. She mouthed urgently, 'Can I come in?' He glanced over his shoulder furtively and then opened the door an inch, stopped it with his foot.

'Go away.'

'There's trouble.'

'D'you think I don't know?'

Her words tumbled over each other. 'They've bashed up the workshop. I saw it on my way back. I wanted to tell Anthony, perhaps someone should go down there. I'm worried what's going to happen.'

'I think it's a little late. They've taken every Italian who lives in Little Italy. Starting on this road next.'

She felt herself trembling. And then she saw a figure step out of the darkness from behind Mr Albertini.

'Anthony!' she squealed.

'Peg. In here, quick,' he said, yanking her by the arm. He nodded at Mr Albertini, who moved aside as Anthony pulled her in.

'They've chucked a stone through the workshop window. Smashed the whole place up. I just wanted to tell you . . .'

'I already know,' replied Anthony, looking serious and afraid.

Peggy knew straight away that something else was dreadfully wrong.

Mr Albertini sighed. 'They've taken his brother. And they're coming for his father. They're looking for him right now.'

'Why?' she asked, shocked.

'They say he has to go to the police station. Show them everything is in order.'

'Well, maybe you should go.'

'Here's the thing though, it's not in order,' said Anthony, slumping into a chair. 'Papa never got his immigration papers signed. In any case, we're on a list, Peg. They think Papa is a fifth columnist.'

'What! They can't – you're in the air force!'

'No one cares about that.'

'Then you can't go back home. At least not tonight. That's the worst place for you to be.'

'They've taken my nephew,' said Mr Albertini. 'He had his sixteenth birthday three weeks ago. This morning they dragged him from his Boys' Brigade marching practice, said they were going to put him in a camp in Huyton. With people who really *are* the enemy. Stuck together with Germans. We Italians hate Hitler!'

'Then you're coming with me, Anthony. I'll hide you from the coppers. This is worse than I thought. I thought it was just about chucking stones through windows, but arresting you . . .'

'Where, though?'

'The dairy. No one's there. Da's doing the Bootle

runs tomorrow. I'm opening up. You can lie low for the night.'

Anthony looked at Mr Albertini.

'Well, you can't go home. And they're on their way here. Peg's right. Go somewhere where they won't find you. Just so we can think until morning and come up with a plan. Then we can get some money to you, make a few phone calls.'

'If you're sure, Peg . . .'

'Never been more sure of anything in my life. Let's go.'

Anthony nodded, began quickly gathering up his coat and tightening the laces on his boots as fast as he could.

'I can tell your mam if you want, that you're safe?' Peg said.

'I'll do that,' said Mr Albertini. 'Only, maybe I won't say it's an O'Shea who's hiding him, eh?'

Outside, they could hear the clanging bells of more police cars, and there was a smell of sulphur in the air.

Meanwhile, three doors down, Enzo sat in Bertorelli's, puffing on a Capstan cigarette, blue smoke rings curling up towards the skylight. The door was locked, the lights out. The men huddled in groups.

'I can hear them,' someone said. Enzo paled, steadying himself on the brass rail. Val, the owner, stood at the bar rinsing glasses under the tap. She cocked her head. A couple of men at a table, trying to distract themselves by playing dominoes, glanced up, startled.

Val set down the glasses, peered through a window

into the street. Footsteps approached, and after a tense moment there was a clamour of impatient battering and hammering on the door. A man shouted 'Open up!'

Val shooed them all behind the bar, urging them to crouch down and go quietly out through the side door, one by one. But someone was waiting there, too, in the alley between the pub's yard and the squat terraces: a man in ARP uniform, his tin helmet sitting on top of his head and bag slung across his body, with a clipboard. He had the expression of someone following orders he wasn't comfortable carrying out.

'You're being detained under the Defence of the Realm Act Regulation 18b . . .' he mumbled, reading from a sheet of paper. His feet were planted firmly apart, his eyes shifting from the clipboard back up to the group of men. He directed them towards two soldiers in uniform with a perfunctory nod. 'All you lot, follow these men . . .'

Enzo Giardano glanced back over his shoulder. The man saw it. 'Don't try and get out the front. The door is bolted.'

Val appeared at his side, teacloth over one shoulder, puffing anxiously on a cigarette.

'Don't I recognize you? Larry? It's Larry Tozer, isn't it?' said Enzo to the guard, in a halting voice. The man didn't respond. 'It's me, Enzo. I know you. We did your mosaics. Your front step?' A look passed between them, one of guilt, shame, and regret on Larry's part, as one by one the Italian men were shoved towards a van, pushed and prodded as if they were cattle. Inside, the small green army van had benches running down either side. More men were already in there, sitting hunched, looking bewildered as the guard shone a torch into their faces.

'Larry Tozer. Can you believe it? He looked through me like I didn't exist. Last Christmas we were sharing whiskeys and enjoying Artie Shaw. The bloody turncoat. I spent months on that mosaic for his shop,' said Enzo to Luigi, who shrugged. Someone said unhelpfully that the man was probably just doing what he had been told to do. Just carrying out orders.

'And isn't that why we're in this mess? *Madre mia.* No one to stand up for us and say how wrong this is,' Enzo replied. Raking his hands through his hair, he crossed himself and raised his eyes towards heaven as the doors slammed and locked with a firm clank and twist of a key.

When Anthony and Peg reached Scottie Road after veering off and making their way through the twisting maze of back alleys and ginnels that she knew so well, she stopped at the dairy.

Furtively looking over each shoulder, Peg fumbled for the key.

'No one will know you're here. There's an empty flat upstairs. My Uncle Seamus left Liverpool and moved out six months ago with his kiddies to go and stay at Davey's farm, so it's just me and my da and my brother working here. It's my turn to do the early milk tomorrow so I can keep them at bay. I saw what that angry mob were doing. Might have looked like it was just lads. But those lads can be pretty vicious.'

He clutched her hand, squeezed it as they stood for a breathless moment under a sky threaded with stars.

'Thank you, Peggy.'

'You saved my life once.' She smiled. 'Remember, when I set meself on fire?'

She opened the door and led him inside. When she closed it behind her, she let out a breath. 'Anthony,' she said, her eyes like saucers. 'It's going to be all right. Let's get you upstairs.'

She led him up the staircase and onto the landing, then into a small room. The place had fallen into disrepair in the months since Seamus had left. There was a smell of damp, a tattered curtain at the window. In the corner was a small, sagging metal bed with a rolled-up mattress on it. It felt calmer here. She took her coat off.

There was tape over the window. Rubbing on the glass and standing on her toes, she peered outside. She could just about see down to the end of the street. There was a van idling across the road.

'Looks suspicious,' she said. 'You wait here – I'll check. And there's some blankets downstairs we use for the cows; I'll bring them up.'

Anthony looked around the room at the bare walls with plaster that had fallen off in places, the damp creeping over the ceiling. It reminded him of some of the photos of the farmhouse they'd had in Italy. There was the obligatory crucifix. An old washstand with a stained and chipped enamel basin. Under the bed, when he leaned down and peered, was a cracked chamber pot. He hoped he could make it through to morning without having to use it. Peggy came back in, wiping her hands on a tea towel and with a coarse horsehair blanket over one arm. 'Coast is clear. Looked in on our Dora.'

'How is she?' he asked.

'She's grand. She's growing fatter. Never been better. That's one good thing about being a pig. As long as she gets her slops, she couldn't give two hoots that the world has gone mad and folks are chucking stones through their neighbours' windows. Here's the blanket. And I brought you milk.' She put a small jug on the shelf. 'It's creamy. But it'll keep you going til morning.'

'Thank you, thank you.'

'Nothing to thank me for. Sit here.' She unrolled and then patted the mattress. 'No one will think of looking here for you.'

He nodded. They sat down together, backs leaning against the wall, legs stretched out long. Somewhere in the distance there was a sudden, loud bang. Peggy jumped, and instinctively he grasped her hand.

'Are you okay?' She nodded. 'You know, Peg, it's worse than just chucking stones. There's rumours that once they get folks to Huyton camp, they're putting everyone on boats and sending them away.'

'Where to?

'Isle of Man.'

'Flippin' 'eck . . . Perhaps you ought to stay here at the dairy for a while longer.'

'And what would your folks say about that?

Giardanos and O'Sheas hated each other before all this. What do you think it's going to be like now? What about tomorrow morning, if your da were to turn up and find me here?'

'I told you. It's my turn to milk early. No one is going to be here tomorrow morning except me. But if there's any trouble, remember that den when we were kiddies, don't you? It's still there – bit of a squeeze, but it's a good place to hide.'

It was beginning to feel cold, and she pulled the blanket over their legs and tucked it under their thighs.

'Did you know this was going to happen?' she asked.

'Well, Mr Albertini has two photos on display in the bar: one of King George, and the other of Vittorio Emanuele the Third. Police came round last week and tried confiscating the Vittorio picture. King George was smashed in the scuffle. I found him in tears, clearing up the glass from the carpet and swearing at both Mussolini and Churchill. But I had no idea it would get this bad.'

She intertwined her fingers with his as he spoke. She felt him squeeze, gently.

'This bloody war. I thought we'd moved on from the name-calling. Tony Baloney Sausage Polloni, Tony spic. Tony Lava-tory, they used to shout after me wherever I went. I always hated it, but it was just lads at school. We got over it. Most grew out of it. Now it's gonna start all over again. As for my dreams of the RAF . . .'

The words cut right into her heart. Lads grow into

men, but some don't change when they grow full beards, she thought ruefully. She shivered and clung onto his fingers. 'I'd die if anything happened to you, Anthony. Just when I found you again.'

'Oh, Peg,' he said. Raising her hand to his mouth, he kissed the back of it. No one had ever done such a thing before. It felt so tender and sweet. Peggy was so overcome that in response she leaned forward and threw her arms around him. She could feel his heart beating as he hugged her back and their bodies pressed against each other.

And it was then that he raised her face to his with a finger under her chin and kissed her gently on the mouth, her eyes, her eyelids. Peggy could hardly believe how it made her feel. That in the midst of all these terrible goings-on, she felt a kind of rush of happiness that she wouldn't have dared imagine even existed.

'Peggy. You're so fierce and honest. I didn't know girls like you existed.'

She blushed. They sat gazing at each other, with the light sloping in and throwing soft shadows across their faces. Love? Was that what she was feeling?

'And you're so beautiful.'

'I am not. Your Italian girls are beautiful,' she replied shyly.

'Beautiful in one way. But you, Peggy O'Shea, well, you're different. Feel my heart,' he said. He took her fingers, pressed them to his chest. 'It's bumping like a hammer.'

'That's because at any minute the police could come here and bash down the doors and put you in one of their cells.'

'No it's not, it's because I'm sitting next to you thinking, do I dare tell you that I want to do more than just kiss you?'

'Oh, Anthony.'

He plunged his tongue into her mouth and she fell back, breathless, onto the bed.

'Don't stop,' she said as she ran her fingers through his hair, and he kissed her harder.

But then he paused, looked down at her and took her face in his hands. 'I love you, Peg.'

She felt herself trembling, a fierce heat rising through her body, but this time it wasn't a candle setting her on fire, it was this boy. It was his skin on hers. It was his breath on her face, the sweet smell of him, his strong hands moving over the contours of her body, the fact he had just told her he loved her.

Clutching the lapels of his jacket, she pulled him closer and kissed him back. 'I love you, Anthony. I've always loved you, you do know that?'

And then they were lying down, getting tangled up, as he tore off his jacket and undid a few buttons on her blouse, then a few more, all the way down to her waist, pulled down the camisole exposing her pale skin, kissed her creamy nipples, running his finger around one and licking the tip of it, and doing it again. She shivered. He then kissed her full on the mouth again, tongue twisting around her teeth. She felt every atom of her body coming alive.

'Peggy, you are the most beautiful thing I've ever seen,' he said, pausing and gazing down at her as she lay there half naked. 'You are so pretty.' A pinkish hue crept over her cheeks. 'But I won't take advantage of you. That's not fair to you, sweet Peg. Even though just kissing you and touching you is burning holes in my skin. I would burst into flames, for sure, if we went any further. Good things come to those who wait,' he said, kindly.

Winding her fingers up through the weave of his chest hair and kissing him gently on the lips, the smell of him, the feel of his flesh against her flesh, so male, was intoxicating. It had felt extraordinary and shocking and shivering, to have his hands touch every part of her, her breasts, her inner thighs, her back, to feel his fingers search out the most private parts of her as she had gasped with such rapture and such bliss. It felt the most natural thing in the world and confirmed what she had known since they were children: she loved Anthony Giardano. He was the man she needed to share her life with. All she had to do was persuade the rest of the world to see it that way.

A short while later, he said, 'Peg, I can't tell you how much I want to stay here kissing every freckle on your sweet face, and everywhere else besides – I don't think I've ever felt happier in my life. But I'm also more worried than I've ever been, so I think you should leave. If someone does come, I don't want them to know you let me in. It's not safe.'

Lying there, legs and arms entwined, the moonlight sloping in from the broken window, their bodies glistening with sweat, she clutched him and moaned. 'I don't care. I love you. I've found you again and I'm not going to lose you this time.'

'I do,' he said. 'Martin Gallagher doesn't sound a

forgiving kind of chap. Go on now. And Peg. If anything does happen tonight, if anyone discovers me, I'll get word to you of where I'm gonna head off to. Probably back to Scotland. But Peg, I promise I'll be back,' he said tenderly, fastening her top button and resting his fingertips on her chest.

'No, I don't want to leave you.'

He smiled and kissed her on the nose. 'Do as I say, Peg.'

She stood up and straightened her clothes, saying bravely, 'I guess it's ta-ra, then.'

He kissed her forehead. 'Ta-ra, for now,' he echoed.

She went over to the door and lifted the latch as he settled back down on the bed.

'Try and sleep. If you have to do a runner tonight for any reason, leave me a note.'

'It's not likely I'd get far. Italians on the list haven't been able to own a car for weeks. Or any motor vehicle for that matter, or a bicycle, in case we do a moonlight flit. Even got a letter saying we're not allowed to own an aeroplane – that's a laugh.'

'Ridiculous. If you get lonely, there's Dora and Glenda and Nettie,' she said with a smile. 'And if you need to hide, there's our den. Don't forget the den! See you tomorrow. I'll be here early. Hopefully Mr Albertini will have got word to your ma, and if the coast is clear, they'll have decided what you should do next. Oh, and Anthony – you're the best kisser in the whole world,' she said, smiling.

'Go, dear. I love you like a heart needs a beat, Peg. But I intend to stay alive to tell you that every day for the rest of my life. So go.'

Twenty-two

The next morning Peggy got up and dressed quickly. The house was still asleep as she left, thankful that there was nobody to ask questions. She hoped she would arrive at the dairy before Anthony woke up, and that the bed hadn't been too uncomfortable.

The sun was rising and the rose-coloured sky bathed the streets in pink light. She got to the dairy clutching a scone wrapped up in a bit of linen. The door was on the latch and she pushed it open, went in and made her way up the creaking staircase. Pushing the door open with the side of her hip, she called quietly, 'Anthony!'

The first thing she saw as she stepped into the room was his coat, lying on the floor crumpled in a heap. That was odd. Then, casting her eyes one way and the other, she felt a creeping worry.

Where was he? Her heart thumped and she felt a little ill. Approaching the sagging bed, she noticed there was a puddle of milk seeping out from behind the door and under the bottom of it. Looking behind it with a sinking feeling, she saw the jug lying there, smashed into three pieces.

There was no other way to read the scene. She felt her stomach clenching. These were signs of a struggle. She knew a fight when she saw one. Racing back downstairs, she made her way into the yard and pushed open the gate of the shippen. The piece of wood where the den was had been moved aside. She got on her hands and knees and peered into the gloom. Nothing. Just an empty black space.

'Anthony!' she called, struggling to her feet, twisting her head right and left. There was no response, just the sound of the cows breathing heavily and the swish, swish of tails, a low moo.

She ran home as quickly as she could after pushing and prodding the pig back into the pen. She slammed open the hall door, slammed it shut behind her, slammed open the kitchen door.

Sheila was rearranging wet nappies on the clothes horse in front of the range and Liam was rolling a marble between the table legs. Philomena, who had recently taken to wearing bright red nail varnish, was painting her nails.

'Sheila!' Walking over to the window, she yanked back the curtains and looked out into the street. 'You need to go down to the dairy, sort out Dora and milk Nettie and Glenda right now.'

'Why, what's happened?'

'Trouble.'

'You mean the rioting last night?' said Peter, who was sitting near the fireplace and polishing a pair of boots. 'News has been spreading like wildfire through the court houses.'

'Mr Lombardi, you know, owns the barber shop called Gino's on Scottie Road?' Sheila said. 'Someone put a brick through the window, just chucked it right through. Could have killed someone. Mr Lombardi was shaving a poor fella, nearly slit his throat.'

'I heard his wife taped it up, and scrawled Open for Business Tomorrow – and guess what the rotters did? Someone put another brick through the side door this morning.'

Martin came wandering through from the parlour, stuffing a piece of bread into his mouth. 'What you doing here, Peg?' he said, taking his coat off and putting it on the back of the chair.

'I could ask you the same. Where did you go after I left you last night?' she said, her eyes flashing angrily at him.

'The Boot. We had a bit of a craic.' He grinned. 'The ice-cream place got smashed in. The windows were whacked in with a cricket bat. And the hair-dressers. The door is off its hinges. Fellas turned up with a cart full of bricks and bottles and made their way down Scottie Road, looting all the Eyeties' shops and bars.'

'And you think that's all right, do you?'

And then he smirked, the faintest hint of a smile, but Peggy could feel the blood thundering around her body, her heart thudding against her chest. She could tell he was waiting to see what she would do next.

'You hear what happened, Peg? They're taking all the folks from Little Italy down to the police station,' said her father, coming in with a bag of coal. He dragged it across the floor and tipped it into the scuttle.

'Yes. And I don't like it.'

'Bloody Giardanos have had it coming for years,' muttered her father, taking up his copy of the *Echo*.

'Aye,' said Martin.

'What are you talking about?'

She moved towards Martin, jabbed a finger at him. 'If Anthony Giardano has been arrested and you have anything to do with it, you've got me to answer to.'

'What are you on about, Peg?' he said, plonking himself into a chair, putting his feet up on the table, crossing one leg over the other.

The cheek of it! thought Peggy. The damn nerve of this man!

'I wanted to help him! I let him hide in the dairy. And now he's gone,' she wailed.

Dennis, in shock, banged his flat palm on the table, making the cups and saucers rattle. Philomena smudged the thumb she was painting, Sheila yelped in fright and Peter dropped his tin of polish.

'Help him! What have Giardanos got to do with you, Peg? Stop sticking your nose in where you're not wanted! It's not your dairy, it's Davey's! How bloody dare you do that!'

The baby came crawling in on her chubby legs. She stuck a thumb in her mouth, startled, her big eyes opened wide.

Peggy looked at Martin, who was grinning. He still sat with his feet on the table, boots unlaced, ankles crossed, hands behind his head.

'Take your muddy boots off the table,' she said.

He carried on smirking.

'Take them off. Messing the place up.'

'Ooh, our Peg's cross.'

And then her blood went cold. 'What's that?' she said, squinting at Martin's foot, at the sole of his shoe.

'What?'

She flew at him in a sudden rage, grabbed his boot. 'Show me your foot!'

He tried to pull his leg away and jerk it off the table, but she held tight and continued to tug and wrestle at his foot furiously. When his boot came off in her hand and she fell backwards and landed on her bottom, he laughed.

'What the flaming hell, Peg?'

'Look! In the tread of your boot! A piece of glass. Tiny piece . . . of blue glass . . .' she said, holding it aloft. She was shaking with emotion.

He sat there, pushing his finger around a plate of crumbs and licking it. He shrugged.

'Did you go to the Giardanos' workshop last night? Was it you? It was all bashed up.'

It was the way he said, 'Yes, what of it?' so nonchalantly, with a shrug of the shoulders and that stupid grin playing across his lips, that made her explode.

'And was it you who told the police where Anthony was hiding?'

His face changed, and he slammed his hand down on the table. Liam, still underneath, yelped, snatched the marble and drew his legs up to his chest. 'Yes, it was. I went to find you and saw you leaving the dairy. Knew something was up. And I'll tell you what, Peggy: I don't care. In fact, I'll be having a drink over it tonight in the Throstle's Nest, and I'll be raising a toast for all those Italians we put away.'

She sprang like a wildcat towards him and pummelled him around the head with the boot as he ducked to avoid her blows.

'Good riddance to them. Someone's got to take a stand. I'm not ashamed of that,' he said, laughing and shielding his head.

The words hit her like a truck slamming into her chest. 'Do you realize what you've done?'

'Just doing my duty. Collar the lot. You heard Churchill.'

'That's not your duty, idiot! You bastard, Martin!'

Her father threw his arms up in frustration. 'Language, Peg! Didn't I tell you to stay away from them Giardanos? They're just getting what they deserve,' he snapped.

She felt her eyes brimming with tears. 'I'm going to find Anthony. I'm going to do what I can to help him. And there's nothing you lot can do to stop me. It's your fault Anthony has been taken away.'

'Who's this Anthony? What are you talking about?' her father said. 'Get up. You're making a right show of yourself, as usual.'

Philomena, who had been about to leave for work at the parachute factory, lingered in the doorway, watching open-mouthed. Sheila had backed off to stand beside her. They both winced in alarm as Peggy threw the boot angrily at Martin, hitting him square in the face.

'Ow!' he yelled. 'That got me in the eye!'

'Stop chucking things around! This kitchen is too small for all this commotion! Stop behaving so daft, you know the Italians getting arrested wasn't Martin's fault!' said Dennis.

'He told them where Anthony was,' she cried. 'I want nothing to do with you ever again, Martin Gallagher.'

Martin's face grew sterner. 'Now, Peg. Stop being such a wildcat. I'll not have you behaving like this when we're married.'

'Married?' said her father, surprised.

'Married?' said her mother, walking into the room. 'Peg's getting married?'

'Peg!' cried Philomena, excitedly. 'When!'

A grinning Liam poked his head out from under the table.

'Don't you have to ask us first?' said her father.

'Now who's the one talking daft? I'm not marrying *him*. Never!' She spun round on her heel to face Martin square on and jabbed a finger at him. 'How could I look at you ever again, when all I'd be thinking was that Anthony would still be here if it wasn't for you?'

'That's enough!' said her father.

'What the heck are you all talking about?' said Moira. 'Leave you lot alone for five minutes and another war breaks out while my back is turned.'

Tears stabbed Peggy's eyes. 'Ask him,' she said, storming out of the door. 'Ask flaming Martin Gallagher!'

Twenty-three

I hate my family, Peggy thought, I hate them.

She said it to herself over and over again as she pounded the pavement, running all the way to Albertini's, where she found Mr Albertini on the front step anxiously waiting for news. He raised his head tiredly as Peggy approached, tucked the teacloth he was twisting in his hands into the waistband of his trousers.

'What can I say?' he replied when she asked him what he knew. 'They arrested Anthony? *Sì*. There's a meeting at church. I'm going there now. Come if you want, only do you mind, not with me? I don't think it's a good idea that I should be seen with . . . you. I'm sorry. Mrs Giardano is in a terrible state. I haven't told her they found him at the dairy yet. I'm leaving someone else to break that piece of unpleasant news.'

Peggy decided the least she could do was to find Mrs Giardano and explain. There was a small throng of people already gathering at the church. After fighting her way through, she squashed into a pew at the back and listened. Most were speaking volubly in Italian. Peggy didn't know exactly what they were saying, but she didn't need to speak their language in order to understand how frustrated and angry they were.

Father Moretti stood at the altar banging a small wooden gavel onto a makeshift table that sat between the altar table and the brass altar rails, with the altar gate open. Beside him on a spindly chair was a man in an ill-fitting suit. The priest introduced him as 'Mr Page, from the Corporation.'

They started with a prayer, a swift Hail Mary, then after making the sign of the cross, the priest said, 'Patience is what's needed.'

'I've heard you want to put them on bloody ships, Mr Page!' a voice shouted from the back of the church.

'Please, stop yelling. Remember we are in God's house,' said Father Moretti, striking his hand across his breast. A few of the women tutted and crossed themselves as they threaded rosary beads through their fingers.

'I'm not yelling, I'm Italian!' the man shouted back.

'It's not too bad, the camp. Sanitary . . .'

'They've no furniture, I heard! When can we go and see them?'

Mr Page from the Corpy faltered, looked over his half-moon spectacles. 'You can't . . .'

'What's to stop us going down there?'

'It wouldn't help things,' said the man.

Peggy shifted in the pew. She scoured the church, looking for a woman who she thought might be Sofia Giardano. More voices were shouting out now, many in Italian. Father Moretti tried to quiet them down, waving his hands and shushing them, patting the air to calm everyone, but to no effect. The man from the Corpy shuffled through his papers nervously. Eventually Father Moretti grabbed the altar bells and jangled them vigorously.

'*In nomine Patris et Filius* . . .' he said.

The words came back from the body of the church like a mantra: '. . . *et Sanctus Spiritus* . . .'

Flustered, Mr Page wiped his brow with the sleeve of his jacket.

'What we don't want is a crowd of people turning up at Huyton. It will do more harm than good.'

Peggy listened as more muttered grievances were aired, and wives and mothers snivelled and sniffed into their handkerchiefs.

'Let us sing a hymn,' said Father Moretti. 'Hymn number 43. For those who they're putting on ships.'

Someone said, 'How the hell will that help us?'

The organ began to play.

'Let your servants be born again from the sea, as you were. Bless him with salt, bless him with stone, bless him with steel . . .' Father Moretti began, under the plaintive sound of the organ reeds.

As Peggy reached the corner of Feather Street, she heard someone come up behind her and a hand appeared under her elbow. It was Frances.

'Peggy – Trevor told me what happened last night. You all right?'

'I've just been to Holy Cross. Oh, Fran, it's terrible. The man from the Corpy said they're sending them to camps. And then on boats. I can't think what I should do. Maybe go to the town hall?'

'Oh, love. Why? For pity's sake, what the Corpy has planned for the Italians has nothing to do with you. Getting tangled up in all this.'

'I should try and find Anthony's mother.'

'No. You'll only make things worse. Promise you'll do as I say?' Frances took Peggy's face between her palms and looked her straight in the eye. 'It has absolutely nothing to do with you.'

'But Anthony . . . I love him, Fran. He was arrested at the dairy because I was the one who took him there. So you see, it has everything to do with me.'

Seeing Peggy's face crease into sadness and her shoulders sag, Frances thought for a moment what she would have done in the same situation. What if it was Trevor who was in danger of being arrested and shipped off to God knows where?

'Anyway, if I don't go to the town hall, I'm going to the camp in Huyton to find him,' Peggy continued. 'They were giving out leaflets outside the church saying where to find it and what bus to get. It's only five miles away, near where Ma took us a few times blackberry picking.'

'How about a nice cup of tea and you can tell me all about it. Fancy it? Life's never dull with our Peg, is it?'

'No, ta. It's not a joke, Fran. I really do love him,' Peggy replied, looking stern and serious.

'I'm sorry, love. But it's true. Trouble follows you like a shadow. If you won't have that cup of tea, go home and sleep. You'll feel better about it all in the morning.'

* * *

There was no answer at Albertini's. It was shuttered up and the curtains closed. Half an hour later, after a bus ride that took her through Knotty Ash and across Queen's Drive in searing heat, Peggy arrived at the camp. It was a huddled-together group of houses in a place called Page Moss at the end of an unfinished road of sand and shale.

Nothing could have prepared her for the grim scene. It couldn't have felt less like the pretty countryside she remembered from when they used to come for summer days out, to picnic amongst the hedgerows and blackberry bushes and fields of waist-high grass. There was a dreadful sense of foreboding about the place.

The housing estate was still a building site. There was nothing much in the way of vegetation or buildings in the surrounding area; no trees or grass verges, just rubble and sandstone, bags of building sand, a cement mixer with solidified cement in it, and jagged lumps of concrete studded with broken bottles. The houses were set in a horseshoe-shaped crescent. But the very first thing that struck Peggy was the barbed wire curled on top of the iron mesh fence surrounding the perimeter. Part of the slum clearance, these sturdy brick boxes, with front gardens and thin strips of back gardens and passages running down the side, had been built in the hope of sunny futures. But that would have to wait. This bloody war.

There were a couple of women who had had the same idea as Peggy. She wandered aimlessly up to the wire fences, just as they were doing. A couple and a little girl, standing looking through the fence, fingers curling around the mesh, seemed unsure of what they should do next.

Beyond the wire fence there was a group of men in uniforms, smoking and playing cards outside a hut. They looked up from their game with mild curiosity, then went back to slamming down the cards on an upturned packing case. One was spitting tobacco as he puffed on a rolled-up cigarette. Peggy heard him laugh, and as she turned away, the sound of a wolf whistle.

'Nice pair of legs, that freckly one, wonder what time they open?' one of the men sniggered. Peggy shot them a look over her shoulder.

'Filthy pigs,' she muttered.

The place had a lost feeling. The sun appeared, and the windows on the buildings flashed. On one side, separated by another barbed-wire fence, there were more soldiers laughing, smoking, bashing a football against a wall; on the other, an empty fore-court. But in one of the buildings there was a face at the window – she saw it move quickly away like a frightened deer.

Two raggedy children approached the fence, poked sticks through. 'Oi, traitors! Show your bleeding faces . . .' one of them said, cupping his hand around his mouth, and the other one laughed. A man came out from the building and shooed them away.

Peggy clutched at her chest. Her stomach somer-saulted and her heart kicked at her ribs. The rumours said there was no furniture in these houses, no lav-atories; the men were sleeping on straw mattresses.

Now that she was seeing them for herself, she had no reason not to believe this. Despite the sunshine, her feet felt cold.

There was a small gaggle of people approaching: a family with suitcases and bags, asking the soldiers if they could deliver them to their relatives. One of them had a set of rosary beads and a Bible. The soldier, shrugging, told them no contraband was allowed. They had a child with them who nervously clutched his mother's skirts.

'This one wants to see his Papa,' the woman said.

'Go home,' said a soldier, coming to the fence. 'There's no point. Your chaps are fine. But you're not going to see anyone. Nothing to see. Diddly squat.'

'Can't you bring them outside?' said Peggy.

'No, love. Orders is orders.'

'Just for a few minutes so we know that they're all right?'

'This isn't a holiday camp,' he said gruffly.

'I'm not moving,' said Peggy.

But then, just as she was about to protest again, a small group of men shuffled out in a line, carrying metal plates. She squinted over towards them. 'Anthony! *Anthony!!* Over here!' she cried, waving frantically.

He peered in her direction, then his eyes widened and he broke from the line and jogged over to the wire fence.

'Anthony. What's happened?' He had a dark smudge over his cheek.

'I'm not sure myself. Me and Roberto and Papa – all arrested. Even old Enrico. He's eighty-two. Even a priest. Made the mistake of renting his parish club to some political types. Mr Ferrari, the barber, and his two sons, Luigi and Paolo. Then Mr Macari, who runs the music shop. They found me at the dairy,' he said sadly.

'I'm sorry. Anthony . . .' She faltered. A tear rolled down her cheek. Behind Anthony, she could see a man approaching with a clipboard. He looked like he was checking names against his bit of paper.

'Hey, Peg. Not your fault. I'm grateful you tried. Someone must have tipped them off. Must have seen us.'

She pushed her fingers through the wire, curled them tighter around the mesh. 'I'm going to get you out of here.'

'Impossible, Peg. My mother came here earlier and left a note for me but they wouldn't let me see her. Da and Roberto are still at Walton police station. The others are here in the camp. My mother is trying to speak to people, I gather, but getting nowhere.'

She thought about kissing him through the wire. God, how she wanted to kiss him again. It made her feel shaky and quivery.

'You! Get back in line!' shouted the man with the clipboard.

Peggy's thoughts twisted to Martin. It was his fault Anthony was here, being shouted at by this oaf. Everything was Martin's stupid fault.

For the next few days Peggy, full of anguish, kept on feeding the pig and cooking pots of stew; but mostly she spent her time scouring the papers for news.

'*Arandora Star*, they say, Dennis. Fellow who works at the docks told me,' Mr Tozer said to Peggy's father when he came into the kitchen to deliver the eggs. 'All hush-hush. Cruise ship. They used to call her the *Wedding Cake*, she's that fancy. That was before they painted her gunmetal grey and took off all her ribbons. Sailing in an hour's time. Taking them all from Huyton to a camp in the Isle of Man.'

Peggy, who was stirring a pan, dropped the spoon into the boiling radish soup and burnt her hand.

The sky was tightly packed with black clouds, and it rained a leaden beat. Urged on by desperation at the unfairness of it all, she raced down to the Pier Head. Every breath she took felt as if there were knives in her throat.

The boat was just as Mr Tozer had described it. Barbed wire curled over the decks. It was a huge ship, but drab and lifeless now, with fencing used to separate the decks and wire entanglements covering every possible escape route. A cannon was mounted on the stern to counter aircraft fire. It was all a far cry from the ship's previous life of card tables, mirrored ballrooms, dancing girls and orchestras.

The men, waiting in a small line on the quayside, were a pitiful sight. Some had bags and suitcases. There were other pale-faced women like her, a few Germans as well as the Italians, standing straining against a chain that looped between posts. One woman was urging a man in a naval uniform with a rope to take something and give it to her husband, pushing it into his hand. A few of those that were already on board were leaning over the rail. Some were even smiling and waving. Peggy felt her eyes smarting. A soldier moved forward, shouting something, and they all moved back behind the coiling barbed wire. Everyone on the quayside looked worried.

The soldier with the stick shrugged. 'Can't trust foreign folks these days. Never know who's in the fifth column. It's for their own good,' he said.

'My husband is Jewish. He survived the Germans in the last war and came here to be safe, and now this,' hissed a woman to Peggy. 'None of it makes any sense.'

'Canada is very lush. Very green. The fresh air will do them good after Huyton. They have lakes and fishing . . .' said a wan-looking man.

'Shut up,' said the woman. 'Canada?'

'Look at the size of the ship. That's not just going for a short trip across the Channel.'

'My heart has broken into a million pieces. I hate Churchill,' she said, bitterly.

'Be quiet. They hear you saying that and they'll be sending you off as well.'

The last few men went up the gangplank. There was clanking as it drew up, and the sound of the ship's engines beginning to grind. The anchor being winched up made a terrible squealing noise, and a mournful belch from the funnels signalled she was leaving.

Some of the waiting relatives clutched at one another. A few waved handkerchiefs. And then the ship slipped out of the dock and into the mouth of the Mersey, moving further away until it became a silhouette against the night sky lit by the pale moon, and then a blur on the horizon . . . and then it really was gone.

People started to drift off. A woman threaded rosary beads between her fingers and crossed herself. Another threw a penny into the water. A priest began to sing a hymn and a few voices joined him on the quayside. '*Hail, Queen of Heaven, Ocean Star, guide of the wanderer here below. Save us from peril and from woe. Mother of Christ, Star of the Sea, pray for the wanderer, pray for me . . .*' the voices sang weakly, the sound floating away on the cold night air.

Pray for Anthony, she thought. That was all she could do now.

Twenty-four

1st July

Somewhere in the Irish Sea, 11.30 p.m.

Below deck, the long cabin of the *Arandora Star* was teeming with life in all its desperate forms, with the sour smell of men's pungent feet and the stink of sweat. Anthony was finding it difficult to shake off the sensation of something gripping his ankles and pulling him off his feet every time he tried to take a step. Stomach churning, he staggered towards the low bunk and lay down.

They had been lumped together in alphabetical order, so he found himself tearfully reunited with his father and Roberto when they had been allocated their cabins. He could hear his father snoring in a camp bed pushed up against the opposite wall. Roberto, who was in the bunk above him, had fallen asleep murmuring the rosary: 'Blessed be the Holy God, blessed be the mother . . .' It was comforting in a strange sort of way, but then a fellow called Larry Rabinowitz had shouted that that was enough popery for one night, they were all trying to get a bit of shut-eye.

At least they each had a bed, thought Anthony. There hadn't been enough to go around; some poor chaps were sleeping on tables. He thought about Peggy. What she was doing, what she was wearing, what she was feeling. Taking out a pencil and a notebook – among the few of his possessions that hadn't been confiscated, unlike his watch and his passport – he began to write.

> *Dear Peggy,*
> *This is pretty grim. I'm in a bunk in a cabin with Papa and Roberto and six other fellows. They keep shouting orders to us in German, thinking half of us are the Hun, but no one here speaks German. So far, I've only met two of them. And one was Jewish. We all speak English or Italian. They've taken everything I have. They shouted at me to shave, but they even took my razor. When things get bad, which is all the time, my mind turns to you. Kissing you, the smell of you, the sweetness of your smile. If I had a raindrop for every time I thought about you, they would make ten oceans bigger than the one I'm sailing across right now. When I'm back, I'm going to marry you straight away if you'll let me.*
> *I love you,*
> *Anthony*

He put the notebook away, and finally sleep came upon him. As he drifted off, clutching his belly, the thundering sound of the engines reduced to a low thrum.

The following morning, he woke with cold in his bones. He turned over, tried to drift off again. Tugging the blanket over his shoulders, he pressed his hands over his ears and squeezed his eyes shut. Must, must, get some more sleep. When he stirred again half an hour later, however, it wasn't the noise of the ship that had woken him, it was Roberto shaking him.

'Wake up, Anthony. We need to go upstairs. Now.'

Anthony rubbed his eyes. 'What? I'm not going anywhere,' he said.

'Something's happened,' said Roberto. 'Didn't you hear it? That thump. Could be an iceberg? Where's Papa?'

Anthony sat up, squinted, trying to shrug off sleep and make sense of his surroundings. He swung his legs over the bed. Iceberg? On the way to the Isle of Man? Where were they? Was he dreaming?

'Get up, Anthony. We need to go on deck.'

'What the . . .' he said as he stood up and tried to steady himself. A strange sensation rocked his senses. Was this more seasickness? He reached out a hand to steady himself.

Oh God, surely not. The boat – was the boat . . . tipping? As if in answer to his thought, Roberto's rosary beads slid from one side of the shelf to the other, then clattered off onto the floor.

Only then did Anthony notice that within the cacophony of sounds – the dreadful grinding of engines, the hissing of steam, the foghorns, the horrible whump, whump – there were also muffled voices, shouting and screaming. He looked down in horror as he realized icy cold water was swilling around the floor, dribbling in under the door, rising up past the soles of his shoes.

'We've been hit, Anthony. We've been hit!' cried his terrified father, rushing in, breathless. He stood there in his stockinged feet. 'I've just been up on deck. Need to get out of here! Need to get out! Now!'

'*Presto, presto* . . .' said Roberto, panic-stricken. Their father was trying to find his suitcase under the bed. 'Leave your suitcase, Papa! Leave it!'

They went into the corridor, feeling their way as it was so dark they could hardly see, and clambered up the narrow stairs to the next deck. There was no time to speak, just to follow the guards' barked instructions to head for the lifeboats. Anthony's feet slipped under him as he walked along. The water swirled about. He felt as if they were already as helpless as the dead.

'Stay with me,' he cried. 'Papa, hold my hand!'

They passed through the ballroom. There were huge shards of glass underfoot – the shattered ornamental mirrors that had fallen out of their frames. As they went through another maze of corridors, ruptured pipes spewed out noxious fumes. Panicked, muffled cries were everywhere, louder now, and an alarm was urgently wailing somewhere. There was a soldier leading men along a corridor. Another with a bayonet fixed to his rifle, still on guard at the door and refusing to allow anyone onto the upper decks, looked shocked and confused as men pushed past him. And to add to their bewilderment, they found their escape route outside barred by the barbed wire that the guards had secured in place to keep them below deck. Tugging and pulling at it with their bare hands, they finally made a way through.

Coming out into the air, blinking against the morning light, they were confronted with a scene from a horror story. One end of the ship was already sloping high into the air, like a small hill of steel rising behind them. All around, clumps of fire floated on the surface of the iron-grey sea. Already there were so many bodies on the deck, there was barely space to move. Some of the men clung onto the rail in terror. This boat was only meant for five hundred, and there were fifteen hundred of them crammed on board. There was a terrible roar and more keeling to one side. A lifeboat was being winched down and people were scrambling to throw themselves on top of those already squashed in.

'Youngest first,' someone cried.

Full of bodies, the lifeboat smashed like a matchbox against the side, then dropped with a splash and swirled wildly around in the sea. The people inside it looked as helpless as washing in a tub.

'Where's Roberto?' cried Anthony, standing behind a coil of barbed wire.

'He let go of my hand,' Enzo said, twisting around to try and find his younger son. Someone barged into them: a soldier, rushing to the front of the queue for the second boat. It happened again. Smashed like a tinderbox, and this time a young man fell over the side and slipped into the sea. Useless.

The third boat jerked and swung back and forth,

hitting and bumping the side of the ship. There was yelling, and then more screaming. One of the lifeboats further along was full of soldiers. This can't be right, thought Anthony. A boy – young, a merchant seaman probably – looked at him with wild desperation. Anthony thought he would never forget those terrified eyes for as long as he lived. But would he live?

'Let me through!' shouted a soldier. The horrible truth was that this situation seemed to be bringing out the very worst in some people. The boy began blubbing like the baby he was, no more than thirteen. Anthony's face contorted as he saw him dart forward and scramble into the boat.

A scuffle broke out between two men. Anthony stumbled, felt himself struck in the back with the butt of a rifle. Then another panicked, desperate person flung himself into the black sea, and others, thinking it was a good idea, did the same. A few climbed down the rope ladders and then others over the side of the railings, clinging on for a moment and then sliding down the sides of the ship.

'Anthony!' called Enzo from the lifeboat he had just been pushed into. His voice was lost in the wind as the boat was lowered.

Anthony faltered, twisting in panic in a desperate attempt to search for his brother, but seeing bodies clinging to the side of the ship like ants, he knew it was hopeless. And then he could think of only one thing to do as he looked back at the burning ship, a hill of fire, slipping under the water. He had to jump like all the others. He thought of Peg. The scaldies. Her words. *Don't be scared. Geronimo!*

The shock when he hit the water momentarily revived him. The terror, the cold, the oil on the surface, made him cry out in distress. But once he was clinging on to a piece of wreckage, an upturned table, it became eerily quiet.

A voice called, 'I'm not dead!'

The faces all around him in the morning mist. The look of despair in everyone's eyes. And then he could see nothing; it was as if black ink had been injected into his eyeballs. He could just feel himself falling, could hear sounds, cries of help, muffled, indistinct, but he could make no sense of them. The pain overwhelmed his senses, the dull ache was all-encompassing. Men's hollow cries hung in the freezing morning fog.

'Help will come soon. Help will come soon. Keep swimming. You have to keep swimming . . . keep . . . swimming . . .'

'Dear Lord, let me give my soul to God . . .' a voice said nearby. Another began to sing, feeble and halting: '*Come, Holy Ghost, our souls inspire, and lighten with celestial fire . . . enable with perpetual light, the dullness of our mortal sight . . .*'

But Anthony could only feel death, not light. Dead bodies and debris were all around him. One poor soul's head was flapping open, as if he were made of feather and hollow bone. He heard more distant voices, muffled, but he had no idea what they were saying.

Someone better go and tell his mother, he thought. Someone better get word to her. And Peggy. Poor Peg. He saw her in his mind's eye. A sob rose up from his throat. More fire and oil now. Fire shooting up. Men all around him, thrashing about in the freezing water, their cries lost in the fog.

Was this real? Or was it something that had happened to him years before? Salt caked his lips, the sea air parched his skin and it stretched tight over his skull and face.

And then nothing. A dread calm that came with the grim realization of the inevitability of death. Blackness.

Twenty-five

'What is it?' asked Peg. She knew straight away, from Fran's ashen face as she stood on the doorstep of Feather Street, that something terrible had happened. Her stomach somersaulted.

'Peggy,' Fran said, her face expressionless at first, but then crumpling, giving in to something dreadful, a stricken panic as she mouthed words and said nothing.

'What's happened? We're all in bed.'

'What's going on?' asked Dennis, coming out onto the landing in his pyjamas. 'It's nearly midnight.'

Frances's eyes darted up to him, then back to Peggy.

'Has something happened?' he asked.

Frances gave a fragile nod.

Peggy shifted wordlessly from foot to foot.

'Come in out of the rain, Fran,' Dennis said. 'Is it bad news?'

'It's Anthony . . . I know it,' Peggy said. 'Fran, tell me?' she pleaded in an urgent, tremulous voice.

'How do you spell his name?'

'What?

'The spelling of his name . . .' Fran looked down at a paper that she had tugged out of her pocket.

'Why?'

'It's too early to say anything definite. But Trevor just got word of this. Peg, he said that there was absolutely nothing anyone could do. The torpedo struck the ship on the port side. Came out of nowhere.'

'Ship?' said Peggy, rigid with fear. Too frightened to breathe, even.

'The *Arandora Star*.'

Peggy's legs collapsed beneath her. '*What?*'

'It sank.'

Peggy let out a wail, a sound like nothing Frances had ever heard. 'Oh God. Oh God. This is my fault. This is my fault! If I hadn't brought him to the dairy, Martin wouldn't have found out he was there and this wouldn't have happened! He wouldn't have been on that ship!'

Frances took hold of her. 'Yes, he would. They would have found him soon enough. And anyway, no one's to blame for this. Apart from the Germans . . .'

'No. No . . . Don't you see, it was my idea to bring him to the dairy . . .' Peggy was wild-eyed with despair, clutching at the sides of her head.

'Peg, stop. Stop, Peg,' said Dennis. 'Let's get you a cup of tea.'

Moira appeared at the top of the stairs, rubbing her eyes. 'What is it?'

But when she saw her daughter's face, she knew death was involved. She just knew.

'Open up! Open up!' a voice shouted through the letterbox.

For Sofia Giardano, the pillow she had been sleeping on had felt like a warm embrace. She heard the rat-a-tat, the calling of her name, but it was a distant sound, only half waking her from her deep sleep. Good God, what time is this? What on earth was this about? It was like the night watchman again, the one who used to come around checking to make sure they weren't overcrowding. 'Not now,' she murmured, half asleep, her eyelids still heavy.

But it was the banging on the door with a fist that made her sit bolt upright, the fierce knocking and thumping that got her jumping out of bed, scrambling for her clothes. There it was again, a bang at the door that was waking the whole street now. A brief cursory rap, and then more fist hammering, followed by a woman's voice this time, calling 'Sofia Giardano!'

Sofia quickly put on her dressing gown to open the door; she clutched it around her with one hand. With trembling fingers, she opened the latch. A policeman stood on the doorstep, rain splashing off his shiny mac – the palms of his hands, she noticed, faintly tinged with grey. There was a woman standing there, too. She was wearing a tin hat with the WVS red letters.

'Can we come in? This is not a conversation we want to have on the doorstep,' he said.

'What? Why?'

'Can we have your husband's and sons' names?' asked the policeman.

'Vincenzo, Roberto and Anthony Giardano. What's happened?'

Gloria appeared, bowling down the stairs, bashing

up against the hat stand so that it almost toppled over. The woman at the door inhaled sharply when she saw her more clearly: cold cream on her face, her usually coiffured hair sticking out in tufts, demonic, wild, staring, frightened eyes.

Peggy sat, waiting for the sun to rise. She had slept fitfully in a chair. She was in a kind of daze. She had said so many novenas through the night that exhaustion had overwhelmed her, but still she hadn't been able to sleep.

Poking her head out of the window, she looked down the street at the newsstand on the corner, where a boy was waving a paper.

Her father came in. Peggy was twisting the wireless knobs back and forth.

'Nothing,' she said dully. 'Why aren't they reporting it?'

'Probably because it's classified,' said Peter. 'How did Franny know?'

'Her Trevor. He works for the government. It happened yesterday morning. He only got word late last evening.'

Exhausted, she dragged on her clothes and headed out to the newsstand. Handing over twopence for an *Echo*, she pored over its pages. But there was nothing. She set off to Albertini's. On her way she saw Mr Tozer outside the barber's, looking serious.

'Not now. I can't think about the pig now, Peg.'

Peggy felt a rush of blood to her head. 'I'm not here about the pig. I'm on my way to Albertini's. I wondered if you'd heard anything?'

'Oh,' he replied. 'Then you'll mean the *Arandora*. Still fishing bodies out of the water over there in Ireland. Now go home, Peggy. Don't bother Luigi Albertini. That's all I know.'

She banged on Frances's door until her friend opened it tiredly.

'Peg,' said Frances.

She wanted to tell Peggy she wasn't to start blaming herself; wanted to remind her that Anthony was Italian, and Italy had declared war on this country. It was unfortunate, but just the way things were. The Giardano family was a member of the Fascio Club, and even if they only went there to play bingo with their cousins, that meant something. She wanted to say that everyone was desperate for news but there wasn't much to speak of, except for patchy details and unverified deaths. The boat was full of Tonys, Trevor had said. All the chefs in Liverpool were called Tony, so it was causing no end of problems.

But she knew Peggy wouldn't want to hear any of that, and it would be cruel.

Peggy could feel herself shaking. She raked her hands through her tangled hair, pulled her threadbare coat around her tiny shoulders. Frances placed a calming hand on her shoulder. 'They received news of it being hit by a U-boat at about 6.15 in the morning. The Giardanos are all missing. That's what Trevor said.'

Peggy jerked away from her friend. She felt as if she needed more air and took great gulps, her hand

flying to her mouth. A picture came into her head
of the ship, one end in the air, the other sliding under
the water, and Anthony standing on the deck, calling
her name as it sank to the bottom of the sea.

When she got back, she heard voices in the kitchen.
Martin.

What's he doing here! she thought. She had told
him to stay away. She had said she didn't want to
see him ever again. But now here he was, sitting at
the table. And her mother was putting a plate of
sprouts and Spam in front of him!

'Heard about the ship,' he said. Peggy froze, then
turned her back to him and said nothing. 'Another
tragedy.'

'Another?' said Moira.

'Well, if it hadn't been the war getting in the way,
we would be married by now,' said Martin. 'That's
a bloody tragedy,' he added, grinning.

'You two set the big day yet?' said Dennis.

'Don't be ridiculous,' spat Peggy, spinning round
to face him. 'Who's talking about marriage? No one's
getting married, Da.'

'You hear that, Mrs O'Shea? Your daughter would
most likely rather have us living over the brush than
getting married.'

'No daughter of mine is living in sin,' she replied.
'Perhaps a wedding is what we all need, Peg.'

'Love a wedding,' said her father. 'Eh, Moira, don't
we O'Sheas love a wedding?'

Peggy looked horrified. 'Are you mad? How can
you even talk about weddings! After what's happened!'

She stormed out of the kitchen, fury raging through her darkening thoughts. 'I never want to see his revolting face again!'

Twenty-six

A month later

Peggy made her way down to the dairy. Taking the bucket, she poured the mush of mouldy cabbage leaves, apple cores and potato peelings into the trough. Dora was getting fatter. She guzzled them greedily, then when she had finished, pushed at Peg with her nose, flopped down and rolled onto her side. Peggy knelt and patted her on her belly.

She was still overwhelmed by sadness. Weeks had passed and still this grief gobbled up her ability to speak, or walk, or stand, or see, never mind collect the slops. She wondered why there was still no news in the papers. The only things she had heard about the sinking were terrible bits of gossip in the Throstle's Nest and on the street when she had been collecting the slops. She had refused to believe it. It was too horrible. Mr Tozer said the Italians had behaved disgracefully. How could anyone say such unkind things? Were they saying that the Italians were to blame for not saving themselves? Did they think that they had a penchant for mass suicide? Ridiculous. A story had already taken hold that there had been fights on board, lots of punches thrown, a scramble to get to the lifeboats, the barbed wire blocking the way; that the Italians didn't stand a chance because they were below decks. So bloody unfair.

The pigsty was barely big enough to hold a pig now, and Dora was huge. Peggy marvelled at how her little legs could hold her up as she waddled around the sty, snuffling and wheezing.

She pulled down the pail from a high shelf, put the slops under the pig's nose. Dora pushed her head into it greedily and made grunting noises, occasionally looking up at Peg from under long, pale eyelashes as she nosed the pail across the floor.

Her mother had been right. How she could think of killing Dora? Let alone see her roasted on a spit. It made her sick every time one of her customers said cheerily, *How's the pig? Won't be long now, Peg, until our feast.* It also made her sick to think of them slavering over Dora turned into slices of bacon and pork chops and sausages. But her neighbours were already planning a party. And now that France had fallen and Hitler had set his sights firmly on Britain, it was becoming a matter of urgency. What had begun as a hobby, now that people were going hungry, began to turn into something more serious.

If the bombing was about to start, and people were about to die, she didn't want Dora to die as well – even though she had no idea what she would do when the man from the slaughterhouse, with his black umbrella and bloodstained apron with the knife in his belt, came sniffing about any day now.

Peg put the bale of straw into the sty. There was still no news apart from Trevor's blessed list, and now Sofia and Gloria Giardano had just disappeared into thin air. Even Mr Albertini seemed to have left. At first Peg had found it hard to believe that Anthony wouldn't just come walking around the corner, give her a warm embrace and ask her if she wanted to go and buy some pear drops from Hegarty's. But as the days passed, that had changed.

Hurrying along the road, she reached Frances's house in Pansy Street and threw a stone up at her window. Frances pushed up the sash, poked her head out, and threw down her keys. Peggy let herself in and went up the stairs to her flat.

'How are you, Fran? Any news from Trevor?' She took off her coat.

Fran carried on scribbling in her notebook as if she was writing things down that made sense in order to remember them, because nothing else did in this world right now. Poetry. Maybe a story.

'Fran? Any news?'

Frances laid down her pen, shut the book, chewed her lip. 'No. Except I've got a job. In Southport. Helping out at a school. Sister Veronica organized it,' she said.

'Oh no. When?'

'Soon. It's a nursery. Looks after children whose fathers are at war.' Peggy looked crestfallen, and Frances went on apologetically, 'This running back and forth to the shelter isn't doing me any good; I can't hear myself think, let alone concentrate on my studies. And it stinks down in the shelter – I hate it. My aunt lives in a flat in Southport usually, but she's living with a few other Wrens at a base in Morecambe now, so she said I can use it. It's on the promenade. Mam is going to Suffolk to help look after my cousins.'

Peggy sank down into a chair as she took all this in. It was good news for her friend, but it still came as a shock.

'And you, Peg? The shells are raining down in Liverpool now. Thirteen were killed last week. A friend of Mam's was in their shelter, you'd think safe and sound, but a water pipe burst and they were flooded and drowned in their own cellar.'

'I can't go anywhere. I've got our youngest to look after.'

'Won't your mam send the kiddies back to Wales?'

'No. Not after last time. Anyway, it's not just the kiddies. There's Dora, and – and . . . what if . . . Well, I'm still hoping . . .' Her throat ached when she spoke.

'And what? Anthony Giardano? Peg. The list that Trevor—'

'Until it's confirmed. The Corporation, the Welfare Officers. I've been to them all. Folks in Little Italy now, they just shut the door in my face. Mr Albertini said I have to be strong, but now he's gone as well. Father Moretti has organized a blessing for the parish as folks are desperate, especially as there's no funerals to speak of – well, if you don't have a body to bury. There's going to be a parade. I could go to that, I suppose.'

'Oh, Peg. Really? Will it do any good?'

'I love him, Fran.'

'Peg – you hardly knew him.' Fran rested a hand gently on hers.

'What? You think I can't love? Just you can, with your books and fancy words?' Peggy said fiercely. She clenched her fingers, her knuckles whitening.

'No, of course not. But he's . . . well . . . dead, most likely.'

'Until you or anyone else can tell me that for a fact, I'll not think it.'

'But you're making yourself ill with it. Look at you. You're thin as a rake.'

Peggy smoothed down her dress.

'Yes. I am ill. I feel so sick all the time. I can't remember when I last had my Auntie Mary. Isn't that what happens when you love someone and you lose them?'

Frances frowned.

'Wait. You and Anthony, you didn't . . . ?'

'No. We didn't go that far.'

'And Martin?'

'No,' Peggy lied, knowing Frances would be shocked if she told her what Martin had done. Besides, he had used a rubber – hadn't he?

'Well, I suppose they do say if you have something bad happen in your life, it can make you physically ill. Like, you might lose weight and your hair might fall out. Or it can play havoc with your monthlies.'

'Can it?'

'Aye. Stop them altogether.'

Peggy nodded, gripped her hand. 'Oh, Franny, you can't believe how awful it's been. It must be that, then.'

'But you should let the Italians get on with finding out about their loved ones. You get yourself better. Get fattened up, like Dora.'

'What, to get roasted on the spit by Martin?' Peggy said darkly.

'Don't be daft. Anyway, we've enough to worry about with the bombings. And on the subject of your red sails in the sunset, I shouldn't worry. They'll come back. You'll be flying the crimson flag soon. Look at you – you're still thin as a beanpole. Skinnier than a toothpick.'

Peggy looked down at herself, smoothed her dress again. 'Well, then, it'll be the shock. True, I look like Mrs Shufflebottom's whippet and my legs are like saplings.'

'Couldn't have put it better myself, Peg,' Frances replied, scribbling down Peggy's words in her little book. 'I'll write that in a novel one day.'

Peggy nodded and kissed her on the cheek.

Not surprising, then, that all this sadness was making her ill. Actually physically ill, to the extent that she would wake up in the morning and be actually sick.

Yes, that was it; Fran must be right. It was the shock of it, of course. The shock was the problem.

Twenty-seven

It was a hot August day. The parade was to come down Scottie Road first and make its way to Holy Cross. Someone suggested they should carry the Virgin Mary statue, Star of the Sea, but someone else said that would confuse things; people would think it was the May procession in summer.

Peggy knew she shouldn't go, but she wanted to see it for herself. She would wear a black mantilla over her face and hope no one recognized her.

She took her place on the pavement outside the Rotunda with a small group of others who had come to watch. As the procession approached, it was the sound of the singing they heard first. Altar boys in lace chasubles, swinging incense and holding a brass crucifix and candles, walked in front of Father O'Mahoney and Father Moretti, who was trying to look as gentle and mysterious as he could, murmuring prayers and singing mournful hymns. Tremulous voices singing 'Ave Maria' filled the air.

At first, everything was orderly and reverent; but as the band of people following swelled, the outpouring of grief turned to rumblings and mutterings of discontent, which edged closer to anger, which led to rage – which in turn led to worried police arriving on horses and telling them all to turn back.

'You were told not to draw attention to yourselves. Bad for morale,' said the policeman, gesturing at the mourners and shooing them off the street. Careless talk costs lives, he said, never mind careless parades with ribbons and violins and girls in white dresses carrying lilies. And the parade was shunted off towards the church.

A memorial service had been planned, and Peggy slipped into Holy Cross church behind the gaggle of people. There was Sister Veronica, gliding about the altar lighting candles and fussing with flowers. Peggy felt her palms sweating as she listened to people around her in the pews talking in low voices. 'It's a terrible thing. There were a hundred bodies floating in the sea. Bloated and disfigured, washed up from Ireland to Scotland, and everyone is fighting over whose body belongs to who. Everyone wants a funeral. Turns out you don't need a whole body. You can have a funeral with a coffin even if you just have someone's finger, so I've heard there are some who've gone over to Ireland to try and claim the bodies that have washed up, fighting over a bit of leg, or parts of an arm, a toe even, insisting it's their Giuseppe or Luigi, just so they can have a burial and a decent send-off. I could never tell Paolo and Mr Giovanni apart when they were alive, so you can imagine the problem. I'm keeping a candle lit, damn this bloody blackout, waiting for my Joe to come home.'

'Government wants to pretend it didn't happen.

Numbers are hard to come by. So many lies. The *Telegraph* said they were afraid of jumping into the water. Knew my Giuseppe should have learned to swim but he always said the water was too cold. Should have taken him to the scaldies. Our Italian lads were just normal folks with jobs who made the mistake of joining the Fascio Club or a trade union.'

Anthony *would* have fought. He would have done. And Anthony could swim. She knew that too. She had taken him to the scaldies herself.

The woman behind her was now whispering to the man next to her. 'They found a foot. Just a foot. Luigi had webbed toes and the foot had webbed toes! But it was only the right foot, and this was a left foot, and maybe there was more than one fella with webbed toes in Liverpool.'

'Terrible. Terrible. Just terrible.'

A few days later, Peggy steeled herself to knock on the Giardanos' door again. Just one more time. Frances had told her it was a terrible idea, Trevor should never have given Peggy their address, did she want to get him into trouble?

'Please,' begged Peggy. 'I'm sorry – I just heard that there had been a meeting in London. And they read names out from a list. Was Anthony on it?'

'So what if he was?' said the old lady who had answered the door in Hunter Street. Peggy still didn't know who she was. 'What do you have to do with Anthony? Nothing. Now go away.'

Peggy smarted.

'He wouldn't have had anything to do with an

O'Shea, even if he was alive,' the old lady added with a sour expression as she shut the door.

'You've got a nerve coming here,' said a man in a string vest who had just stuck his head out of the window.

'I just wanted to ask if you wanted to join my pig club,' she stammered.

The words sounded hollow. They didn't deserve a response.

'He would still be here if it wasn't for you. Just like an O'Shea. You keep away from us, you hear?'

Frances sat with Trevor in the front room of her flat. She spread the piece of paper he had just handed her over her knee and read it out loud.

'*The* Arandora Star *sank stern first just after 06.40. As she went down, Captain Lee could no longer stand on deck owing to the angle she had taken. He jumped overboard and swam away from the ship to avoid the suction. The ship went up at one end and slid rapidly down, taking the men with her* . . . oh God, Trevor. I can't tell Peg any of this.'

'I know you can't. I've told you enough. I could lose my job over this.'

She read on. '*After being categorized as Class A – high risk – they were selected for deportation. Trade union members, refugees, socialists. Four hundred and seventy Italian men died* . . . Oh, Trevor . . . *However, deportation has continued. Two thousand seven hundred internees departed for Australia on the tenth of July aboard the* Dunera, *some of whom had been on the* Arandora Star.' She paused and looked up in shock. 'That was only eight days after! No, I can't possibly show Peg that.'

'Three more bodies were found on the beach last week,' he said quietly. 'Bodies have been buried in the local churchyard in Ireland, but no one knows who they are.'

'Stop. I don't want to hear it. What if one of those bodies was Peg's Anthony?' Frances handed the paper back to Trevor, her hand shaking. 'Hearing all that will finish her off, that's for sure. It's finished me off and all.'

When Peggy woke the next day, she felt the strange sickness again. She turned her head away from the light and winced. She heard her mother's voice, shouting up the stairs.

'Peg! Peg! I need you.'

Wearily she came downstairs. Her mother was stoking the fire. 'Help me do the grate.' Peggy scowled. 'What's the matter with you? Have you got your Auntie Mary or something?' Moira asked her.

'Wait,' said Peggy.

She rushed out of the room across the yard to the privy. The retching was not enough to hold back the vomit. It was as if her body had taken leave of its senses and just wanted to empty itself. Perhaps she was ill. Perhaps she had the same fever Phil had had the previous week.

'Don't speak to me. I feel sick. I'll be better in a little while,' she said, wiping spittle from the side of her mouth with the sleeve of her blouse.

Moira frowned as she moved around the parlour,

picking things up and putting them away in cupboards. 'Weren't you sick yesterday?'

Peggy shrugged. 'I'm always feeling sick.'

'Come here,' said her mother darkly. She took Peggy's chin roughly with her fingers and thumb, turning her face to the light. 'Stand up straight. I want to take a proper look at you. That's the third time you've been sick this week, isn't it? Unbutton that top. You look fatter to me lately. How you can be putting on weight like this when we're all starving to death, I don't know.'

Peggy's eyebrows knitted together. 'What do you mean? I'm thin.'

'Good grief,' Moira said, her eyes widening as she pulled Peggy's blouse open. 'Look at your bosoms. Your arms and legs may be thin, your face hollowed out . . .' She stood back. 'But your breasts! And you've got a huge belly!'

Peggy cast her eyes down. She frowned. Her breasts were pillows of flesh.

'Let's just say I'm an expert on this. Are you sure you're not pregnant?'

'What?'

'Pregnant. You heard me.'

'No.'

'I think you are. When did you last have the curse? Have you missed any of your monthlies?'

Peggy frowned and bit her top lip. Thinking about this made her brain hurt. 'It's been a while. But Franny said it's because of the shock.'

'What shock?' her mother asked.

'The shock of Anthony and the ship.'

Her mother slammed her hand on the table. 'How many more times do I have to say, I will not have that boy's name mentioned in our house! Anyway, I don't know what you're talking about. What do you mean?'

'Frances said if you have a terrible shock or sadness, your monthlies stop.'

'Oh, Peg,' said her mother, sinking down into a chair. 'Do we not live every day in this house with trauma and shocks and sadness? It's all around us. But it's never going to stop a baby coming. There's no shock big enough to do that, sadly.'

Peggy's lips trembled. 'Oh, Mam.'

'How could you not know?'

'Because Franny said . . .'

'Franny this, Franny that!'

'Franny's going to be a teacher. She's cleverer than me. She's cleverer than any of us.'

Moira walked over and pulled the door shut. 'So she knows more than me, does she?' she hissed. 'The fact that I have eight children doesn't mean that I might know more than Little Miss Schoolteacher? Or am I just stupid? You can tell precious Franny that all the learning and books in this world can't stop a man from taking what he thinks is his God-given right. So whose is this baby?' She faltered, and her hand flew to her mouth. 'Oh, God. It's not Anthony Giardano? Oh good God! Don't tell me this baby is his. Is this why you keep going on about him?'

'No, of course not.'

'Then is it Martin's?'

'No one's.'

'So, either my eyes are playing tricks on me and that's not a baby in your belly, or you're the Virgin Mary. Which is it?'

'I don't know. I don't care,' Peggy wailed. 'I didn't want to do it.'

'So you're saying this nobody, whoever it was, forced you to do it? Have you not heard the word "no"? You stupid, stupid, girl.' Moira shook her head.

'Stupid like you, you mean? Stupid eight times over?'

'Less of your cheek, madam,' Moira said furiously. 'Are you saying those horrible things to hurt me?'

'I can't be pregnant, Ma. It was Martin. But he used a johnny.'

'Oh, Peg. Did he? Or did he just say he did? Besides, if you don't know what you're doing, French letters are as useless as chocolate teapots. Well, that settles it, you'll just have to marry him.'

'No. I'm not going to do that. I can't have this baby and I can't marry Martin.'

'Oh, don't talk daft. How many times do you think I've said that? *I can't have this baby.* It doesn't matter what you say. The baby will still come along. Martin will marry you, thank God, we know that. You'll come round to it.'

'No, I won't.'

'Peggy. Every time I find out I'm pregnant, I think the same: not another baby, ruining my life. And then the baby comes along, and it's never so bad. You change. You don't wish your child away once you see

256

it with its little ten toes, and pink feet, and little soft head. D'you think when Kitty was born and she was so sick, I hoped she had died?' Peggy thought of Kitty coughing her guts up. 'Do you think I was relieved when little Alice did actually die and . . .' Her words tailed off.

'Who's little Alice?'

'Never mind; it was before you were born. But no one wants to hold a dead baby in their arms. It's the saddest thing in all the world. Where was I? We were talking about you, not me. I shouldn't be having this conversation with you.'

'So you're telling me I should marry Martin?'

'Of course. Why on earth not? Who will want you with a baby if you don't?'

A head poked around the door. It was Sheila, round-eyed with excitement. 'Marry Martin, Peg? Have you changed your mind? Are you getting married?'

'Can I be bridesmaid?' said Philomena, joining her at the door, standing on tiptoes, eyes shining.

'Get out,' said her mother. 'Get out!'

'Ah, ey, Mam,' moaned the two girls in unison.

Moira rubbed her temples. 'Well, it's a blessed relief it's Martin's, the way you've been going on about this Anthony, seeing as he's dead. All this moping about the place. You'll have to stop all that. Now, you'll have to have a quiet wedding, Peggy. I can get a dress from the charity, maybe. Sister Veronica might help. And what a time for it! Bombs dropping all around the place, but we'll make the best of it. No one will ask many questions. We'll do it quickly. I'll go and see Father O'Mahoney. How many monthlies have you missed? Three, four?'

'You're not listening, Mam. I'm not marrying Martin.'

'What?'

'After what he did to Anthony.'

'What on earth are you talking about? He didn't do anything to him.'

'Yes, he did.'

'Peggy, have you gone loose in your head?'

'It's not fair. Anthony has died. None of you care.'

'Give over, Peg,' Moira snapped. 'Now, I'll give you a chance to deal with this. But you know what you have to do. Go and see him, and tell him. You'll do that tonight?'

Peggy let the question hang in the air. Her brain felt like it was going to explode. Making a vague gesture in response, she moved past her mother and swept out of the door.

'Peg! *Peg!*' Moira shouted out of the window.

'Got to feed Dora,' Peg called back.

'What's all this the girls are telling me about our Peg getting married?' said a beaming Dennis, coming in from the yard. 'Have they finally set a date?'

Sheila followed him in. 'Can I be bridesmaid? Can I get a new dress? Like that one in the window in George Henry Lees? With frills around the neck and the sticky-out skirt?'

'Get out, you silly girl,' said Moira.

Twenty-eight

Peggy went straight to the dairy.

'Hello, Dora,' she said. Dora wobbled over to stuff her snout into the pig bucket, then flopped onto her side. She was fat now. Fatter than any pig any O'Shea remembered. And it was as if she and Peggy were growing fatter together.

It was the one thing that had kept her going: collecting the slops, feeding Dora up, exchanging news of her progress with her pig club members. The change in the pig, gargantuan now, was remarkable.

Am I going to end up like that? Peggy wondered glumly, as she sloshed water over Dora's back. She could still just about hide her bump with the right clothes – her older brother's baggy dungarees and oversized shirts – but one day soon, she would be wobbling on her legs too.

Ten minutes later, she led the man from the abattoir into the yard. She had been dreading him coming. He stood leaning over the pen, chewing on a matchstick, wiping his hands on his bloodstained overalls.

'Jolly good. Jolly good, you've done a grand job,' he said. He leaned in and slapped Dora. 'What's wrong, love?' he asked, when Peggy didn't respond.

'I'm not sure if she's ready.'

'She's ready, all right. Do you have the pig club list? The forms for the Food Ministry? She looks more than ready to me.'

'I'd like to keep her a bit longer.'

He turned down the corners of his mouth. 'Really? Folks won't be happy with that. Bit of meat will be what they're looking forward to.'

'I know, but . . .'

'But what? There's no way back from this, love. Even if you could return the money. And all the effort you've put in? I've seen you walking the streets, seen you and the lads asking for leftovers. And now you're going to go to everyone and say they're going to have to wait for their precious sausages and bacon?'

Please go away, she screamed inside.

'You can't go getting attached. Never ends well.'

'I know,' she said, and her hand subconsciously drifted downwards to her belly. It was true not only with animals, but with humans as well.

But what should she have done? Built up a hard exterior shell? She had tried that. She feared that all this was making her angry and bitter in a way eighteen-year-olds should never be. She clenched her fists, digging her nails into her palms so hard that it hurt, as if it might draw blood.

'Give me another few days,' she said.

That evening, Peggy stood at the range. There had been more awful news on the radio. Despite Churchill's fancy words about blood, toil, tears and sweat, there had been a dreadful blitzkrieg in Rotterdam.

Suddenly there was the sound of the front door

being flung open so hard that it hit the wall with a
bang, followed by Martin rushing in.

'Preggers!' he cried.

Peggy was ashen. 'Who told you?'

'Your Pete. Pregnant, Peg? Is it true?'

'Mebbe.'

He beamed and picked her up and whirled her
about the dairy.

'This is grand. I'm going to be a dad. You've made
me very happy, Peg.'

'What?'

'I'm pleased as bloody punch! We can marry quick.
Eh, Peg, what'll we call him?'

'Stupid.'

'That's not a very nice name,' he said and grinned.

'*You're* being stupid! I'm not marrying you!' she
said, squirming out from his embrace.

'Why not?!' He leaned into her. 'Eh, Peg, who'd
have thought that night on me ma's sofa would have
led to such happiness as this?'

She opened her mouth to give a response, but
nothing came out. She turned away.

'Eh, Peg, is it in there? Can I feel it? Bet it's a boy.
Bet he has my red hair,' he said, coming towards her
again, snaking an arm around her waist.

'There you go again. We've finished, Mart!'

'Not now we haven't,' he said. 'Bet he's got my
red hair and your temper.'

She choked on the words she was about to say. Her
eyebrows knitted together fiercely. 'As a matter of fact,
why are you so keen it's a boy? Because it'll scrap and
fight and play rough and hard, just like you?'

'Because I don't bloody understand women, Peg. And that's the truth of it. Now, I'm off. Sort yourself out, work off this silly strop, and then we can start organizing the wedding. Whatever you say, I'll not be downhearted. I'm going to be a dad. And I'm happy about that.'

He lurched forward, kissed her on the cheek. 'And don't you look grand with them big boobies. Sexy,' he said, and clapped his hands on each one of her breasts and squeezed them. Horrified, she pushed him away forcefully, shoving him in the chest.

'Gerroff me,' she said, scowling up at him. 'You're a brute, Martin. Leave me alone!'

He winked. 'Love my firecracker. Come to my house soon, Peg, and we'll tell me mam. Whilst I go and pick me wedding suit and get that ring out of its box again.'

The plate came hurtling towards him first. He ducked to avoid it. As she picked up a second from the dresser, he circled the table and came up behind her, then lurched forward and put his arms around her waist and lifted her right off the ground. Yelping and huffing, she writhed and wriggled in his arms like a wet fish. It made him laugh so hard that when Jimmy came rushing in to see what the racket was about, he thought it was some sort of game they were playing.

'I hate you, Martin Gallagher,' Peggy snarled through her teeth. 'Get your filthy hands off me!'

'You need taming.'

He let go of her but she snorted and ran at him, head down, kicking out at him.

'Jeepers,' he said, clutching his shin. 'You're a little devil, you are.' He was still laughing as he wrestled with her and lifted her off the ground again. 'But you want to watch it. Always winding me up like this. There's only so many hot stoves you can touch before you're locked out of the kitchen!' Then he laughed, and dropped her.

Peggy landed in a crumpled heap on the floor, seething. This time she seemed unable to fight back, but it was only the silent brooding rage welling up inside her that was stopping her.

Martin left, and what was worse, he left smiling. People came and went, seemed to move noiselessly around her. Philomena with a tray of shortbread cakes, Sheila with a torn underskirt that needed stitching. Jimmy to do the grate. Another conversation was had with her mother where Peggy insisted that she couldn't bear to even look at Martin, let alone consider marrying him. Didn't she see what he had just done to her? Aye, and you gave as good back, Moira retorted. And then an hour later, Moira came back in, looking more serious and worried than Peggy had ever seen her.

'Sit down, Peg. Me and your father have decided. You should go to the flat at the dairy to consider all this, the marriage proposal, and hopefully that hot head of yours will cool down. Don't come home until it has.'

'The dairy! That damp, awful place! There's rats upstairs!'

'There's rats here an' all, in the yard. It's your da's

idea. Thinks that it will concentrate your mind. A few days in that hovel will make you realize how stupid you're being, refusing Martin. Knock a bit of sense into you. See what real life is.'

Peggy stood with her fingertips on the window pane, looking out into the street. Moira came over and held out a plate of leftover potato cakes.

Peggy stood, put on her coat.

'What are you doing? Have a cake.'

'No.'

'You're so stubborn!' she said, banging down the plate on the table. 'Maybe your father is right!'

'A bit of peace and quiet will do me good at the dairy.'

'Don't give your mother that cheek,' said Dennis, coming into the room. 'I heard you. Go, then! Git. See how you like life without your ma and pa, your brothers and sisters, in that place with just the pig and the cows and the bloody rats for company!'

'Aye. I will! And I'll go right now!' Peggy spat back.

She snatched up her cardigan, huffing, then marched out of the room and let the door slam behind her.

'I didn't actually mean it, Denny,' said Moira, shocked. 'I didn't actually want her to go and live at the dairy! What did you do that for?'

'That girl needs to be taught a lesson. Don't worry, she'll be back with her tail between her legs before we know it. Mark my words. She'll come round, she always does.'

'But she's probably frightened, she just won't show it. And with the baby . . .'

'Sometimes people have got to learn the hard way.'

Moira dropped her head into her hands. How much harder could life be for Peggy? This war was getting more real every day. They had no money. She was pregnant and out of wedlock. To say nothing of the pain of losing this Anthony.

'She needs to get a grip. Get that Giardano boy out of her system,' said Dennis, as though he could read her thoughts.

'And perhaps you need to as well,' Moira said pithily. 'We ought to feel sorry for that family instead of flying into a rage whenever the Giardano name is mentioned. Terrible things I've heard about what happened on that ship.'

He narrowed his eyes. 'Like I said, love, there's terrible things going on all around us.' He grabbed a newspaper and waved it under her nose. 'Have you not read this? Ten dead in Wallasey. Mayhem in France.'

Moira brushed this aside. 'She's also worried about the pig. It's the only thing she's got and she doesn't want it to go to slaughter. I've noticed people are asking me all the time. When do we get our bacon?'

'Well, that's another thing. Facing up to consequences. She pestered for that pig. Nagged us until she was blue in the face.'

Moira sighed. Part of her knew he was right. 'So what am I to do now? Are you saying we really should let her go to the dairy flat? I shouldn't go and bring her back? It's a pretty unpleasant kind of place now no one is living there.'

'Leave her. She needs to face up to her obligations.

It can start with the pig. She needs to take it to slaughter.'

'What about if she gives everyone the money back?'

He slammed his fist on the table. 'What are you talking about? You're as bad as our Peg! Just give her a few days at the dairy. Trust me, she'll come around. I'll have a word with Martin. Poor lad. And then we'll have a wedding. Wouldn't that be grand? Something to celebrate?'

The room swam before her as her eyes filled with tears. 'What a mess,' she said. 'What a bloody mess.'

'Stop whingeing, woman. You can buy yourself a hat. And we can tell the girls they can be bridesmaids. I'm sure we can cobble together some frocks and new clobber. I can borrow a suit from our Seamus. We'll hire out a room above the Boot. Push the boat out a bit. We can invite all the cousins and I'm sure they'll chip in. Wouldn't it be something to look forward to?'

She looked at him mournfully.

'Let's get a date set, but let's not wait too long; we don't want our Peg waddling up the aisle like her pig. Don't want her showing. Martin is mad about her. She decided her future when she was happy to let him put his hands all over her. We'll have a grand time.' He put an arm round his wife. 'I'll send him round to speak to our Peg in a few days. Don't worry about her, she's just headstrong – needs to calm down. She and Mart are like steel and stone: rub them together and you get fire, that's all. Like you and me, Moy. Fire keeps things hot for a time, but eventually, it dwindles to warmth.'

Twenty-nine

Peggy needed air. Hurrying along, following the railings of the park, she saw a small boy push a paper boat into the water with a twig. The leaves were turning red. She was wearing a dress ruched under her breasts, but she felt people were looking at the swell of her stomach. She met Frances on the corner of the road and told her the whole story in a rush of words all the way back to Frances's house.

'They think I'll go to the dairy and loathe it and change my mind. *What are you going to do, Peg*, they keep saying. What they really mean is, where am I going to go if I won't marry Martin? Only I have no idea what to do. Oh, I'm a useless waste of space,' she said, sinking down into a chair in Frances's front room.

'Slow down, Peg,' said Frances, fetching her a glass of Vimto. 'Don't say those things. You're the bravest person I know. You'll get through this.'

Peggy picked up and idly flicked through the pages of a book she had never heard of that was sitting on the table beside the chair. Frances took it from her. 'You've never been afraid of anything.'

Peggy slumped. 'So what should I do? Sail the baby down the Mersey in a wicker basket like Moses and then go and top myself?'

Frances gave her a faint, pitying smile. Even now Peggy could still find the energy to lighten the mood, she thought.

'I just hate it that Martin and everyone else *assumes* I'll marry him,' Peggy went on. 'Just because I'm up the duff. Like I have no part in it. Perhaps I should say it's not his.'

'You mean, say it's Anthony's?'

She sighed. 'No. I would never do that. Maybe I should say I'm the Virgin Mary.'

'Sister Veronica would love that.'

Flicking through another book lying on the table, Peggy paused. 'I don't understand a word of this. I told you. I'm hopeless,' she said, flinging down the book.

'No. Well, it's Chaucer. I wouldn't expect you to, Peg.'

'I could ask me ma to say it's hers. But she'll just say we don't want another baby around the house. She's always saying she never wants to see another baby in her life.' She tailed off, remembering that the last time Moira had said this she'd immediately picked up baby Kitty and kissed her on the stomach and murmured, *Not you, of course, I wouldn't swap you for the world.*

'What did your da say?'

'Da was furious. I heard him through the walls.' She mimicked his low voice. '*Tell her to wheel her flamin' pram elsewhere, if she won't marry Martin.* They hate me.'

'Your ma and da will come round. It takes a lot of energy to hate someone.'

'Well, they're all making a pretty good job of it,' Peggy replied glumly.

Fran sighed. 'Perhaps you should speak to someone.'

'Like who?'

'I don't know. Father O'Mahoney.'

'Father O'Mahoney! Why?'

'I don't know.'

'I could never do that.'

'Sure you could. You can talk to anyone. I wish I could talk to people like you can. Look how you talked everyone into joining the pig club. Even mean old Mrs Hardstaff handed you over a five-bob note. How did you do that?'

'That's different. Anyway, Mam has said Da's making me live at the dairy because it's the only way to get some sense into me, but you know that place. It's awful. I'd go to the Giardanos – I found out where they live, Gloria Giardano is working with our Phil at the parachute factory – but they hate me. They won't even answer the door to me now.'

Frances was taken aback. 'The Giardanos? You've been hanging around their house? I told you not to go there,' she said.

'I couldn't stop myself. I thought it might help me somehow. Part of me thought it might mean that if I could find out what happened to Anthony, I could have a clearer idea of what to do about the baby. I went to the ice-cream bar, but this time even Mr Albertini told me to leave.'

'Oh Peg. You know what happened to Anthony. Still, at least there's better news on that front, now

269

they've stopped sending the Italians away on ships. Trevor says the government is full of guilt over the sinking of the *Arandora*.'

'That makes it even more painful,' said Peggy. 'It's Anthony I care about.'

'If I were you, I'd stop worrying about Anthony and think about this baby.'

'I knew the police would come after him if Martin told them I was hiding him. If they hadn't put Anthony on the *Arandora*—'

'Peg, they sent them off on that boat for their safety,' Frances said. 'The world's not against Peggy O'Shea. They didn't do it just to be mean.'

Peggy wasn't convinced. 'That's what it feels like.' She felt a twinge, a little shard of pain in her side. 'Ow,' she said, clutching her side.

'See, your baby thinks so as well. Peg . . .' Frances hesitated.

'What?'

'Well, Martin. Even Anthony would want Martin's child to have a father, surely? And Martin does love you. He always has. Would it be so bad?'

'Oh, Fran.'

'You know, I can hardly believe Martin doesn't know about Anthony. Perhaps he loves you so much, he's prepared to turn a blind eye about it. That's pretty rare. I know he's a bit of a dope, but if it means this baby would have a father and you would have a roof over your head . . . couldn't you at least just consider it?'

Thirty

'You're as stubborn as the will of kings,' her mother had said to Peggy, exasperatedly. When repeatedly faced with her father's stark choice of either living at the dairy or marrying Martin, Peggy had insisted on the former. Now, here she was, with a small bag of clothes, a pocketful of pennies and a few ribbons in the room where she had last lain on the bed with Anthony that had felt so sweetly romantic, but now seemed dismal and wretched. It smelled of sour milk. A bottle that someone hadn't washed out was stinking the place out. The surface had fuzzed over with green mould. She poured it out into the cracked sink and it glugged into the basin in lumps.

Black mould spotted the ceiling. There was a box of matches and an oil lamp that she tried to light. The matches were damp, and it took four attempts. Finally, the lamp flickered and noxious fumes filled the room. The bed was hard. There was a thin, moth-eaten blanket. This is no good, she thought.

There were buckets set here and there across the sloping floorboards. The curtains at the windows were no more than rags hanging on a sagging wire. Outside was like a bombsite. The city seemed to have been

271

torn up; every day more bulldozers, more corrugated iron, more smashed-up buildings, more bombing.

She could hear the rain pounding the roof. Looking out of the window, she saw rings appearing on the surface of the puddles. There was the sound of water trickling between the grids in the gutters. The streets were empty and in the distance she could hear sirens.

She looked around her. She felt lonely. Was she mad? The pathetic fire in the grate was doing nothing to warm the room. She really did feel like the Virgin Mary in her stable. What on earth was she doing here? The crack in the window pane brought a sharp draft inside the room that started to make her neck ache. Sitting on the bed, she pulled her skirts over her knees and hugged them close to her.

She hadn't believed it at first, that she was having a baby. How can anyone be as stupid as me? she thought. She'd seen her mother year after year, her belly swelling and another baby coming bawling into the world, and she had heard the refrain, 'How could it have happened again!' so many times.

She had also seen the chart, crudely drawn with little squiggles and red marks. And she remembered her mother crying out in despair, 'How am I supposed to remember all these little red ticks and crosses!'

And yet here Peggy was, expecting, after just one stupid moment. Martin had said he'd used a rubber, but she hadn't actually seen it. And she wouldn't have known what the difference was, with or without. Annoyed with Martin, herself, her ma and da, annoyed with the nuns, annoyed with everyone and blaming them all, until finally she had no one else to blame, so she blamed God.

She touched her stomach gently. Every day she had steeled herself to look in the mirror, feeling a rising panic as she watched her body change. Alone in this room, she allowed herself to move her hands over her bump, something she had been too frightened to do before now. When she stood sideways, the shadow of her silhouette against the flickering candle-light, the rise of her belly below her belt, told the story that she had been denying for a long time. Yes, her wrists and legs were still like sticks. But her stomach felt huge, and she had noticed the difference in her breasts. She was aware her nipples were growing and changing colour to a dark nut-brown. She was beginning to get strange cravings for bully beef, and she even liked the smell of coal and found herself wondering what it would be like to eat.

Going downstairs, when she heard one of the cows groaning, she went into the backyard. She could see the shapes of Nettie and Glenda moving in the dark. Dora was unsettled, trotting back and forth, bashing into the sides of the sty, her breathing swirling in the air. Peggy crawled into the little den where she and Anthony had once sat. It felt warm. Warmer than upstairs. Her eyes began to acclimatize to the dark-ness. She was used to the smells. She had grown up with them. Somewhere far off, she heard the distant wailing sound getting louder: sirens again. Finding a milking pail, she put it over her head to protect herself if a bomb was to fall on the dairy and hoped she would survive until morning.

Thirty-one

'I'm dandy, Ma,' she said. 'It's going to be all right.'

She didn't like the way her mother was standing in the doorway of the shippen, staring at her as she moved around Nettie and Glenda with a bucket, eyes roving over her body, trying to read the subtle changes.

'How? If you won't even speak to Martin.' Her mother sat on the milking stool, rubbed her temples. 'Peg, you're stubborn. I thought you'd last a night, but two weeks! And last night we had our first proper bomb. I was worried sick about you. Docks have been hit. Brunswick, North Coburg and South Queens Docks. Just missed Caryl Gardens.'

'Oh no. I heard the roaring sound. And saw all those fires. Was anyone hurt?'

'No one we know. But this is just the beginning, Da says. It's dangerous, Peg. And if you're still refusing to marry Martin . . .'

'I won't, Ma.'

'Well, you have to face up to the consequences. I would drag you home by your hair if I could, but your da's still furious with you. He says it has to be your decision. So what are you going to do?'

'Mam,' Peggy moaned, and suddenly rushed

towards her, falling to her knees in the muddy straw, burying her face in her mother's lap.

Moira caressed her hair and shook her head. 'If you hadn't been so busy messing about with that pig – if you had told me sooner – you could've done something about it.'

Peggy lifted her head. 'Done something about it? You don't mean . . . ? Get rid of it? With a knitting needle or gin or something? What about Edie from across the road who died?'

'Edie? Who told you that?'

'Everyone knows. And her ma too ashamed to have anyone to the funeral. I heard the woman who was supposed to sort her out didn't have a clue and stuck a dirty needle up her and it went wrong.'

'We don't know the details. We never will. But no, of course I don't mean that. I don't know why I even said it. Just desperate, I suppose.'

'Oh, Mam,' she said. Her sad eyes brimmed with tears.

'Da has only sent you here to make you understand how serious this is, Peggy. He wants you to come home and say you'll marry Martin.'

Peggy's lip quivered. 'Da won't talk to me. Every day, when he comes here to do the cows or when he helps me in the shop, he won't even look at me.'

'D'you blame him?'

'Ma, couldn't you pretend to everyone it's yours?'

'Don't be daft. We've no room for another baby at Feather Street.' She paused. 'So, have you had any more thoughts?'

'What about? Dora?'

'God help us, Peg! The baby! Martin! A wedding?'
Peggy shrugged.

'Well, then, if you won't speak to Martin, we need a conversation about giving the baby away to the nuns. I don't know what else to say,' Moira snapped, and pushed her away, coldly.

'The nuns! The nuns were awful to me!'

'No, they weren't. They only wanted the best for you. You led them a dance and drove them to distraction, that's all. Like you're doing with me and your da and Martin.'

Peggy stared at her mean surroundings. Everything looked as sad as she felt.

'Please say you'll talk to Martin? He is desperate for you,' said Moira. 'I don't know how much longer your dad and I can hold him back from fetching you from this awful place. Da just keeps promising him you'll come home. Says he's not to poke the hornet's nest.'

Peggy sighed. 'Mam, do you love Da?'

'Of course I do.'

'Why can't I have the same?'

Her mother drew herself up, angrier now. 'Peg, stop going on about love and concentrate on the matter in hand. Your father can hardly look at you. We want you to come to your senses, that's all. No one feels as bad about this as I do. You'll understand that once you have children of your own. Uncle Davey and Seamus said you can stay at the farm to lie low, but Doreen's against it.'

Peggy narrowed her eyes. 'What about the pig?'

'Will you stop worrying about that blessed pig!

Why are you so mad about the pig? It's just a flippin' pig! If Cary Grant popped by, you wouldn't even come in the yard to look at him if you were messing about with that flaming pig!'

'I wish I was dead,' Peggy wailed, and threw herself onto a bale of hay, pummelling it with her fist.

'Don't talk like that. Go and pack your bag. Come home. Please, love. I can't have you sleeping here like one of the animals. I'll take care of your father. He's actually happy for you. He's still planning the wedding as we speak.'

Peg chewed her lip. 'Does Martin even still want this baby?'

'I don't know. I don't know what anyone wants anymore. I hope so. He's not a bad lad. You'll grow to love him again in time.'

'No, I won't.'

'Why not?' Moira said, exasperation all over her face.

'I can't stand the way he uses a handkerchief . . . when he blows his nose, he opens it and examines it. It makes my stomach turn over and I feel sick.'

'Heavens to Betsy. Is that all you can come up with? If I had a penny for everything that your father did that made me feel queasy, spitting, grunting, growling, drinking, belching, I'd be a rich woman. That's just fellas. Try and like him. He'd put a roof over your head and make an honest woman of you. Look at this place.'

'Mart's hardly going to take me off on his white charger to his palace on a cloud. I'll still be having the tin bath and doing the coal hole if I marry him.

He's a docker. I'll still be mucking in with the cows and doing the milk rounds to make ends meet. I wanted to marry someone who played the violin and would take me to the Adelphi for a gin and French . . .'

'What are you on about? Gin and French? Where do you think you're getting these highfalutin' ideas from? Since when have you got fancy hat notions? Is this the Giardano boy putting these thoughts into your head? He was the enemy, Peg. And what difference does it make to anything, knowing he's dead? No difference at all. And yet think of the difference you are making to that child you've got growing in your belly, if you won't marry Martin.'

'It's all so hopeless,' she said in a small voice.

'Get your bag,' said Moira. 'Come home. I can't bear to leave you here like this. You won't have to see Martin. Not yet.'

'Promise?' she asked plaintively.

'I promise.'

And Peggy, too tired to argue and too sad to care, allowed her mother to lead her off in the direction of home.

When she got in, she went straight to the small bedroom. It was a relief to be back amongst the bustle and comings and goings of home – clean sheets, warming her bottom on the kitchen range – but she still tried to keep out of everyone's way. A couple of weeks passed and she carried on, up early to the washhouse, coming home late from the market. Her father, despite stern words from Moira, who had explained she was trying another tack, barely spoke to her, and she was relieved about that as well.

But one evening, when she came downstairs, she found Martin sitting in front of the hearth.

'What are you doing here?' she gasped.

'Are there any rules that say I can't come around and see your ma and da?'

Her mother placed a spoon and a glass of milk in front of Martin, moved away without a word. Peggy flashed her a black look.

'I've not decided anything,' she hissed to Martin.

He leaned into her, gripped her arm and whispered in her ear as Moira went into the scullery and rinsed a bowl. 'I've missed you, wildcat. Look at you. You're enormous. Don't let's put this off any longer.'

Moira bustled back in with a tea towel over her shoulder and a bowl of baked raisin pudding. 'Peg, stop pulling a face. It's not Martin's fault. All he wants to do is marry you,' she said flatly. She turned to Martin. 'I'm sorry, Mart. Don't know what's got into her.'

Peggy snapped her head round and scowled. 'I can speak for meself!'

Moira flashed a nervous smile at Martin. 'What's the matter with you, Peg? Another terrible night with the air raids, Martin. Giving us all the jitters.'

'Overwrought, aren't we, love?' said Martin. 'Some folks would think she should be grateful to have my offer, wouldn't they, Mrs O'Shea?'

How could he be so calm! Anthony would still be here if it wasn't for him, she thought, darkly. Martin Gallagher – the nerve of him, coming into this house!

279

He was just sitting there, stuffing raisin pudding into his mouth, as if everything was the same as it always had been.

'How's the pig?' he asked.

'Dora. She's got a name,' she snorted.

'You don't give a pig a name. Never heard of such a thing.'

'Why not?' she said and turned away. You're not getting any of it, she thought crossly.

'Oh, and we're going to have a big roasting, are we?' Martin raised his eyes and shook his head. 'And you're going to waddle out dishing out sausages and bacon, a fallen woman, for the whole world to see. Let me save you from the shame, Peg.'

'I'm not ashamed.'

Moira flinched. 'Sometimes I want to crack you one, Peg.'

'Sure, you're not ashamed. You're not half showing now. You haven't got much time left before them in the court houses and the streets round here will start gossiping. It'll be all round Greaty and Scottie before you know it.'

Her eyes darted up to him, flashing with fury. 'None of your flaming business,' she said.

'None of my business! Peg, I'm just trying to make you wake up. You might feel sore now, but I love you. I want you to be my wife. I could make you happy. I don't care what others will say. There's not many who would say that, is there, Mrs O'Shea? I'm prepared to put all this Anthony Giardano stuff behind us. No one else is going to save you. How would you survive for money without me? The

Corporation won't help you. They don't care about anyone. Especially with the war, and having to look after people who are really in trouble.'

'He's right, Peg. The Corpy were the ones who made your Auntie Colleen burn her piano for firewood before they gave her a single penny when her Mick broke his legs, don't forget. No one could play "Oh to Be in Doonaree" like Colleen, and the heartless beasts took that away from her.'

Martin's face became serious, his chin thrust out and obdurate. 'If you won't say you'll marry me . . .' His voice sounded bitter; he suddenly seemed twitchy and spiky.

'If I won't . . . what? You'll wallop me?'

'Be quiet, Peg!' said Moira.

'I shan't be quiet! Cover your ears if you don't want to hear me!' She stood, pushed the chair away from underneath her.

Martin shrugged and turned to Moira. 'Don't worry, Mrs O'Shea. I've handled plenty of cows that have gone wild when they've been neglected. I can handle our Peg. Just needs a little bit of loving.'

Peggy just looked at him, her mouth falling open in protest, but not a single word came from her lips.

The fear of what might happen next in this war meant that every night, it seemed, somewhere was having a lock-in and a sing-song and a knees-up to take the edge off. And tonight was the same as every other night.

'Come on, Peggy, you're coming with me. Let's go

and have a drink at the Rialto,' said Fran, who had turned up unexpectedly at the front door.

'I can't,' she said mournfully. 'What if someone sees me?' She opened her cardigan.

'Good grief. I see. You are coming on. Let's go to mine for crumpets instead. Mam's doing her mobile teas with the WVS.'

'That's what I wanted to do,' moaned Peg, mournfully. 'Before this mess.'

Half an hour later, they sat in front of the range with their crumpets toasting in the fire on a fork. 'I'll not have you going back to live in that pigsty,' said Fran after Peggy told her the sad story.

'It wasn't so bad. At least it got me away from Martin. And I had Dora to keep me company.'

'I'd ask me mam if she could take you in. But you know her. If I was here it might be easier to smooth things over, but I'm leaving for Southport this weekend.'

Peggy's eyes flicked to the crucifix on the wall, and then to the one on the mantelpiece; the yellowing palms in the shape of crosses in a jam jar; a little font of holy water screwed into the wooden panelling; the faded framed pictures of the Pope.

'She'd probably have a fit if she knew you were even talking to me, Fran. Imagine if she could see me in this state,' said Peggy.

'Can I feel it?' said Frances.

Peggy unbuttoned her cardigan and pulled up her blouse, revealing the rise of her stomach.

Frances knelt at her feet. 'It's like the moon,' she said, enthralled.

Peggy smiled. 'You have a nice way of saying things. Put your hand there, further up. Sometimes I can feel him moving. Just tiny little fluttering feelings, sometimes actual kicks.'

'What makes you think it's going to be a boy?'

'I can tell.'

'How?'

'I had a dream where I was wearing pink slippers and a pink negligee and eating strawberries. You dream about girly things, means you have a boy.'

'Don't be silly. What are you going to call it?'

'Anthony.'

'You wouldn't dare.'

'Why not?'

'You still feel sad about Anthony?'

'Every day and every second of the day. Sometimes I wish a bomb would fall on me head and do me a favour. Do everyone a favour. Everyone just says life goes on, but the thought of that, life carrying on as normal when all I'm thinking about is Anthony being snatched away from me, and now me carrying Martin's baby – that's the hardest part of it. Can you imagine being married to Martin and how unhappy that would make me? How could I even find room in my sad heart to love the child? Oh, I wish I could be a teacher, like you.'

'Why?'

'Then I could keep my baby and look after him on my own, because I'd have a proper job and I wouldn't be poor. That's the only reason I can think of to marry Martin. Because I'm so poor.'

'What makes you think if you were rich you would

be able to bring up a baby on your own? No one likes a mother without a husband. People would still call your baby illegitimate. Or worse. No respectable job can shield you from that. Anyway, I don't want to be a teacher. I want to be a writer. I want to write stories about you, and your pig, and stupid Martin.'

Peggy managed a half-smile. Frances sat back on her heels.

'Oh, I just felt it moving again! It's lively tonight,' Peggy said, smiling. 'Perhaps if you put your ear on my tummy you'll be able to hear it?'

'You can't hear babies. Good God, Peggy, do you really know nothing?'

'I should've stayed at school, like you said.'

Frances stood up and sat beside her and put a comforting arm around her shoulder.

'How did I get myself into such a mess?'

'Well, we both know the answer to that.'

'I didn't have a clue you could get pregnant the first time. And we only did it once. I thought Mart used a French letter, but ma said that can go wrong. It wasn't nice, Fran.' She lowered her head. 'Martin just pushed himself on me. Said he just got carried away because he loved me so much, but even so.'

'You mean . . . ? You poor lamb.' Frances sighed. 'No one told us anything, did they? Apart from, don't let any filthy man's hands touch you. Sit with the Bible on your lap in case a gust of wind comes along. Don't wear patent leather shoes or your knickers will reflect in them. I used to think if you did it standing up, you couldn't get pregnant. Someone told me that. And when I asked Trevor, he said he thought it was

284

true as well and we should try it. Now I think he was lying just because he wanted to get his bloody leg over. That's what fellas are like, even mild-mannered ones like Trevor. You heard of taking the kettle off before it boils? Or driving a car without petrol? Trev's always saying that's the safest way, but I still won't let him.'

'No. What's that?'

'Before the fella finishes his business, he pulls out of you at the last minute. Thought you'd know the ins and outs of that, what with the cows and your pig.'

'Didn't know about the boiling kettles and petrol, no,' Peggy said glumly.

Frances squeezed her hand. 'So what next?'

'I dunno. Shout and stomp some more and then give in and marry him, I expect. This stomach is growing bigger every day. What else am I to do?' she said sadly. Looming defeat showed in Peggy's face.

Frances kissed her. 'Oh Peg, I'll miss you when I go.'

'I'll miss you too, Franny. More than you'll ever know.'

When she got home, her mother had laid a white tulle dress over the chair.

'Here you are. D'you like it?'

Peggy looked horrified.

'Phil's confirmation dress. I kept it. Good job, too. Unpicked it and got a bit of white satin from Greaty and made the skirt. Try it on. I can take out the waistband. Put a bit of elastic in it.'

Peggy backed away as though she had seen a ghost, with her hand to her mouth.

'You'll look beautiful. And when I put that extra bit of material under the bodice, a few flounces stitched below the bust, you'll hardly be able to notice you're up the duff.'

Peggy shook her head and ran out of the room. The sound of her thudding up the stairs vibrated through the house.

Moira called after her. 'Peg! Come back here! What's the matter now?!'

Thirty-two

After Peggy had been thrust into the parlour by Moira to tearfully tell her father she had changed her mind about marrying Martin – who had turned up on cue with a bunch of wilting dahlias and knelt down with the ring and, grinning, pushed it onto her finger – the wedding had quickly been arranged for three weeks' time. 'No time to waste!' Moira had cried. Arrangements had been made. Peggy had prayed for an air raid warning, something, anything – a bomb landing on the roof of the pub, or the church. Or even better, landing on her and killing her stone dead, which would bring an end to this nightmare.

'Close your eyes,' Moira said, the night before the wedding, leading her by the hand into the parlour.

Peggy had refused to play along with this charade at first, but she couldn't think of an excuse not to. She felt as though she was being led to the gallows. As she opened her eyes, her mother said, 'Ta-dah!'

She stood there looking around at the parlour decorated with white bunting, with crates of beer piled up in the corner, plates for sandwiches, pretty china cups and saucers that had mysteriously appeared from nowhere.

'Isn't it grand? Just what we need to cheer us all up. Mrs Hardstaff made those macaroons. They're Father O'Mahoney's favourite.'

'Oh Mam, you haven't told her! Who else have you told? Why have you gone around blabbing your big mouth off?'

'We all want good news. I haven't told them about the baby. I just said that you were getting married, and they were delighted. They're so grateful for what you're doing with the pig. Who could have known how desperate we would be all these months on for a bit of ham or a pork chop? Everyone loves you, Peggy. Stop making a face. I could bloody crown you. The wind will change and you'll stick that way, and then Martin will change his mind and tell you he doesn't want to marry you after all.'

Peggy awoke to a foggy grey September morning. She got on her knees, rested her elbows on the side of the bed, and tried again.

'Dear Jesus, please get this baby out of me somehow, or let me wake up and find this is all a horrible dream. Or send the Nazis to Liverpool this morning and bomb us all so I don't have to go through with it.'

But it was daylight; they hadn't had raids in the day yet, and she knew the other request was so far-fetched that even the Lord Almighty would just think it was plain stupid.

She hadn't been able to sleep. It might have been the strange sensation she was feeling in her belly. Dragging herself out of bed, the first thing she did was stagger down to the privy, sink to the floor on her knees, and retch.

'That'll be the baby. Or wedding nerves. You'll be right as rain after a spoonful of cod liver oil to settle your tummy,' called her mother, who was pegging out the napkins in the backyard to air. Peggy came out of the privy and looked at Moira leaning over the peg basket. If there had been a garden fork to hand, she would have plunged it into her mother's back. If there had been a spade, she would have hit her over the head with it.

'Sister's here to see you,' called Grammy Nora, who had arrived early.

Peggy looked into the kitchen through the open door, horrified to see Sister Veronica sitting at the table.

'What on earth is she doing here?' she hissed to Sheila, who was holding up her skirts and gingerly walking across the yard in her bare feet, on her way to use the privy.

'Dunno,' replied Sheila.

Peggy went inside, glowering.

'Ah, Peg. I was hoping to see you in your wedding dress, not your nightie. I'm just here to wish you well and to give you this. I've heard all about the pig. People have been getting very twitchy, wanting to know when they're getting their meat, but the hog is finally going to slaughter any day now, I heard.'

So that's what she's after, Peggy thought: a good nose and a bit of bacon. Sister Veronica handed her a set of rosary beads in a little white satin bag. They were pretty, but Peg thought they'd also be good for strangling her.

'And of course, the wedding. It's just what we all need at such a terrible time. Didn't I tell you, though? You follow your path in life and you'll get there in the end.'

Was this what she thought her path in life had been leading to? thought Peggy. The sister must be able to see she was as big as a house. Why wasn't she telling her she would be going to hell? She nodded dumbly and turned away, pushed a clump of matted hair behind her ear. Philomena and Sheila were standing at the door, grinning, Sheila covering her mouth with a hairbrush and Philomena winking at Peggy.

'I think we should make you look like Myrna Loy in *The Great Ziegfeld*,' said Philomena, bouncing around her excitedly. Peggy tried to swat her away as if she was a fly.

Brendan, who had just walked in, laughed out loud and slapped his side. 'More like Grumpy in *Snow White and the Seven Dwarves*. Can't you do something about that hair?'

'Or,' said Sheila, 'the Scarlet Woman.'

'What's a scarlet woman?' said Liam, standing on a stool at the sink.

'Our Peg.'

'Shut up, Sheila,' said Moira. 'Go to your room! Sorry, Sister, where were we?'

'Scarlet woman. I'll go. Thank you. Good luck, Peggy. God bless you,' said Sister Veronica.

Peggy slumped at the table. 'She always hated me,' she moaned when the nun had left. 'She just came to gloat.'

'No she didn't. Come on, now, love. We'll have a grand time. There's going to be a party. And guess what, jellies and pop, and Gram's making suet pudding, and even a hot plate. Ham and taters, what a treat,' Moira said, with a wink.

Peggy hardly listened, just sat with her head in her hands. She wished Frances was coming to the wedding, but she had already left Liverpool. Despite everyone buzzing around her, all these people, she had never felt so alone.

Half an hour later, she struggled into the flounced dress. The seams gaped and it felt tight across her breasts. 'Look at the state of me, I can't go like this,' she murmured to her reflection.

There was a knock at the door.

'Can I come in, love?'

'No.'

Moira opened the door anyway.

'I'm too fat,' wailed Peggy.

'No, you're not. Anyway, you're not fat, you silly girl. You're pregnant. You look lovely. The dress will hide it. Hold your flowers over the bump. I never really showed until I was six months, just like you. You're glowing. Positively blooming. Here.'

She gave Peggy the veil. It was the same one she'd tried to persuade her to wear all those years ago, for her communion. Peggy had refused then and she refused now.

'Oh Mam, it's too much of a palaver,' she said as Moira fussed around.

'Of course it's not. You look beautiful,' her mother said through a mouthful of pins.

Peggy's shoulders drooped. She sat down, kicked off her shoes and rubbed her swollen feet.

'Come on, sweetheart. Chin up. Your da is waiting outside.'

Peggy slumped again, rested her face on her forearms.

'I'll leave you to wipe them tears off your face and see you downstairs. Hurry up now.'

Half an hour later, Moira called up the stairs. 'Peg! Get a move on! Peg? Peg, you there?'

Dennis came in, smiling. 'Just seen Mart. Happy as a whippet wi' two willies, he is.'

'Tsk. Don't be such a potty mouth,' said Moira. 'Stop laughing, Gram. Don't encourage him.' She turned to Sheila. 'Go and fetch Peg.'

Sheila stopped reapplying her lipstick and went upstairs.

'Mam!' she called a few moments later.

'What?'

Sheila reappeared, ashen, in the doorway. 'Our Peg. She's gone.'

Thirty-three

Moira's hands shook as she read the hastily scribbled note that Sheila handed her.

> *Dear Ma and Da,*
> *I'm sorry. I know you're probably feeling that you might never want to see me again. And I know I've let you all down. But I can't marry Martin. It feels so wrong. Please don't worry about me. I'll write to you with news of where I'm going in time, but for now, I feel as if I might die or suffocate, or tie a stone to my feet and jump into the Mersey if I go through with this. I need to get away. I just need some air to fill my lungs. Don't try and find me. Please ask Sheila and Pete to look after Dora.*
> *Your daughter, Peggy*

Disbelief turned to rage, and then that turned to sadness, then to drink. Despite the dreadful circumstances, the result was another booze-up for the O'Sheas.

'What shall we do with all this?' Dennis had said to Martin. 'Peg has done a runner, lad. Some folks have come for miles. We can't let it go to waste.'

'It'll keep,' said Moira.

'It'll keep – what for? She's not coming back tonight. And we might be dead if this bombing gets worse. Who's for a bevvy? Martin?'

Martin looked downcast.

'Don't worry, lad. She's got no money and nowhere to go. She'll come back. But we'll not go after her this time. She came back before. She'll do the same again. You'll feel better after a few brown ales.'

The shippen was warm. The air was thick with the smell of sour milk. She heard Nettie and Glenda snorting gently, saw the shape of them moving in the half-light, swishing their tails, and took some solace from the scene. Stepping further in and patting Glenda's hide, she said, 'You understand, don't you, lass?' The cow blinked up at her and snorted. She noticed the bucket of slops in the corner of the shippen, picked it up to take to Dora's sty.

'Dora . . . ?' she called, leaning over the fence of the sty. When the pig didn't appear, she picked up the skirts of the wedding dress, tucked it into her knickers and heaved herself over the low wooden gate. 'Dora? Flipping 'eck. Get out here. I've got yum-yums.'

She tipped her head to one side. Where on earth was Dora? She crouched down, the hem of the wedding dress dropping into the mud. The heels of her white shoes had sunk into the soft mush of straw. She tutted, lifted her foot; wet brown stains were rising up from the soles. Ruined.

'Dora!' she said again, poking her head through

294

the opening into the small enclosed space at the back of the sty. The smell was overpowering. Squinting into the corners, she was overtaken by a rising panic and a sudden realization. No Dora.

Her legs began to shake. A grim picture came into her head, of the man in the overalls stained with blood. His toothless grin. The knife tucked into the belt he wore around his waist. No! Had he taken Dora? She thought back to something her mother had said with creeping horror. That casual remark about ham and boiled potatoes for the wedding. *Ham.* How could they afford that? Where was that going to come from?

No. It couldn't be. Was it Dora that they were going to be eating at her wedding? *Her own wedding!* Her whole body began to tremble. Is that why they had kept her away from the dairy? Because they'd taken Dora to the slaughterhouse without telling her? All she could think of was more betrayal.

And Martin. Had Martin put the fellow up to this?

She remembered a conversation she'd had three days earlier with her father. 'It will be a difficult job, Peg. It's only natural that you'll feel upset. But it's all done safely and humanely, Martin says so. People will start to come and claim their cuts as soon as it's done, and we'll put some aside for you.'

'No!' she wailed now, slumping to the floor. 'No, Dora!'

She grasped fistfuls of straw and kicked her legs. She felt sick to her stomach. That did it. Her mother had wanted her to eat Dora at her own wedding.

Peggy shivered with the shock of it, but it just made her even more certain that she was making the right decision.

She couldn't stay in Liverpool a minute longer.

Thirty-four

Peggy hurriedly made her way towards Lime Street Station. There was a man sitting at the saloon bar at the end of the platform, swirling ice in a glass. He turned and looked her up and down, staring at her: pregnant, standing there in a wedding dress caked in mud, and with a piece of straw sticking out of her hair.

She was beginning to grow used to it now. People staring, trying to get the measure of her. But she wasn't going to let anyone make her feel bad about herself any longer. She did enough of that herself.

She went towards the barrier, clutching the ticket she'd just bought with the five pounds she had kept hidden in a jar at the dairy, and made her way onto the train. It was empty and she headed to the Ladies Only compartment. Relieved, she chucked her small bag into the overhead netting shelf, shut the door and sank down into the seat with its balding tufted covering.

As they set off, she rested her head against the window and the rocking of the train lulled her into a kind of trance. She was only vaguely aware of the scenery as they chuffed past Anderson shelters in gardens and allotments crammed together on the railway sidings, and then as they continued on through the flatter open spaces: dunes peaking in the distance, fringed by pine trees and then levelling to sand.

Finally, her eyes became heavy and she slept for a while. She was awakened by a guard shouting: 'Southport! Everyone off, Southport!'

'Peggy!' said Frances, when she opened the door of her flat. It was part of a small terrace in a side street off pretty Lord Street, with its lacy Victorian iron-mongery, elegant shop fronts, fountains and symmetrical rose beds arranged around a jolly band-stand. 'What on earth! And what a state you look! I thought you were getting married today?'

'Aye,' said Peggy. 'Can I come in, Fran?'

'Of course. Let's get you out of those filthy clothes and you can tell me all about it while I make you a cuppa. You know what's the best thing for a broken heart? A nice cup of tea and a good cry,' she said warmly, seeing Peggy fighting back the tears.

The kettle whistled on the stove as Frances bustled about the kitchen. Peggy sat on a window seat framed with red and white gingham curtains.

'Dora's dead.'

Fran, scooping out tea leaves from the tin, paused. 'Dora? So you've not been jilted?'

Peggy didn't answer, just continued to talk about the pig. 'They didn't even tell me. Did it while I wasn't there. I reckon it was one night when I was in the shelter when there were those terrible raids. Of course, everyone will be delighted. Pork chops and sausages and bacon to stuff their faces with. And can you believe my ma was even going to try to make me eat her? And at my own wedding? Ham with boiled potatoes on the menu. It was Dora, I'm sure of it.'

'Oh, love. We knew that wasn't going to end well, didn't we?'

'I suppose. You'd think they would have told me, though. I didn't even get to say goodbye.' She wiped a tear from under each eye with her forefinger.

'But that isn't why you're here, is it? You've not come all this way because of the pig.'

'I couldn't do it, Frances.'

'So what are you going to do now?'

'I was hoping you might have an idea. You're cleverer than me, Fran,' Peggy said, stifling a yawn.

'Well, then. My idea is that you finish that cup of tea. Drink up. You've not had a drop. And then we'll get you cleaned up and into a nightie and into bed, and have a proper conversation in the morning.'

Peg woke up late. She had tossed and turned in the night but Fran had covered her with the eiderdown, given her a spoonful of cod liver oil and told her to rest. When she opened her eyes, Fran was there with a tray containing a hard-boiled egg in a yellow spotted eggcup and toast cut into soldiers.

'Dippy egg,' said Fran.

Peggy thanked her and sat up. Fran propped a pillow behind her back.

'I've written to your mam. Put the letter in the postbox while you were sleeping.'

'What did you say?' asked Peggy, looking alarmed, the piece of toast hovering between egg and mouth.

'Just that you're safe with me here. And that she shouldn't worry.'

Peggy nodded, and didn't ask any more questions. She felt a vague sense of disappointment that Frances hadn't asked her first.

Half an hour later, when she had tackled her hair and was dressed in a borrowed baggy jumper and loose skirt, Frances suggested they take a walk along the promenade.

'Here,' she said, giving Peggy a ring. 'Twist it round so the rubies face the inside of your finger and people will think it's a wedding band. Not on your right hand, you dope, you wear it on the left.'

They went outside and, linking arms, made the short, bracing walk along Lord Street towards the promenade. Peggy thought how different it looked to Liverpool. There were fewer soldiers about, not so many places boarded up, and no bombed-out buildings. It was almost as if there wasn't even a war on, never mind the Blitz. They wandered along looking in shop windows, then went into a large department store, choosing clothes they liked but could never afford, trying out lipsticks on the backs of their hands, marvelling at the sheerness of stockings, squirting perfume on their wrists.

Halfway along the promenade, Frances ducked into a side street leading to the Copper Kettle cafe. By now Peggy's ankles were swollen and her feet ached. She was glad when Frances said, 'Come on, let's have a cocoa.'

300

'Cocoa!' replied Peggy. 'I haven't had that in ages! Just powdered egg and more powdered egg in Liverpool.'

'I've got a friend, Hazel. She's a waitress here. She'll sort us out.'

They sat at a little table in the bay window. Hazel, a pretty girl with a snub nose and almond-shaped eyes the colour of her name, brought them cocoa on a silver tray. It was the most delicious thing Peggy had tasted in months: piping hot, with a dollop of cream on the top. Hazel had even slipped a tiny florentine underneath the saucer. Peg enjoyed the sweetness of it melting on her tongue.

'Thanks, Hazel,' said Frances.

Hazel smiled. She has such luminous skin, thought Peggy.

'This is Peggy, who I told you about,' Frances went on. 'Hazel lives in the flats by the Queen Vic memorial. We used to play on the sands together when I came here for summer holidays. Buckets and spades. Punch and Judy. Hook-a-ducks and dodgems at the fair.'

'Hello, Peg,' smiled Hazel. 'Hours we spent on the beach, up to mischief on the pier.'

'Remember the love boats?' said Frances. 'That boy with the *eyes*.'

They both grinned as if to suggest some wicked secret.

'Well, it's nice to meet you, Peg. But I've got to dash, Fran. I'm going dancing tonight. The passion wagons roll in in an hour and I'm meeting my Wally.'

'Wally is Hazel's new fella,' said Frances to Peggy.

'He's stationed at the barracks. He's grand. What time do you finish tomorrow?' she asked brightly, smiling between sips of her cocoa.

'Five o'clock.'

'So, can we come for a chat then?'

Hazel shrugged a nod.

Peggy watched this exchange uncertainly. Frances's manner seemed a little unnatural. Something didn't feel right.

The next day, Frances set off early for the little school where she worked. She was helping the nuns teach children whose fathers had gone overseas to fight, and whose mothers either couldn't cope or didn't want to try.

She came back carrying a pile of books: *Five Children and It, Milly-Molly-Mandy* and a few others Peggy hadn't heard of. Flinging her bag on the sofa, she sank into a chair.

Peggy jumped up. She had prepared tea and made some scones, and she had spent the day dusting and tidying, plumping cushions, scrubbing pans and washing pots.

'You didn't need to do that,' said Frances, sipping the tea Peggy had poured into a mug. 'You're so kind. Shall we go now? Hazel will be waiting.'

'Aren't you going to finish your tea?' said Peggy.

'No. Let's go.'

'Why are we going back to see your friend?'

'Never mind. You'll find out when we get there.'

They hurried along, heads down against a blustery wind, clutching their coats around them. When they arrived, the little sign on the door had been turned round so it read CLOSED.

'Oh no. It's shut,' said Peg.

But then Hazel stepped out from behind the counter, waving, taking off her apron on her way to the door.

'Come in and sit down,' she said, pulling out a chair at the same table in the window where they had sat the day before, with the flowery pink curtains. She plonked herself opposite and crossed her long legs, wrapping one around the other. Then she lit a cigarette and blew smoke out of the side of her mouth.

'How far gone are you?' she asked Peggy.

Peggy's mouth fell open in shock. Obviously, her loose clothing had done little to disguise her bump.

'Six and a half months,' answered Frances.

Peggy felt every fibre of her body on edge.

'Oh well, at least she'll be over the sickness. That was the worst part for me. Chucked up nearly every morning. Yep. She looks about six and a half months to me.'

Who's she? The cat's mother! thought Peggy.

'So Frances tells me you don't want this baby?'

Peggy felt the room swaying even though she was sitting down. She gripped hold of the tabletop.

'Her mam has eight kids, so she won't take the baby. There's no room for another in the house.'

'It's not that,' muttered Peggy.

'What is it, then, love?' said Hazel kindly. 'Is it the shame? Terrible what the world thinks of girls like you and me. Never the fellas, is it?'

Peggy shot Frances a black look. Frances read the

303

look, reached out and placed a hand gently on hers. 'I just wanted you to talk to Hazel. I don't want to scare you. I just wanted to give you some hope.'

'Come on, tell me, duck. Believe me, I know the hell you're going through. You hope you'll wake up and it will all have gone away, but you just get more fat and more desperate, don't you?'

Peggy looked up from under her fringe. 'I won't be able to love this child,' she mumbled.

'Sorry, dear. Speak up. What did you say?'

'I won't be able to love this child.'

The girl smiled. 'Why?'

Peggy fiddled with the edge of the tablecloth, pulling a thread that had come loose at the hem of it.

'Don't do that to Hazel's tablecloth, Peg.'

Peggy glanced up. 'Sorry, I . . .'

'It's all right,' said Hazel. 'Why d'you think you wouldn't be able to love this child?' she asked again, more gently.

Peggy blinked away tears and didn't reply.

Frances spoke for her again. 'She's got it into her head that the father was somehow responsible for the death of her sweetheart.'

'Anthony wasn't just my sweetheart. He was more than that.'

'Whatever, Peg. It's all mixed up in your mind, isn't it.'

'That's what happens. Jelly brain,' Hazel said. 'But love, you've got to understand that when the baby comes, doesn't matter who the father is or what you feel about the louse – you'll love the child like you wouldn't believe. And even if you only spend one hour with it and never see it for the rest of your life, you'll still love it. Father will be long forgotten, but baby never will. I still cherish those six weeks I spent with my daughter and always will.'

Peggy frowned. 'I can't have this baby.'

'Well, if you're sure about that. I'll tell you my story.'

Peggy listened, fighting back tremulous tears, as Hazel told her about how she had met the father of her baby at a dance at the Smedley Hydro in Birkdale.

'He was kind to me. Big blue eyes. Gift of the gab, you know the type. And he could play the piano, stride piano and jazzy, you know? "You Are My Sunshine". Which of course finished me off. He kept telling me he lived with his ma and pa, religious types, and that was why I couldn't go home to meet them. Any road, like a fool I believed him. He used to walk me home, but one night . . . well, I was waitressing here as a Saturday girl, and that evening I happened to have the key. And that's when it happened. Here. Behind the counter. Amongst the pots and pans and with the tea urn still warm. And then another night, it happened again, and before I knew it, I was knocked up. I was so green, I honestly had no idea I might end up in the club.'

Hazel's story reminded Peggy of herself. *I had no idea either*, she wanted to say.

Hazel continued. 'Anyway, my ma and da, religious types like his, I couldn't tell them. I didn't dare. It would have broken their hearts. But Ma found out – well, how could she not, I was like a whale by then – and she told Da and it was just as if the very sight of me threw him into a rage. They got a priest out, put their hands on me and tried to pray the baby away. I wished they could have done. Because see, the problem was, Peg, I had plans for my life. I always wanted to go abroad. Still do. I want to see the world. I couldn't have a baby. But here's the thing, and I think this is why Frances has asked me to speak to you, I'm thankful for the nuns. Now I'm not saying it's easy: be prepared for a shock, when your baby comes out, because you have this rush of feelings and you just fall in love with them. That's something you have to live with. But despite that, I'm glad I went to the nuns. It was the most difficult thing I've ever had to do, but they saved me, Peg.'

Peggy shuddered. She frowned, blinked away sadness. What was she actually doing here? she wondered. Why had Frances thought this would help? It was just making her feel worse.

Hazel took a picture out of her purse and slid it across the table. 'My little girl. Patience.'

Peggy's heart lurched. Until now, for the most part, she hadn't really thought of her baby as a baby – just as 'the dreadful situation' or 'the awful problem'.

'She's happy. She's going to be adopted in three weeks. The war has made it difficult, but the nuns have found a nice couple for her. Dad's a chemist. Mum's a cello teacher. Hey, Peggy, what's the matter? Chin up. I'm your poster girl. Look at me, I've got a job. I've got a decent fella, I'm going to join the Wrens soon, hope I get sent abroad somewhere. Somewhere hot, I hope – Greece, Africa – where I can get a nice bronzy and drink rum punch in the sun.'

Peggy dropped her head into her hands. She felt Frances gently stroke her limp hair.

'You have to be strong, though,' continued Hazel. 'Some of these babies are sent as far away as Canada. And some of the crueller nuns don't like a fallen woman and are not afraid to show it. Make sure it doesn't break you. I've seen some who've gone under. Especially when you go back home and your baby's gone and you really miss all those little kicks and jabs and punches in your tummy; that's the worst.'

Peggy nodded and sniffed.

'Hey, love. The sisters really can give you back your life. Who else is going to help you? I tried to solve the problem on my own and I nearly died from slippery elm. Let them help you. Apart from anything, it's nearly impossible to have your baby in a proper hospital if you're a fallen woman. Sister David at the home, look out for her, she's kind. And mousey Sister Mary – but keep away from mean Sister Mary. There's two of them. And avoid Sister Assumpta if you can. She's the boss. So there you have it: unless your fella is going to marry you . . . mother and baby homes is where girls like us have our kiddies.'

'What's slippery elm?'

Frances and Hazel exchanged a glance.

'It's bark from an elm tree. You stick it up inside you and I don't know how, but it's supposed to make, you know . . . make the baby come out. Early.'

'You mean. Like . . . get rid of it. Like the gin and knitting needles?'

307

'Aye. No baby any more. Just ended with me in the hospital though, with a terrible fever and me ma crying the place down and a priest standing by my bed giving me the last rites. *May the Lord free you from your sin . . .*' She laughed.

'It's the spores on the bark,' explained Frances. 'When the tree gets wet it builds up this kind of yeast that causes an infection. So if it's inside you, the idea is, the infection spreads to your womb.'

'Ooh, well, you're clever, Fran,' said Hazel. 'Anyway, that's how my ma found out. I was writhing around in agony on the bedroom floor. They called the doctor and the game was up.'

Peggy stared blankly ahead.

'You're too far gone for slippery elm, Peg. Besides, like I said, I wouldn't recommend it.'

Slippery elm. She was learning about things she could only have imagined. That girls would put bits of trees inside them; that hospitals wouldn't want you if you were a fallen woman; and that mean Sister Mary or mousey Sister Mary might send your baby all the way to Canada.

Two weeks passed. Then another two weeks. Peggy moped around the house, falling asleep in the afternoon, taking a walk. Sometimes she would sit in front of the mirror for hours, dragging a brush through her hair, borrowing Fran's lipstick and applying it to her generous mouth; but then feeling downcast at what she thought was a grotesque version of herself looking back at her.

Despite Fran's gentle enquiries about Peg's day,

Peg's plans – *Any more thoughts?* she would ask each evening – Peg wanted to tell her that far from helping her, Hazel's conversation had seemed to build invisible walls around her that imprisoned her more each day.

One day she asked Fran, 'D'you think Hazel is really happy? It sounds such a sad story.'

'What's happy?' Frances replied.

'I dunno,' Peggy said, her voice quavering.

'Her story is sad, but no more than so many others. No more than yours, Peg. But she seems happy enough to me. You should've seen her before. Not knowing what she was going to do, where to turn. Her whole life disappearing before her. It was like the nuns had thrown her a rubber ring and saved her from drowning.'

'Don't say that,' Peggy said, a shadow crossing her face.

'Sorry, Peg.'

'The nuns always liked you, but they hated me. Imagine if they could see me now.' Peggy spoke in a deep, throaty voice. 'Depart from me, ye cursed, into everlasting fire which has been prepared for ye, Peggy O'Shea . . .' she said, waving her arms.

'By the devil and all his angels . . .' chorused Frances, smiling.

'I'm not sure I believe Hazel, that she's happy. Or that that place isn't a hellhole,' said Peggy, falling sombre again.

'None of us are happy right now. Look what's happening with this terrible war. Poor little kiddies that I'm trying to teach, worrying why they haven't seen their das, and their mas can't be bothered. The news from Liverpool is just awful. My ma says she thanks God every day that I came to Southport. Thank God for Sister Veronica getting me this job at the school, too. But what can anyone do – just make the best of things, eh, Peg? And I suggest you start thinking about doing the same. You can't keep hiding under the eiderdown. You're getting so close now.'

Thirty-five

'Here you are,' said Frances the next day, plonking a book down on the table. The pages flapped open as if it were a dead pigeon. Peggy picked it up and looked at the title: *A Medical Dictionary for Expectant Mothers*.

'Looks like you're not the only one to find yourself in this situation. That book is well thumbed,' Frances added. 'It's a nursing manual. Got it from the nuns' library.'

Turning over the pages gingerly as if she might catch something from it, Peggy began to read. There was a picture of a pregnant woman pointing to her stomach as if she had been cut in half; more of a diagram that she couldn't make much sense of. She flicked over to another chapter, read a paragraph about the waters breaking. In another, she read a few lines about things that were familiar to her: the sickness, the cravings.

But there were other, startling things that were new to her. The gristly-looking snake attached to the baby's stomach both horrified and fascinated her. Why didn't she know about that? And then there was a picture of a curly-haired baby's head coming

311

out from between the legs of a woman, whose head was cropped out of the image.

It didn't say much about the pain. That was one thing Peggy did know about. She had heard her mother screaming on the other side of the bedroom wall with Kitty, and with Liam, and Jimmy. There were more red arrows pointing at unrecognizable sinewy, ropey parts of the inside of a woman's body.

'Did you know about this, Frances?'

'What?'

'The gristly snake?'

'The snake? The umbilical cord, you mean? Yes. From biology lessons. It's pretty much the same in humans as animals. Don't you know about all this because of the cows and your pig?'

'I just do the feeding and milking; birthing happens at Davey's farm. Sister just used to call me a silly goose all the time. Said I had stuffing between my ears and nothing else. She was right.'

Frances smiled. 'It's never too late to learn. Books are no substitute for real life anyway. You'll know more than me or the sister soon. Have a good read. It's useful to know what to expect.'

That night, she pored over pictures of forceps and balloon inductors and babies with strangely pointed heads. And for the first time she touched her stomach tenderly, not with horror and fear. My baby, she thought. The book kept talking about 'mother's baby'. Hazel was right. Giving a baby away was the most difficult thing for a mother to do.

* * *

The following day, Frances set off to school and Peggy, overcome by a sudden urge to beat carpets and clean under beds, went into her room to shake out the eiderdown.

The letter was just lying on the bedside table. Peggy glanced at it, recognized her mother's spidery handwriting, and saw her own name scribbled halfway down the page. It was screaming to be read.

Dear Frances,

Thank you for your letter. Please take good care of her. And yes, do keep trying to persuade her to go to the nuns. I'm sure seeing your friend has helped her face up to the reality of her situation.

I live in hope that she might change her mind about Martin, but at least I feel relieved to know that you and your friend will soon make her see sense and go to Saint Jude's to give birth to the child and then if she still doesn't want Martin they will arrange for her to have the child adopted. The dreadful thought of her having her baby in a hospital, everyone else getting gifts and flowers and visitors, and Peggy with no husband, or mam, just lying on her own with her baby, shunned, is too awful. The nuns will look after her at Saint Jude's, I'm sure of it. I love Peggy with all my heart. But I think you taking charge means she'll listen to you over me.

I just don't know what to do. I am ill with worry. I'm hoping when the baby comes she

313

will fall in love with the child and come
running back to Martin. But like I say, if I
tell her that, she'll just do the opposite. My
contrary Peg. So in the meantime, I'm
grateful that you have given her a roof over
her head. Especially as there's more terrible
news here. Can you believe we've had
daylight bombing? The chemical company in
Norfolk Street was destroyed by fire and
Milner Safe Works on Smithdown Lane was
hit. It's very generous of you to take her in
on that count as well. And I know what
strong words your mother would have to say,
thank the Lord she's in Suffolk. You are a
good friend, Frances. Please find some money
for her keep. Sorry it's not much. We won't
turn our backs on her, whatever she decides. I
pray to God she survives this somehow.
    Moira

Frances! What a betrayal. Why had her mother said
that thing about Saint Jude's? And the money! She
had been sending money to Frances! So that's why
her friend had allowed her to stay here so long. All
those little treats she came home with – cakes,
lemonade, a new lipstick – had she just used Moira's
money for them? She sat there, her hands shaking.
But when Frances walked in the door an hour later
and Peggy thrust the letter in her face, she just
shrugged.

'Your ma cares about you. She loves you. We all
do. Is there anything wrong in that?'

Peggy felt confused, angry and oddly grateful all at the same time.

Frances sighed as she filled the kettle and put it on the electric ring of the cooker. 'So there you have it. Nothing has changed. Your mam says either you say yes to Martin's proposal, or you have your baby adopted. What's it to be, Peggy dearest? You can't wander around behaving like a shot dog forever, love. It's been ages now. You look close to me. Have you thought any more about what Hazel said? She's already spoken to the nun who helped her. Their door is open for you. That's what they're there for. For girls in need.' She came and sat beside Peggy, wiped her hands on a tea towel and took her hand. 'How about if you just come and have a look at Saint Jude's with us? It's only you we're thinking of.'

The following week they met Hazel at the bus station on Lord Street to get the number 12, which would take them down the coast road to Freshdale.

'Gosh, you can't hide that bump now, can you? You're cooked, surely. Bet baby keeps you up at night, does it?' Hazel said as the bus rattled along. 'Put a bit of mint in your tea. Helps.'

Peggy knitted her brows together. Had she really grown that much since she had last seen Hazel? As if in answer to her thoughts, she felt a hard jab in her stomach.

'Any excuse to catch a glimpse of my Patience,' Hazel went on breezily. 'I've already said goodbye to her, but I keep sneaking back to have a peek over the wall at her sleeping in her pram. She goes off next week.'

Sand hills rose up on either side. Heaps of sand were blown over the road, in some places obscuring most of it. As they rattled down the bypass, Peggy looked out of the window blankly and saw an airfield with aeroplanes parked around the edge of it.

'Woodvale barracks,' said Hazel.

Peggy thought sadly of Anthony and how he would have loved to have been there, tinkering with planes, looking dashing in his uniform.

They swung off the road and passed a small church and a few thatched cottages, then turned into a wide, tree-lined avenue with imposing houses that looked as if they must belong to rich people. Getting off the bus, they headed towards a railway crossing. The white gates clanged open. 'Come on, stop daydreaming,' said Frances.

They walked together, passing large Gothic buildings set back behind wrought-iron gates, with turrets, sweeping driveways, rhododendrons and rose beds. Peggy wondered what this place was that they were taking her to. The houses, which all looked the same, were even bigger than the ones she'd seen from the bus, and more intimidating.

Eventually Hazel and Frances stopped in front of a huge red-brick building. Hazel clutched Peggy under her elbow and pulled her to one side. They stood peeping out from behind a gate pillar.

'Stone the crows, that's my Patience in that pushchair wearing the bobble hat. I'm sure of it! Look how happy she is. She's smiling!'

A small girl holding a nun's hand tottered along the path. The nun bent to give her a pine cone that had fallen onto the path from the branches of a huge pine tree. She smiled and placed it into the child's little open palm.

'That's Sister David. She's lovely. And the other one over there snipping the rose bush, mousey Sister Mary, she's kind. Mean Sister Mary, well – let's hope you don't have much to do with her. But they weren't all awful,' Hazel said. 'Some of those kiddies are evacuees. They've started taking them in from Liverpool. Even mean Sister Mary and Sister Assumpta will be kind to them.'

'What about you, though?' asked Peggy.

'Me?'

'Are you happy?'

'Musn't grumble. I muddle on.'

For another week, Peggy sat in the flat, sewing gloves and socks while an exasperated Frances sat at the table and scribbled in her books. Occasionally when Frances went to the school, Peggy tried to hide her bump with layers of jumpers and coats and ventured out along the promenade. No one knew her here, and she wore the cheap ring Frances had given her as she walked along the promenade towards the fair, breathing deeply in the fresh air. The hump-backed Big Dipper rose up on the horizon, and the candy-striped seats of empty deckchairs dotted around the bandstand bucked and tossed in the wind. It all seemed a world away from Liverpool.

Every day, despite feeling her baby kick and turn

and even hiccup, Peggy tried to detach herself from this child, remembering Hazel's cautionary words. She would walk the other way when someone came towards her pushing a pram, and head towards the wilder seashore and the vast emptiness of the beach. The blustery wind would hurt her ears and her hair would become matted and stiff with the stinging salt air. She walked miles each day, over sand hills planted with marram grass that pricked her shins through her stockings, and silty marshes. She ignored the signs at the flatter part of the beach saying there were dangerous tides and mud that would swallow you up, and didn't care that the ground underfoot was slimy. Often, she could feel her boots being sucked off her feet.

'You can sink to your neck in minutes,' Frances said to her one day, after she returned from one of her walks. 'You're spending too much time at the beach. I know you go out when I'm not here. There's sand everywhere. I can feel it under my toes, and in the bed, and in between the floorboards.'

'I'm sorry. I need air to think.'

'And has the fresh air given you any answers?'

'Yes,' Peggy said, with a sigh.

Thirty-six

Frances noticed the small suitcase by the door when she arrived home from work. Wordlessly, she took Peggy's hand and kissed her on the cheek. She offered to go with her – it was four o'clock, and already getting dark – but Peggy said no.

She got off at Freshdale. Setting off down the road, she tried to remember where she was going, but she had never expected that all the buildings would look so similar. She tried to remember the gate. Which one was it? All these big houses looked identical: the same Gothic turrets, the same sweeping drives and flower beds, walls covered with ivy, windows looking dolefully out onto manicured front lawns.

Then she recognized the statue of Our Lady in one of the gardens. Taking a deep breath, she pushed open the large, ornate gate.

This was it. The net curtains, the crucifix on a rockery with a little wooden roof. In a recess on one of the walls was a statue of the Virgin Mary with a jam jar full of freshly cut white lilies at her feet. Peggy walked up the path, gravel crunching under her feet as she approached the large wooden door and rang the bell.

She was a little surprised when a priest opened

it, wearing a black cassock and battered leather slippers.

'Hello. I'm here to see . . . Sister . . . erm . . . ?'

He glanced down at the suitcase. 'Three houses along,' he said wearily. 'You've come to the seminary.'

'Seminary?' She paused. 'Seminary?'

'Yes, child. I'm assuming you want Saint Jude's?'

She opened her mouth to speak, closed it again. *Seminary*. That word.

He was growing impatient. 'What is it? I have confession in five minutes.'

'Sorry for asking. But I had a friend. And I'd forgotten . . . Roberto Giardano. Do you know or . . . have you . . . is he . . . ?'

'Oh dear, is that why you're here? I'm sorry to have to tell you, if he was important to you. He died.'

She felt this news as a crushing blow, even though it was something she knew already. 'Oh . . . I knew the family. I didn't know it had been confirmed.'

She could see the priest glancing at her stomach, then down again at the small suitcase of her belongings.

'Yes. A tragedy. He would have made such a good priest. One of our finest young men. Such a terrible shame. Can I help you, dear? Is that why you're here? Do you want Saint Jude's?'

'What about his brother – Anthony Giardano? Do you have any news of him?' she asked urgently. The priest, with his baggy eyes, paused. He shifted from foot to foot. It felt as though he was about to say something. 'Anthony Giardano,' she repeated.

'He died too.' A bell rang softly somewhere inside

the house. 'I have confession. That's the bell for evening Mass.'

Peggy nodded sadly. But the way he hurried to shut the door, the way he turned away so quickly, left her with an uneasy feeling in her heart.

The nun was waiting for her on the steps, bathed in the porch light. She smiled, showing yellowish, protruding teeth.

Peggy froze. She wanted to run away. Was this really the answer? She had no idea. Should she have just waited and gone to the hospital? Could she have had her baby at Frances's flat? Her mother had had her last four at home. But Hazel had told her how awful hospital was – being on a ward surrounded by mothers with husbands and visitors bringing flowers and knitted booties, while she would have to lie there alone and ashamed. And Frances wouldn't know what to do. At least here at Saint Jude's, there were others in the same dreadful mess as she was.

'Peggy O'Shea?' said the nun.

Peggy nodded as the nun took her small bag and led her inside, down corridors that smelled of candlewax and polish, to a cramped office. She didn't seem unkind – more like she was someone who wasn't easily shocked.

'So. Peggy O'Shea, I'm Sister Mary. What's brought you here? Apart from the obvious?'

She smiled all the time. Even when Peggy crumpled in an outpouring of grief, she smiled. She even smiled when Peggy started to tell her the story about Martin and Anthony, smiled as she held up a hand and said she didn't want to hear any more.

'My dear, I have had enough of men. They're all the same. I've heard so many tragic tales and I'm beginning to think it's all their fault. There are some sisters here who blame the women – most, actually. They can't understand why Catholic girls make mistakes, when they surely have had so many years of being told about hell and damnation and the consequences of sinning. But I find it always comes down to a man with no morals who can't keep his hands off a girl, or has lied, or taken advantage. And they leave you with a river of pain to wade through, don't they? That's the thanks you get. Never let a man give you something that he got for nothing. Cheap, that's what that is. And it makes a girl cheap as well.'

Was she being nice? Peggy couldn't work it out. Was this mean Sister Mary or mousey Sister Mary?

'How far gone are you?'

'Nearly eight months, I think.'

'We'll get the nurse in.'

A woman – not a nun, but a nurse in uniform – bustled into the room, and Sister Mary made her excuses about evening prayer and left.

'I'm Nurse McCarthy. Don't be frightened, dear.'

'I'm not, just . . . I thought it was only nuns here.'

'I'll let you into a secret. I used to be a nun. But I'm married now. I had a baby myself. Grown up. Doesn't stop the nuns asking me if I might consider coming back to God one day.' She winked.

Just like the sister hadn't wanted to hear about

Anthony, Peggy didn't want to hear about any of this.

'Do you know who the father is? For the birth certificate. You have time to think about it, but you should consider whether you want his name recorded there.'

'If it's a boy, I want to call it Anthony.'

'Any reason why?'

'I'd rather not say.'

The nurse left briefly and then bustled back in with a bundle of papers, followed by Sister Mary.

'And what if it's a girl?' the sister asked once the nurse had explained Peggy's wishes.

'Antonia.'

The two women exchanged a look. It would have been cruel to tell Peggy that this name would only stay with the child for the six weeks Peggy would spend with her at the convent.

The nurse told her to go into the next room. 'Get up on the couch there, and I'll check you.'

'Check me for what?'

'To see where the baby is lying. You look quite close to me, dear. Have you had any pains?'

Peggy blinked. For so long now, the physical pain, her aching back and her head throbbing every morning, had been nothing compared to the pain in her heart. But now that she thought of it, although the sickness had stopped, there were other things that were almost worse. Sometimes it hurt to look at the light, to drag her feet over the side of the bed. The tiredness was debilitating, and sometimes it hurt just to breathe.

'Any indigestion?'

'Yes.'

'And I see you have quite a lot of swelling in your ankles. It looks to me as if the baby has dropped.'

'What does that mean?'

'It means you might be closer than you think. Have you seen a doctor?'

Peggy shook her head dolefully.

'Your mother didn't take you?'

'My mother isn't talking to me.'

'I see,' said the nurse, not sounding the least bit surprised. 'Now I will measure the uterine height and girth. That would all have been done if you had seen a doctor, and the fetal heart listened for, and the urine tested. Still, look on the bright side: your mother might be unhappy about your baby, but the government will be pleased. Another of Lord Woolton's babies. He calls girls like you his preggies – he wants us all to have lots more babies. Of course, he'd prefer his preggies to be married, but did you know you were helping with the war effort?'

'No,' she said glumly. 'I had a pig for the war effort, but I didn't know about my baby.'

'Pig? You should try his recipe for Woolton pie. It's delicious,' the nurse added.

After Peggy had been poked, prodded and peered at in the examination room, she was given a linen pinafore and clogs to put on. Nurse McCarthy took her up a wooden staircase and showed her the dormitory.

'This is Peggy,' she said to the girls in the sparsely

furnished room. 'She'll go in Noreen's bed.' Each bed had a nail hammered into the wall above it with a set of black rosary beads hanging from it.

There were five girls playing cards, all except one were visibly pregnant, a few of them wearing nightgowns. Two of them perched on the edge of a bed and two others were kneeling; one lay on her side, cradling her stomach.

'Jesus, she always gives me a fright,' one of them said after the nun closed the door, 'creeping up on us like that.' She sucked on a cigarette. They returned to their card game, laughing and whooping as they slammed their hands down on an upturned trunk, ignoring Peg. She went over with her bag to the small iron bed.

One girl with blonde curls, shuffling the cards, nodded over to her and said cheerfully, 'You know how to play Egyptian Ratscrew? You want to pair up? It's easy, I'll show you.' She pulled up a wooden chair, patted the seat. 'Follow me in this game. You just have to get six hearts. Watch.'

Peggy came over, sat on the chair and watched silently as they dealt and slammed cards down and giggled, scooped them up and cheered.

'I'm not sure I got that,' she stammered.

'How about a game of charades, then?' said a pretty West Indian girl with sloping brown eyes. 'I'm bored. She'll never get Egyptian Ratscrew.'

'Ooh yes, Pearl, I'll start,' said the third girl in an Irish accent. 'Two words. Fillum.' She mimed cutting her wrist, pointed at her heart, then she ran around pinching everyone's cheeks.

'Cheeks! Red cheeks! Scarlet cheeks! Yes? Scarlet! *The Scarlet Letter!*' they shouted.

The girl shook her head, pointing wildly at the cheeks of a spotty girl with curtains of greasy hair.

'Scarlet . . . Scarlet Woman?' said the fourth girl, lying on the bed. They all laughed. The one with curtains of hair jumped up. 'That's us. Oooh, we're all fast, ain't we?' she said, putting her hands on her hips and thrusting them back and forth.

The girl who had suggested the game was now hopping from foot to foot, her eyes bulging. 'Jenny's pimples! I've got it! Scarlet Pimpernel?'

'Bravo,' said the Irish girl, collapsing onto the bed, exhausted.

A woman in the corner, who had been quietly knitting throughout all of this, smiled coolly. Aside from the fact that she too was heavily pregnant, she was different to the others, more like Peggy's mother's age – she was at least thirty-five. Maybe even forty.

'Oh, that was a good one,' said Jenny. 'It's eight o'clock, though. Old Assumpta will be doing the rounds.'

Everyone started to get into their beds.

'Look at this, Pearl,' said Win, the older woman. She produced a small glass bird from her pocket. 'Hubby sent it to me from Africa. My ma posted it on to me.'

'He still doesn't have a clue you're preggers?'

'Not a clue. He's on his way to Greece, thank God. My sister is with the kiddies. I haven't told him and I shan't. I can't. We don't have the money and I don't want him saying we'll get by. Things were bad enough as they were. And now, with this war . . .'

Peggy lay staring at the ceiling with the sheet pulled up to her chin, and hoped no one would see the tears spilling onto her cheeks.

She awoke in what felt like the middle of the night. A nun was shaking her and saying, 'You're the one with suspected toxaemia? Come with me.'

'Toxaemia? What's that?'

'Nothing to worry about. Mild. But we need to get you moving, just in case.'

Confused, Peggy left the other sleeping girls and followed the nun to the bathroom. It had six baths in it. She had never had a bath before with water that gushed out of taps. Hot water! The room filled with steam as the nun watched water splashing into the tub.

'Get undressed,' she said. Peggy took off her clothes shyly, hung them on the screen. The nun glanced at her shivering, covering her naked body with her arms. 'Bit late for modesty now,' she said as she swept out of the room.

Peggy switched off the taps when the bath was half full, like the nun had told her to, and gingerly climbed in. Sliding under the water felt heavenly, and for a moment she forgot the horror of her situation and luxuriated in the warmth. No noxious smell like the scaldies, none of the embarrassment of the tin bath; just a soothing blanket of watery calm. Submerging her whole body, then her face, she lay perfectly still with her eyes shut. She re-emerged, gasping, when she could no longer hold her breath and saw a figure standing looking down at her.

'Oh,' said the girl, staring at her. She was holding a towel. 'Thought you were dead for a second. I'm Ivy, by the way.'

Peggy crossed her arms over her chest. Ivy pulled her dress over her head, took off her brassiere and then her knickers, stepped right out of them, and stood there naked. Peggy blushed and turned her head away, but not before she had noticed the purple line Ivy had, just like her own, running vertically down her stomach, the protruding belly button, the enlarged nipples.

'I'm close. They've told me to get a bath to try and bring it on.'

She started to step over the side. Peggy was shocked. Would they even fit in this bath together, when they were both heavily pregnant?

'Budge up. We have to share the water. Can you sit at the other end? Good job they're big tubs,' Ivy said, flumping in with a splash, sinking under the water. Peggy flinched as she felt a leg slide against her thigh and was even more embarrassed when the girl stretched out and her thatch of pubic hair fanned out, floating and bobbing on the surface like a hairy black sea anemone.

Ivy winced, pressed her hand into her side. 'Oh God, that's another contraction. A bad one.'

She stretched out further. Her feet stuck out of the water next to Peggy's head beside the taps. 'Sorry,' she said, sticking her big toe into the end of the tap. 'When are you due?'

'They say any day now,' Peggy replied.

'They shut us away here in the annex, away from the main house. Over there there's a few preggy girls whose parents can afford to slip them cash; but now they've started taking kiddies in, the evacuees, we're told to stay out of the way even more. Everything's harder now with this flipping war, even giving birth. Easier for a fella to get off the hook, though. Mine's buggered off to God knows where. Said it was classified. Classified! Not likely. And so here I am. Me ma and da have thrown me out. Still, at least I can pretend he got shot and say he was a war hero. What about you?'

'Same. Pretty much.'

'You can change your mind and keep your baby, you know. If you do, speak to mousey Sister Mary.'

Peggy went back into the dormitory, leaving Ivy to wallow in the suds. The older woman and another girl, Jenny, were sitting up in bed and knitting.

'Am I doing it right, Win?' Jenny said. She held up a little pair of booties.

Win glanced over. 'You'll need three needles for the toes.'

She looked at Peggy, needles clacking. 'You know how to cast off, Peggy? Will you show Jenny? I'm just getting into my stride.'

Peggy nodded, took the needles. 'There you are.'

The girl smiled a thank you. 'Fancy a jelly baby?'

Peggy took it gratefully. The sugar melted on her tongue.

'When are you due?' Jenny asked her. 'If they've told you to get a bath, I guess you're pretty close.

When your waters break, call them straight away and someone will come. If you're lucky.'

That evening, Peggy fell asleep to the sound of the girls' chatter all around her: about the chores they most hated, the Jeyes fluid that stung their hands, who was the prettiest nun, the meanest nun, the nun who had deliberately spilt a whole bucket of dirty water onto the floor after a girl had spent all morning scrubbing it clean; how they could get out of confession; who was the dreamiest movie star and who was top of the hit parade; the good-for-nothing men who had let them down; and about unfeeling mothers and hated fathers. It had been strangely comforting. Most of the girls were funny and lively and didn't seem at all as scared as Peggy was.

'What's your story, Peg?' asked Ivy.

'Oh. My fiancé. He died.'

She lay there in the dark. Please don't ask me anything more, she prayed.

'Mild toxaemia,' said the nurse the following morning, when Peggy was called away from polishing a table in the corridor and taken back down to the medical room. 'We need to get you moving straight away.'

Peggy looked at her ankles and feet. They were so swollen that they bulged over the strap and sides of her shoes.

'Let's take your blood pressure, dear.' The nurse slapped a band around her arm, pinned it and pumped on a small ball that attached the tube to the band. 'As I thought,' she said, 'let's get cracking. Come with me to the labour ward and put this gown on. No, not that way. You unbutton it at the front. When you've had your baby, you can unbutton it at the back. That's a badge of honour for some girls.'

She bustled out and bustled back in. 'Rightio, we'll break your waters. If that doesn't work, I've decided we need to induce you. I've called a doctor.'

A doctor. Did that mean she was going to die? She remembered her mother's grave face whenever they had called the doctor to one of her births – normally it was a midwife. So this must be serious.

'Am I going to die?' she asked the nurse.

'No, no, don't be a silly girl. No, we just need to help this baby along. There's no reason this baby should end up in the dying ward. Now, go next door to the ward and get on the bed and put your feet in the stirrups. Sister Mary will be along in a minute. Here – spoonful of syrup of figs before you go. I swear by it,' she added as she moved towards her with a dark brown bottle and a spoon.

Peggy lay alone on the small, narrow bed, covered with a towel, and thought grimly about the dying ward.

A nun swept into the room. 'Peggy O'Shea?' she asked. Before Peggy could reply or object, she pulled the towel and gown aside and peered between her legs. 'Start massaging your nipples,' she said, flatly.

'What?'

'Massage your nipples. It helps get you started. Produces oestrogen. Or do you want me to do it?' she sighed.

331

'N-no,' Peggy stuttered, reaching up and touching her breasts, scared and confused. Always the same with nuns: you did what they said if you wanted a quiet life.

The nun walked over to the sink. There was the sound of snapping as Peggy lay there, fiddling with her nipples as if they were knobs on a wireless. The nun turned back and came towards her, pulling on a pair of blue rubber gloves. She held up her fore-finger. Peggy saw something glinting. The glove had a short hook, like a crochet hook, protruding from the tip of the forefinger.

'I'm going to do an amniotomy. It won't hurt as long as you don't move. This little hook will pierce the sac and your waters will break. Hopefully. Have you a towel under you?'

Peggy nodded, then screwed her eyes shut as she felt a cold, rubbery finger poking and prodding and wiggling up inside her. She wanted to cry out – not because it hurt, but because she wanted to die.

'That'll get things going,' said the nun, removing her hand and peeling off the gloves. 'It wasn't so bad, was it? You should feel the water trickling out of you. Use the towel.'

Peggy squinted at the ceiling and winced as she felt herself wet between the legs. 'Nurse McCarthy will shave you now,' the nun said, presenting an indifferent back as she started filling a bowl from the tap above the sink.

Nurse McCarthy appeared in white shoes and a white coat, took the bowl and the brush and began lathering up the soapy water. 'Hold still, dear,' she said, pulling up Peggy's gown to her waist and smearing her exposed pubic hair with the brush dripping in foam.

Peggy began to shake as she felt the cold, blunt blade scrape against her skin. Her whole body went into a kind of spasm.

'All done,' said the nurse, wiping the razor.

Peggy rolled onto her side, curled her knees to her chest and lay there.

'This is all natural. This is what's supposed to happen, dear. Contractions will start soon, hopefully. Someone will be along in a while,' said the nurse, and left.

In a while!

Peggy lay there whimpering. Why wasn't anyone coming? She felt the pain coming fast and hard. Soon it began to worsen, like a hand gripping her insides and twisting. She pummelled the side of the bed. Martin Gallagher! '*Martin Gallagher!* This is all your bloody fault!' she cried.

Another nun, one she didn't recognize, put her head around the door. 'Be quiet! No good asking for this Martin Gallagher now. Don't waste your energy on him. Concentrate on getting this baby out of you. There's another girl has started contractions and we'll need the bed soon.'

Peggy moaned, and the nun left. More time passed. Why, *still*, was nobody coming? The strip light in the ceiling was cold and harsh. Finally, the nurse came back, carrying a jug of water.

'My head hurts. Everything hurts. I'm scared,' said Peggy.

'You're safe here, lovey. Quite up to the minute.

Quite modern. It's actually much safer than having a baby at home; often you can't see a thing in those cramped houses, where the bed is stained and mucky. Full of germs. All this lovely whiteness. The nuns make a good job of keeping it clean.'

'It's not the nuns that keep it clean, it's the girls. Scrubbing this place night and day. Even when they're so far gone,' she muttered.

'Stop prattling,' said a nun with a long, pointed nose who had just come in with fresh towels and calico. She disappeared again as quickly as she had arrived.

'The light hurts my eyes,' said Peggy.

'Well, if it's only your eyes you're complaining about then we're going to be fine, dear,' said Nurse McCarthy. She placed a soothing hand on Peggy's forehead. 'Call us on that bell pole if you need anything,' she said, leaving the room again.

'Come back!' cried Peggy to her retreating figure.

'In a minute,' the nurse called back, brightly. Peggy could hear the squeaking tread of her rubber soles on the linoleum as she walked away.

It was more of a trolley than a bed that she was lying on, scared and alone. It was on wheels. When she kicked a foot against the wall, it moved back and forth and squealed on its runners.

The pain was like nothing she had felt before. It started in waves, then increased to cramps and fierce contractions. Peggy clutched her stomach, got shakily to her feet and pulled the bell pole. Another sister, who she didn't recognize, came to the door.

'I think it's coming,' she said.

'I see. You feel the contractions coming more quickly?'

Peggy nodded. She remembered that in the book.

'Take some of these Epsom salts.'

'Will that stop it hurting? Am I dying?'

'Of course not. You're having a baby.'

'Can I see the nurse?'

'In a minute.'

'But the pain, Sister . . . I think something is wrong.'

'Bind yourself up in this towel, that will take care of it . . .'

Peggy did as she was told and climbed back onto the bed. The lightbulb seemed to come in and out of focus, swaying on a cord.

She lay there for what felt like an age. Occasionally, one of the sisters would put her head around the door and then leave. Each time, she felt as if they had forgotten her, and it made her feel even more desperate and alone. The towels did little. Gradually, afternoon turned to evening turned to night and still nothing happened, except the pain went on and on and on.

At eight o'clock, the doctor arrived.

'Why won't it come?' she said.

'Because they come in their own time,' he answered.

'Please help me . . . I feel like I'm about to burst into flames . . .' she whimpered, grabbing his sleeve.

'I can either get your temperature down or deal with the pain. I can't do both,' he said matter-of-factly.

'I don't care, just get this bloody baby out of me!' she screamed, clutching the sopping sheets. Sweat was running in rivers down her face, beads breaking out in clusters, pearling on her forehead and above her top lip.

A moment later the nurse appeared, this time wearing a mask. She handed Peggy a clean, calico-covered pillow, took a look between her legs and said, 'I can see the baby's head! Ready to push now?' Peggy gripped her arm and pushed. 'One more time!' cried the nurse. 'One more big push!' And there was a baby slithering out of her, whisked away over to the sink by mousey Sister Mary, who had appeared on cue.

But then . . . nothing. A moment suspended in time. No sound at all. Just a strange silence filling the room. The nun and the nurse glancing at each other over the bloody bundle. Peggy's heart lurched, and she twisted her head. She screwed up her eyes.

'Live,' she murmured, fear consuming her. 'Please, please live . . . Dear Lord, I'll do anything . . . anything if you let my baby live . . .'

And then there was a wail, and relief flooding the room, and the nurse saying, 'A girl! And she has red hair. Isn't that wonderful!'

After they'd cut the cord with a flash of scissors and wiped away the mucus and blood, Peggy's head lolled back on the pillow. 'Can I hold her?'

'Of course,' said the nurse, smiling and bringing the baby over.

'She's perfect,' murmured Peggy, in awe at this beautiful, slippery creature Nurse McCarthy had placed on her breast. Straight away the baby searched out her nipple and began suckling.

The nurse rinsed her hands under the tap, washed

her arms up to her elbows. 'You look exhausted.' She came over and pushed Peggy's hair off her face, now in a big clump, matted with sweat. 'Well done, love. We need to deliver the placenta now. I'll leave you and baby alone for a minute and go and ring the bell, then I'll come back . . .'

'The bell?'

'Rings three times in the dormitory to let everyone know another baby has just been born. Listen for the applause. It's always nice to hear. I'll tell them it's a girl.'

Peggy nodded, her gaze fixed on her child with her mess of red hair and soft squashed-up face, her big blue eyes roaming around the room, the little bent ear that she smoothed out with her finger. How long? How long before they would take her away? She counted her eyelashes. The rise and fall of her chest. The curl of her fingers, tiny pink nails. Would she be able to memorize this scent? She breathed in the smell of her skin.

Hazel was right: she felt overwhelmed by love. And no, she didn't look at the baby's face and see 'the problem', or Martin Gallagher. She saw a baby. Her baby.

Her eyelids felt heavy. Perhaps . . . perhaps she should marry Martin, after all . . . perhaps her dislike of him would be possible to bear, compared to the pain of giving away this child? She lay her head back on the pillow as shapes moved vaguely around her. She could hear voices, but she had no idea what they were saying.

'Take this to help you sleep,' the nurse said. Peggy

tried to lift her head a little, but she couldn't even do that. 'Open wide, dear.' She wrapped herself up in the sheet, let the nurse put a pill into her mouth and turned her face to the pillow.

The nurse tugged the bell pole. A distant cheer echoed down at the end of the corridor, followed by faint applause from somewhere far off.

Thirty-seven

A few hours later, she opened her eyes and turned blearily to see the baby still lying in a plastic cot beside the bed, wrapped tightly in a white crocheted blanket. For a moment, she thought she was still asleep and dreaming.

'I'm taking her downstairs to the nursery. Sister is waiting for her,' said mean Sister Mary, her face sharpening into focus.

'Why?' asked Peggy groggily, sitting up and propping herself on her elbows.

'Because that's what happens next. She needs to be with all the other babies. Need to keep track of them.'

She handed Peggy another piece of clean calico. 'I'll be back to give you a breast pump in a second.'

'What?'

'Your milk. You express it, put it in a bottle, nurse will label it. You won't have to do it for long. In a week or so we'll give you a piece of calico which you'll tie around your breasts which will send the milk back in and eventually you will stop lactating. Hopefully soon, so you can get out of here.'

Peggy looked horrified.

'Don't look so worried. We don't want to send

you back home when all this is over with your milk leaking, do we?'

'When can I see my baby again?'

The nurse leaned into her and whispered. 'Soon. You'll go back to the dormitory for now. But soon.'

She made her way back to the dormitory as instructed, feeling numb. Her legs wobbled underneath her as she shuffled along the corridor, clutching her stomach. It hurt when she walked.

'Well done. We heard the bell. Little girl, they said. Baby gone to the nursery?' said Win.

Peggy nodded.

'Don't worry. You'll be going down there in a while. As long as she's not on the dying ward?'

'What's the dying ward?' said Peggy.

'It's where the babies who don't look like they'll survive end up, the ones with TB and the others. Congenital abnormality, they always say. Though how they know so soon after they're born, God knows.' Peggy looked shocked. 'Your baby will be fine. They don't usually ring the bell when it's like that. Hey, Bridge . . . they didn't ring the bell with your Sally, did they?'

A waif-like girl with a tic, over in the far corner of the room, shook her head sadly.

Peggy spent the rest of the day jumping up the minute anyone came into the dormitory, hoping it would be the nurse telling her it was time to go to the nursery. Relieved that she didn't have to scrub any floors, or spend hours rubbing brass cleaner onto some ugly bit of ecclesiastical cutlery – she wouldn't have put it past mean Sister Mary, even today – she was desperate to be reunited with her baby.

Finally, one of the nuns put her head around the door. 'Buckets waiting downstairs, girls,' she said breezily. 'And exciting news. We've lovely new mops.'

'Ha, bloody ha,' muttered Jenny. 'Isn't she hilarious.'

'She doesn't mean me? She can't expect me to start cleaning floors again? I've only just had my baby – I can hardly walk. I just want to see my baby. She can lump it.'

'Good luck with that. They'll tell you to offer it up to God. I would keep your head down if I were you.'

The rest of the day passed with Peggy curled up in bed, drifting fitfully in and out of sleep. Evening prayers came and went. She pulled the covers tight over her. At eight o'clock, the nurse popped her head round the door again. 'Peggy O'Shea, follow me,' she said.

They made their way to the nursery together. Moonlight sloped in from the high windows and fell onto the rows of cots. Most of the babies, six or seven of them, were sleeping. Peggy followed the nun, staring into each cot. Sister David, standing by the window, was holding a child swaddled in blankets.

'He's a little diamond, this one,' she said, handing Peggy a bottle of warm milk.

'Don't you mean she?'

The nun faltered. 'Oh, Peggy, didn't the sisters tell you? Or the girls? This isn't your baby that you'll be feeding. Sister Assumpta says it doesn't do getting attached.'

Peggy's hand started to shake. 'What do you mean?'

'This is one of the other girls' babies. Such a sweet little one.'

'But where's my baby?' Her heart pounded. 'Not on the dying ward?'

'The dying ward? Who told you that? There's no such thing. That's nonsense.'

'Then where is she?'

The sister waved her hand vaguely at the cots and left the room.

Peggy stared down at the baby she had been handed. He looked up at her with huge eyes, bewildered and curious. 'There, there . . .' she said. The baby squirmed towards her. The milk bottle was warm. It felt cruel not to feed this child, even though he wasn't her own.

She looked around the room as the baby sucked greedily on the teat of the milk bottle. From behind a curtain drawn around a bed, a head popped out. It was Jenny, her face lit up silver from the moon. She had a child on her knee and was holding its chin up, rubbing its back.

'Don't you worry, queen. The girls are canny. They'll soon help you find which one is yours. Have you looked at the dates on the cots? You'll work it out.'

Tears welling in her eyes, Peggy turned deathly pale with sadness. 'I think she's mine. That baby you're holding. She has red hair.'

'Do you want to take her, then?' said Jenny.

Peggy nodded.

'That's a relief,' said Jenny. 'I'm exhausted. Put that little fella back down. He's falling asleep.'

Peggy gently put the baby back into his cot, and Jenny placed the bundle she was holding into her arms. A wave of love, a gush, once again overwhelmed her in an instant. This baby's beautiful eyes, her downy skin, little squashed face and crinkled ear. There was no doubt this was her daughter. Her baby was the most beautiful thing she had ever seen. And she was supposed to be brave enough to give this child away?

On her way out, Jenny leaned over a cot beside the door and bent to kiss the forehead of the child inside, whispering something. What she said to her baby, Peggy didn't hear, but she felt sure that love was involved.

Thirty-eight

There were smouldering embers and ash in the grate, but Moira didn't have the energy to light the fire properly again. She just threw in a ball of screwed-up newspaper that burst into flames and dwindled in seconds.

The chill of winter was in the air. Outside it was raining, the kind of rain that sent a river of water down the hill. Pushing the iron back and forth over the board, she paused and went over to take the boiling pot off the range, but not before the bean soup had frothed and bubbled over the side and she'd dropped the spoon in it. She couldn't seem to do anything right these days. Not even bean soup. Taking it off the stove, she stirred the pot, gazing at a blank spot on the wall. The room was full of steam. She could hear coughing from next door. Kitty looked so pale lately and she had the croup again.

'I told you it was a mistake,' she said to Dennis, who was sitting in front of the range, smoking. 'I can't bear to think of her on her own in that awful place. What if she never comes back? She's been gone for so long now. She'll hate us for it. Forever. Should I go and get her?'

'No. Our Peg will come back. With or without

344

the babe. She's always been one to stomp off in fits of sulks and then forget about it the next day. At least she's safe for now, out in the countryside.'

'No one's safe with them nuns. Trust me. I haven't heard a thing from Frances since the last letter. What if she's had it? Imagine that? She's had a baby and not even told us. We don't know if it's a boy or a girl. *Martin's* baby. He's a right to know. He'll be back asking any day now. He has no idea she's giving the child away. Still thinks Peg will change her mind after she's cooled off. Like you.'

'Help me with this. These blackout curtains are coming down. And I need to put more tape on the windows. Aigburth and Anfield were hit bad last night. Sefton Street an' all. More folks dead.'

'Do it yourself. Anyway, so what. I don't care. Everyone around here is dying. Everyone's desperate. Except you, it seems. Carrying on like everything's normal.'

He banged down the bowl of soup Moira had just handed him. 'I've looked death and desperation in the face these last few months with this flaming Blitz, Moira.'

'I meant carrying on knowing your daughter is all on her own having a baby. And no you haven't. Not like Peg has. Giving up your baby. That's worse than dying.'

The bombing had devastated the city. Day after day, the blackouts were relentless and the air raid shelters stank of pungent human smells; no one wanted to go there, so they often just sat around under the table with saucepans on their heads. Peter and Jimmy had been sent off to the farm in Lancashire; Davey had agreed to have them this time, saying they could do with an extra pair of hands. So that was one thing amongst a sea of troubles.

'I'm going to check the post. Perhaps we'll hear today.'

'Leave it, love.'

She started to cry, tears plopping and splashing onto the oilcloth.

'What's the matter, Mam?' said Philomena, wandering in with a jug of milk.

Moria blinked away the tears. She kept asking herself when things had gone so badly wrong. How had it come to this.

'Nothing.'

'Is it Peg? Any news?'

Moira shook her head sadly.

'Going to be trouble tonight. More bombing,' said Dennis. 'Going to be a lot of sorry folks waking up round here again tomorrow morning.'

How would you know? thought Moira, buckling her money bag around her waist, as she prepared to drag herself off to Paddy's market for more flipping turnips and potatoes. Stupid man.

Thirty-nine

A week had passed. Peggy had swept, boiled and scrubbed every day. But she had managed to feed and wash her beautiful baby, too, and each night she crept down and held Antonia close to her while the nuns slept.

It had all left her exhausted. Frances had sent her a letter congratulating her when she'd got word from Hazel, and had asked a raft of questions about what she was going to do next, though Peggy didn't really have an answer. There was talk in the dormitory of a couple coming to have a tour of the nursery, and the very thought of it made her shudder.

She stood over Antonia's cot, dangling a ribbon. The baby's big blue eyes followed it, left and right.

'What are you doing here? Shouldn't you be dusting? I need you to go to Saint Paul's and deliver the messages.' It was Sister Assumpta.

'Saint Paul's?'

'The seminary.'

The nun practically snatched Antonia out of the cot and whisked her off down the corridor. Peggy decided fresh air and a walk down the road might take away the sting of sadness, at least for a short time.

Her first shock, on stepping out into the outside world, was encountering a woman who walked quickly past her and smiled. Then a man in a scarf and hat passed by on a delivery bicycle, whistling, with no idea of Peggy's torment. Why should they know?

She walked on, hunched against the wind. Even here, even in Saint Jude's, they had all heard the terrible news of what was happening in Liverpool. Frances had told Peggy about a bomb hitting Durning Road with untold numbers of people killed – more than a hundred and sixty. It should have been heartbreaking to hear about people dying, sometimes even whole families, but she felt strangely detached from it. She didn't want to hear about bombs, and turned her gaze away from the newsstand as she scurried past the parade of shops. She had asked Frances not to tell her unless it was news that directly affected her; she wanted to build a shell around herself, to shut out the terrible things that were happening in the world. It was too much. A girl could only stand so much.

Feeling the ration books in her pockets, she went up the long drive and rang the doorbell.

'Sister sent me with the messages,' she said to the young priest who answered.

'Take them through to the father. Just finishing Benediction. You'll find him in the chapel.'

'Thank you,' she said haltingly.

The small, high-beamed chapel was at the end of a long corridor. Standing at the back of the pews, she saw the priest murmuring through a final prayer on the altar.

'May the Lord protect us from eternal sin. Amen,' he said crossing himself. 'Ah. From Saint Jude's? Come into my office.'

Peggy followed him into the dusty panelled room, handed him the envelope, stood watching as he leafed through the bundle of ration books. Feeling that she shouldn't know about this, she looked away, stared out of the leaded window.

A man was raking leaves on the lawn. A gardener, probably. Perhaps her eyes lingered a little too long, but when he turned to pick up the handles of his wheelbarrow, it was as if he stared straight at her. She frowned. A shiver went up her spine and goose-flesh prickled up on her arms.

He looks a bit like Anthony, she thought, taken aback, as his eyes slid away and he moved off pushing the barrow, soon becoming a blurred figure in the distance.

'Take this to Sister,' said the priest, opening a cupboard and then giving her a packet of Woodbines. 'What is it, dear? You look like you've seen a ghost.'

'No – no. I thought . . . it was . . . Sorry. But . . .'

How many times had this happened? That she had thought she'd seen Anthony and it had turned out to be some other person who bore a passing resemblance? But this man: he had a beard and his hair was long, but he *had* looked like Anthony. And now here she was, about to ask a complete stranger – a priest, no less – if the man outside was a dead person, someone she had been told had drowned at sea, had even seen it written down.

'Off you pop, dear,' said the priest.

'Father. That man . . . the gardener. He looks like someone I once knew. Robert Giardano's brother. Anthony Giardano.'

'Who?'

'The gardener.'

'No gardener here,' the priest said.

Peggy nodded and left. She walked along the corridor with her head down, concentrating on her battered shoes. How many times had she tried to summon Anthony up in her head?

'Is there something the matter?' said a priest carrying prayer books, nearly colliding with her.

'No, of course not. I'm sorry. I'm sorry,' she said, turning away.

She came out of the seminary and stood staring across the empty lawn where she had seen the ghost – for that's what she had decided it was – then turned and headed back towards Saint Jude's. As the road grew wider, she noticed sand had blown into small heaps in the gutters. The beach must be nearby, with its huge sky, where she could sit and breathe in the salty, cleansing air.

If she had to choose one thing she could share with her baby before she gave her away, she would swaddle her up and bring her to the vast windswept shore. And she would call out across the waves in fury, and ask God to stop playing cruel tricks on her with ghosts.

She decided to go back by the small path that ran behind the houses. It was wilder here, and the wind hissed through the leaves. Beyond the sycamores, where the path narrowed, it was lined with densely planted pine trees. Here the wind made a different sound, like someone breathing.

The path was littered with tiny pine cones. The roots looked like old, clawed fingers pushing up from under the sand. Some of the trees were as straight as telegraph poles, the branches sticking out at perfect right angles, a wood full of ladders. And on top of the pine trees were brushes of needles like birds' nests, sturdy enough for a person to sit in. Beyond a barbed-wire fence there was a field of feathery asparagus, planted in uniform lines.

'I'm sorry,' she mumbled, nearly colliding with someone. 'I'm sorry,' she repeated, barrelling past. She had perfected the art of averting her eyes, either too ashamed or too wrapped up in her own thoughts to have room for anyone but herself.

It was the gentle touch on her upper arm that made her whirl around. Then it was the shock, slamming into her chest, of seeing the ghost again.

She started to shake. She felt her legs buckle under her. 'Oh God. I – Anthony . . . ? I'm . . . Am I dreaming?'

It was as if time was moving faster than she was living it. She was finding it difficult to make sense of what was before her eyes.

He raked his hands through his hair.

'Peg? Peg?' And then he paused. 'How did you find me?' he asked.

'I didn't. You found me.'

Forty

Words tumbled over words. Tears coursed down Peggy's face and she repeatedly touched his arm to see if it really was true. Disbelief turned to joy and then to more confusion, relief and bewilderment as they each tried to make sense of what the other was saying. Finally, slow realization came to Peggy as she pieced together snatches of Anthony's sentences: he was telling her about clinging on to an upturned table; about being plucked, half dead, out of the cold sea; about days spent lying in a hospital bed in Ireland, unable to speak, barely remembering his own name. Finally, his mother had found him and arranged for him to be sent to Roberto's seminary, to avoid transportation to Australia with his father the following week.

'So . . . you're not here to report me?' he faltered.

'Good God. Report you? Why would I do that? God, Anthony . . .'

'They said it was you and your fella who called the police.'

'Who said? What? *Me?*'

'My ma, and Gloria. They said that it was a trick . . . you taking me to the dairy . . . They showed me a letter you wrote. Said you only turned up at the camp to make sure I had been arrested.'

'Oh, Anthony. That's why you didn't tell me you were alive?'

'I tried to find you, to ask you myself. But you'd gone. Disappeared into thin air. Then I heard that you'd got married to Martin Gallagher – which only confirmed it.'

'They just wanted to keep us apart. Don't you see? I never wrote any letter.'

'They kept saying I should never have trusted you. That you were an O'Shea, and that's what O'Sheas did to Giardanos.'

'I didn't marry Martin. I can't ever forgive him for what he did to you, the way he behaved those last few weeks before you were sent to Huyton. You were right about one thing: he was the one who told the police you were hiding in the dairy. But it was nothing to do with me. I hate him for it. I can't spend the rest of my life with someone I can't bear to even look at.'

He took her hand, traced a finger on her palm. He had dirt pushed under his nails, she noticed. 'You feel warm and real. I'm not imagining it.'

'No.' Then she dropped her eyes. 'And Roberto? You said he drowned?' He nodded. 'So it's true. I'm so sorry. But your father? He's in Australia?'

'Melbourne. Barely a week after he was fished out of the sea, they sent him away on the next boat. As if those poor men hadn't been through enough. They would have done the same to me, if they'd known I was alive. That would have killed my mother, so Father Moretti said I could come here to lie low – but my ma is still scared. Until I get my release papers, she wants me to stay put. I had hoped they would have sent them through by now.'

'Terrible.' Peggy fiddled with the tassels on her woollen scarf. 'Anthony . . . there's something you should know. I've just had Martin's baby.'

'Ah,' he said in a quiet voice. 'Saint Jude's?'

She squinted away. 'Martin's baby. Out of wedlock. Everyone tells me I should be ashamed. They all say I should let the nuns find someone who will give her a better life.'

He squeezed her hand. 'Really? Is that what you're going to do?'

She shrugged. Tentatively, he held her hand again and she let his fingers curl around hers.

Then, expelling a huge breath, he hugged her close to him and rested his chin on top of her head and kissed her hair. She could smell his cologne mixed up with the smell of soil and cigarettes. 'This is too important a conversation to be having out here in the rain. But for now, Peg – I'm just so happy I've found you.'

They walked together down the path, where the branches of overhanging trees met above their heads, down to the back gate of Saint Jude's. They were still holding hands tightly, still in shock, still bewildered.

'Peggy O'Shea!' a voice shouted impatiently.

'Sister Assumpta. She'll have a fit. Me talking to a boy. I'm for it. I have to go.'

'When can I see you?' he said urgently.

'Soon,' she replied, feeling a mixture of intense joy and, suddenly, intense sadness, like a dead weight pressing on her heart.

'Peg? What's the matter?' he said. 'Is it difficult to get away from that place? You look worried. Don't make any decisions yet.'

'It's nothing,' she replied.

He waved as he left, walking towards a tangle of winter honeysuckle growing in the sandy earth, interspersed with tall nettles. The creamy flowers looked seductive and dazzling, but the sting from a nettle if you dared to reach out and pluck a bloom was like fire. It summed up the feelings raging through Peggy's head as euphoria quickly gave way to despair. Antonia: Martin's baby. He would be forever tangled up in her future, whether she were to keep her or give her away. If only she had fallen pregnant with Anthony's child instead. It complicated everything.

'Get here, you shameless hussy!' called the nun, tutting and flapping. 'Where are my cigarettes?'

Forty-one

Dear Mrs O'Shea,
Grand news. Peggy has had a baby. A girl.
Peg tells me she has red hair and that she's
the most beautiful thing she's ever seen. I'm
meeting her next week. We are going shop-
ping to buy a christening outfit. The nuns let
them out of the home to do that before the
baptism. It's quite a thing. The birth was
straightforward from what I understand,
mother and baby are doing well. I will
update you with Peg's plans but for now,
she's spending precious time with her
daughter.
Frances

'A girl!' Moira's eyes filled with tears and her legs turned to jelly.

Dennis was pouring the battery acid from the wireless. It splashed onto the floor.

He nodded gravely. 'Martin Gallagher's girl. She say when she's coming home? She say whether she's given the kiddie over to the nuns?'

Moira shook her head sorrowfully. Kitty wandered around, grabbing at the tablecloth, sticking her fingers

356

into the coal scuttle. Moira just raised her eyebrows and shook her head vaguely, as if Kitty pulling a hot cup of tea off the table was nothing to do with her.

Peggy sat in the dormitory, darning a frayed doily she had been told to mend, counting the minutes until her nursery shift so she could go down and see Antonia. The strange ticcing girl in the corner, Bridget, was flicking through a copy of *The Lady*.

'Anything in there?' asked Win.

'Housekeeper,' said the girl. 'Seamstress.'

How could they casually pick out jobs? Peggy thought.

'You want me to look for you, Peggy?' asked Bridget.

'Note for you,' said Pearl, barrelling in through the door. 'Just met a fellow at the gate and he gave me this. Good-looking sort of chap.'

Peggy took it, knowing straight away who it was from, her hands shaking so that the paper fluttered like a hummingbird's wings.

> *Dear Peggy,*
> *My head is in such a whirl. I don't know where to begin. I can think of nothing else but your pretty face. I expect you are as confused as I am. But Peggy, where do I start? I knew in a heartbeat, the moment I saw you, that I loved you. I have loved you forever. Do you believe in love at first sight? Well, this feels like love at first, second, third, fourth sight. I just want to kiss you and hold you in my arms*

and carry you away with me. My wild, funny, carefree Peg. If only that nun hadn't dragged you off. I want to be with you, Peggy. My heart leapt with joy to hear that Martin was no longer in your life. I want to marry you, Peg. There, I've said it. Please don't think I'm ridiculous. Can we meet at that little cafe in the village? Perhaps tomorrow? Is it difficult to get away from the sisters? I expect so. But I'll wait for your reply.

Love, Anthony

'Who's the lovely fella, then? He your sweetheart?' asked Pearl. 'He changed his mind? Says he wants to marry you, and you can live happily ever after with your wee one? He's handsome. Looked like one of Jenny's matinee idol cigarette cards. Gary Cooper and Robert Montgomery.'

'Ooh, I love a happy ending,' said Bridget.

'Me too . . . I'd leave this place now, Peg. Go running into his arms, like Vivien Leigh did with Clark Gable in *Gone with the Wind*.'

Peggy faltered. 'I've got the christening next week.'

'Why hang about for the christening? Surely he wouldn't want his daughter christened in this hell-hole?'

It's not his baby, she was about to say, but she kept quiet. It was certainly not the straightforward happy ending they were all talking about. And the fact that Anthony hadn't even mentioned the child in his note made her think that this could only be a story with a sorrowful twist to it.

'Where's baby's red hair from? Your side of the family?' said Bridget.

Peggy shuddered. She had to get out. Needed to breathe. Picking up a convenient mop, she said she wasn't sure, and left the room.

Frances and Peggy sat together in a small cafe in Wayfarer's arcade just off Southport's Lord Street.

'And do you still love him?' asked a shocked Frances, after listening to Anthony's story and reading the letter from him that Peggy had thrust into her hands. Peggy had related every detail: the mud on his boots, the length of his hair, the way he had kissed her on each finger.

Peggy nodded. 'More than anything. But I'm a different person now. Not the same Peggy that Anthony fell in love with. There was never a baby in the dream of finding Anthony alive. Or at least, not another's man's baby.'

'You really can't see a way forward?'

She shook her head sadly. 'I've thought and thought about it. In my wildest dreams I'd have us go off into the sunset with Antonia, to live in one of them cottages in the lanes down by the beach. Grow strawberries and roses. Sit stroking our cat in the sun. But Martin would come after us, that's for sure. He would never let another man bring up his child. And then every time Antonia did something wrong – and believe me, I know about toddlers and tantrums and how vicious and selfish teenage girls can be – well, Anthony would just think of him. How could he ever love Antonia, hating Martin as much as he must do? And as for the other scenario, me leaping with joy into his arms and forgetting I have just given her up – my baby – well, maybe that's what Anthony is hoping for. But it's impossible. It will haunt me forever. Who would want to live with a person carrying sadness for the rest of their life? It's changed me, Franny.'

'You mean you're not the same girl who used to balance on walls and kick a can down the street and make recorders out of carrots? Maybe you've just grown up a little.'

'I'm different, but not in a good way. It wouldn't be Peg he was marrying. Just a sliver of me. I'd soon grow resentful and mean. He doesn't deserve that.'

'Well, that's awfully noble, Peg. But shouldn't you give it a try?'

'I don't know. I'm a mess. I don't know what to do.'

'So what now? Back to Martin with Antonia?'

'Never.'

Frances took her hand and squeezed it, assuring her that things had a way of turning out for the best, whatever that might be.

'I wish you could see Antonia, though, Fran. She's beautiful.'

Frances could tell straight away from the look on Peggy's face that she was so in love with this child, she wanted someone, anyone, to see her. 'I bet she is. Like you.'

'It's Martin she looks like. Got his red hair. But I love her like . . . like . . . there are just no words . . .'

'The sisters will make sure she'll go to a good home, if that's what you decide.'

'They left me alone after I went into labour, you know, for hours. And it was so strange when she came out. I thought she was dead and I prayed and prayed that she would live. Funny, knowing how everything would be solved if she had stopped breathing, and I wouldn't have had the pain of giving her away. But no. I just wanted her to live. Live, I said. Please live . . .'

'Hazel was right about that, then. The love.'

'You can't imagine. I wish some of those nuns could understand. They've been kind to you at the school, but you haven't sinned like I have. The nuns in there are crazy about sinning.'

'They were pretty crazy at Saint Joseph's about sinning as well. Remember Sister Veronica's list?' Frances nudged her playfully. 'Girls, what will we not tolerate? Idleness, intemperance, improper dances . . .'

'Immodest dress, indecent conversations, bad companions . . . *boys* . . .' Peggy replied, blackly.

They left the cafe and walked along Lord Street. Arms linked, they gazed into the window of Boothroyd's at a display of mannequins, all neatly clothed in boxy dogtoothed suits and wide-shouldered dresses. They went inside and straight up to the counter, Frances gently pulling Peggy's hand, and looked at baby clothes laid out on wooden trays: little knitted jumpers, quilted matinee jackets, pretty booties threaded with pink or blue satin ribbons at the ankle.

'How old is baby?' said the woman behind the

361

counter, with a bright smile. Peggy and Frances glanced at each other.

'Two weeks,' stuttered Peggy.

'The pink one is nice, isn't it, Peg? With the little pearl buttons and the daisies,' said Frances quickly. 'It's for baby's christening.'

Peggy's heart leapt to her mouth. The woman must be thinking, where is baby, then? Please don't ask me, she thought. It was bad enough having to choose christening clothes for the baby she was about to give away. Her cheeks felt hot as she handed over the five-shilling note. The woman wrapped the outfit in tissue paper and tied it with a ribbon, and Peggy thought her heart might explode.

They came out into the fresh air.

'Oh, Peggy, this can't happen,' said Frances.

'It has to . . .'

'It can't!'

'But what d'you suggest I do? It's hopeless.'

'I don't know. But fearless Peg is still in there somewhere, surely. So what if Anthony's family hates you? So what if Martin goes crazy? You wouldn't be the first to do such a thing. If Anthony loves you, he'll love the baby. She's your child as well as Martin's.'

They walked over to the fountains, sat on a bench beside the bandstand. Seagulls screeched and wheeled above them.

'You told me the nuns let the fathers come to the christening? God knows why . . .'

'Perhaps to absolve their sins,' replied Peggy, darkly.

'But perhaps if Anthony came? Perhaps when he sees the baby?'

'What?'

'You might feel differently if you see him with her. And it might also be easier for him, if he has any doubts about accepting the child into his life, if he were to see her as a real, tiny, breathing person, separate to Martin, and not just his baby. Give it a go, hey?'

'But even if Anthony were to get over Martin – and I'm not so sure that would ever be possible – what about our families, if we were to try and have a future? Can you imagine? Can you imagine *Martin* getting over Anthony?'

'Everyone has sorrow and drama in their life, but sometimes it just wakes us up to find happiness,' said Frances.

'That sounds like something out of one of your books. Not real life, Fran.' Peggy took an envelope out of her pocket. 'I've written him a letter. Will you post it for me? I don't have a stamp, and I don't want to walk up that long drive at the seminary and face all those priests.'

She handed it over. Frances put it in her pocket.

The woman from Boothroyd's emerged from her shop and ran over to them, waving something in her hand. 'You forgot this,' she said, holding it out. Peggy took it, surprised.

'Baby's first teething ring. Complimentary. You'll need it in about three months. Enjoy your daughter. Best of luck for your future happiness.'

Peggy thanked her, and looked down at it sadly.

Future happiness? Finding Anthony alive had gone some way towards smudging the hard line of pain; but happiness? She would never be happy again.

That evening, Frances went into the room where Peggy had slept. Peggy had left the grubby wedding dress hanging untidily on the back of the door. A lipstick, powder puff and a brooch remained on the dressing table. The bed looked crumpled. She decided she would take the sheets to the washhouse. Pulling off the eiderdown, she went to remove the pillow. Underneath it was a small muslin bag. She picked it up, thinking it might contain a lavender sprig or something of the sort; but it felt hard and jagged.

Curiosity took hold of her. She undid the ribbon. Peeking inside, she saw six or seven small pieces of glass. They were pretty: blue and silver and pearlized pink, one that looked like it had been painted gold. Mosaic tiles. How long had Peggy been carrying this around? For years, surely?

That confirmed it for Frances. Peggy loved Anthony. And Peggy might be a realist with her no-nonsense attitude to life – but even so, thought Frances, didn't that just show that love conquered everything? Wasn't that what all her books and beloved poets and writers said?

She fetched the letter Peggy had given her and stood with it over a boiling kettle to loosen the envelope. The paper began to crinkle. Slipping her nail under the seal, she peeled it open and began to read.

Dear Anthony,

My heart is breaking. I can't describe how elated I am that you are alive. But as my father has said so many times, I made my bed. It's one of thorns, that's for sure. I just keep thinking, I dreamt so many times of finding you. But now I have another life to consider. And even if I kept her, she's Martin's child. Well, how could you bear it? Every time she lost her temper, every time she brushed out that red hair, every birthday, Holy Communion, walking her down the aisle, Martin would be there like a ghost looking over our shoulders, even if he wasn't actually there in person. I couldn't do that to you. To live with the fear of his fury. And how I wish it could be so simple as to say that when I give her up for adoption, I would be free to love you and I could live my life as I wish. But the truth is, I worry that a future with you would be one that I would destroy. Who knows, in the end I might even blame you. I feel doomed.

Please realize, though, the joy at knowing you're still on this earth has brought me some kind of peace. We hardly know each other, you and me. It's just a silly romantic dream.

Peggy

No, thought Frances. No.

Forty-two

Peggy took her baby's tiny, curled-up fist and pushed it into the arm of the pink dress. She gently lifted Antonia up from the bed and did the same with her other arm. She tied the pink ribbon in a pretty bow and smoothed out the skirts of the frock.

She wished she had a camera; one of the other girls had taken a picture of her baby, but she had left the week before. For a moment, she just stared down at her. Her brain would have to be her camera, and she prayed she would never forget how beautiful, how pretty, her daughter looked.

The chapel was lit by candles. Shadows moved across the whitewashed walls. It was a strange time of day to have a christening: the quiet, shameful hour of six o'clock. Shame was everywhere in this place. It whispered in corridors, in the hallways, in hidden alcoves. Her whole life she had known shame, muttered behind hands in the court houses, spoken quietly into the ears of gossips. It rarely raised its voice. Much easier for shame to slink off to somewhere like this mournful place, head down, eyes cast to the floor, cheeks flushing and palms sweating. Those poor girls and their babies. Poor, poor girls.

Next to her on the bench sat Ivy with her little

bundle. She turned to Peggy. 'Win's not coming,' she whispered. 'New ma and pa came and practically snatched her wee one out of her arms, I saw it all from the window. She's in a bad way. Not surprising.'

Peggy nodded and chewed her lip. Would she be in a bad way when it was her turn? She stared down at her child. Antonia's face was so serenely pretty. She leaned into her, gently touched the tip of her nose.

'Your Antonia looks gorgeous,' whispered Ivy. 'My little Delilah hasn't stopped crying,' she said, smiling.

'Delilah's a pretty name,' said Peggy.

'Aye,' replied Ivy, with a tinge of sadness, knowing her daughter might never be called Delilah again after today.

A nun prodded Peggy in the back. 'Sit up straight. Lift your head up. Father Dolan is about to arrive. Is Ivy to be your godmother?'

Peggy nodded. Ivy squeezed her hand.

The sister closed her eyes. 'Virgin most pure, virgin most chaste, mother most pure, mother most chaste, mother undefiled,' she prayed in a low voice, striking her breast with a fist, but just loud enough for everyone to hear. Was that deliberate? Peggy wondered as she cradled her baby. Antonia began to mewl, and she rocked her back and forth to quiet her. She looked so calm and pretty.

'Who's this?' Ivy whispered, and nudged Peggy. She was looking towards the back of the church. 'Is he yours? Your fella?'

Peggy twisted around. She gasped. Anthony – newly shaved and wearing a suit, with Brylcreemed hair and carrying a mackintosh draped over his arm – was walking towards them.

Taking his place beside her on the bench, he sidled up next to her. 'Don't say anything,' he whispered. 'I came with Father Dolan. The nuns know me from the seminary. They said I could come and be with you for the service. They won't dare cross me.'

She felt his fingers twine with hers. He could feel her trembling.

'Is this Antonia?' he whispered, peeling the covers back.

She waited for him to gasp or recoil, she didn't know what, when he saw the mop of red hair. But he just said, 'Beautiful. My God, she's beautiful, Peg.'

'But Anthony . . .'

'Shush, here they come.'

The priest murmured through the prayers she'd heard said a thousand times before, and all the time Peggy stood rigid with joy, fear and shock, all mixed up together.

'Peggy O'Shea,' said the nun. 'Get up to the font.'

In a daze, Peggy came forward with Ivy, holding Antonia. Standing over the stone font, the priest murmured through his prayers: '*Go forth from her, unclean spirit, and give place to the* Holy *Spirit, the Paraclete.*'

Peggy and Ivy dutifully renounced Satan. Peggy glanced over at Anthony, who winked and grinned. The water splashed onto Antonia's head. Antonia looked startled for a moment, but to everyone's relief, she just snuffled and squeaked, then yawned and began to doze. The priest smiled, made the sign of the cross on her forehead with his thumb dipped in oil, then dried Antonia's forehead with a white linen cloth. He finished by saying *'receive this burning light so as to be without blame,'* as he handed Peggy a lit candle and murmured a final blessing.

Peggy glanced up and exchanged a smile with Anthony as she blew out the candle. They returned to the pew. The nuns remained stony-faced. 'Shush,' said one of them, when Ivy whispered to Peggy, saying what a little star Antonia had been. Peggy took Antonia from Ivy. She felt the comfort of Anthony standing beside her. 'At least you didn't set yourself on fire this time,' he whispered.

After the service, Anthony turned to Sister Assumpta. 'Sister, Peggy and I would like a few moments together.'

The nun frowned. 'Very well, you'll find me in my office. But don't be long. She has to sign the papers.'

Anthony took Peggy's hand when she had gone. 'Dearest, I love you. And if you'll let me, I'll try my best to love this baby as well.'

'But I'm supposed to sign the papers.'

'Peggy, if you're not ready to do that, don't. This could be the biggest decision of your life. I've spoken to Frances, and she says you can bring the baby back to her flat. She was the one who told me to come here today.'

Peggy's head was a whirlwind of conflicting emotions. What had just happened? Anthony turning up at the chapel hadn't really changed anything. But somehow, for the first time in so long, she felt rooted to the ground. Hope, that's what he had given her.

And when he had said he loved her, he had also looked at the child, and not with bitterness or regret. He had held Antonia in his arms and said she was beautiful. Could it be . . . was it possible? A future?

'So what do you say? Surely you owe your daughter a short time to think about it?'

Sunlight flooded in through a window. Mousey Sister Mary would have said it was a sign.

Forty-three

Sister Assumpta had taken off her spectacles, laid them on a stack of Latin missals and stared icily at Peggy from across the desk as Peggy explained that she and her baby were going to stay with Frances. As to what she was going to do next, she didn't know, but she would decide soon enough. Mean Sister Mary had whisked in and thrown down her bag wordlessly. Elated, she and Anthony had walked down the gravel drive to the front gates. Peggy had turned to see the girls from the dormitory standing at the large window, fingers and faces pressed to the glass, and waved.

'Let's hope you'll give some of them the courage to do the same, Peg,' Anthony said.

The following morning, after Peggy had woken from a deep sleep, Frances came into the bedroom to find her sitting up with Antonia suckling her breast. 'Amazing you know what to do with her, Peg. You're a good mam.'

Two days later it was Anthony, sitting on the end of the bed, who smiled and said the same.

'It's natural,' she said, as the baby nuzzled into her. 'And anyway, I don't need books to show me – I've seen my mam do it.'

As she spoke, Anthony was paging through the

index of the maternity book. 'Feeding baby . . . reflux . . .'

The baby started to cry, and Peg rubbed and patted her back in a circular motion. She laughed. 'A million times I've done this with my brothers and sisters. And the crying, I don't mind. Just means they're hungry. They don't understand the difference between day and night, that's all.'

Anthony kissed Peggy on the cheek and Antonia on the top of her head and left, saying he would return the next day. Frances watched from behind the curtain as he walked off down the street.

'Peg. All the time he was here he was watching you with the baby. He couldn't keep his eyes off you. But you know, the nuns will be sending someone to find you as we speak – you can't just walk away like that. They'll come looking for you. Social services will get involved.'

Peggy looked up at her from under her curtain of hair and shivered. Already? When she had walked off through the gates of Saint Jude's with the baby she had been told that wouldn't be the end of it, but it hadn't occurred to her that they might come after her so soon.

Another few days passed. Whenever he could, Anthony came to visit Peg, and the first thing he did each time was take the child with her red hair and hold her in his arms. He jigged her, rocked her, cooed over her.

'He's been here so often, Peg. He's absolutely potty about the baby. And you, of course.'

'I can't keep him away, bless him,' she replied, as they heard him bounding up the stairs two at a time.

'Hello, ladies. Hello, darling,' he said to Antonia. He leaned into her as she kicked her stubby legs in the bassinet, smiled and extended his thumb towards her little nose, letting her grip it.

'Here you are,' he said, taking a handkerchief-wrapped bundle from his jacket pocket and opening it. It was full of treats Peggy had not set eyes on for months. A Kunzle cake. Cinder toffee. A packet of sugared mice. Even a stick of rock. And then he produced another small bag as he sat on the ottoman and crossed his legs.

'Flying saucers!' cried Peggy, opening it and peering inside. 'Like at Hegarty's. How did you get these?'

'Let's just say all the nuns are crazy for the priests. They bring their rations to the seminary every Friday. No questions asked as to how or where they got them from.'

Peggy smiled. 'Families are encouraged to give the nuns money to take your child. Some of the girls' families give them ration books. That's how.' She looked at the sweets sadly.

'One day,' Frances said, 'this will all come out.'

Anthony bit his lip. 'There are those like Roberto who truly believe they are on this earth to serve God; he didn't have a bad bone in his body. Folks like him will be tarnished by some of these nuns.'

Peggy turned to Frances. 'It's not all of the nuns. Hazel was right: Sister David and mousey Sister Mary have good souls. Sister David is wonderful with those kiddies. I'm done with it, though. The church stuff.'

'Good luck with that, when you have centuries of it running through your blood,' said Fran, leaning her backside on the sideboard. She nibbled a sugar mouse, examined it and then put it back in her mouth.

'I got to know some of the priests well. They're my friends. I think with our Roberto, though, he was too young. He was sent to the seminary as a boy.'

'You ever think, where was God when he was standing on the side of the ship?'

'God can be found in the strangest places,' Anthony replied, looking down at the baby.

'I don't know about that. I don't know about anything at all,' said Peggy. 'Except it's good to be here in this room with you both, and this little chubby chops.'

Anthony took the baby, cradled her in his arms. 'Despite everything, when I marry you, I would like it to be in a church.'

'Marry Peg, did you say?' said Frances.

'I did.'

'Would we even be allowed to?' Peggy stuttered.

'Who would stop us?'

'My ma. Da. Your family.' She paused. 'Martin,' she said, gravely. 'The nuns. They'll come and find me. Follow-up, they call it. Report me to social services.'

'We could run away? I fancy the idea of eloping. Gretna Green. Martin would never know. No one would.'

'But me ma. And yours. I never imagined I would drop out of their lives forever. I miss my brothers and sisters. And your ma, she needs you. And Gloria.

Then when your da gets back, well . . . they would never accept it.' Her face clouded over. 'You'd really bring up Martin's child as your own? It's impossible. Besides, there's a war going on. Had you not noticed?'

He shrugged.

Frances dropped her eyes to the floor. 'Peggy. Stop talking like that. Think about it. You don't want to take the baby back to the sisters, do you?'

Peggy shook her head sadly.

'Then there's only one answer,' said Anthony. 'We go home. Face the music. And tell them that we're getting married. Unless, of course, you don't want to marry me.'

'Martin would kill you. You have no idea what he's capable of.'

'I know his type – all talk. Mouth and no trousers. Besides, us marrying doesn't mean he can't see his daughter . . . though perhaps the name Antonia is pushing it too far.'

'Hope,' murmured Frances. 'That's what you should call her. Antonia can be her second name – only don't tell anyone just yet.'

'Hope,' Peggy repeated. 'Hope. That's nice.'

For another week, they sat in Frances's flat, drank more tea and talked, all the time amazed and enthralled by the baby. Christmas was approaching. One morning, Antonia was asleep in her makeshift cot, and Frances had gone to school with armfuls of holly, tea towels for the shepherds and a cardboard baby Jesus to make a crib for the nativity celebrations. Peggy was perched on the end of the bed, crocheting a small blanket with pink wool that Frances had bought. Anthony let himself in with the spare key. While he sat cradling a smiling and gurgling Hope, Peggy started moving around the room, gathering up clothes. She paused, looked over at them both.

'She's bonny,' he said.

'Anthony, what if Martin is so furious, he wants nothing to do with her? Will we still tell her who her father is?'

'Of course. It's only right she should know. To be honest, it would make it easier for me if he turned his back on her; the shadow of Martin will be with us forever. But if he does want to be in her life, I daresay that's something I would have to live with. Stop fussing around. Come here, Peg.'

She moved over to the bed.

'I meant what I said about marrying you. I want you stuck by my side forever, like glue.'

'Oh, Anthony.'

He pulled her down beside him, carefully brushed a strand of her hair off her face. 'Peggy, you are the most beautiful thing I've ever seen,' he said as he ran his hands gently through her hair and traced a finger under her chin, down the slope of her nose, over her lips. 'We can't change the past, but we can certainly try to make a future. I do love you, Peg.'

Forty-four

Moira gestured at Phil to leave the room, but then her hand flopped back onto the bed. She turned her head away from the light that flooded in as Sheila drew the threadbare curtains back sharply. Still in her tatty nightgown, she looked dishevelled, distracted with worry. Lately, finding the energy to get out of bed – even just to lift her legs over the side – felt hard.

'Go away,' she cried, and Sheila looked at her as though she had turned into a madwoman.

It will pass, everyone said, *it will pass*. But things had just got worse. Sister Veronica had suggested that Moira should go to church. She had lit candle after candle, but it wasn't doing much good. She had knelt in the pew and said so many prayers, but still Peggy hadn't come home to Martin, and still Kitty's cough rattled through the walls in the night and left them all staring at the ceiling, wide-eyed with worry. To think I wished some of my children away, Moira said to Jesus.

'Letter, Mam. From Southport.'

Moira propped herself up on her elbows. She snatched the letter out of Sheila's hands, opened it and began to read.

> *Dear Mrs O'Shea,*
> *Peg still has the baby here with me at the flat. She weighs eight pounds now, we put her on the kitchen scales, and she has even more of that lovely red hair. She's healthy. And for the time being, Peg has decided not to give the child to the nuns after all. I don't know whether that's what you want to hear or not. I will leave her to tell you more. But hold tight in Liverpool. I think she will be coming home soon with her daughter to tell you about her latest news.*
> *Best wishes,*
> *Frances*

Moira held the letter on her lap. The war had destroyed so many families already with this terrible Blitz; everyone had fear in their hearts about the knock on the door or the dreaded letter with bad news, but this was the good news she had been waiting for. Tears stabbed her eyes. She faltered and looked up at Sheila, who was anxiously waiting at the side of the bed. 'Oh thank God, she's kept it! This must mean she's changed her mind about Martin, surely?'

Sheila asked, 'Can I read it?'

But Phil, who had just charged up the stairs, came over and took the letter from Moira's hands, scanned it. 'Da!' she called.

There was the sound of his steps clomping up the stairs. He came into the room. Moira threw back the eiderdown, staggered to her feet, pushed her wild, straggly hair from her face. Her eyes shone. 'She's coming home, Dennis. With the baby.'

'Well, Martin will need to know.'

Moira faltered. 'Don't tell him,' she said worriedly. 'He still doesn't know she's had it. Please don't tell him. Not yet. He'll be furious. You know what he's like.'

'I won't. Maybe we need to hear her plans. That girl's head is stuffed with stupid notions.' He turned to Philomena. 'Look after your mam while I'm out.'

Philomena nodded. Nothing more needed to be said. They had all grown used to Moira's erratic behaviour. Wandering around in the night, refusing to go to the shelter, forgetting Kitty in the pram outside the grocer's; but now, for the first time in months, she was smiling.

'I don't need looking after. And Phil needs to get to work. What a thing to say. Now where's Kitty? Where's that little girl of mine?'

That evening the Throstle's Nest was crowded. A sailor in uniform was bashing out 'Knees Up Mother Brown' on the out-of-tune piano. A cigarette drooped from his bottom lip and a few girls gathered around him, singing and holding their skirts up around their thighs and jigging about. As soon as Dennis arrived, the air raid siren went off.

'Everyone out!' yelled Maisie the barmaid, banging a saucepan with a metal spoon.

'I'm not leaving. I'm finishing my pint,' said Martin from his usual place at the bar, lifting his glass and draining it. 'And I'll have another, Maisie.'

Dennis approached him. 'Martin.'

'Eh, Denny? Fancy a pale ale? You bringing news of Peg?'

The sirens grew louder.

'Everybody out!' shouted Maisie, coming out from behind the bar with a broom. 'And that includes you, Martin. Going to be a big one, I heard. Maybe this is the night we cop it. I'll not have you huddling under the tables here again, get down to the shelter. I'm locking up.'

She shoved the broom in the few drinkers' backsides. 'Bugger off. Time waits for no man. Full moon. The Jerry'll be coming along the river. There'll be fires all over the city.'

'What were you going to say, Denny?' said Martin, speaking over the noise of clattering chairs, the sound of people putting on coats and leaving.

'A girl. She's had the baby. And she's coming back.'

'No! My Peg!! She's finally seen sense! My little Peg. And I'm a da! I'm a da! You hear that, everyone!' His eyes shone as he clapped his hand around Dennis's shoulders. A few in the pub raised their glasses and cheered.

'Congratulations,' said Maisie. 'Now, vamoose.'

'You'd still have her, Mart? After what she's done?' asked Dennis.

He shrugged. 'I love her,' he said. 'Simple as that. She's crazy as a wet hen. But I love her. And I have a daughter! Maisie! Go on, give us a lock-in?' he cried, shouting over the sirens. 'We're celebrating! I'm going nowhere! Drinks on me, lads!'

* * *

'Your ma has sent another letter to me,' said Frances, as they sat eating baked beans on toast. 'I'm not sure how to answer it. She's threatening to come here and get you.'

'Perhaps it's time to tell her, then,' Peggy replied. 'No point putting it off. Anthony says so.'

'Will you take the baby?'

'Aye. There's going to be trouble. Such trouble.'

The next morning, Anthony arrived earlier than usual. He burst in through the door, beaming. 'Look at this!' he said, spreading out a piece of paper. 'My release papers! Mamma sent word this morning. No one can arrest me now.' He looked up.

'Does that mean it's safe to go home?' asked Peg.

'Well, they say I'm no threat. They've changed their tune after what happened with the ship. There's been plenty making a stink in parliament for months, so bravo to them. No one's got the appetite for locking us up and sending ships full of innocent men and children across the sea, only to get torpedoed. And you know what else? Italy. It's not going well. Hitler has met strong resistance at home, let me tell you, no matter what the Iron Prefect Mussolini might say. We had word of my uncle chasing German soldiers away from the village with a shoulder of mutton. It will drag on, but there's no appetite to fight, Peg. I wouldn't be surprised if they swap sides like they did in the last war. Let's hope we'll be free soon.'

'Free in the eyes of the law – but free in the eyes of Martin Gallagher is an altogether different thing.'

'There's always some who will still see me as the enemy, but who cares? Anyway, first things first. No one can shove me in a van now. That's official. I can go home and see my mother and our Glo without worrying. And you and Hope are coming with me. I miss my mamma. I want her to see the baby. I want to tell her our news.'

'We're getting married, Fran,' said Peggy. 'Anthony's already made enquiries about a date. And those nuns haven't caught up with me yet. So we're going to do it quickly.'

Frances's eyes widened. 'Oh, that's grand!' she said, and kissed Peggy. 'Something to look forward to! A new hat!'

Anthony was puffed up with pride. He squeezed Peggy's hand. 'Can't wait to get back home.'

'Good luck with that,' Frances murmured as she turned away to boil the kettle.

Meanwhile, in Liverpool, Gloria sat in Cooper's restaurant at a table in the window with a cigarette stuck to her lip, fiddling with the feather on her hat that she had placed on the white linen cloth beside her teacup. Across the room strode Martin Gallagher. You couldn't miss him, with that red hair and his broad shoulders that blocked out the sun.

'All right, love?' he said, taking a seat.

Gloria twitched a smile. She looked nervous. Pretty in a peacock-blue dress with white piping, her brown hair tumbling over her shoulders, brooding nut-brown eyes. She thrust out her chin and, with the sugar tongs, put two sugar lumps in her teacup.

'Bombing was bad last night round our way. How about you?'

She nodded. 'Worse down by the docks. The woman over the road, windows all blown in.'

He looked at her. Then over to the small genteel orchestra playing 'Tea for Two'. There was an awkward silence. He had been surprised when he'd read the note pushed under his door: '*Please meet me at Cooper's. I need to speak to you about my brother. And Peggy O'Shea. Urgently.*'

'So, I got your note.'

'Obviously. You are here,' she said, then tried to row the words back in. She didn't need him to think she was against him. Being twitchy and bitter wouldn't help. 'I'm sorry.'

'So, what is it? Why did you bring me here to sit amongst all these flaming pot plants and those jokers?' He gestured to the man scraping his bow across his violin. 'What's up?' His fingers seemed too big for his china cup. He looked stupid and clumsy holding the tiny handle.

'I'll try and be brief. My brother, Anthony, he—'

Martin flinched. 'He died. Drowned. Look, love, I know. I did something I shouldn't have. I nearly lost me sweetheart over it, so I've paid all right. And I'm sorry, but if you've brought me here to give me a drubbing—'

'No.' She put out a hand to stay him. 'Anthony is alive.'

She saw the muscles in his face relax. 'Alive?'

'Yes.'

He paused, slowly took in what she was saying. 'Well, I'm glad about that.'

'But here is the thing. He's coming back. To

383

Liverpool. With your Peggy. Apparently, they want to marry. Or some such nonsense,' she said, twirling the spoon, licking the cream off and stirring the tea.

It sounded so ridiculous that he laughed and spluttered, spraying a mouthful of lukewarm tea. He wiped his chin.

'They're in love,' she continued. There was a startled silence as the smile slid from his face.

He frowned, put down the cup, raked his hand through his hair, trying to make sense of what she was saying. 'No. She's just had my child. She's coming home.'

'Seems having your child is not going to make a jot of difference to anything. Like I say, they are in love. That's *amore*,' she sighed, rolling her eyes at him over the gold rim of the teacup.

His eyes flashed with rage. She saw his hand clutch the napkin, blood rush to his face. 'So what are we going to do about it?'

'I – well . . . I . . .' she stuttered, alarmed by the furious expression on his face. 'I just thought you should know. Please don't do anything stupid . . .'

'I'll kill him. I'll break his bloody neck,' he muttered through clenched teeth, then banged his fist on the table, causing the cups and saucers to rattle. The startled violinist scratched his bow across the strings, a jarring sound that made everyone turn and look. Not that Martin Gallagher cared. He was up from his seat and stamping off out of the place, barging between the tables, leaving Gloria panicked and frightened and feeling sick to her stomach that she hadn't really thought beyond the tea and scones, or what was going to happen next.

* * *

The beer helped. One, two, three, glasses. Four. And another after that. Maisie knew something was wrong as she poured Martin a whiskey chaser. She saw him tense, press his knuckles and crack the bones in his huge hands as she slid each pint over the bar. 'Collar the lot . . .' he murmured drunkenly into the bottom of the glass.

'Don't be daft. That's all over now,' said Maisie. 'They've practically closed Huyton camp. Releasing them all.'

'Not over for me,' he said.

He looked up, glowering, a force of pent-up fury and rage. From the other side of the room, Colm Delaney, Pat Coggins and his cousin Mickey, dockers and draymen, were making their way over.

'You all right, Mart? You wanted to see us?'

Martin stood, tried to focus, swayed unsteadily on his feet.

'Collar the bloody lot,' he said again, drunkenly. 'Anthony Giardano's coming back to town.'

They glanced at each other. Colm shrugged. 'What is it you want us to do? Smash up the mosaic place again?'

'If you hear word, find him and bring him to me. Bring him to the dairy. I'll be waiting.'

'There's trouble brewing,' murmured Maisie to the barmaid rinsing glasses with her. 'Mark my words, that boy's after giving someone a good hiding and more, by the looks of it.'

Half an hour later, Martin jammed his cap on his head.

'Mind how you go, love. Parky out there,' said

Maisie, shoving a teacloth up into a large glass and twisting it vigorously. Martin, bleary-eyed, shrugged and muttered something under his breath, his words unrecognizable and slurred. 'You've been drinking all day, Mart. Be careful.'

'Aye,' he said.

'Blessed blackout.'

Martin shrugged, turned up his collar and began weaving his way unsteadily through the tables. When he came outside, he blinked, mildly surprised to discover that the streets were no longer bathed in the strange pink estuary light of the Mersey but were now shrouded in swirling fog.

The car came roaring down Scottie Road, just a smudged black silhouette, its headlamps covered with metal covers so that only thin blades of light shone through the strange slits in the gloom.

Meanwhile, at Hunter Street, by the soft glow of candle-light, Gloria Giardano sat down and began to write.

> *Dear Anthony,*
> *Please stay at the seminary. This Martin Gallagher will kill you. He's told me himself. You won't be around to marry your precious Peg once he gets his hands on you. He's a brutish sort of fellow. We'll face this together as a family. But for now, I beg you, don't come back to Liverpool.*
> *In haste, your loving sister,*
> *Gloria*

Forty-five

'Don't worry,' Frances said, as she helped Peggy pack her bag. 'His sister is the one you'll have to manage. But you'll be grand if you stick together.'

'I'm scared,' said Peggy, shoving in the soft toy and the pretty romper suit.

Frances was wearing a smart dress and a blue cardigan buttoned at the top of her neck, draped like a small cape. She looked like a proper school ma'am, thought Peggy.

'Don't be, dear. Your ma and da love you, I'm sure of that. Here, let me do that. Fold them up, don't just stuff them in. It will leave more room.'

'Anthony might not have the strength to face me ma and da when he actually meets them. One thing to leap about this room all lovestruck, saying he'll take on the world and Martin Gallagher. Still, if he doesn't have the courage, it's best I find out now. If he can't stand up to my folks and his – or his sister, and believe me, I know they'll go crazy – then that's my answer about whether marrying him is the right thing.'

Frances nodded. 'I'm proud of you, Peg. Whoever thought you would be this brave? You're the bravest person I know. I hope it has a happy ending.'

'It's easy to be brave when love is the only thing that matters. You said that to me once.'

'I did, love. I did.'

'It's just, I'm not sure anyone's love is strong enough when faced with Martin's fists . . .'

'Of course it is. Now let me know the minute you arrive how you get on,' said Frances, waving Peggy off from the front doorstep.

Peggy walked out into the cold air with Hope in the pram. The winter sun was shining and Hope kicked her little legs, her foot in a pink bootie sticking out from under the covers. Soon it would be Christmas. People were decorating their houses with paper chains and trees, and the shops were full of toys in their windows, Santas and elves and pretty snowy village scenes.

'That child will catch her death,' said a voice behind her as she walked down Lord Street towards the bus station to meet Anthony. Peggy froze, sucked in air. She recognized the harsh voice straight away. Sister Assumpta.

She felt her insides clench, and gripped the pram handles tightly. 'Leave us alone,' she stammered, head down, hunched and hurrying away.

'Peggy O'Shea, don't you turn your back on me, you little Jezebel. I need to examine the child,' the sister shouted after her.

'The child is fine,' Peggy replied, picking up speed. She hoped the nun wouldn't run after her. They never ran. Never broke into a sweat. Mostly they just glided, as if they were on wheels. She'd never catch her.

But Sister Assumpta was fast. 'Have you seen a

doctor yet? That child needs her check-ups,' she said, jogging up behind them, eyes narrowing as she peered into the pram. There were tight, furious lines around her lips.

'I'll do that in Liverpool.'

'You can't just take her away! I have a very nice couple. They've already given us some money.' Sister Assumpta's eyes were bulging.

'I've changed my mind,' blurted Peg. The nun flinched. 'I'm keeping my daughter.'

The nun held up a piece of paper that she produced from inside her sleeve, wafted it under Peggy's nose. 'But you were ready to sign.'

'I was never ready.'

'Then you owe us money,' said the nun flatly. 'Doctor's fees, board. That pram you *stole*. This all comes at a cost. And we're struggling now that we have more evacuees arriving.'

'Send the bill to the priests. Tell them Anthony Giardano will settle it.'

'So you're getting married? This illegitimate child will have a father after all?'

'Yes,' Peggy said, moving off.

Sister Assumpta, full of rage, grabbed hold of the pram handle, jerking it towards her. 'Give me back that pram. It's not yours!' she cried.

They grunted and tussled for a few seconds, the nun and Peggy, a sight that made a shopkeeper come out and gawp. Inside the pram, a startled Hope began to cry.

'Have the damn pram!' said Peggy, lifting Hope out of it and hurrying away.

'Peggy O'Shea, you're a disgrace!' Sister Assumpta called after her.

'Fudge off,' she replied. She tossed back her head. 'That feels better, Hope. Been wanting to say that to a nun all my life!'

She met Anthony at the station just as the train was about to leave. They got on together, Peggy relating what had just happened in urgent sentences with dramatic hand gestures. Chuffing off down the tracks, they rolled and rattled on from countryside to the city. With Hope nestling into Peggy, they cooed and fussed over her, barely noticing what was going on around them: ticket collectors, a woman with a child squashing into the carriage, a soldier, a boy with a suitcase. It felt like they were the only two people in the world. Half an hour later, the scenery began to look familiar but different, and they arrived at Lime Street Station. At the thought of what might lie ahead, Peggy took a deep, deliberate breath.

Getting out of the train and walking down the platform under the huge curved glass roof, and out onto the steps, for a moment she had to remind herself where she was. Everywhere looked so different – it was shocking to see the devastation from the bombing. Places boarded up, broken bricks, army trucks, more blimps.

'Are you ready for this?' she asked Anthony. He nodded, and they kissed lightly. He had arranged to go first to Granelli's cafe in Bold Street in town and find his sister.

'Meet me at the witch's hat at three?' she said.

390

'Yes. Stay strong, Peg.'

'And you.'

'Whatever else, we have each other.'

'And Hope.'

'And Hope.'

Ahead of her she could see that Saint George's Hall was still standing, sturdy and majestic, but to the left there was a gaping hole where a pub had been – just piles of rubble now. Windows were shattered, making buildings look like toothless old men. It was shocking to see, and even though Frances had kept her updated as much as possible with news from Trevor about what was happening in Liverpool, nothing could have prepared her. How could such devastation have occurred on such a vast scale in only a matter of months?

There was barbed wire everywhere, curled on top of walls, across roads, in front of houses. A few soldiers had gathered in a small group on a corner for a smoke, a couple of ARP men in their tin hats were knocking on the door of a house with lights on in an upstairs bedroom.

She got off the tram with Hope and made her way to the maze of back-to-back terraces where the dairy was situated, only a few streets away from Feather Street. It was a bewildering journey; she seemed to go round and round in circles. Large sections of the neighbourhood had simply vanished. Nearly a whole road was gone. When she finally saw the sign for O'Shea's Dairy she realized she had already walked past it, maybe because so many of the familiar landmarks had disappeared. Everywhere was unrecognizable, covered in grime, windows boarded up, street signs lost.

But here it was, right under her nose. There was a lock on the door. A piece of wood had been thrust through the two handles, barring the entrance. Still cradling Hope, she climbed onto a dustbin, shaded her eyes and peered in at the window. It looked empty.

When she finally got to Feather Street, down a narrow passage and up an entry, that looked different as well. There was brown paper and black tape on nearly every window. A mobile tea van stood where the newsstand had once been, the butcher's was boarded up, and the cobbler's next door now had a sign above it saying SIGN UP HERE FOR WVS. The smell of sulphur hung in the air, making her throat feel dry.

Across the road there were a few kids playing with an old tyre in front of a gaping hole that had been the Tozers' house. One of them, a scruffy-looking thing, was lobbing a stone through the empty window of another bombed-out house.

'Liam! What are you doing here?'

'Missus?' he said, and stood with his messy head cocked quizzically to one side.

'Liam! Don't you recognize me? It's Peg!'

His eyes lit up. He ran over and buried his head in her skirt, his arms encircling her knees tightly. She looked at him tenderly. 'I've come home.'

'A babby!' he cried. 'Your babby?'

Peg nodded and smiled.

'Ma's not been good,' he said. 'But since she heard

yer news, she's better. She's already up and out of bed.'

'But it's one o'clock in the afternoon,' Peg said, surprised.

'She normally stays in bed all day. Bumps around in the night doing the chores, then sleeps in the day. She doesn't like us to wake her.'

'Why? What's the matter?'

'It's her nerves, Phil says. She didn't get out of bed last week at all. But yesterday she came downstairs smiling.'

Peggy frowned. 'Here,' she said, handing him a stick of rock and then hurrying towards the house as fast as her legs could take her.

Moira raised her head from the pillow when she heard the front door slam. She threw back the crochet blanket, came out of the bedroom and stood at the top of the stairs, looking over the banister.

'Peggy! My Peg! You've come home. With the baby!' she said, her hands flying to her mouth and her eyes filling with tears. She smoothed down her crumpled housecoat and came unsteadily down the stairs.

'Our Peg's brought sweets!' cried Liam, standing beside Peggy. He had already sucked the rock to a sharp point, mesmerized by the dissolving letters saying 'Southport' and the way it prickled against his tongue.

'Can I hold her?' said Moira, arms outstretched. The baby gurgled as Peggy put her in her arms. 'Oh my. She has your smile. She's a beauty, Peg. Don't cry. There's no need to cry. What are you skrikin' about?'

A tearful Peg wiped a thumb under each eye. There were no words for the feeling it gave her to see her mother cradling her child like this. Just a wave of relief. But then Moira raised her head and furrowed her brow. The lines on her forehead were deep and dark as a ploughed field. Her smile became laced with some kind of terrible anguish. 'Peggy, sweetheart,' she said. Straight away Peggy knew something was wrong. Her mother's voice was quivering strangely.

'Ma, please don't start on about Martin. Please don't say anything. I've so much to tell you. So much has happened.'

'Oh, Peg . . . Sit down. I've some awful, awful news.'

Forty-six

At Hunter Street, Gloria was pacing nervously up and down the kitchen. Anthony had just delivered his speech.

His mother sat in the armchair, twisted her hands in her lap, pulled her black shawl around her birdlike shoulders. Her eyes were full of glassy tears. She had stopped him several times, clutching his hand, sobs rising to her throat, begging him to tell her it wasn't true, this terrible news that he was going to marry Peggy O'Shea. Talking too quickly, hands flapping, her words interspersed with Italian phrases he had forgotten. 'Anthony. You're back. And so much has happened since you left. But you don't really mean you want to marry the O'Shea girl?'

'Yes, Mamma. I'm coming back to Liverpool. But I'm bringing Peggy with me.'

'Peggy O'Shea. *Idiota*. She's trapped you,' spat Sofia, her hands flying up in the air.

'No, she hasn't. I've fallen in love with her. Mamma, if you don't accept this, if you don't give us your blessing, I'm gonna walk out the door and you will never see me again. Is that what you want?' he said.

'And what about Roberto?'

395

'Roberto? What's that got to do with anything? His death was not the fault of the O'Sheas. Roberto was arrested at Lime Street Station. I was the one they found at the dairy. Besides, it wasn't Peggy who told the police.' He shot a look at Gloria. 'You lied, Glor. I don't even know why you hate them so much. We will be married in church. I expect you there. If not . . .' He shrugged, palms upwards, in a gesture just like his father.

'But you said she's got red hair! This baby! Everyone will know it's not your child.' Gloria stood there biting the skin around the base of her thumbnail.

'So what?' he said.

His mother stood up, pushed the chair away from under her, busied herself running the tap and filling a saucepan.

'Oh, aren't you two a proper little Romeo and Juliet?' snapped Gloria.

'Well, yes, maybe. But they both ended up dead in a church,' he said. 'We'll be alive and kicking, walking down the aisle together.'

'Don't be clever, Anthony,' said his mother, still with her back to him. Her tone was bitter.

'Well, I suppose that's my answer. But Mamma, one more thing. You spent all this time hiding me away at the seminary, trying to find a way of keeping me in your life, and now you're telling me you don't want me? Just because I'm gonna marry the girl that I love?'

She pursed her lips. 'Stop, Anthony.'

Gloria finished a cigarette, screwed it into the

ashtray with her thumb. 'Are you gonna tell him, Mamma? Or shall I?'

'What?' asked Anthony.

Gloria blew smoke out the side of her lips, with a cold stare.

Forty-seven

'Dead,' said Peggy, standing in the kitchen of Feather Street, numb with shock. 'Martin, dead?'

Moira nodded sadly.

Peggy's hand trembled as she reached out to steady herself on the range. 'How?'

'Came stumbling out of the Throstle's Nest. Blind drunk. A car hit him – they swerved but they couldn't avoid him. There was nothing they could do. He died straight away. So many people run over by cars because of this stupid war.'

'No,' said Peggy, her voice quavery and panicked.

'I know, love. I'm sorry.'

For a moment, Peggy considered not telling her about Anthony. This terrible news hadn't changed anything she had planned to say, but she knew how cruel it would seem. However, the truth, even though it would hurt, was surely better than a lie.

'Mam, I wasn't coming back to Martin. I was coming back to tell you I'm marrying Anthony Giardano. He's alive, Ma. I love him. My mind's made up.' Haltingly, she showed her mother the ring.

'Good God. So it's true? Gloria Giardano was banging on the door two days ago, fuming. She heard from one of the nuns about you two carrying on,

398

but I didn't want to believe it. I mean, what about Martin's baby? I can't bring up another child. I'm so tired and I can't . . .' she stammered.

Peggy placed a hand over hers. She could see now what Liam had meant about Moira's nerves, how fragile she was. 'I'm not asking you to, Mam. Anthony says he'll bring up Hope as his daughter. Anthony knows Father O'Mahoney. He's already spoken to one of the fathers at the seminary, who has arranged a wedding for next week.'

'I see,' Moira replied, even more shocked.

'What d'you think Da will say? About the Giardanos?'

'Leave that to me. But are you sure about this Giardano boy? You hardly know him. What about if you have another of your own, and when Hope wallops her sister or brother, because that's what kiddies do, how's he going to feel then? And with Martin's red hair?'

'I don't know how it'll turn out. But I can at least try. If you don't give someone a chance, how do you ever know how it will end? Like I say, I love him, Mam. And . . . well, with Martin dead . . .' Her eyes filled with tears again and she felt a lump in her throat that she felt sure she wouldn't be able to swallow down.

Moira reached a papery hand across the table to Peggy's. 'Well, I expect that's the end of the conversation, love. I do love you, Peg. It's not the ending I imagined, but then, I never imagined I'd be sitting here with bombs raining down on us, either. Or me in my nightie at one o'clock in the afternoon. I'll handle your father, Peg. This Giardano and O'Shea nonsense has gone on long enough. A funeral and a wedding in a week. My oh my.'

An hour later Peggy, wearing the gloves and scarf that Moira had insisted she put on to keep warm, was sitting on the bench of the witch's hat huddled up next to Anthony, who had an arm around her shoulder. It had started to lightly snow, drifting across the playground. 'I still can't believe it,' she said.

'Me neither.' He brushed a snowflake off the end of her nose.

'Ma fell in love with her granddaughter the minute she set eyes on her.' A tear rolled down her face. She wiped it away with the cuff of her sleeve. 'I should be happy that Martin's dead. Makes everything so much simpler. And yet I haven't been able to stop crying.'

'Oh Peg. This damn war.'

'He wasn't a monster. Just a stupid boy. Perhaps if I—'

'No. It's not your fault. Flaming Hitler. If that car hadn't come hurtling along with those stupid covers on the headlamps, I expect he'd still be here.'

'But—'

'No buts.'

'The funeral is tomorrow.'

'Will you go?'

Peggy was silent for a moment. 'I guess so. I'll not be popular but at least it will save Martin Gallagher's ma's blushes. No one ever need know that I didn't come back to marry him. She'll make up her own story.'

'They say he came charging out of the pub to find me, all wired up to give me a good walloping. If it was anyone's fault it was mine.'

'But he was drunk. I know how he is when he's in his cups. Poor Martin didn't stand a chance.'

'So now what happens?' he said.

She gazed ahead. 'We have to move forward. Martin would have wanted his daughter to have a roof over her head, food in her belly and someone to love her.' She worked a finger under her eyes. 'He certainly wouldn't want his baby to be given to the nuns. He never wanted that . . .' Anthony kissed her lightly on each fingertip. 'How was your ma?' she asked him. 'Gloria?'

'Glad to see me in the end. I think this whole business has made everyone realize how precious life is. There was a bit of stamping and waving arms about, slapping on the table, but I expected that. That's the Italian way. Gloria will be the hardest. But I think when they realized that they were going to lose me, Mamma started to see sense. Gloria has a temper on her, but I can't do anything about that. They're the ones who will have to decide what to do with their lives.'

'My sisters will get excited about the wedding. They'll be jumping around the kitchen and chattering about dresses as soon as they hear. That will cheer everyone up. But I don't know about Da; I haven't seen him yet. That might be a different matter altogether.'

* * *

Back at the house, stomping the snow from his boots on the mat, Dennis arrived, bringing the cold winter with him. He looked stern and flinty.

'Before you start: meet your granddaughter,' said Moira.

The baby was squeaking and snuffling a little in a makeshift cot Moira had made out of a drawer in the hall. He pulled back the shawl.

'Crikey. Martin's red hair,' he grunted. 'Fiery red. She'll always have Martin's hair.'

'Dennis, we've lost Martin. I'll not lose Peggy. Such a waste, all this hurt and hate. And now death to add to that pain.'

'She is bonny,' he said. He held his index finger up to her face and she grasped it, pulled it towards her open mouth. His scowl, the one he had passed down to Peggy, relaxed. And he smiled. Moira seized the moment of softness, quickly put the baby in his arms, and when she started to cry, instinctively he rocked her back and forth, and she soon settled into sleep. 'Hey, I've still got the knack,' he said to Moira. 'What do you say we go for another?'

'Are you crazy, Denny O'Shea?' she laughed. He smiled at her, thinking that finally his old Moira was on her way back.

Ten minutes later, Peggy, pale-faced and a little frightened, stood at the door. Hope was sleeping in the cot. Dennis, sitting at the kitchen table eating a dry piece of bread, turned his head to see Peggy. She came in and sat down nervously. He opened his mouth, but he didn't know what to say.

'She's called Hope,' she said, her voice quivering.
'Aye.'

'Anthony and I like that name.' Dennis glanced at
Moira. 'We're getting married.'

Immediately her eyes filled with tears. She watched
her father, waited for his reply as he let the words
sink in, drumming his fingers on the arm of the chair.

'A wedding!' said Moira, clapping her hands. 'You
wouldn't miss a knees-up, would you, Dennis
O'Shea?'

He grunted. 'So you're going to be a Giardano?'
he said.

And Peggy still couldn't read what he was thinking.
Maybe they would heal. And maybe they wouldn't.
But she decided that was up to them.

Forty-eight

Dear Frances,
I miss you very much. I would much
rather sit face to face with you and tell you
what I'm about to write, but there it is. I
have the most terrible news. Martin has been
run over by a motor car. I wish his death
could have been something more noble. But I
can only tell you the facts. He was coming
out of the Throstle's Nest. He was hit by a
military car driven by a soldier, so in a way if
there is anyone to blame, it's the Germans
again. The funeral was yesterday. I tried to
stay unnoticed, slipped in at the back. I wore
my black dress with Ma's velvet hat. The
dockers and dairy lads had a procession all
the way down Scottie Road with the dray
horses with black ribbons in their manes and
their tails, and lovely brushed feet. Ma and
Da have been better than I expected; they
love Hope, though Da is finding it difficult to
accept Anthony and even though I'm staying
at the house, he's hardly spoken to me.
Anthony and I have arranged a wedding.
Father O'Mahoney has agreed. Anthony has

*friends in high places eh? Father Moretti has
also helped.*

*We've found a little house in Smithdown
Road to rent. Sister Veronica was at the
funeral, of course, sniffing around. But I held
my head high, and there was no poking and
prodding me in the back telling me to stand
up straight this time. Will you be a bridesmaid? I'm not even sure who will turn up,
knowing we've made it clear it will be both
the families. Please say yes.*

    Peggy

The sun was bright, the River Mersey glittering.
Moira had suggested a walk along the front in the
cold, fresh air. A soldier who was patrolling the
promenade, checking the guy ropes of the blimps,
stopped and looked admiringly into the old pram
that Moira had dug out from the cellar. 'She's a
beauty,' he said.

Moira was pushing the pram. 'I love babies,' she
said to Peggy as they walked on. 'They make the
world act kinder.'

'Do you think she'll always look like Martin?'
asked Peggy.

'Too early to say. They change.'

A tanker slipped into the estuary. A seagull
swooped over the river. 'I like to think you would
eventually have come home. But to have you home
with the baby – it's wonderful, Peg. I'm sorry, for
everything . . .'

'Mam. It doesn't matter. I know you were writing

to Fran. I know how worried you were. Will Da come to the wedding?'

'I'm working on him. But this is not the year to get everything you want; it's the year to appreciate everything you have. Remember that. And what about Anthony's family?'

'We live in hope.'

'What about food?' Moira said brightly, trying to change the subject. 'We need a wedding breakfast. Sarnies? What about if I see who will chip in with their rations? No ham this time though, with this war. No ham anywhere. Egg, maybe?'

'Ham butties? Even if we weren't in the middle of a war I'd still never let a piece of ham cross my lips. I've never recovered from Dora,' said Peg. 'Chopped up by that awful man. I still see him standing there in his bloody apron with his knife in his belt saying *jolly good, jolly good*, and I have nightmares.'

'What are you talking about? Dora is in Lancashire.'

'What?'

'Been there for months. Davey's prize sow stopped heating. It only takes two monthlies missed with sows and that's the end of breeding, so he swapped Dora for an old pig from his farm who was ready for slaughter. Everyone round here in the pig club was delighted, as they still got their bacon. But Dora is giving birth to piglets right now, and will be doing for years. As happy as a pig in muck, quite literally.'

'Oh, Mam!' she cried, flinging her arms around her mother. 'I thought the ham at my wedding was Dora.'

'Don't be daft. Da's pal, he's a butcher at Greaty, he gave us that ham. And you thought it was Dora!'

'That's the best news I've heard in ages. It had almost put me off meat for good!'

'Not me. What I wouldn't do for a bit of bacon,' laughed her mother. 'I'm not half sick of turnip pie and carrot roast.'

The week of the wedding came around more quickly than anyone expected. There was a steady stream of people at the house with dishes of parsnip pie and scouse and more news: someone's house bombed out one minute, somebody miraculously escaped death the next. The bombing had been terrible, but for a week there had been a lull. Moira had made enough sandwiches to feed the five thousand: egg sarnies, jam, Spam, fish paste.

As to who was going to turn up, so far, Brendan had agreed to be best man, so it was lucky he was on leave; Phil was taking the morning off work; and Sheila wouldn't miss the chance to wear a pretty frock. Even Pete and Jimmy were coming back from the farm in Lancashire. Gloria and her mother were still refusing; Mr Albertini had said he would try. And Dennis . . . well, Dennis was anyone's guess.

The wedding dress that Philomena had produced, borrowed from a friend she worked with at the parachute factory and made with leftover silk, was plain but elegant, with long lace sleeves and a pretty scalloped neck. Peggy would wear a matching ribbon in her hair and white shoes to finish it off. It fitted perfectly, but it had needed a hem. 'Take it to your gram's,' Moira said. 'She'll sort it for you.'

So Peggy's Grammy Nora had spent days stitching and hemming and putting the final touches to the wedding dress.

'Gram,' said Peggy, as she watched Nora take down the dress from its satin-covered hanger, hooked over the picture rail. She had sewn a chiffon ribbon onto the waistband and spent two days embroidering the cuffs of the sleeves. 'If I could have one wish for my wedding, it would be that there'll be no falling out between O'Sheas and Giardanos. Just for a day.' She sighed. 'So silly. No one even really knows why they hate each other.'

Nora paused. 'I know,' she said. 'But I'm embarrassed to tell you,' she added, through a mouthful of pins.

'Why?'

'Well, because it was so stupid.'

'So no one was murdered? There wasn't a tragic romance?'

'No, dear.'

'It wasn't over a terrible betrayal? I heard someone went blind in a fight?'

Nora laughed, laid down the bundle of sewing and sighed. 'It all started with a button.'

'A button!'

'The Giardanos and the O'Sheas fell out over a box of buttons. One button, to be precise. Doesn't mean it didn't turn into something else that led to broken hearts and bitterness. But that silly argument between their daughters over a button lodged like a bad seed in their heads, and that's how it started.'

'What on earth do you mean? Why would a button tear two families apart?'

Her grandmother folded her hands in her lap. 'There was a little girl called Isabella, daughter of the Giardano mosaic family. Well, when she was six years old, she had a box of buttons. She liked the little pearl ones. One particular rose-coloured pearl button. Eleanor, an O'Shea, was Isabella's best friend – they were at Holy Cross School together, joined at the hip, those two girls – anyway, Eleanor asked her to share the buttons. Isabella refused. So Eleanor stole one. A single button. Isabella soon found out, and the girls fought like wildcats in the playground. The nuns called the mothers into school to stop the bickering. But it was the mothers who started all the trouble. Each one blaming the other girl. Terrible names flew back and forth. Isabella's mother said Eleanor was wicked and a thief. Eleanor's mother said it was only one button, Isabella was petty and cruel. Thieves. Vagabonds, bitches, more insults. And so that's how it started. The two mothers stopped speaking, then the girls weren't allowed to see each other, then the families began crossing to the other side of the street to avoid each other. You want to hear more?'

Peggy nodded.

Nora took a deep breath. 'Well, the wife stopped buying from the Giardanos, who had a grocer's shop on Scottie Road as well as the mosaics. And then she told the rest of her family not to go there. Then the O'Sheas stopped delivering milk to the Giardanos and got their friends to do the same. And so it went

409

on. Of course, in the end it was this kind of nonsense that drove a wedge between the families. Especially when the businesses began to suffer. And that led to fisticuffs and rows in pubs. And yes, one of the Giardano boys had his face punched in, I seem to remember. Went blind in one eye. The little girls had both grown up by then and had children of their own but to this day you'll hear different accounts, whether it was the O'Sheas' fault or the Giardanos' fault, who started it first . . . no one knows.'

'What parts are true?'

'Sometimes I wonder if any of it is. But each family blamed each other for every little thing that happened. And big things. Your ma, well, she had a baby. So sad . . .'

'Alice?'

'Yes, Alice. When Alice died, there was a stupid rumour going around that the Giardanos had unhooked the O'Sheas' washing line and the baby's blanket had fallen into a dirty puddle and the baby had caught something from it. Then someone said they had seen a Giardano sneezing into the pram. Then when Enzo Giardano had to leave Liverpool suddenly, someone said that your father had tipped off the police saying the all Giardanos should go on the blessed 'people of interest' list, because of Alice. Such nonsense. It was Mussolini's thugs who came over from Bardi wanting protection money who were to blame for that.'

Leaning over, she touched Peggy's hair, tucked a piece of it behind her ear. 'Such a long time ago now.'

'I'm not sure who will come to my wedding. But

if the Giardanos have any argument, it should be with Martin Gallagher's family, not the O'Sheas. Martin was the one who went to the police.'

'People have long memories. And yet hardly anyone remembers that the feud all started over a button. Now, here you are . . .' She pinned the veil, attached to a white wreath of silk flowers that were yellowing slightly but still pretty, onto Peggy's head. 'Perhaps you and Anthony will bring an end to it. Now then – something borrowed? Here.' She took something out of the sewing box, a small tin, rattled it, opened it. And then pressed something into her granddaughter's hand.

Peggy uncurled her fingers, peeking into her hand, and gasped. She looked at her grandmother in shock. 'The button!'

A small rose-coloured pearl nestled in the crease of her palm. It was beautiful, the way the light caught it and it flashed lilacs and blues and soft pinks.

'Yes.'

And then it dawned on her. Eleanor. Nora. 'The girl who stole the button from Isabella – it was you?'

Grammy Nora nodded. 'I think it's about time we stopped all this nonsense, don't you?'

'Aye.'

Nora smiled. 'You know there's no difference between us two families. The Italians got tired of slaving away under the boiling hot Mediterranean sun. Our people got tired of digging the peat bogs in the cold Irish rain. There had to be something better. Anthony's family, like so many others round here, stopped by on the way to New York, and when they realized that there was money to be made and a future, they never got back on the boat. Our family came from Dublin to find work and fill their aching bellies with food, and never looked back. Liverpool reminded them all of home. Scottie Road welcomed them with profiteroles and chocolates, ice-cream parlours and accordion players, and Irish stew and Guinness; and, of course, Jesus. All those crucifixes, the May processions, the Bambino di Christis on everyone's windowsills, gave comfort to everyone, the Giardanos and the O'Sheas. No worse than some, and no better than others. Both families are in the dirt and in the wind of Liverpool. It wasn't that they were bad people, just that a few bad things happened along the way. Like an argument over a button. Time to put all that behind us now, don't you think?'

'Aye, Gram. As for this war, it's been the ruination of so many lives; why ruin more? Anthony's family has been destroyed because of a stupid man called Mussolini. Martin's life has been ended because of Hitler. Arrogant eejits with egos the size of a small country and pea-sized spoilt children's brains.'

'Well said, dear,' said Gram.

'Please God, some of the O'Sheas and Giardanos will turn up tomorrow at least. I don't care who.'

412

Forty-nine

The following morning, Peggy came out onto her grandmother's front doorstep. She had stayed the night, sleeping fitfully in the spare room. Gram flitted around her nervously, arranging the ribbon on the dress.

Waiting on the pavement was Frances, in a woollen coat and a blue velvet dress, and Trevor, in a smart pinstriped suit. He was wearing a pretty white carnation in his buttonhole, and gave one to Frances and Gram. They all walked together to the church, Frances excitedly telling Peg that Trevor had just proposed and showing her the ring he had bought her from Lewis's, which brought squeaks of happiness from both girls. There had been a flurry of snow in the night, and it disguised the scars of the city and made everywhere look beautiful.

But when they arrived at Holy Cross, Peg's spirits dwindled. 'There's no one here. Looks like it's just us, Fran.' They stood shivering on the porch, peering in around the door at the empty church.

'Maybe your da wouldn't let them come,' said Gram.

Frances pressed a posy into her hand, nodding up to the front pew. 'The bad weather doesn't help. But

413

look, your Brendan's here, just come out from behind the pillar. And Anthony, of course.'

'That's all that matters. I guess it's not the ending that we hoped for. Too much happiness would seem greedy. I don't care that no one has come.'

'Don't give up yet. You and Anthony: it's a start. And Anthony's father is still in Australia. Word is, he's softened. When he gets back, things will change. This isn't the end. This is a new beginning. If your da's not here, I'll walk you up the aisle myself.' Frances nodded ahead to where Anthony was standing with Brendan in front of the altar. 'He looks like Gary Cooper,' she whispered.

As they prepared to walk up the aisle to meet Father O'Mahoney at the altar with Father Moretti standing beside him, the candlelight and the snow falling quietly gave the church a feeling of calm. Shadows of the drifting snowflakes moved across the walls, and when they fell on the faces of the statues, the stone saints seemed almost alive.

Peggy smiled bravely. 'Perhaps it was too much to expect of me da. Walking me up the aisle to marry a Giardano. Gram's right. He must have told me mam and all the kids to stay at home.'

She took slow, steady steps, gripping Frances's arm.

Anthony turned to see her, smiled and winked. 'You look beautiful,' he whispered, when she reached the altar.

The priest cleared his throat. 'Dearly beloved—'

'Peg!' cried a voice. 'Peg, wait!' More voices. More noise. Rattling and shuffling. 'Wait! Stop!' someone

414

yelled. Peg whirled around and there was a clattering, a stomping, a rush of bodies coming through the double doors.

'Are we too late?' Phil said, jogging up to the altar. 'They found a flaming incendiary in the road. Have we missed it? We had to go all the way round the back of Lace Street! They wouldn't let us through!'

Peggy started laughing. She looked at this ragtag little band of people. There was her father, and her mother – and, most surprisingly of all, Mrs Giardano, extravagantly dressed in a red coat and matching gloves. And beside her, Gloria! Hiding her face under a huge wide-brimmed fawn hat as though she didn't want anyone to see her, but here nevertheless. And all of the O'Sheas including Uncle Davey and Peter and Jimmy in shirts and ties. And Mr Albertini – of course Mr Albertini was there, wearing his best double-breasted suit. Philomena, in a new plaid dress with a fox-fur stole, dashed forward and swapped the bunch of posies for a larger bunch of snowdrops and ivy, all tied together with vine and curling white ribbon.

'Father, can we start again?' said Moira.

The priest frowned. The O'Sheas: some things never change, he thought.

'Now, let's do this properly,' said Peg's father, joining her. He reached out and shook Anthony's hand. 'You have my blessing, son. Don't you look lovely, Margaret Mary. Don't you look a picture, queen.'

She felt her father link her arm, strong and sturdy as he took her a few steps back down the aisle, straightened his tie and prepared to walk up it again. As she passed the family group shuffling into the pews, she saw them all leaning over and shaking hands with each other. And in the rush, amidst all this confusion, whose was the groom's side? Whose was the bride's side? It was impossible to know. And what did it matter anyway?

'Let's just get started. Stay where you are,' said the priest impatiently. And Peggy turned her head and smiled as she looked around the church. There was her mother holding Hope, standing shoulder to shoulder with Sofia Giardano . . . who was standing shoulder to shoulder with Peter, who was standing shoulder to shoulder with Mr Albertini. And Sheila in a pretty summer frock despite the freezing cold weather, standing shoulder to shoulder with Gloria and Phil. With Kitty and Jimmy and Liam. And they were all in their best clothes – or as near to best as they could be, with bent feathers in their hats and holey gloves and mangy stoles and well-polished boots.

The priest began to speak. 'We are gathered here today . . .'

Outside, they could hear the clanging of a fire engine. Please God, there wasn't going to be a raid. And even if there was, nothing was going to stop them enjoying this wedding.

After a quick *Sanctus, Sanctus, Sanctus, Dominus Deus*, they all set off to the pub. Peggy noticed winter violets struggling up in between the cracks in the pavements, tiny clusters of purple flowers. Little knots of happiness in the snow. Everyone finds some joy in this city somehow, she thought.

The wedding cake was tiered, decorated with pink roses in glittered icing.

'Mr Albertini's present. He went around to all the pig club members, got everyone to give you their rations and baked a cake within hours!' said Sheila, leading the way to the upstairs room of the pub. Peggy gasped. For people to have donated treasured ingredients from their bare larders was kindness indeed. Mr Tozer had provided two bottles of gin and whiskey; Mrs Shufflebottom, a plate of rock cakes and sticky iced buns.

Brendan took her aside. 'Peggy – if this all goes a different way to what you expect, you know we're here for you.'

'It's going to be fine. My baby came into the world to find love. Our lives will be filled with love from now on. And if there are enemies to be found, they're not going to be found on our doorstep.'

Perhaps the lack of a mention of the baby's red hair, either from her parents or Anthony's mother, was a sign of things to come, she thought. That others might be ready to forgive.

Dennis climbed onto a chair. 'A toast!' he cried. 'To Peg and Anthony. God made 'em and matched 'em. Let the festivities begin.' And everyone raised their glasses, Giardanos and O'Sheas alike. 'Who am I to stand in Peg's way?' he whispered to Moira, who squeezed his hand tightly.

Frances grinned. She whispered in Peggy's ear. 'Look at them all. All so happy. That's the point of you, Peggy. To bring people together. No greater thing to be proud of.'

'Now, who's for a bevvy and a sing-song?' Dennis cried.

Mr Albertini arranged for them to spend their wedding night at Rossi's Hotel in New Brighton. It overlooked the estuary and was everything Peg had dreamt of: white linen sheets, fresh winter flowers on the table, plump cream cushions on the window seat. And as they fell onto the bed and Anthony kissed her and undressed her, she wasn't shy or ashamed. Because over the past year, she had come to know this body of hers. This body that had been invaded by Martin and then taken hostage by pregnancy but, now that it had delivered such joy as her daughter, she was ready to embrace and enjoy. Her body was to be celebrated, and she was ready to take comfort in it. Most of all, it was *her* body.

And in Anthony's arms – as he peeled off the rest of her clothes and she lay naked on sheets as soft as clouds, as he kissed her tenderly on her lips, her breasts, her thighs – she knew that every tingling fibre and every shuddering nerve ending would soften forever the blunt blows of the world. As he touched the silky soft parts of her, she was ready to love and be loved.

Epilogue

Summer 1945

The Union Jack bunting, tied from flagpole to flagpole around the perimeter fence of Woodvale airfield, fluttered in the sunshine. High above it, the engines of aeroplanes thrummed.

Peggy squinted up into the golden sunshine. Anthony had decided that he would continue in the RAF for at least the next year. How much worse it had been when he had been going on actual sorties.

His aeroplane was a Tiger Moth, like the one he'd learned to fly in. I expect he'll be doing this for a little while longer, she thought. He was making up for those lost years before Italy had finally joined the Allies and he had been accepted back into the RAF. On the day that had happened, Anthony had gone down to the town hall and given the officer his papers, and they'd been happy to take him. She remembered how bleak she had felt the first time she had been here, trundling down the coast road on her way to Freshdale. As though her life was over before it had begun.

Peg had discovered a new love: ice cream. How could anyone resist ice cream? And she'd had a bit of help from Gloria, who had thawed and come

419

around to the 'situation' now that her father would soon be back from Australia and there was another baby on the way. The envelope that Peggy had posted through the letterbox addressed to Sofia had also gone some way to heal old wounds. Inside, with a note from Grammy Nora, there had been one rose-coloured pearl button that flashed lilacs and blues and soft pinks. Mr Albertini's firm words had also played a part in persuading the Giardanos to see sense. Peggy had soon had people coming to the house in Smithdown Road for her concoctions and ice-cream sundaes. The pig club had taught her that she was good at selling. Good with people. One followed the other.

She looked around. There were women in pretty tea dresses wearing colourful hats and sunglasses. Children had been allowed into the enclosure, and the younger ones ran about in summer frocks and linen shorts with white socks, laughing as the planes looped and soared overhead. Frances was late, but when she arrived wearing a jaunty sky-blue turban and yellow trouser suit and kissed Peggy on the cheeks, she forgave her.

'I still feel sick to the stomach every time I see him up there,' Peggy murmured.

'I hear there's a bit of a knees-up next week? Another celebration for your Brendan coming home from Africa at last? I'll get us all an ice lolly,' said Frances, disappearing through the crowd.

The room at next week's gathering would be full of Giardanos and O'Sheas. Torta di Mandorle and *millefoglie* would sit next to Victoria sponge cakes and sticky buns. There were still parties all over Liverpool celebrating the end of the war, even though VE day had been nearly three months earlier. Peggy could hardly believe that they had got through it. That her beloved Anthony had survived it. Brendan. Peter. The O'Sheas were all still alive, despite the horror of the Blitz. Three of Anthony's air force pals had been shot down and another was in a wheelchair, but each time Anthony left, he had come back. Peggy was well aware that she had been lucky, in so many ways And especially now, with the new baby coming.

Thinking about this, she smoothed out her daughter's pretty lace collar and kissed her gently on the crown of her head.

Anthony's plane landed, bumping across the tarmac and coming to a stop on the grass with a phut-phut-phutter. Climbing out to applause, he strode across the airfield to repeat the display in a Spitfire. The uniform was a perfect fit. He looked dazzling. Hope, full of pride, waved to him. A woman cut a ribbon. Anthony waved back and smiled.

The plane took off. It climbed up, up, then plunged and climbed again, plunged and climbed, then swept over them in a wide arc.

'That's my daddy up there,' Hope said cheerily.

Peggy knelt beside her. 'Yes, it is, Hope. Showing off. Up there with your other daddy,' she added. She had never wanted a lie to take hold. She knew where that led.

'Here he comes!' Hope cried. 'Is he going all the way up to heaven?'

Peggy smiled. 'Not quite, love. Nearly.'

Touching heaven, brushing up against Martin Gallagher, whose child had healed their two families. Both of her men up there, with the sun burnishing their golden wings, as the buzzing and thrumming plane curved, dipped, scoured and swooped in the cloudless blue sky.

Acknowledgements

Thank you to my editor, Gillian Green, for once again helping me find the light in the stories I bring to her. Thanks so much also to my indefatigable agent, Judith Murdoch. Thank you to all the team at Pan Macmillan for their extreme care and detail. Thank you to my sister, Ruth, my best friend: for all those conversations we have shared where we remember the people from Liverpool who populated our childhood and who have made it into this book, not least our resilient grandmother, Catherine Heery – a mother of ten who was widowed in 1937 and brought up her young children on her own. Thank you also to my grandfather, Ernest, whose work as a head waiter at the Queens Hotel brought so many Italians into our lives and into our home, which was how I first learned of the tragedy of the sinking of the *Arandora Star* and the Huyton internment camps in Liverpool. This book is dedicated to the 805 casualties, 470 of whom were Italian, and their friends and families. Thank you to all of those who have taken their time to share their life experiences with me. Finally, for keeping the show on the road whilst I disappear to write, as ever, grateful love to my sons Louis and Joel, and to Peter.